SIREN WARRIOR CHRONICLES

by

Michelle Marquis & Lindsey Bayer

WHISKEY CREEK PRESS
www.whiskeycreekpress.com

Published by
WHISKEY CREEK PRESS

Whiskey Creek Press
PO Box 51052
Casper, WY 82605-1052
www.whiskeycreekpress.com

ISBN 978-1-60313-414-9

Credits
Cover Artist: Nancy Donahue
Editor: Sue Vetter & Chere Gruver

Printed in the United States of America

WHAT THEY ARE SAYING ABOUT
MIDNIGHT BECOMES YOU

"Having had the pleasure of reading other compilations by Michelle O'Neill and Lindsey Bayer I wasn't at all surprised at the exciting tale of a woman with uncontrollable powers and her attempts at love. *Midnight Becomes You* was an interesting story about two gifted individuals on opposite sides of the control spectrum that come together in a clash of wills."
Fallen Angels Review

Other Books by Author Available at Whiskey Creek Press:
www.whiskeycreekpress.com

Midnight Becomes You

Dedication

To all those who strive to break the glass ceiling
every single day.

SIREN WARRIOR SERIES BOOK 1: MAIDEN'S CURSE

by

Michelle Marquis & Lindsay Bayer

Chapter 1

Today was the day.

Gypsy Theron reached the weapon master's shop at dawn, just as she planned. The low early morning fog that left her boots damp had begun to dissipate. She watched from across the road as the old man folded aside the wood panels that fortified his shop front. He seemed intent upon his work, mesmerizing her with his easy grace as he set his merchandise out for sale. His long gray robes were clean and pressed but hung heavily off his gaunt frame. The gray was a poor choice for him, making his green skin look ashen and dusty with age. His weathered face was deeply carved with heavy lines and his body moved with the stiffness of arthritis.

When he had finished setting up for the day, Gypsy moved forward and greeted him. "Good morning, old father," she said.

He squinted at her and leaned against a thick wooden post that held the roof up. "A good morning to you as well, young miss," he said, returning her greeting with a suspicious grin. "How may I serve the general's daughter? Come to purchase a new weapon for your father?"

"No," she corrected, running her finger gently along the blade of a battle-axe set out for display. "This weapon is for me."

The weapon master stared at her, his mouth set in a thin line. He picked up a leg sheath with a small knife buried within. "A dagger, perhaps?" he offered. "Definitely suitable protection for a young lady."

Gypsy turned to face the man. "I don't need a dagger. What I need is a battle-worthy sword for the tournament this morning."

The old man cast his eyes to the ground. She knew he thought she was insane. They all did. To look at her, he would have every reason to think so, for she looked every inch the humanoid her mother was. She was no obvious match for a six-foot-plus Æssyrian warrior. But the warrior's life was what she'd chosen, even if she did have to break all the known rules of womanly conduct.

A few thin clouds veiled the twin suns for a few moments, then passed quickly away as they stood there in silence. When the weapon master looked up to meet her gaze again, his eyes were clouded in shame. He looked as if she'd undressed herself in public.

Clearing his throat, he said, "I have a few blades that might meet your needs." He moved deeper into the store, his boots scraping heavily on the wood planks. He came to a wall where three short swords hung. Two of the blades were straight and one was curved.

Gypsy chewed her bottom lip. Her sword knowledge was seriously sparse. She had tried to learn as much as she could by reading the books in her father's library, but most of them were somewhat dated. She didn't recognize any of the swords in the shop and thus knew nothing about them. She decided it was better not to ask, he probably would mislead her anyway. *Certainly one blade was as good as another.*

Two grizzled soldiers stalked into the shop and gave her a curious glance. *I'd better not take too long or I'll look like a novice.*

Finally, she pointed at the curved short sword. "That one," she said. "I'll take that one."

* * * *

The main gates to the arena were massive wooden doors that dwarfed the guards before them. They were usually open to allow for visitor access, but they were now closed, indicating the tournament had begun. Gypsy approached the posted guards, her stomach twisting nervously.

Walking up cautiously, she approached the shorter of the two guards—a warrior of about six-foot-two with a scarred lip and a corporal's insignia on his uniform. He eyed her suspiciously.

Gypsy arched her back, trying to look taller. "I need to get inside," she said in her most commanding voice. "I'm a contestant."

The corporal's face settled into an angry scowl. "What is this, a joke?"

Gypsy cursed under her breath for getting here late. If she'd arrived a few minutes earlier, she would have blended in with the crowd and avoided this annoying interrogation. "No, it's not a joke," she said coolly. "Check your list. I'm on there as one of the combatants."

The corporal snorted and shot a look at his companion. The other man shrugged and they both opened the gates. Squeezing her sword tightly, Gypsy slipped inside and melted into the crowded darkness.

Chapter 2

The ready rooms beneath the arena were packed with young warriors hungry to prove their fighting skill. The smell of nervous sweat hung in the air as men took any spot they could to get ready. Some sat on the floor reinforcing their heavy boots and securing their shin armor, others stood with their arms out while friends secured their chest armor. Drake Trolis didn't need to join in all the fuss. He'd come to the tournament armored up and ready to go.

He placed his hand on the hilt of his saber and watched the latest match through the entryway. Because of his weight, he was in a more senior class and had at least another hour to wait before his match came. As he stood waiting, he caught an unusual scent. He turned around and drew it in with a deep breath through his nose. It was sweet and earthy and he yearned to find it. *Female.* A small kernel of lust pulled at his gut, arousing and awakening him.

Then he spotted her.

She was humanoid and he immediately knew who she was. Indeed, everyone did and everyone was reacting the same way. Sitting on the floor by a chest of discarded armor, she swore softly as she rummaged through it, trying to find anything that would fit her small frame. Her black pants were snug and tucked neatly into her boots and she wore a long-sleeve light cloth shirt a few sizes too big for her. A tense hush quieted the noise and clatter of the men getting ready as all eyes turned to the woman.

Her name was Gypsy Theron and she was tall for a human. Well, technically she was a *half-breed*. Standing somewhere around

4

five-foot-nine, she had dark brown hair that hung in long waves down the middle of her back and the golden eyes of her father. She was a stunning beauty, her Æssyrian blood gifting her with a body of lean muscle and long graceful limbs. The daughter of a famous general, she was a good catch for any man hoping for a career in the military. Unfortunately, she was considered brazen, willful and very crazy. At nineteen—while most young woman were dating like crazy to find a good husband—she was here hoping to qualify by fighting the most dangerous men in the empire. A normal woman wouldn't have been caught dead here.

Drake stalked over to her. She was so intent on getting ready she didn't hear him coming. He crouched down next to her and picked up her sword.

"You're going into the arena with *this*?" he asked.

Gypsy tried to snatch it back, but he held it just out of her reach. She got up off the ground and glared at him. "Give it back."

Drake instantly hated her. What he wouldn't give to teach her some respect in private. "Take it from me."

In a flash of speed, Gypsy pulled a knife from her boot and pushed it between the joints of his codpiece. A rush of hot rage filled him, but he remained cautious. He had no doubt she'd hurt him.

"Gypsy Theron!" a voice called from the arena entrance. "Your match!"

"Give it back now or your breeding days are over," she said through clinched teeth.

Drake slowly held the weapon out to her. She reached for it and he dropped it on the ground. Keeping her knife at his groin, she knelt and picked it up. She came up, slipped the knife in the holster, and backed toward the arena.

"That thing will break with the first solid blow you get," he called after her.

* * * *

Gypsy emerged into the hot morning sun to the roar of the crowd. Standing before her was Thog, the smallest warrior in the competition. He wasn't small to her though. Standing at six-foot, he was easily two hundred and fifty pounds. His hair was long, stringy and black, hanging loose just past his shoulders. He advanced to the middle of the arena to join her and wore the same piecemeal armor she had on. *At least his equipment isn't better than mine.*

The referee rattled off the rules and stepped back. Thog touched his blade to hers then lunged in for an attack. Gypsy blocked the first blow but immediately knew something was wrong with her weapon. As Drake had warned, the steel was weak and began taking dings with every blow that struck it. Gypsy panicked and stumbled back, working her sword from side to side to ward off the punishing attack. A horizontal chop bent her blade badly and embarrassment burned her cheeks. Her first match and she was going to lose because her sword was crap. It hardly seemed fair. It was one thing to be defeated fairly but this…this just sucked.

Chapter 3

General Gavin Theron climbed the brown stone steps of the arena to his reserved seating. He stopped for a moment and glanced behind him to make sure he hadn't lost his wife, Harlan in the crowd. He had pulled her out of her clinic duty for this and she was none too happy. Still wearing her bright blue scrubs and crisp white lab coat, she was easy to find in this crowd. It also helped that she was one of only a handful of humanoids scattered throughout the stands.

"Come on, darling," he said impatiently. "The first set of matches has already begun."

Harlan was momentarily trapped behind a group of old gentlemen trying to decide on a place to sit. She gave him an annoyed glare. "You go ahead. I'll be there in a minute."

The men turned around and, noticing her, made a gap for her to pass. She smiled at them and rushed up the steps to catch up to Gavin. Finally at their reserved seating, Harlan and Gavin settled into their seats. Gavin looked down at the arena floor. A lot of promising young men had come of age for military service this spring, and he was eager to see how they fought. He stared down, unable to process what he was seeing.

Gavin stood up. *By the gods…*

Gypsy was down there, and not doing too well. Her weapon had broken in two and she was doing everything she could to dodge her opponent's savage attack.

"What's wrong?" Harlan asked, setting her jacket down on the seat next to her.

"Gypsy's in the match."

Harlan stood up and stared down. "Don't be ridiculous." She stared at the arena and her face paled. "What the hell is going on! Is that why you brought me here?"

"I swear I had no knowledge of this. Surely you know I wouldn't be a party to something like this."

Gavin and Harlan cringed as Gypsy dodged another vicious blow that almost cost her head.

"Oh my God, Gavin, get her out of there!" Harlan yelled.

"I can't. If I interfere, she'll be a laughingstock. Right now she only looks like a crazy fool."

"I don't give a crap what she looks like! You get her the hell out of there before she gets killed!" Harlan screamed at him.

Gavin quickly swept his gaze over the reserved military seating one row below them. "Where the devil is Caraculla?"

He finally spotted him, sitting just a few rows down. The colonel wasn't looking at the arena, preferring instead to kiss his girlfriend of the day. Gavin tried to yell down to him, but the roar of the crowd drowned him out. Picking up a small rock, Gavin threw it at him to get his attention. It bounced off the back of his neck. Caraculla glared in the general's direction, then seeing who wanted him, climbed the steps to join them.

"What the hell is wrong with you?" he said, rubbing the back of his neck.

"Gypsy is in the arena *fighting*," Gavin replied.

Caraculla looked down and frowned. "What is she doing fighting? She's going to get maimed or killed down there."

"Go tell the referee to call the match off. He should listen because she no longer has a weapon to defend herself," Gavin said, pushing Caraculla toward the steps. "When you've got her, bring her to my office for a little chat. And hurry up!"

Gavin turned to Harlan, but before he could say anything, she was up and following Caraculla down the stairs.

Chapter 4

Gypsy came into her father's office, escorted by his bulldog, Colonel Caraculla. Her father's office felt small and cramped with files stacked high on tables, the floor, his desk, everywhere there could have been open space. Gavin may have been a gifted soldier but he wasn't known for his administrative skills. Unfortunately, his people skills were even worse and most secretaries were unable to stand him for more than a few months. The air which normally smelled like cigar smoke, now held the strong stench of mint oil. It smelled awful. She sighed, not even trying to hide her annoyance. She was tired, humiliated, and not in the mood for one of his long-winded lectures.

Gavin was lying on his belly on top of a folding table, being rubbed down by an attractive young woman. Her father had persistent back problems from his many years of combat, and often sought all kinds of remedies. Gypsy wondered if her mother had any idea one of his treatments involved such a pretty woman. She doubted it would surprise her.

Gavin waved the masseuse away and got up off the table, stiffly. He pulled his uniform tunic on, but left it unbuttoned. "Have you lost your fucking mind? Do you realize you could have been killed in the arena today? What were you thinking?"

Gypsy bristled. She hated being sworn at by him. It made her feel dirty. "No, I haven't lost my mind. Of course, I realize I could have been killed. That's the point of tournaments. I was trying to gain some points to qualify," she replied flatly.

"You can't qualify. First, you're a female—no female has ever qualified. Second, you have no training. All you're going to accomplish is to get yourself slaughtered," he said angrily.

Caraculla went to a corner chair and removed some files stacked on the seat. He eased himself down as though he didn't want to attract attention. "Your father's right. You can't just go into the arena and hope to qualify without any training."

She turned on him. A flash of heat warmed her neck and face. "So train me or mind your own damn business." It came out much nastier than she had intended.

Gavin shook his head and took a seat behind his desk. "That," he said, "is out of the question."

"What? Training me, or minding his own damn business?" she said.

"Both," he replied.

"Why? Just because I'm a woman? There are no rules against women competing."

Caraculla glanced at Gavin, who stood up and pointed at Gypsy. "There doesn't need to be any rules. Women, you included, simply don't have the strength to compete. Those matches are brutal and long, and most women are smart enough to realize they wouldn't stand a chance."

This was pointless. They were never going to support her in this, so why even try reasoning with them? She didn't need them anyway. Gypsy took on her most pleasant tone. She was eager to get out of here and confront the thieving craftsman. "Is that all?" she said to Gavin.

"No, it isn't," he said. "Where did you get that useless weapon?"

"I saved up and bought it," she replied.

Caraculla shook his head. "Whoever you bought it from cheated the hell out of you."

Gypsy scowled at the colonel. "No kidding. Was I not holding it when it broke? I'll deal with it myself," she said. He was only here to aggravate her and back up his master, Gavin. She pointed to where he sat on his chair. "Why is he still in here? Don't you have some other monkey errand you can send him on?"

Gavin shrugged. "There's no need to be pissed at him, he's just trying to help you, Gypsy."

"I don't need his help or yours," she said, staring at Gavin. She could feel Caraculla glaring, and a happy thrill filled her. *There, how does that feel?*

Her father stood up, arching his back. It cracked a few times. She hoped it hurt. "Now listen, Gypsy, you've terrified your mother and endangered yourself recklessly. I'm placing you on restriction until I'm confident you won't do anything foolish like that again."

Gypsy opened her mouth to protest, but Gavin held up his hand.

"I also want you to go by the clinic and apologize to your mother for scaring the crap out of her, and promise her you won't do it again. Are we agreed?"

"Sure. Fine. Whatever," she said.

"Colonel Caraculla will escort you there," Gavin added.

"I can find my way to the clinic on my own. I don't need a babysitter!"

Caraculla stood up. "I'd love to escort her, but I can't, Gavin," he said. "I have a match myself in a few minutes."

Gypsy seethed at the hint of smugness she detected in his voice. She bit her bottom lip before something vile escaped from it.

Gavin studied Gypsy for a moment. Then he said, "Go straight to the clinic and then straight home. Do you understand me?"

Gypsy turned her back on him and headed for the door. "I don't think I'll ever understand you," she said.

11

Chapter 5

Since this was going to be her last chance at freedom for a while, Gypsy took her time getting to her mother's medical clinic. The five-minute bell for the next match sounded throughout the city, and Gypsy scrambled up the steps of a nearby rooftop to watch. It was early afternoon and the twin suns blazed. This was the time when the most experienced fighters had their matches. The intense heat and humidity of the afternoon added additional challenges to the combatants. Sometimes it stormed which, strangely enough, brought out an even larger crowd. Matches weren't called for anything elemental.

When Gypsy was a little girl, she loved watching the fights at the arena. Tournament nights she'd sneak out of her room, up to a rooftop and watch the men compete, fighting for a coveted slot at the military academy. It was terrifying and thrilling all at the same time. She'd seen all the great ones, her father included. But he didn't usually fight anymore. He was at the top of the food chain and had nothing to prove to anyone. She'd also seen the tragedy of men die. But what a death they'd had! The whole empire attended their funerals and they were remembered with respect and honor. It was inevitable that one day she'd dream of being among them.

Out onto the arena floor stalked Caraculla, the handsome young Razorback who had climbed the ranks faster than anyone of his race. It was unusual for a Razorback male to pursue a military career as most were fairly docile, unlike their Æssyrian cousins. The Razorbacks were a matriarchal society ruled by a dominant queen who made sure the males stayed in their place. Males who showed too much aggression were usually exiled or sought lives in the ÆEssyrian Empire, as Caraculla had.

As Gypsy watched the match, she was reminded how skilled the colonel was. Within seconds, he had his opponent struggling to fend him off as he pressed his advantage with punishing blows. As Gypsy studied him fight, she couldn't help but admire Caraculla's hard, rugged beauty. Every muscle seemed to move with feline grace as he effortlessly drove his enemy back. Reality slipped away and she imagined herself in her room with him. In her fantasy, she was in a white robe and wore nothing underneath. He was advancing on her, a dangerous warrior glint in his eyes, his long dark auburn hair around his broad shoulders, except for the two braided scarlet locks at his temple—nature's warning of his venomous abilities. A current of sexual hunger took her deeper into the hidden recesses of her soul. She closed her eyes and smiled as she stood before him in her room, his lips touching hers with a crushing, demanding kiss. For a moment, she let go and lost herself in his seduction.

Running her fingers into his hair, she reveled in its silken texture. His kisses were becoming more insistent, demanding more than she was willing to give. He picked her up and laid her on the bed, his heavy body on top of hers, both frightening and exciting her. She wanted him with every fiber of her being. Then the crowd cheered and pulled her from her thoughts. She looked down at the arena and watched Caraculla raise his sword in triumph.

He had won.

Gypsy envied him. *What a great moment that must be. Someday, no matter what I have to do, that's going to be me.*

Chapter 6

Harlan sat in her office trying to concentrate on the patient file at hand, but just couldn't. *What could Gypsy have been thinking, going into the arena like that?* Combat was a dangerous prospect for even the most well trained soldiers, and in all the years Harlan had lived here she'd never seen a human compete, let alone a woman. The thought of her daughter being battered to death sent an icy terror through her. There was a soft knock on the door.

"Who is it?" Harlan said, not welcoming an interruption.

The door cracked open and Gypsy poked her head in. "It's me, Mom. Gavin made me come to apologize."

Ever since Gypsy could speak, she had called her father by his first name. Harlan had tried to teach her to call him dad or father, but she always came back to Gavin. Gavin thought it was cute when she was a child, it annoyed him when she was a teenager, and now that she was a young woman, he was just used to it. Harlan stared at her daughter standing in the doorway and fought to hold her temper under wraps. Like her father, Gypsy responded poorly to aggression in any form. "Come in and sit down," Harlan said.

Gypsy came in and sat. Harlan took a moment to scan her for any sign of injury and found none. "Are you really sorry or are you just humoring your father?"

Gypsy shrugged and chewed her thumbnail. "I'm sorry I scared you, but I'm not sorry I tried to compete."

Harlan's heart sped up. "So what are you saying, that you're going to try again?"

"The first chance I get," she said, as she stood up.

"Gypsy!" Harlan said, getting to her feet. "Don't you realize you could have been killed today? Those men in the arena study for years to fight. What makes you think you can just waltz in there and win a match? Please don't do that again."

The moment the words left Harlan's lips, she knew she'd wasted her breath. Her daughter was so much like her father—headstrong, aggressive and bold. A feeling of hopelessness took hold of Harlan as she worried for Gypsy's future. Perhaps Gavin had been right. Perhaps she should have let him arrange a marriage for her. Maybe that would have been enough of a distraction.

But Harlan knew she was fooling herself. Gypsy would never have accepted an arranged marriage, even if the man were the most handsome in the empire.

"I'll tell you what," Gypsy said, "I can't promise I won't compete again, but I will promise to try and get some kind of training for the next time."

Harlan wanted to scream. "Competing against these Æssyrian warriors is suicide! Please, Gypsy—"

Gypsy held up her hands to ward off her mother's protest. She paced the room. "Okay, all right! If I promise, will that make you happy?"

"Very."

"Interesting that nobody gives a shit what makes me happy, though."

"Now, Gypsy, that's not fair."

"Why can't I just be who I am? Why do I always have to conform to what you and Gavin want me to be?" Harlan opened her mouth to speak, but Gypsy wasn't listening.

"I'm sick of everyone trying to control my future," she said, storming for the door.

Harlan felt a sudden surge of panic. Her daughter had a tendency to act first and worry about the consequences later. "Where are you going? Your father wants you home."

"Don't worry," Gypsy tossed back, going out into the hall, "I won't disappoint my big asshole jailer. I'm going home."

Chapter 7

After coming home and doing all the grunt work her father gave her, he finally allowed her some private time in her room. Gypsy traded her battle clothes for some loose-fitting gray pants and a thin, dark blue T-shirt. She dressed quietly and turned off her light. She could hear her parents having a tense discussion in their bedroom, and she quietly padded down the stairs in her bare feet, shoes in hand. Gavin would kill her if he caught her, but she just had to get out of here for a while. A group of her friends usually hung out at Hollow's Ford, and she was curious what the buzz was about her arena appearance. Since it was only a short distance from her house, she walked and enjoyed the mild evening temperature.

The minute she arrived at the Ford, she knew something was wrong. Everyone was there—Angel, her best friend, Stella Brock, a few of the noble's sons she didn't know the names of, and Gregor Savion, the son of a once-exiled Razorback grand duke. They all stared at her like she'd killed someone.

A delighted squeal erupted from the crowd, and Angel rushed for her, slamming into Gypsy for a friendly embrace. Angel pulled back and smiled. "By the gods, Gypsy! Everyone is talking about you! Nobody can believe you went into the arena!"

Gypsy suddenly felt like coming here might not have been such a good idea. Æssyrian men didn't approve of women fighting, and her being human probably didn't help matters. "I was just trying to rank."

The group of young men chuckled and went back to their conversation. *They think I'm an idiot. I shouldn't have come.*

"Whatever your reason was, I think you were very brave," Angel said.

"Thanks, Angel," Gypsy said, now wanting to leave more than ever.

"I think it was pretty brave too," a voice said.

Both women looked up to see Gregor strolling up to them. Angel gave him a dazzling smile. "You Razorbacks like women who fight, don't you?"

He met Gypsy's eyes and she felt her cheeks warm. He was achingly handsome and all she could think about was kissing him on those full, sensual lips.

"We don't just like women who fight, we like strong women," he corrected.

"Gypsy's a strong woman," Angel offered. Gypsy shot her a warning look.

"She is indeed," Gregor said.

Gypsy was vaguely aware of Angel sneaking off to leave her alone with Gregor. She made a mental note to scold Angel when she saw her again for playing matchmaker.

Gypsy folded her arms across her chest. "You're Grand Duke Savion's son, aren't you?"

Gregor sat down on a fallen tree and gestured for her to sit. "Yes, I am. And you're General Theron's daughter." Gypsy sat, keeping her distance from him. There was some bad blood between their fathers and she still didn't know if this was some kind of cruel trick to embarrass her. "Yeah, that's me."

"I meant what I said. I think you were very brave for trying to make rank. Too bad your weapon broke."

She plucked a few pieces of bark off the tree. "Someone in the preparation area tried to warn me it was crap, but I didn't listen. I feel pretty stupid."

"We all make mistakes, especially when we're driven by passion."

Gypsy smiled. At least he was doing a good job of *pretending* to understand her. "I assume you got your ranking at the tournament."

"Yes, I did, but don't worry. You still have two more chances this year. You still might make it."

"Yeah, but if I don't make rank this year, I'll never have a chance at the military academy."

"Is that what you want? To be a soldier like your father?"

Gypsy ran her hand over the bare spot where she'd stripped the bark. "Yes, but that's not what he wants me to be."

"I would think he'd be very supportive."

"Well, he's not, because I'm female. There's never been a female in the military academy and he certainly doesn't want his boy's club soiled by me. It doesn't matter. He doesn't believe I can make it, anyway."

Gregor reached out, moved a lock of hair from her face, and draped it behind her ear. "In the Razorback Queendom, they call that the Maiden's Curse."

"What do you mean?" Gypsy asked.

"The queen is openly critical of how the Æssyrians treat their women. She thinks it's criminal. I'm surprised you haven't heard talk of her views before. She speaks out every chance she gets."

The misery of the afternoon was starting to fade. "No, I hadn't."

"What do you believe in your heart? Do you believe you can make it?"

"I don't know anymore," she said, getting up. "Listen, I've got to go before I get caught not being where I'm supposed to be."

"Meet me here tomorrow. I'd like a chance to talk to you alone."

Gypsy smiled at him. "We'll see, but I'm not promising anything. My little tournament stunt has got me on restriction until I'm dead or longer."

Chapter 8

Gavin was the most graceful man Gypsy had ever seen with a weapon. Alone and naked to the waist in their villa's courtyard he seemed somehow complete, like the last practitioner of a long forgotten religion. He and his sword were a single entity and as she watched him work with such skill and focus, she both envied, and admired him.

When she was a small child, he'd lost an eye during a campaign in the jungle. What should have been a career ending injury only made him more determined to get back to his previous skill level. He trained for hours every day, having to relearn even the most basic fighting skills. Her mother had helped him with vision exercises to retrain his one eye to work as two. His frustration level was intense, and didn't help his already surly personality. Gypsy remembered avoiding him a lot during that time. It had taken years for him to recapture his proficiency, but he'd done it and some said he fought even better.

A person would think a man with one eye blind would exhibit a more cautious fighting style. Not her father. He fought with the endurance and ferocity of men a fraction of his age. The black eyepatch he wore should have been a beacon of weakness to his opponents. But it only increased the brutality of his appearance, and made him more intimidating.

Sometimes—although she hated to admit it even to herself— she longed to have a better relationship with him. But she knew that was never going to be. Her father was a difficult man to get close to, especially if you were one of his children. She would have to settle for the thin truce they always exercised when they were together, and try never to hope for anything more.

Gypsy stood in the shadows for a few seconds, then ventured over to a stone bench to sit. She was annoyed at herself for being so quiet, as if she had no right to be here and interrupt him.

He stopped and looked at her, not with the warmth of a father, but with the scrutiny of an adult being annoyed by a small child. "Did you apologize to your mother like I asked you to?" he asked.

"Yes," Gypsy replied, fighting to keep the sarcasm out of her tone.

Gavin lowered his saber and picked up a towel to wipe the sweat from his neck and chest. "I trust you won't be trying that stunt again."

Gypsy rubbed her palms on her pant legs. "I *am* going to try that stunt again. I have two more chances to qualify, and next time I'll be better prepared."

"Have you lost your fucking mind?" Gavin snarled. "It's going to take a lot more than a few more months of practice to get you ready for the caliber of fighters in the arena, my dear. And even if by some miracle you did have the training, you'll never match the men in size and strength."

"I don't need size and strength. I have speed and agility," she said, feeling her anger bite deep, but keeping her voice calm.

"Your speed and agility isn't going to amount to shit if one of them gets a hold of you or one of their weapons makes contact with your flesh." Gavin laughed.

He was baiting her, taunting her for a fight, but she wasn't in the mood. She knew this conversation was going to have to end soon, before she got herself in more trouble.

"So what should I do? Should I just keep my mouth shut and get married to the man you chose for me?"

"Well, that would be my choice, yes."

Gypsy stood up from the bench. "You can forget it! I'm going to make it all the way to the military academy in spite of you."

Gavin sheathed his weapon and gave a low menacing chuckle. "If you manage that, my dear, I certainly would be impressed. But be realistic, Gypsy. No one is going to give you the training you need because you're a girl. You have no weapons, no armor worth a damn, and at the rate you're going, you'll never qualify by the deadline."

Gypsy felt like she was loosing ground by the minute. "Why won't you train me?"

"Because that's not the life I want for you. I have no desire to see you beaten up in the arena match after match, trying for a dream that can never be yours," he said.

"You've trained men without half the talent and determination I have," she retorted.

Gavin laughed. "You think quite a lot of yourself." Reaching into his saddle, he pulled out an extra saber and tossed it to her. It hit the ground with a loud thump. His hyperia jumped at the noise. "Here," he said, with an evil gleam in his eye, "let's see how good you are."

She wanted to fight him, but she knew this was just his way of amusing himself.

"Forget it. I'm not in the mood to be humiliated," Gypsy said.

He watched her with his golden eye, like a cat watching its prey. Gypsy hated him. "Some other time then," he conceded.

Chapter 9

The new armor was splendid. Caraculla turned in the mirror, admiring the polished silver cuirass he wore. Although not the type of man in the custom of purchasing new equipment every time he got a raise, battle hardware was different. It was always taking a beating and the armor smiths were constantly coming up with lighter and harder armor to feed the army's appetite. For a high-ranking soldier in the empire, it was expected he'd keep up with the trends.

Caraculla lifted his saber and noted that the armor rose uncomfortably high on his neck. "It's still a little bulky," he said to the smith.

"I see that, sir, and I will make adjustments," the old man said, waiting for Caraculla to lift off the cuirass.

"When will the rest of the armor be ready?" Caraculla asked.

"Another week or so, sir."

The door to Caraculla's office opened and Gavin stepped in. The smith bowed his head in respect. Gavin strolled over to the shiny new cuirass. He stroked his hand along the muscle sculpture on the breastplate. "Very nice," he said. "This your work, smith?"

"That's correct, sir," the man said, keeping his head low.

"Perhaps I'll stop by your shop later today to see what else you have on hand," Gavin said, taking a seat across Caraculla's desk.

"I would be honored, Excellency," the smith replied. Then glancing at Caraculla, he added, "I'll bring the adjusted armor in a few days, lord."

Caraculla nodded and saw the man to the door. He closed it and sat at his desk, watching Gavin. Although Caraculla's office was not as large and dark as Gavin's, it still held a masculine charm, with several sculptures and murals depicting eras in Razorback history.

"It's kind of early for you to be in here shooting the breeze," Caraculla said, amused.

Gavin propped his boots up on the edge of Caraculla's desk. He hated when the general did that. It left nasty scars on the wood's surface, but then every desk in the empire bore the marks of Gavin's spurs. "I need your thoughts on a subject."

"I'm flattered," Caraculla said. "What subject?"

"My daughter."

Caraculla grinned. "That's an interesting subject, indeed." Gavin would never admit it, but his daughter was just like him. Her recent stunt in the arena proved she wasn't like any of the Æssyrian women his general was used to dealing with. The more Gavin tried to bully her into becoming a good and obedient daughter, the more she resisted him. She was as beautiful as she was mysterious, and she always stirred deep feelings inside Caraculla every time he encountered her.

"I'm worried about her trying to get into the arena again," Gavin said so low Caraculla thought he might be talking to himself.

"I don't think she'll try, I think she'll do it," Caraculla said. "She's pretty headstrong. If she wants to make rank this year, she's going to have to go into the arena again."

Gavin sighed. "You know her. What do you think I should do?"

"First of all, I barely know her, and second, I don't know that there's anything you can do."

"Perhaps I could send her away. The distraction would buy me some time. By the time she came back, it would be too late to gather enough points to make rank. She'll never get into the military academy."

A sudden feeling of dread came over Caraculla. So this wasn't just a personal goal, Gypsy wanted an invitation to attend the military academy in a few years. "Short of locking her in a cell, I don't think she'll go anywhere you suggest. Even if you force her to go, she'll just come back in time to compete."

"Unless I can interest her in something else."

Caraculla leaned back in his chair and rocked it slightly. "What about sending her to the Razorback Queendom? Maybe life in a new place will change her perspective. They have tons of opportunities for women there. She's bound to find something that interests her."

Gavin rolled the idea around in his head for a moment. "That's brilliant. I'll suggest it to her. Her mother won't be thrilled, but I can handle her. Now for that other matter."

"What other matter, sir?"

"Your promotion, of course," Gavin said with a sly grin. "I have been thinking of promoting you to lieutenant general."

Caraculla's heart was beating so fast he could barely breathe. This was what he'd been working for his entire career. "I'm honored, sir."

"Don't thank me too soon," Gavin said, getting up. "You'll have to go through a year of mentoring with me, and I'll be testing you all the way. I'll also expect to see good matches in the arena, am I understood?"

"Yes, Excellency."

"Right now I've got to go and find Gypsy. We'll discuss this later."

Caraculla stood up as Gavin left the room. *Finally, I'll achieve what I've always wanted.*

Chapter 10

The hardy smell of freshly cut meat met his senses as Gavin came into the villa. He made his way into the kitchen and wrapped his arms around his wife, Harlan, who was laying out a plate for him. She was as beautiful as the first time he'd seen her, with long silky black hair and bright emerald eyes. She could heat his lust like no other woman he'd been with. At five-foot-seven-inches, and one hundred and forty pounds, she was the small one in the family, but as nature often has it, she was the one in charge. Harlan threaded his tumultuous soul with serenity. With his every breath, he wanted to touch her and make her happy. Unfortunately, right now he knew Gypsy was making her very unhappy. Their daughter often placed strains on their marriage with her wild antics, which he blamed on Harlan's allowances for personal freedom, but he always yielded to her decisions. He had no doubt Harlan was the better parent.

The meat was just as he liked it, thinly sliced, raw and soaked in blood. As was her human custom, Harlan had cooked her own serving. "Is Gypsy here?" he whispered in Harlan's ear.

She turned around in his arms and kissed him. "Of course, she said you grounded her."

Gavin chuckled darkly. "That doesn't mean she listened."

"Very true. Let me rephrase that. The last time I saw her, she was in her bedroom because you grounded her."

Gavin gave his wife one more kiss and stalked toward Gypsy's room. He was about to open the door when he hesitated. He knocked instead and waited. Gavin had been working harder on respecting his daughter's privacy, and waiting to be invited in was a difficult step in the right direction.

"What, Gavin?" she said without opening the door.

"I'd like to come in and talk to you."

"We've already talked today. I don't have anything else to say to you."

Gavin frowned and felt his temper escaping his control. "Open the fucking door," he snarled.

"Why don't you try the handle? It's not locked, remember, another one of your ridiculous rules," Gypsy said through the door.

Gavin took another moment before opening the door, because if he walked in now, he would smack her for sure, and Harlan would get pissed. He certainly didn't want to incur the wrath of both of the women in his life. One was bad enough. Slowly he turned the handle, pushed the door open and stood in the threshold.

This was already going poorly. He was half-tempted to get Harlan in here to suggest the trip. "I just have a suggestion. How would you feel about taking a trip to the Razorback Queendom for a few months?"

His daughter's eyes blazed at him. She wasn't falling for it. "A few months? Like say, just long enough to miss the next two tournaments?"

"There are a lot of careers there open to women. Why not take a little time off and see if there's something else out there that might interest you?"

"No, there isn't."

"So you don't want to go?"

"No."

"Why not?"

"Because I know what I want. Just because you don't want it for me, doesn't mean that I'm going to give up. This is just a way to distract me until the season is over. Well, Gavin, it's not going to work. I'm staying and I'm going to compete no matter what you try to do."

Gavin glared at her. "You seem very confident of that."

"What are you going to do, chain me to the bed?"

"Perhaps I'll request that the emperor prohibit women from entering the military academy. That would derail your little quest, and all your future arena humiliations would then be for nothing," Gavin snarled at her.

"Oh, they wouldn't be for nothing, because I'll just pursue a career as a mercenary and then you won't ever have to see me, or be embarrassed by me again," Gypsy said, her voice trembling.

He folded his arms across his chest. He needed to leave now, perhaps after she'd cooled down she might reconsider the trip, but if he made her too angry, she'd dismiss it to spite him. "Make no mistake, Gypsy. I'll do whatever I have to do to keep you from getting killed. Now before you say another word, why don't you just think about it? It's a great opportunity and I think you'd enjoy the culture."

She leaned back on the bed with her hands behind her head. "Oh yeah," she said sarcastically. "I am so enamored with cultural diversity. Don't bother me with this crap, Gavin, I'm not going and if you try to make me, you'll regret it."

Chapter 11

Gypsy couldn't wait for everyone to go to sleep. Lying in her bed, she listened carefully to her father's late-night ritual just before he went to bed. Her mother usually went to bed long before her father did. He'd read military history for a while, then when he was sure everyone was asleep, he'd break out the bottle and consort with the demons that lived in his memories.

Gavin's memories of war were a terrible thing to behold.

She must have been twelve when she'd first seen the effects of them. Her father had been drinking until late that night. He'd staggered to bed sometime past one in the morning. Gypsy drifted off into a light sleep, her thoughts hopping from one thing to another. Sometime before dawn, just after she had taken a bathroom break, her night was shattered by the soul-crushing sound of her father screaming. She'd heard his nightmares before, but this one must have been made worse because of his drinking. She could still recall the pitch of his screams, and it chilled her blood. Jumping up out of bed, she raced across the hall to where her parents' bedroom was and quietly pushed the door open.

Her father was kneeling on the floor, his face in his hands, weeping like his heart had been torn from his chest. He spoke in ÆEssyrian, something he rarely did when at home with them, and his voice sounded so tortured and broken it brought tears to her eyes. Her mother moved toward Gavin, speaking to him softly, reassuring him everything was all right. Her mother knelt down next to him and placed her hand on his shoulder. Gypsy was frightened for her mother and wanted to warn her to get away, but then something strange happened. Her father's body softened and he collapsed forward, his great head coming to rest on her mother's lap. He placed his thick powerful arms around her mother's waist and squeezed her. Gypsy had never seen this side of their relationship, this quiet and compelling expression of love between them, and she was deeply moved by it.

Silent tears escaped her eyes. She wept for her father's past, of the pain and suffering he'd experienced in his career, the friends he'd buried long before their time. But she wept too for her mother, who loved this man with a passion Gypsy feared she would never know.

During all this, neither of her parents had known she was there. Deciding to leave them to what was left of the night, she backed away from the open door, her heart beating like a wild bird in her chest. As she returned to her room she felt guilty, as if she'd taken something from them she could never return, but she also felt more joyful and perhaps understood them just a little bit better than before.

* * * *

She heard Gavin walking to the bathroom just past her door and it snapped her back to the task at hand—getting out undetected. He coughed a few times, then returned to the living room where he began putting his bottles and books away before going to bed himself. Gypsy always waited out these quiet drunken rituals, having learned the hard way that her father was a really unpleasant drunk. Anyone who came downstairs for a drink of water or a midnight snack was fair game for a spirited argument, and she knew he'd like nothing better than to start in on her again.

After several moments of puttering around, she heard him stagger off to bed a little after midnight. Now was her chance. She slipped out of bed and pulled on a pair of soft black pants and a loose white blouse. She glanced in the mirror and noticed her hair hung in wild wavy locks. She smoothed them with her hand in a feeble attempt to tame them, then just gave up. Gypsy was not accustomed to fussing over her appearance and the urge to do so felt strange. Once satisfied she looked decent, she crept downstairs and slipped out the servant's entrance.

* * * *

The night was beautiful. The three Æssyrian moons, all different sizes, illuminated her way as if she were a magician and the light was a spell she'd cast. She wondered if Gregor had been serious when he'd invited her to meet him at the Ford. Hopefully, this wasn't a cruel joke. She guessed she had nothing to lose. Having Gregor show interest in her was both frightening and titillating, especially because he had no love for Gavin, who had kicked the crap out of his father in a combat match. She was surprised he even wanted to speak to her. But her mother saved Gregor's life when he was a toddler, and he was always gracious whenever he saw her.

As Gypsy walked down the path, she thought about her troubles relating to men and wondered how her personality difficulties would ruin this. Most men would initially become interested in her because of who her father was, but once she failed to meet their expectations as to what a proper woman should act like, they usually never came back. It didn't bother her really, she had her sights on other horizons, all they did was waste her time. This would be different, maybe not good, but different.

She arrived at the clearing fully expecting to be alone, but he was there. He was sitting by a small fire, snapping larger twigs into smaller ones and tossing them on the flames. Gypsy walked over cautiously and stopped.

He smiled up at her. "I'm glad you came."

She sat down and stared into the flames. "So," she said, feeling tense. "What did you want to talk about?"

Gregor reclined on his side, propping himself up with an elbow. He toyed with a small leaf on a stick. "Nothing in particular, I just wanted to get to know you. How did your parents take you competing in the arena?"

Gypsy glanced at him and lifted her brow. "Just like you'd expect, they freaked. Especially Gavin, he's really pissed."

"You call your father by his first name?"

She shrugged. It never occurred to her to call him anything else. Dad seemed too intimate, and didn't fit their relationship. "Sure. I've always called him that."

"Do you call your mom by her first name, too?" Gregor asked.

"No, she's always Mom," Gypsy said, smiling. She dared to look Gregor in the face and was shocked by how attractive he was. The flickering light from the fire cast a healthy glow over his green skin, and his amber eyes shone with a warm amusement. She knew from the rumor mill he was very popular with the ladies, and judging by how he looked now, she could see why. There was a calm sexuality about him, a relaxed hunger, that made her skin long for his touch.

Gypsy hated the sudden lull in the conversation, and racked her brain to fill it. "How come you don't have a girlfriend?"

He shrugged and dragged the tiny leaf along the flesh of her arm. "I did," he said casually, "I don't anymore. What about you? Why don't you have a boyfriend?"

"Most men think I'm weird."

Gregor laughed warmly. "I don't think you're weird," he said. "I just think you're misunderstood." He reached out and took her hand, softly kissing the delicate skin on her wrist.

A rush of heat raced into her cheeks and Gypsy's body was charged with energy. Gregor sat up and pulled her against him, burying his face in her neck. He smelled so good against her that any urge to resist him melted away. Closing her eyes, she ran her lips along his throat and pushed her fingers into his thick dark hair. He moaned into her ear, his kisses growing hotter and more aggressive. Gregor pushed up her shirt and pulled one of her breasts into his mouth. Gypsy gasped as pleasure raced through her senses.

Unable to wait any longer, Gregor fumbled with her pants, finally getting them unbuttoned and peeling them off. He rolled on top of her, hastily taking off his shirt and pushing her legs open with his thighs.

Gypsy was nervous, and having never had sex before, she had no idea what to expect. Gregor was feverish with lust and before she knew what was happening, he was inside her. The pain was a shock. In all her scenarios of sex she'd never expected it to hurt this much. She tried to talk to him, to tell him to slow down, but he was lost to her, buried in the haze of his own lust.

After a few brief and uncomfortable minutes, he groaned and got off. He dressed and kissed her roughly. "Come and find me at the Spring Festival tomorrow, promise?"

Gypsy buttoned her pants up, feeling confused and awkward. *Was this what sex was all about? Why did anyone bother?* She grinned at him hoping he couldn't tell there was anything wrong. "Sure," she said. "I'll see you tomorrow."

Chapter 12

The Spring Festival was one of the most attended events in the empire. Everyone was there—the royals in all their expensive clothing, making sure all the right people saw them, the merchants with samples of their crafts to drum up customers, even the emperor himself attended. Colorful banners hung from all the tallest trees and the smell of freshly cut meat drifted through the air, making Gypsy's mouth water. She had dressed in loose gray sweatpants and a large sweater, to conceal her competition clothes underneath.

As soon as she broke away from her parents, she pulled off her layers, ditched them behind a tent and immediately ran into her friend, Angel. Angel had dyed her hair an interesting shade of brown that didn't flatter her light green skin. Gypsy decided not to say anything about it.

Angel grabbed her arm and pulled her away from the crowd. "I'm so glad you're here. This place was *Boresville* until you arrived," she said, looking Gypsy up and down suspiciously.

"Where is everyone?" Gypsy asked, scanning a group of young people as they passed by.

Angel shrugged. "Some are here, some are there. You know how the clicks roll. I saw Gregor earlier. He asked if I'd seen you."

Gypsy's cheeks grew warm. "Where'd you see him?"

"Over by the tournament field. Everyone's gearing up for the practice bouts." Angel covered her mouth as if she said something wrong. "You're not going to try and compete again, are you?"

Gypsy started walking toward the field. "That's why I'm here." This was a perfect chance to win some points toward her junior ranking. Angel raced along next to her, talking a mile a minute. "Gypsy, you can't! You don't have any armor, and going in there without armor is suicide!"

That at least was true. Gypsy didn't want to go in without any armor, but she didn't have much of a choice. There was always the 'poor chest' nearby with a collection of stuff other warriors discarded, but few things ever fit her right. Unfortunately, she didn't have time to wait, if she didn't get enough points this year she'd never be considered for an academy slot. *Never.* If she wanted this dream, she was going to have to risk everything to get it, or she'd regret it the rest of her life. However long that turned out to be.

An armored warrior stepped out in front of her, and Gypsy almost stumbled into him. She glared up at him and recognized him as Caraculla, her father's colonel and right-hand man. He looked handsome and dangerous in his silver and black cuirass. His face was battle-hard, but it held a hint of wanton sexuality Gypsy always found alluring. His auburn hair hung loose down his back, accented by the scarlet streaks at his temples. His pale green eyes shone with cunning as they swept over Gypsy's body. "Where are you going in such a hurry?"

A fireball of fury burned in her belly. "Where I'm going is none of your business, Colonel." She attempted to walk around him, but he moved in front of her, forcing her to stop.

He squinted at the growing crowds as they moved into small groups to gossip. A stray breeze blew a lock of hair across his neck. Those green eyes met hers and she suddenly felt fearful he was going to stop her. "Your safety is always my business."

"I am going to compete. And don't try to stop me or the scene I'll cause will be legendary," Gypsy said.

"She doesn't even have a weapon!" Angel blurted out. Gypsy glared at her and made a shut-up gesture with her hand.

Caraculla folded his thick arms across his chest. "How are you going to compete without a weapon?"

Gypsy shrugged. "I'm sure I can find something in the poor chest."

"What faith you have in the trash of your fellow warriors," he said teasingly.

"Please don't tell my father."

For a moment, it looked as though that was exactly what he was going to do. Then, without a word, he turned away from them and walked toward some vendors. Gypsy grabbed Angel's arm and rushed toward the tournament field. "Gypsy," Caraculla called after her. She froze. This was it. He was going to stop her, to tell her father what she had planned. She turned around and stared at him. With a slow, graceful movement, he pulled his saber from its scabbard and held it out to her—handle first.

Gypsy was so stunned she didn't know what to say. She walked over to him and placed her hand around the handle. It was a fine saber, strong and light. If her father knew what Caraculla had done, Gavin'd surely have killed him. She watched the blade gleam in the bright morning sunlight and pulled her hand back without taking it.

"I can't take this from you. This isn't your conflict. Gavin would be incensed and you know how spiteful he can be," she said. "But I appreciate the offer more than you know."

Caraculla grabbed her forearm and pushed the handle of his saber back into her hand. "I've known your father longer than you've been alive. He would be even more incensed if I let you go in there defenseless. Don't worry about me, I can handle Gavin."

Gypsy took the sword from him. "I don't know what to say."

"Don't say anything," he said to her, "just win."

Chapter 13

Caraculla braced himself as Gavin stalked up. This would probably get ugly pretty fast. The general stopped and studied Caraculla as if he'd exposed his genitals in public. Harlan, who wasn't far behind the general, hurried past them headed toward the field. Gavin chewed his cigar. "Was that Gypsy I saw you talking to a moment ago?"

The general's daughter was one of the few human-looking women in the empire, which made her rather unique. It wasn't likely Gavin didn't know her from a distance. Caraculla placed his hand over the empty spot in his scabbard. He hoped he'd done the right thing in giving his weapon to Gypsy. "Yes," Caraculla replied. "It was."

"And where was she going in such a rush?" Gavin asked.

"To fight, Excellency."

"And why didn't you stop her?" Gavin asked, his tone growing hostile.

Caraculla watched some young women pass by, giggling and smiling at him. *Why can't the general's daughter be more like every other woman on this planet?* A pang of regret filled him, thinking his help just might have cost Gypsy her life. "There is no stopping her, she would have fought me just as soon as anyone on the field to pursue this," Caraculla said.

The general's gaze tore down Caraculla's uniform. He stopped at the missing saber. "Where is your weapon?" Gavin asked.

"Gypsy didn't have one so I loaned her mine."

"What the hell did you do that for?"

"Gavin, you know Gypsy, there was nothing I could say that was going to stop her. It was the only thing I could think of to give her a fighting chance. You remember what happened at the last fight. What was I supposed to do, arrest her?"

"Yes!" Gavin snarled, pushing past Caraculla and heading over to where Harlan was trying to reason with her daughter. Gypsy hurriedly put some discarded armor on while craning her neck to hear the announcer so she wouldn't miss her cue.

Gavin stormed up to them with Caraculla in tow. Gypsy glared up at them. "Don't try to stop me, Gavin."

Caraculla was surprised to hear her call her father by his first name. He'd heard her address him like that before, but today her tone carried even more distance than usual. He searched Gavin's face to see if the general felt any pain from the icy reception, but he showed none. The general was a hard man to reach, most of the time his emotions were completely hidden from view.

"This is madness," Gavin said. "Stop what you're doing or I'll throw your ass in jail myself."

"I don't care," she retorted, continuing to buckle what few pieces of armor fit.

"You won't have anything to fight with," Gavin said. "Caraculla is reclaiming his sword."

Gypsy's stunning golden eyes fixed on him and Caraculla felt his stomach drop. *Here's where the ugly starts.* "No, I'm not," Caraculla said.

Gavin turned on him like a hungry lion. "I'm ordering you to take your weapon back now!"

Caraculla held his hand out to Gypsy. She turned to Harlan. "I'm going into the match if I have a weapon or not. Do you really want me to go in there unarmed? Or with a pauper's sword that's going to break at the first blow?"

"You won't go in there at all if I arrest you," Gavin said.

"And how long are you planning to keep me? A month? A year? How long do you plan to try and control me because I'm not doing what you want me to do?" She turned to Harlan, pleading. "Let me try, if I don't win at least one bout, I promise I'll pursue something else."

"It only takes one bout for you to get killed. Gavin can't have a fight stopped every time it looks like you're going to lose," Harlan said, her eyes filled with pain.

"I didn't ask him to stop that fight. Besides, I'm offering you a deal. Give me this one chance. If I don't win a match, I'll stop for good. Let me keep Caraculla's sword and at least try."

Gavin seized Gypsy's arm and pulled her closer to him. In the background, the announcer was calling her name. Gypsy struggled to get loose.

"Let me go, you son of a bitch! You're going to get me disqualified!" Gypsy yelled, trying to wrench out of his iron grasp.

Harlan looked miserable. "Let her go," she said to Gavin softly. He stared at her as if she'd spoken another language he didn't understand.

"What?" he asked, letting go of Gypsy's arm.

"She's right. We can't keep her from it forever. Let her try and we'll see after that."

Gavin took a step back and Gypsy rushed into the field to take her position. "Are you sure about this?" he asked his wife.

Harlan shook her head. "No, Gavin, I'm not."

Caraculla placed his hand on Gavin's shoulder. "We'd better go sit down before all the seats are taken." The general nodded and they all made their way up the steps to watch Gypsy's first real match.

Chapter 14

Gypsy marched into the arena with a cocktail of fear and adrenaline coursing through her veins. Her opponent was Sorg, a low-ranking warrior who'd also failed to earn any points during the first tournament. Gypsy knew from the grapevine that Sorg had grown up in a whorehouse on Dama Road. Like most men and women whose parents were whores or criminals, he had a lot to prove and tried his hand at just about everything from silversmith to now, soldier. Like her, he wore mismatched armor. But unlike her, he held a badly dented saber while hers gleamed with excellent craftsmanship. Gypsy felt a moment of pity for him. Good equipment was very expensive and unless one had wealthy parents or a good side job, they were doomed to whatever cast-offs had been left in the poor chest.

Sorg wasn't a tall man by Æssyrian standards, but he made up for it in bulk. Gypsy guessed his weight at something close to two-eighty, well over a hundred pounds more than her.

He moved to the center of the arena with a slight limp to his step. He wasn't a very handsome man, his features dominated by a large, flat nose.

They circled each other, each one waiting for the other to make the first strike. Sorg was slow and awkward in his movements and Gypsy studied him closely to try and predict his plan. "I don't care who your father is," he said in a voice slightly too high for a man, "I'm going to kill you, bitch."

Gypsy didn't waste her time trading insults. This is what she had waited for. Like her, Sorg had no formal training, but she had the advantage of having watched one of the greatest warriors in existence for years. Gavin had no idea that during all of those hours she watched him fight and practice, she was actually studying his every move. She did everything she could to secretly learn from him. If he had known her intentions, he would have banned her spectatorship many years ago. But now she was here, and she was here to win.

Spotting an opening, Gypsy lunged forward, driving her blade toward Sorg's throat. Her opponent snarled and stumbled back, but the crowd cheered her boldness. Their approval was like a narcotic, driving her to fight harder. She attacked Sorg again before he had a chance to recover. This time her blade found its mark, cutting deep into the flesh of his jaw. Sorg roared in pain and rage, punishing her with a series of bone-jarring strikes aimed at her face and neck.

The world around her melted away and a new sensation took over, a heart-pounding fury she'd never experienced before. It surged through her body with such intensity that it made her hands shake. A surprise blow to her weapon knocked her onto the ground. Gypsy scrambled to get up, barely missing a nasty downward cut that would have opened her gut. She had to stop him and *now*. Knocking his saber out of her face, Gypsy got to her feet and rained a series of aggressive blows at his chest. One of her blade thrusts slid off his saber sending the knife-edge of his weapon into the meat of her forearm. She hissed in pain, as her arm grew wet from blood. Sorg chuckled.

Gypsy launched herself at him with all her strength. Holding her saber straight out in front of her, she aimed for the most vulnerable spot she could think of, his abdomen. Sorg grunted and crumpled over the blade. The crowd jumped to their feet cheering and chanting her name. Medics rushed onto the field and pulled Sorg off, pulling her weapon out and tossing it at her feet.

Picking up the saber, she went back to the sidelines to try and understand what had just happened. A master-at-arms came over and handed her a large mug of water. He slapped her on the back good-naturedly.

Gypsy sipped the water and made a face. It tasted like it had come from the sewer. "What happens now?" she asked, tossing the water out of the mug and returning it to the soldier.

He smiled and pointed to the arena floor. Another warrior had come out, slicing the air to loosen his arm. "Now you go out against your next opponent. When you lose a match, they move onto someone else." He pushed her toward the arena. "Good luck!"

Chapter 15

"Why is she going back in there? She hasn't even been treated for her injury!" Harlan said, gripping the arena handrail so tight her knuckles were white. She hated feeling helpless, and that's exactly how she felt. Her only daughter had not just fought a man twice her size, but now it looked as though she was going to have to fight another. She gripped Gavin's wrist tight, as if she were trying to restrain Gypsy from continuing this lunacy.

"She's got to keep fighting until she loses," he said calmly, voicing her deepest fear.

She turned to him, barely keeping the rising anger out of her tone. "Well, she's had her one fight and she managed to win. That's it now. She needs to come out. No one said anything about her staying in until she is maimed or killed!"

The lines around her husband's mouth gave him a harsh, severe expression. "What do you want me to do, darling?" he said. "The only way to stop her is to arrest her. Is that what you want me to do?"

Down below, Gypsy moved to the center of the arena and circled her next opponent. He was a larger Æssyrian man than the first, and handled his saber with ease. It was obvious he'd had a lot more training than Gypsy, who as far as Harlan knew, had none.

"No," she said. "I don't want you to arrest her." She looked at him, searching his rugged face. "Is that the only way?"

"At this point, yes. You're going to have to wait until she loses before you can intervene. Perhaps you can have a talk with her afterward. God knows I've tried. Perhaps she'll listen to you."

The fight in the arena picked up steam and both combatants looked to be giving it their all. Harlan remembered all the matches she'd seen Gavin fight and a new sense of dread came upon her. Combatants were often badly scarred from these encounters, and sometimes even lost limbs. A battle-hardened Æssyrian warrior could inflict an unbelievable amount of damage. They could also take an injury that would kill a human and survive by going into hibernation. But Gypsy was half-human and the jury was still out on what part of her favored her Æssyrian blood and how much of her was human.

"What do you think her chances are of winning?" Harlan asked.

Gavin glanced past her to Caraculla, sitting on Harlan's right. "What would you say, Colonel?"

Caraculla shook his head. "I don't think she'll do as well against this warrior, he's a lot better than the last one."

"The two of you could show a little more concern," Harlan said, furious at their calm exterior. "She's going to get killed down there."

"Don't worry, Harlan," Caraculla said. "It's not likely she'll be killed in a match like this. Besides, you want her to get a good taste for what this is like. My guess is she'll change her mind about being a warrior once she gets a little dose of reality."

Gavin wrapped one of his large arms around Harlan and squeezed. "We want her to lose," he told her. "Once she loses, she's out of the arena and out of danger."

Harlan nodded stiffly. It pissed her off they were treating this so casually. The crowd was shouting and cheering, encouraging the fighters to inflict more damage on each other. Harlan watched

Gypsy's opponent knock her to the ground with a shoulder tackle and place his blade in her daughter's face.

For a full minute Harlan couldn't breathe, Gypsy held up her hands conceding the match and then the master-at-arms came out and called the bout in the Æssyrian warrior's favor. Harlan bolted from the stands and headed for the arena to check on Gypsy's injured arm. Behind her, Gavin told her to wait until Gypsy rejoined them, but Harlan simply couldn't. She pushed through the crowd and found her daughter standing over a rickety wooden table arguing with some old matron. They were both pointing at a thick list on the table. Finally, Gypsy swore at the woman and stormed off.

Harlan caught up with Gypsy, but she barely acknowledged her. "Can you believe those bastards?" she snarled. "I only earned *two* points for those bouts. What a total rip-off! Sorg got *three* for losing to *me*! This place is so fucking crooked I can't even believe it."

Gypsy hastily pulled her armor off and tossed it into the cast-off chest. Harlan grabbed hold of her wounded arm, relived to see the bleeding had stopped, but it would need stitches. "We need to go to the clinic for this," Harlan said.

Gavin walked up with Caraculla in tow. Gypsy turned on him in a fury. "Did you tell those monkeys to screw me out of my points?"

Her father raised an eyebrow. "No, I didn't. You lost points on technique, dear," he said in an acid tone.

Gypsy shook her head and glared at him, the energy of the fight still flowing through her like electricity. "That's a load of fucking crap and you know it."

"Watch your mouth," Gavin said, pointing at her.

"This from the dirtiest mouth in the empire," she spat back at him.

Gavin slapped her. Gypsy lunged at him, her face contorted in rage. Harlan managed to intercept her before she made a terrible mistake. "Gavin," Harlan said, holding her daughter back from trying to attack him. "Why don't I meet up with you later?"

But the general wasn't finished yet. He leaned forward and said, "Give Caraculla his saber back. You haven't earned the right to use such a blade."

Caraculla stared at Gavin, stunned. Gypsy relaxed and held up her hand to her mother, indicating she didn't need to be restrained anymore. Harlan cautiously released her, but stayed ready. Gypsy slid the dazzling saber from the battered scabbard she found in the pauper box. Harlan could read the pain on her daughter's face from the slight frown on her lips. She held the blade out to Caraculla. "Thanks for helping me out. At least you sort of understand."

Caraculla didn't make any motion to take the blade from her. Instead, he stepped back and said, "Why don't you keep it for awhile? You fought well with it and I've got others."

Gypsy gave him a slight nod and then she turned her back on everyone and walked toward the clinic before Gavin could say another word.

Chapter 16

The day was ruined. Leave it to her father to hurt her like no one else could. It hadn't always been like this between them. When she was much younger, they'd been closer. She remembered him playing war with her, teaching her chess, taking her hunting in the ÆEssyrian forests and sometimes putting her to bed with fantastic stories of the many battles he'd fought. She'd always wanted to be just like him. Now she just wanted to be away from him.

Gypsy wandered around for close to an hour looking for Gregor. He seemed so different from any of the other men she known. Maybe it was because of his Razorback upbringing. She thought he actually understood her. That was a nice feeling. For a few fleeting minutes, she allowed herself to think about marrying him and having a family of her own. The thought brought a smile to her face, she'd never thought about that kind of thing before. She shook off the smile. That was exactly what everyone was hoping for…a distraction from her crazy military dreams. But that life would never make her happy. She had to follow her soul and her soul was infused in the fight. That was never as true as now.

Ever since the first blow struck against Sorg, she knew she could never duplicate that feeling of completion with anything else. It was all she ever wanted. Of course, she had doubts. What if she couldn't get the points she needed to qualify for next year's bouts? What the hell was she going to do then? She had to get training, somehow. There had to be someone who was willing to train her.

She rounded a corner and passed some of the food vendors, pausing to take some free samples. Then, after she'd almost given up on him, she spotted Gregor.

But he wasn't alone.

He was with some earl's daughter named Shauna and they weren't discussing the weather. They were kissing like they'd been going out for months. She should have known he was messing with her head. He was probably seeing an army of women besides her.

Gypsy ducked back behind a vendor's tent so they wouldn't see her. Her face grew red-hot as she remembered she had slept with him. She was so stupid. How could she have trusted him? Every man in her life was a lying, oppressive, son of a bitch. All she wanted to do was go home and figure out how to prepare for the next competition.

As she turned to head back in the opposite direction, she saw her friend, Angel, making a beeline for her. Gypsy thought about pretending not to see her. She turned to make a hasty departure, but then thought better of it. Angel knew how to use guilt to punish her and Gypsy would pay for a snub the next time they met up, so instead, she stood there, waiting for her.

"That was amazing! You're absolutely nuts in the arena," Angel said, before laughing.

"Thanks. I'm glad I could provide you with some entertainment." Gypsy knew the words were wrong the minute they came out, just by the look on her friend's face.

"I didn't mean that you were entertaining. I meant you were really good and you must be so happy that you won your first fight. That's all," she said, wounded.

"I know. My win was the highlight of the day and it's been spiraling down ever since."

"Your father?"

"He's part of it, a major part."

"Did you ever find Gregor?"

"Oh yeah, I found him. He's a little busy so I doubt he saw the match," she said, gesturing toward the area where he was still canoodling with the earl's daughter.

Angel frowned when she spied them. "That really sucks. *He* really sucks."

Gypsy shrugged. "You know, I don't really care. I just used him to ditch my virginity so no one will want to marry me."

"You don't mean that. It's okay to admit he hurt you. It was a crappy thing he did and I don't blame you for being upset."

And that was her friend Angel, forever trying to get Gypsy to face and embrace her emotions. When it came to interpersonal relationships, her friend was the smartest person in the empire.

Angel's mom always thought Angel would have made a wonderful psychiatrist. Unfortunately, there wasn't a market for crazy doctors on Æssyria. The only person Gypsy knew of who was actually crazy was her uncle, Dragon Theron and no Æssyrian doctors ever dared treat him. But Angel wouldn't have pursued a career like that anyway. She was like most Æssyrian women, she wanted to land a good husband and rule her family's inner circle. Gypsy knew Angel was very smart and would do well in that world. Angel was Gypsy's best friend. The only person Gypsy knew who accepted her completely.

Thanks to Angel, Gypsy's childhood and teenage years were much easier than they otherwise might have been. Angel was popular and, oddly enough, very nice. She took a lot of crap being Gypsy's friend, but she never wavered in her loyalty, and it never cost her anything in the popularity department. She was grateful for Angel's friendship.

"Do you want to go over there and tell him what a bastard he is? I'll go with you if you want," she suggested.

"That is positively the last thing I want to do right now. All I want to do is go home and avoid my father."

Chapter 17

Gavin sat down in his favorite chair and sipped his whiskey. He was trying to shake off the sting of his confrontation with Gypsy. He should have handled it better. It seemed as though they grew further and further apart with each passing year. Gavin knew he was primarily to blame for the split. It was a pattern with him. Over his eight hundred years, he'd had many children—from wives, concubines and whores. But with few exceptions, all of his relationships with them had soured. When he was honest, he traced his poor parenting back to his own whorehouse upbringing and the tortured confusing mess that was his childhood.

Born of a human woman and an evil ÆEssyrian wizard, he had not known his father, and he had a volatile relationship with his mother. She'd been from Earth, an English woman with more adventure in her soul than cash. Her intergalactic wanderings brought her to ÆEssyria, an unexpected stopover until she could move on, but unfortunately she'd picked her new residence poorly. What she didn't know, was there were few jobs for unskilled foreign women on the planet. After months of searching, she fell into desperation and became the only thing she could—a prostitute. Since walking the streets, selling one's body was suicide, because of aggressive ÆEssyrian clients, his mother decided to join the ranks of other unprotected women and went into one of the city's many brothels.

Gavin, who was born five years later, was her only child and he'd paid dearly for the privilege. Growing up, he'd had little adult supervision and the dubious distinction of frequently having to share a room with his mother and her many guests. He began drinking and smoking early, indulging in all the vices of an adult by the time he was thirteen. His first sexual experience was with three of the brothel's whores who taught him pleasures most men only dreamed of. But Gavin wasn't like most brothel bastards. He'd grown quickly and soon dwarfed most of the men who solicited the house of ill repute. He was also a skilled fighter, having to defend himself often in the rugged streets around the brothel.

One evening he'd defended an old couple from a pair of robbers and impressed them so much they offered to help him get into the military academy. His dedication and skill took him all the way to the rank of general, a rare thing among Æssyrian males. Most died somewhere along the way.

Gavin unbuttoned his tunic and ran his hand along the many scars that marred his massive chest. How many horrible fights had he been in? There were too many to count. And now his beloved daughter wanted this difficult and dangerous life. He took another sip of his drink as the sorrow twisted his heart. Why couldn't he tell her how he really felt, how much he loved and worried about her? Why did everything turn into a nasty argument? Perhaps Harlan was right, perhaps she was too much like him.

He lit up a cigar and puffed hard, blowing a thick stream of smoke into the air. The front door opened and closed as Harlan came in. She frowned and opened a window. He watched her long black hair caress her back and the erotic swell of her breasts as she walked. His love and hunger for her rose up in him like a tidal wave headed for shore.

"Are you angry with me?" he asked.

"Yes," she said. "But no more than usual. Why does everything with you two have to be a confrontation? Why can't you be civil to each other?"

Gavin didn't answer her. There simply was no answer. He practiced blowing smoke rings in the air.

"What are we going to do about this, Gavin?" Harlan continued after a long silence.

"Perhaps we can find her a boyfriend. Maybe that will be enough of a distraction to convince her to give up this crazy plan," he said.

Harlan took a seat on the leather couch. Her lovely full lips set into a pout and his lust for her grew. How beautiful she was when something vexed her. He crushed his cigar out in the ashtray and patted his lap. "Come here, my love."

Her green eyes flashed anger at him. "Gavin, this is serious."

"I know it is, but I have an idea. There are a few young officers just fresh from the academy. They're complete gentlemen and I think she might take to one of them."

"I thought we agreed—no matchmaking."

"It's not matchmaking. I'll merely bring it up to her. She's a young woman now, Harlan, surely sex is on her agenda somewhere."

Harlan came over and sat in his lap. He kissed her, letting it linger until the fire inside him was a furnace of desire. "I don't think you're taking her ambition very seriously. She's not going to go for your idea and that's going to make you furious."

"Nonsense," he said, nuzzling her neck. "Since when does Gypsy make me furious?"

Harlan groaned and let a slight smile escape. She laid her head on his collarbone and sighed. "I feel like we're losing this fight, Gavin, and it's barely begun. I'm terrified she's going to get cut down in the arena and I won't be able to save her. I'm so lost in this and I don't know what to do."

Gavin felt her tears on his flesh and it burned agony in his heart. *By the gods, I don't know what to do either.*

Chapter 18

The armor was almost impossible to bend. Gypsy stood in front of the mirror wearing a cuirass she'd gone back and stolen from the poor chest. The chest plate had been an expensive piece of armor a few years ago, but now it was just one-step above junk. But it was better than the nothing she had. She'd been trying for over two hours to bend the metal so it fit her better, but so far, her efforts only resulted in several hand cuts and four broken nails. She took the armor off and tossed it on the bed, exhausted. A knock sounded on the door.

"Wait!" she shouted. "I'm naked." Gypsy grabbed the cuirass and pushed it under the bed. She rearranged her blanket to cover the hiding place and stepped back to inspect her work. "Okay, you can come in now."

Gavin stepped inside, his massive bulk crowding her small room. The sight of him ignited her anger all over again. Afraid to be slapped, she folded her arms across her chest and kept a respectable distance from him.

"May I sit down?" he asked, gesturing to the only chair in the room he could fit in, an old wing chair she had taken from his office on its last remodel.

"You were very brave in the arena, Gypsy."

She glanced away from him. *Now what's his game? I went from not being worthy enough to use Caraculla's sword, to now being brave. This should be good.* She decided to accept his pathetic excuse for a compliment to move the conversation along. "Thanks. But that's not why you came in here."

"No," he admitted.

"What do you want to talk about? As if I don't already know."

Gavin leaned back in the chair and interlaced his fingers across his chest. "I was wondering if you'd given any thought to how this career might affect your future."

"What are you getting at?" she asked cautiously, as if she were talking to a convicted criminal.

Gavin held his unbuttoned uniform open so she could see all of his scars. Gypsy had seen them before, but always from a distance, while he was practicing with his saber in the courtyard. They were quite shocking this close. "Come here," he said.

Gypsy unfolded her arms and cautiously walked up to him. He took her hand and placed it on the worst of the visible scars. It was raised and a paler green than the skin around it. Her father pushed her hand into the scar until she could feel how deep the wound had been. It should have been a fatal wound. Sorrow overtook her, knowing the pain the wound must have caused him. She pulled her hand away like she'd touched an open flame.

Gavin studied her in silence. Then he said, "Have you given serious thought to what this career will cost you? Your beautiful young body will be battered and scarred every time you limp out of that arena. What about a family? Have you given any thought to attracting a mate? You're already considered quite mad by most of the officers, but a few are still interested in you. Don't throw your future away on this. I don't mean to be cruel, my darling, but if you continue, you're probably going to spend the rest of your life alone."

She lowered herself onto the bed, hating him for what he'd said to her. So far everything had been all desire and instinct, she hadn't really thought about how it might impact her love life. The words were hard to hear but she knew he was right. In that split second she knew it didn't matter, she would give up everything for this. "I know I'm risking the chance to have normal life, but I've never wanted anything like I want this. This is more than just a dream—this is *who* I am. I know you understand that, if you don't understand anything else about me. I do someday want a family but I'm willing to give all that up for just one chance at the academy. Besides, no one's going to want me anyway, I've already had sex."

Gavin got up out of the chair, his chest flexing with rage. "*What?*"

Gypsy met his iron gaze with a tinge of smugness. "I said I've already had sex."

"With *whom?*"

She swallowed. "Gregor."

"Savion's son?" he hissed back at her.

She nodded.

He shook his head and buttoned up his tunic. "That's just perfect, Gypsy. I'm sure it's all over the empire by now. What on Earth possessed you to do such a thing?"

"I liked him and I thought he liked me. Unfortunately, I was wrong. At any rate, my virginity was a liability and I wanted to get rid of it."

Gavin stalked over to the door and opened it. He leaned in the doorway, his face harsh and stern. "Then you've made your decision. You're intent upon screwing up your life. Unfortunately, I don't foresee it being such a long life if you continue this idiotic pursuit."

"It's my life to screw up, and it pisses me off to no end that if I had a penis this conversation would be a lot different."

"It's more than just your lack of male genitalia, my dear. You lack size and strength, both of which are vital to your success in matches. You cannot successfully compete against men who are at the minimum double your body weight."

"You're wrong, Gavin. I can, and I'll be successful, no matter what it costs me. Now if you'll excuse me, I'm going to bed," she said, advancing on him.

"I know you won't believe this, but I want you to be successful, because the alternative for you is death. But I won't help you. I'm not going to have a hand in your unwavering desire to ruin your life. I just hope you're not too badly injured by the time your senses return to you," he said as he walked out the door.

Gypsy closed the door behind him and leaned her back against it. *I'll show him; I'll show all of them. But if I'm going to get enough points next time, I need to find a trainer and fast.*

Chapter 19

Throughout Gypsy's entire life, she'd heard the whispered stories of her grandfather Titan and none of them were good. Some of the whisperings came from her parents who had no idea she'd sneak into the hall late at night to listen to them talk about his many crimes and misdeeds. Others in the empire whispered out of fear that the very mention of his name would bring misfortune. She'd never met the man and any questions she'd asked were met with curt, tense answers from her mother. Her father refused to answer any questions at all. He'd just sit in his favorite chair reading some military history book and puffing on a cigar. Just a mention of her grandfather's name was enough to turn her completely invisible.

From what she'd gathered from other people over the years, she knew he was a powerful wizard, but wasn't very discriminating on how he used that power. In fact, he used his powers mainly to amuse himself. There were terrifying stories of Titan turning her father into a lion for a year, and others told the story of the wizard blinding her mother and keeping her captive until Gavin was able to rescue her. Some of the worst stories were about fortune seekers who would come to him for help, but always ended up worse off after they received it.

But none of the stories were very clear on details, so they may as well have been rumors. Nevertheless, since no one else would help her, Gypsy thought a little supernatural assistance might just be in order, so she decided to sneak out and go visit him. She knew she would probably end up in huge trouble for this restricted violation because she was bound to be missed. The trip to his properties was about four hours long on hyperia. An old noblemen, who was just a hair shy of crazy, had drawn her a map after she'd bought him a drink and listened to his hour long disjointed tales of Titan. She really didn't know how much of it was true, but a least she had a map. She hoped it was accurate.

The nobleman did insist, however, that when she reached the edge of the empire, she would know. Once she crossed onto Titan's lands, everything was dead. Gypsy had no idea what he was talking about...until she got there.

She stood before her grandfather's dark castle, starting to rethink the wisdom of this strategy. The castle was huge, with sharp, towering spires that pierced the sky. It rested on a land island surrounded by a four hundred foot drop. The only way to reach the castle was a narrow land bridge that stretched out from a dangerous looking cliff. The bridge arched high in the air like an animal's spine and touched the earth on the opposite side right in front of massive double doors.

For an hour prior to reaching the castle, Gypsy had traveled on dry, cracked ground with not so much as a weed or an insect. The crazy old nobleman was right, nothing lived here and the silence made her heartbeat pound in her ears. Across the bridge, was a different story as she could just make out vines creeping up the castle walls and entwining the iron fences.

Gypsy spent twenty minutes wondering how such a thing could have been built, seeing there was no place to put the scaffolding, and the land bridge would never have held the weight of the stones used to build it. After wasting a substantial amount of time, Gypsy summoned all of her courage and marched across the bridge to the front doors. She reached out to knock, but the doors creaked open as if they'd been expecting her all this time. *Nice touch.* Cautiously, she walked in and was immediately overwhelmed by the size of the interior. It was all she could do not to turn and run. She glanced down at the polished black stone floor and it looked as though she were standing on liquid. The dark stone walls were decorated with strange and frightening paintings. One showed a young woman, her dress partially torn from her body, raped by three small dragons. Another showed a man dying on a pike, his eyes plucked from his head by crows.

As she stood there transfixed by the images around her, she noticed the air turn colder. She shivered. The low seductive sound of whispering came to her ears. Gypsy tried to make out the sex of the speakers but soon realized it was a mixture of voices. They spoke of beautiful perversities and their passions mixed inside her, arousing her curiosity. She closed her eyes and let their hunger taunt her and to her horror, she found herself enjoying the way the voices made her feel.

A vision spilled into her mind, smooth and sticky like melted chocolate. She was in what she believed to be Caraculla's bedroom. It was night—like now—and the beige curtains billowed in the window like long-forgotten ghosts. The gentle breeze from outside stroked her skin and glancing down she realized she was naked. She approached the bed slowly, cautiously, fearful of what she might find.

Caraculla lay there sleeping peacefully, his uniform draped across a nearby chair. Even partially covered in a thin blanket, Gypsy knew he was naked too. Another breeze caressed her skin and her nipples grew hard and stiff. Within her, a smoldering fire began, awakening her hungry body. She reached out, touched the blanket covering the colonel, and pulled it back to reveal his stunning body. He was beyond attractive or handsome, he was simply *sexy* in all the ways that word had meaning. Gypsy ran her gaze down the thick chiseled muscles of his chest and belly. The sight of him drove her to a heightened sense of sexual awareness and in that quiet, simple moment, she had to have him inside her.

Her lust became a form of madness and before she realized it, she'd leaned down and placed a savage kiss on his luscious mouth. The kiss awoke him and his eyes opened in surprise. Gypsy moved up over him, pulling the blanket completely off. Caraculla opened his mouth to speak but she placed her index finger over his lips and kissed him hard again. Resigning himself, he placed his arms around her and his hands on her back. He pulled her closer.

But it wasn't pedestrian lovemaking Gypsy wanted. She wanted him to ravish her. Straddling her hips over his already erect penis, she lowered her pussy down just enough for him to feel the wet heat over his aching shaft. His green eyes blazed with a sudden dangerous fire that made her mind explode with need. Grabbing her waist, he rolled over on top of her and pushed her into his mattress. His mouth devoured hers with wild, demanding kisses until Gypsy thought she would die if he didn't put his cock inside her *now*.

Reaching down, she grabbed his throbbing shaft, but he placed his hand over hers to stop her. Before she could protest, he lowered himself down to her hips and slid his forked tongue deep into her channel. He'd barely begun to tickle her swollen clit with his tongue when the first orgasm seized her with mind-bending ferocity. She bucked against him, gasping and clutching the sheets until she tore them and the climax faded.

"Please, Caraculla," she groaned, twisting like an animal in heat. "Fuck me. Fuck me now."

Caraculla crawled back up over her, his predatory grace making her tremble with longing. Grabbing the shaft of his cock, he drove it hard into her with one long thrust. Gypsy arched her back and cried out. Shockwaves of incredible pleasure rode up each nerve ending to explode in her brain. Caraculla pumped violently into her, rocking the bed so hard the headboard dented the wall behind it. She'd never seen him like this, lost—intoxicated by her bottomless lust. She wrapped her legs around his powerful hips and called out his name over and over again until her climax pulled her back into a mindless sea of carnal delight.

The second orgasm locked up her muscles and left her breathless. Caraculla's own pleasure peaked as her channel rippled and milked his cock. He roared his climax loudly into the room, delighting her. Then, just as suddenly as it had come over her, the vision was gone.

Gypsy opened her eyes and blinked. She was on her knees bent forward with her hands clenched so tightly her nails cut tiny wounds into her palms. Titan stood before her.

Although they'd never met, she knew it was him. He was a regal-looking man with a face so handsome she found it hard to look away. His long black hair hung loose in thick shining locks right down to the middle of his back. There was a diabolical edge to his beauty and a savage evil gleam at play in his stunning yellow eyes.

Gypsy stood up, her legs feeling like clay. *What just happened to me? Was that real or did he bring it on?* The need to escape threatened to overwhelm her, but she stood her ground. *Mind games. Parlor tricks. Don't get spooked.*

"Granddaughter," he said in a voice as smooth as glass. "What a pleasure to finally meet you."

Gypsy swallowed, suddenly realizing she hadn't thought of exactly what she would ask him for. "I was curious," she said, her mind racing. "I'd heard all kinds of things about you and I wanted to meet you."

He smiled and there was nothing warm or kind about it. "Nonsense," he said. "You came here for the same reason everyone else comes here. You want something."

She took a few breaths and willed her heart to slow down. "Well yeah, that too."

Titan walked toward a stairway and gestured for her to follow. The steps were wide and short, leading up to a simple throne at the top. Titan sat on the steps and toyed with a small carpet fiber. He looked slightly bored. "What can I do for you? Power? Fame? A husband as handsome as a prince?"

"No." She got the distinct impression he was taunting her. "I want to win tournaments."

"You mean you want to be a warrior?" he asked.

"Yes. I don't know what to do and no one will help me." She leaned forward and whispered, "Did you help Gavin become a great general?"

Titan stiffened, his eyes narrowing slightly. "I never helped your father. His career has been all his own. We're...not close like that."

Gypsy felt her stomach drop. "So you're not going to help me either, are you?"

"What has your father said about your ambition?"

"He thinks I'm crazy. He keeps trying to marry me off."

"Did he tell you what happened to the many sons who dreamed of the career you do?"

"Not really, no. I know they're dead."

Titan laughed. "Yes, Gypsy, you're right. They're *all* dead by Gavin's hand. He always dreamed of having his sons follow in his footsteps, but that dream has given him nothing but grief. Every one of the children he trained to be warriors, with the exception of one, either were horrible disappointments or turned on him. The ones who had the most promise turned on him. In order to be the best, they had to kill the greatest warrior they knew, and that man was Gavin. I have most of them spellbound in the throes of death as statues in my garden. It's my version of family portraits, you see."

Gypsy folded her arms. "I'm not like his other children. I don't need his approval nor do I care what he thinks of my abilities or me. This is what I want for myself, not him. Are you going to help me or not?"

"Every fiber within me wants to help you but, alas, I cannot. You see, my dear, my help comes with a horrible price and you never know what it will be until after the deal is struck. I will tell you this—you are destined for greatness, but you will have to achieve it all on your own."

Gypsy nodded and turned to leave.

"Wait," he said so softly she almost didn't hear him. "Before you go, I insist you speak to your brother Northe. Of all Gavin's sons, he was the one with the most promise. If anyone can help you, he can. And his assistance won't cost you a thing."

Chapter 20

The garden her grandfather spoke of looked more like a ceme-
tery, except there were more statues than tombstones. The sky was
dark with heavy steel gray clouds adding to the somber mood of the
surroundings. Narrow paths overgrown with vines, wove an intri-
cate tapestry over everything they touched. A few panels of broken
wrought iron fencing were scattered through the garden. Everywhere Gypsy looked, there were statues of men, women, and even
some children. All frozen in the throes of some horrible tragedy.
None covered with vines. The plants stopped at the foot of each
statue as though afraid to touch the pale stone. One statue woman
clutched her dying son to her breast, cursing the gods above with
frozen lips. Another showed a humanoid woman hanging from a
withered tree. Titan walked up to a sculpture of a handsome
ÆEssyrian warrior clutching his belly in agony where a sword
pierced him through. The warrior looked a lot like her father.

This must be Northe. Titan reached for the sword, pulled it from
the statue, and the figure immediately came to life. The terrible
wound in his belly healed and his features calmed. He jumped
down from the pedestal startling Gypsy and making her jump back.

Titan grinned. "I'll leave you two alone," he said. "You have
ten minutes, Gypsy."

Northe fixed her with the most stunning green eyes Gypsy had
ever seen. They glowed with the intensity of his supernatural
power. "I see Gavin in you," he said. "You must be another one of
his unfortunate offspring."

Gypsy nodded, trying to overcome the icy fear that gripped her gut.

"You wanted to ask me something?" he asked.

"Yes. I want to be a warrior, but I need more training. Gavin won't do it because I'm a woman and no one else will take me seriously. Titan told me you could give me some advice."

Northe didn't seem surprised by her ambition. He folded his arms and leaned against the stone pedestal. Something tight relaxed inside her. *Maybe he isn't so scary after all.*

"You wouldn't want Father to train you," he said. "He's very good but he'll drive you into the ground. He almost killed me in my third year to qualify. We trained night and day nonstop. But I have to give it to him, when I was done no man could match me."

"No man but Gavin himself," she said.

He watched her for a moment, his mouth a grim line of pain. Then he said, "Why don't you ask Father's Master Sergeant Rakon to help you? He's a Razorback and trains all of Father's soldiers. He's crude but perfect to start you out. He'll also be the last one to care you're female, in fact it will probably turn him on that you want to fight."

Gypsy didn't really know Rakon. She'd only watched him drilling Gavin's soldiers in the military complex. He was a notorious bully. She wasn't looking forward to approaching him.

"Don't tell me you're afraid of him."

"No, it's not that. I just don't know him. I'm not sure how he'll react. Won't he be afraid of Gavin's wrath?"

Northe shrugged. "Rakon's no stranger to discipline issues. He respects Father but isn't smart enough to be afraid. That's what makes him extremely effective in the field during real combat. Keep in mind the warrior life doesn't come easy for anyone and you'll have to work harder than any of them. But you'd better get to work fast because if this is your first year qualifying and you don't have many points yet, you're quickly running out of time."

Gypsy watched him climb back up onto the stone pedestal and her throat tightened. He really did understand her ambition and she wanted to talk to him some more. "Why can't you stay?"

"Because I've been dead a very long time, there's no coming back for me."

"Let me ask you one more thing before you go," she said, feeling suddenly very alone. Northe had been the only one who'd treated her dream as if it were a definite possibility and she desperately needed that. "Why did you try to kill him? Why did you stage a coupe and try to assassinate him?"

His smile was cruel and filled with sorrow. "Because I hate him. I hated him more than I've ever hated anyone before or since. I hated him for using my love for him against me, for pushing me so hard I almost went insane from the pressure, for the millions of miseries he visited upon my mother and the many beatings I took in the name of fight practice. I hated him for never loving me nearly as much as I loved him. And someday, Gypsy," he picked up the sword and placed the tip at his belly, "you'll grow to hate him that much too. Be careful, or you will have your own spot in this garden."

He pushed the weapon deep into his body and turned to stone once again. Gypsy stood there for a long time listening to the crows squawking in the distance. After a while, she wiped the tears from her eyes and headed home, a little more frayed and a touch more hopeful.

Chapter 21

"Caraculla," Maura said, shaking him awake. "Wake up, there's someone knocking at the door."

Caraculla sat up and rubbed his face. The bedroom was dark except for the dim streetlights bleeding in through the drapes. He stretched and got up, crossing the room to open a window. He glanced at Maura and wondered why she hadn't gone home yet. She did that more and more lately, especially after he'd told her he wasn't planning to get married for a long time. They'd embarked on this sexual relationship over a month ago, and things were rocky to say the least. From the first week, Maura made it clear she wanted to get married. It soon become apparent to Caraculla she didn't much care who she married as long as it was an officer. He wasn't quite sure why she still hung around or why he kept sleeping with her.

"Aren't you going to get the door?" she asked, looking tense.

He grabbed his black robe and left the room without answering her. Leaning against the door, he glanced through the tiny window and was shocked to see Gypsy. He opened the door, looked around to make sure she was alone, then stared down at her. "What's happened?" he asked.

She met his gaze and his soul melted. Her full lips plumped into a sexy frown as she held his saber out to him. A raging lust came upon him so suddenly he had to fold his arms across his chest to control the urge to grab her. "Nothing's happened," she said. "I just stopped by to give you your saber back. I hope Gavin didn't give you too much of a hard time for letting me keep it."

He caught a whiff of her scent and found himself at a loss for words. A moment passed, then two. She watched him, her brows knitting in confusion. "Are you okay?"

Caraculla nodded. "I'm fine," he said, glancing over his shoulder to make sure Maura wasn't coming up behind him. He came outside and pulled the door closed. "I'm just surprised to see you here so late. What time is it anyway?"

"I don't know. Almost dawn, I think. I had something to do and I just got back."

"You shouldn't be out wandering around this late, Gypsy," he said angrily. "Anything could happen to you. Where's your mount?"

"I put him in one of the emperor's pastures. There was no way I could sneak him back into our barn without being heard," she said.

"Let me get my pants on and I'll take you home."

Gypsy rolled her eyes at him and took a step back. "I don't need you to take me home, Caraculla. I can get there on my own. Just take your blade back."

His eyes swept her body and he thought he saw a slight grin curl the side of her mouth. "I know you can," he said, softening his tone. "But I'd feel better if you let me take you."

She took another step back from him and playfully cut the air with his saber. "All right, if it'll make you happy, but you're not to tell Gavin I was out this late. And I want you to drop me off down the road or that noisy hyperia of yours will blow my cover. Got it?"

He was angry, but he knew better than to argue with her. If he tried to impose his will, she'd reject his offer completely and leave before he could dress. "Wait right there," he said. Rushing inside, he pulled his pants on, carefully buttoning them over his straining erection. Maura groaned and sat up. "Where are you going?"

"Go back to sleep," he said. "I'll be right back."

Caraculla came out and took his sleepy hyperia from the barn. He put the bridle on but decided to forgo the saddle. Gypsy came over and he placed his hands on her waist, lifting her onto the beast's back. Taking a few steps back, he jumped up behind her.

The moment her body settled back onto his chest and groin, he realized this was a terrible mistake. With her this close, his passion became a savage beast desperate to devour her. She innocently scooted her butt into his aching erection. She turned her head to the side and he caught her smirking. "Sorry if I interrupted something," she said.

He urged the hyperia forward. "You interrupted me sleeping."

"I said I was sorry. Like I told you, you don't have to take me home. I can take care of myself."

"I want to take you home."

"Apparently you want to do a lot more than that." She laughed. "So do you want this saber back or not?" She pulled it from the scabbard and admired the blade.

"No, you keep it. I gave it to you."

Because she didn't want to be noticed, Caraculla took a lesser used trail that wound around a heavily wooded area. A potent silence fell between them that grew in intensity with every step the hyperia took. He could detect a slight quickening in her breath and she was using any excuse to push her backside into his throbbing shaft. Annoyed by her teasing, he leaned forward and placed his lips to her right ear. "Stop moving around," he said firmly.

"I'm just trying to get comfortable," she complained.

"Well whatever you call it, stop doing it."

"Why? Does it bother you?"

"This is not a game, Gypsy. Don't tease me."

She laughed. "What are you going to do? Ravish me? How would you ever explain that to Gavin? He'd never promote you again if you defiled his little girl," she said in a mocking tone. "But I'm not worried, because you're afraid of me."

Caraculla licked his lips. "I'm not afraid of you," he barely whispered. His desire was killing him and starting to make him physically ill. *Only a few more yards.* He spurred his mount and rode to the end of the trail within view of Gypsy's home. From this distance, he could easily see her get inside safe. She turned around and faced him. He stared into the fire of her eyes and felt his back begin to sweat. "I don't understand your fear, but I see it. Thanks for the ride," she said softly.

Caraculla moved closer, his mouth less than an inch from hers. She closed her eyes and placed one tiny kiss on his lips. She slid off his mount and trotted toward her home, leaving him there, alone and burning with a hunger that threatened to devour him alive.

Chapter 22

The tavern was quiet tonight and Caraculla was grateful. He'd come in for a drink early in the afternoon and stayed for hours, trying to sort out his feelings for Gypsy. He'd known her since her birth and always thought there was something very special about her. In general, he neither liked nor disliked children. He just never really paid much attention to them. But he always enjoyed being around Gypsy, even when she was a small child. Her explosive, inquisitive nature always fascinated him, and her bold, fearless antics—especially with Gavin—amused him to no end. He never knew what to expect each time he saw her. Now, thinking back on last night, he couldn't get her out of his head. Could it be he'd been in love with her all this time?

Sexual fantasies flowed from his thoughts like spring water bubbling from the ground, and filled him with an aching hunger. He strained his mind to recall what her kiss tasted like and was miserable it hadn't lasted longer. He imagined her long, athletic body naked in his arms, with his cock buried deep within her. His arousal increased with every fantasy he entertained. They flashed across his thoughts like slides at a peepshow—her on her hands and knees in his bed, her legs wrapped around him as they made love in the forest, her tortured cries as he tasted her essence. Trying to pull himself back, he took a long drink and ran his fingers through his hair.

Someone sat down at his table and he glared at him. It was Gavin, and Caraculla's quiet sexual torture, with nowhere left to go, turned to rage. He watched his general light a cigar and sip at his whiskey. "We need to talk," Gavin said.

Caraculla was in no mood to have a conversation with Gavin. He already knew the general was mad he'd given Gypsy his saber at the tournament and their discussion guaranteed to turn ugly quick.

Gavin leaned forward and pointed two fingers at Caraculla. His cigar smoldered between them. "I don't want you to help Gypsy any more, do you understand me?"

Caraculla leaned back, a strategy to put some distance between them. "Should I have let her go into the arena with such an inferior weapon that she gets herself killed?"

"Nonsense," Gavin said. "She wouldn't have gotten herself killed, but she would have gotten hurt. I think one good injury is enough to end this madness once and for all, don't you?"

"What if that injury is a severed arm? Will you still feel the same way?"

"No one would dare do such a thing to a woman, arena or not."

"Are you serious? You're fooling yourself if you think those fighters won't hurt or kill her to win. You don't hear what they say when they watch her, everyone wants a piece of her. They all hate her guts. Those who don't hate her because she's a woman hate her because she's your daughter. You know as well as I do these are inter-kingdom competitions and you have a lot of enemies."

Gavin was thoughtful for a moment. "All the more reason why you must stop helping her. I don't want to drag this out any longer."

"Forbid her to leave the house then," Caraculla offered, knowing Gavin could never enforce a rule like that. Gypsy would only become more defiant.

"I have, but I suspect she's sneaking out while I'm asleep," Gavin said. "To make matters worse I can't even marry her off to anyone of any significance. No one will have her. She's gone and slept with the grand duke's son, Gregor, just to spite me. Of course word of that has spread like wildfire and she could care less."

Caraculla stared at Gavin, his fury smoldering. "Is she still seeing him?"

"No," Gavin said, sipping his drink. "I think he dropped her."

"Did you say anything to him for using her like that?"

Gavin watched Caraculla and chewed his cigar. "No I didn't. Let it be a lesson to her."

"Well, I'm going to talk to him."

Gavin frowned. "No, you're not. You stay out of it. She wanted to be a warrior, then let her fight her own battles. If she wants him punished for gossiping about her she can do it herself."

Caraculla stood up. He'd had enough. "Would it kill you to show her a little support? Is she just an amusing curiosity to you?"

"You're very defensive, what's crawled up your ass?"

"Nothing. I'm just sick of you throwing her to the wolves in the name of nurturing her independence. Why can't you be her father for once, and not just the sperm donor who happens to be married to her mother?"

"Fuck you, Caraculla," Gavin said with a surly scowl.

"Fuck you too, Gavin." Caraculla stormed out of the bar leaving Gavin to pay his tab.

Chapter 23

Harlan invited Gypsy to help her at the medical clinic, hoping to get some time alone together. At first Gypsy resisted, saying she had other obligations, but after some well played hands of guilt she finally relented. As usual, the morning was crowded and bustling with activity. The clinic attracted everyone from soldiers to prostitutes to wealthy merchants. Harlan denied medical care to no one, much to the irritation of the nobles. Harlan was fortunate the emperor gave her carte blanche with the medical operations of the empire.

Gypsy was pleasant, engaging in small talk and asking questions about some of the diagnosis and equipment, but it soon became apparent to Harlan that her daughter was just being polite and was hopelessly bored. Nevertheless, Harlan did her best to keep Gypsy busy. They straightened the exam rooms and were double-checking the medicine cabinets when out of the blue Gypsy said, "Mom, I need some birth control."

Harlan's heart sank. It wasn't that she was a prude about sex, but she was worried about Gypsy's choice in men. She'd heard the rumor about Gregor and knew he was notorious for his womanizing. "Do you have a boyfriend?"

Gypsy leaned against the wall and picked at a broken nail. "No," she said casually.

Harlan folded her arms. Casual sex with Æssyrian men was a huge blunder she'd seen many women live to regret. They were notoriously territorial and had no qualms about killing another man or an unfaithful love interest. "May I ask whom you are sleeping with?"

Gypsy gave her mother a patronizing look. "I'm not sleeping with anyone right now. I had sex and probably will again, so I guess some protection is in order. I wouldn't want to derail my military career. Besides, I'm surprised Gavin didn't tell you. He tells you everything else."

"He's worried about you and frankly so am I. You know how men can be when they think you belong to them."

"Trust me, I don't belong to anyone. Gregor is the only man I've been with and he isn't going to start a fight over me. He's far too busy foraging new alliances," Gypsy said sarcastically.

"Why do you need birth control then?"

"Like I said, so when I have sex again I won't get pregnant."

"Why can't you just come to me then?" Harlan said, knowing it was a feeble attempt at control.

Harlan scowled. She knew she should be happy Gypsy wanted to be responsible, but somehow this wasn't how she'd wanted her daughter to do it. Harlan guessed she wouldn't be as upset if Gypsy was in a committed relationship. Without another word, she pulled a small clear bottle off the shelf and drew a viscous yellow fluid into a syringe. This would stop her daughter's ovulation for five years or until the antidote was administered. "Roll up your sleeve."

Gypsy did. "Are you mad at me?"

"No," Harlan said, swabbing the arm and giving her the shot. "I'm just very worried about you. I don't want you to fight anymore and I don't want you having casual sex because I'm terrified one or both of those things are going to get you killed."

Gypsy rubbed the injection site with her thumb then rolled down her sleeve. "Don't worry about me," she said. "I have a plan."

"What kind of plan?"

"I'm not telling you anything about my plan because you'll tell Gavin and then he'll interfere. Let's just not talk about it anymore because you're not going to be happy with anything I say and we'll just end up fighting the rest of the day."

Before Harlan could respond, the bell up front sounded indicating a patient had arrived. They made their way to the waiting room where a large ÆEssyrian warrior stood. He was a young man dressed in a trainee's gray uniform. He was handsome in a hardened sort of way with a wide jaw and dangerous narrow eyes. Harlan guessed him to be around two hundred and fifty pounds of pure muscle. His long dark brown hair was pulled back into a ponytail that ran halfway down his back. His gaze immediately fixed onto Gypsy and he didn't look happy to see her.

"Can I help you?" Harlan said.

"My name is Drake Trolis. I've come for my physical," he said, keeping his eyes fixed on her daughter. Harlan glanced at Gypsy and was horrified to see her staring right back at the enormous warrior.

"You only made two points in the last match, little girl," he said to Gypsy in a low, growling voice. "You'll never qualify for the year."

"I'm touched by your concern," she replied. "But don't worry. I'll do even better than that next time and I will qualify. You wait until next year. I'll make it to your level just so I can shove my saber up your ass."

"Why wait?" he said, holding his arms out in welcome. "Do it now. I'd love a chance to grind your face in the dirt and have at that pretty pussy of yours."

"Drake! Gypsy!" Harlan said. "That's enough out of both of you!"

He looked at Harlan for the first time and bowed his head in respect. Gypsy just glared at him and leaned against the wall. Harlan gestured to the rear exam room and he started toward it, his boots scraping on the floor. Harlan hoped Gypsy would break off the conflict, but her daughter had to have the last word.

"You don't have to put on a macho show for Doctor Ambrose!" she shouted as they rounded a corner. "Everyone knows you prefer the company of other men!"

Drake turned to go back to the waiting room, but Harlan put her hand in the middle of his back and pushed him into the exam room. She whipped back around and pointed at Gypsy. "Close your mouth and go wait in my office, now!"

She came into the exam room after Drake and pulled the door closed behind her. The exam room felt hot and cramped with him in here, and her daughter had already made an awkward situation much worse. She took a deep breath and smiled at the warrior. "Now," she said in her most pleasant voice. "Where shall we begin?"

* * * *

"What is the matter with you?" Harlan said as she closed her office door. Gypsy slumped in her chair with one of her feet on the edge of Harlan's desk. She absently played with some stitching on the instep of her boot and didn't look up at her mother. Her mother sat down on the other side of her desk, leaned forward and knocked Gypsy's boot off the edge.

"Sometimes you act as though you weren't born and raised here. You know your father's protection only goes so far. It won't do you much good if you incite someone to a rage and end up dead."

Gypsy got up angrily. She didn't know who was better at pushing her buttons, her mother or Gavin. "Nothing I do or say has anything to do with some misguided sense of divine protection. I don't need or want his protection and I certainly don't speak my mind because I think he's got my back!"

"Sit down. I'm sorry I said that. It's just that I wish you would be more careful about how you treat these men. If anything happened to you...I can't even entertain those emotions. Do you realize how sick I am over the possibility you might get yourself butchered?" Harlan said, rubbing her eyes. "You're killing me."

Harlan wasn't crying but she was close. Gypsy hated upsetting her mom. It made her feel as low as she could get. Her mother was the rock in her life. There were no surprises and no restrictions. Her mother had always been open and available, always encouraged Gypsy to do what made her happy. That was until now. Gypsy couldn't look into her mother's eyes. There was too much pain in them. She settled on staring at the multiple spur scars gouged into the wood of her mother's desk and retook her seat.

After a long silence Harlan finally said, "So tell me about Drake. Obviously you have encountered him before."

"He's just a big pompous jerk I had the displeasure of meeting at my first fight. He was the one who told me my sword would break. After he took my crappy sword from me, I had to threaten his manhood with a knife before he would give it back. I almost missed my match, and we've been great friends ever since," Gypsy said, finally venturing a look at her mom's face. It relaxed and carried some amusement, but the sadness was still there.

"Promise me you'll be careful with him. These things can get out of hand very quickly, and young ÆEssyrian men are not known for considering consequences before actions. Most of Gavin's sons are a perfect example of that."

Gypsy smiled and stood up. "Well, I can't make any promises, but I will try to keep my mouth shut when appropriate."

Harlan shook her head. "I just know you're not going to try hard enough."

Chapter 24

The nightmare was one of the worst Gavin ever had and it shook him to his core. Leaping out of bed covered in sweat, he tried to banish the horrible image of Gypsy, clad in a blood-drenched wedding gown, dancing in Titan's stone garden with Northe. He knew it was a not-so-subtle warning from his father and although he hated the man, he was grateful for the message. Storming down the hall, he burst into Gypsy's room and turned on the light.

She sat up blinking and shielding her eyes from the glare. "What's going on?" she said groggily. "What's happened?"

Gavin heaved her from her bed and flung her in a chair. She glared at him with pure venom. "Get your fucking hands off me!" she snarled, slapping his hands. "What the hell is your problem?"

She tried to get up but he leaned down and pinned her to the chair by placing a hand on each armrest. Gypsy pushed back into the cushion trying to escape his wrath. Gavin was vaguely aware of Harlan coming into the doorway wrapping her robe around her.

"Did you go and see Titan?" he roared at his daughter. "Answer me, did you?"

Gypsy glanced from him to her mother. She shook her head and her voice cracked as she spoke. "No I—"

"Don't lie to me!"

"Okay! I did, now get off me!"

Harlan gasped.

Gavin took a step back and looked back at his wife. Harlan was as pale as a sheet. All she did was watch Gypsy in horror. She took a few halting steps forward. "Did you make a deal with him? Did he give you anything?" Harlan asked frantically.

"No." Gypsy cast nervous glances at Gavin. "I swear I didn't take anything from him." She had good reason to be afraid. Right now, he wanted to break her neck.

"Why did you go and see him?" Gavin asked.

"I went to him because I wanted help in the arena. But before you throw a clot, don't, because he refused to help me."

Gavin watched her in silence for a moment. He heard Harlan sniffle. She was handling this better than he was. "Titan must have done something for you," he said. "I can't see him not showing off his power to his granddaughter. What did he do for you?"

"He let me talk to Northe for just a few minutes. That's all, nothing else."

That name—Northe. After so long, hearing it was like a blade in his gut. His stomach turned in grief and his hands began to shake. "What did Northe say?" he said in a voice barely his own.

Gypsy's lip trembled. "He didn't think I was crazy. He said he would have been surprised if I hadn't wanted to be a warrior. He did tell me to watch out for you. He said one day you might end up killing me too."

"And do you believe him?" Gavin asked.

"I don't know what to believe about you, Gavin. We barely know each other anymore," Gypsy said. "I guess we have to wait and see."

Gavin didn't want her words to be true, but they were. It seemed like he'd spent years pushing her away because he couldn't relate to her. He'd always had a hard time relating to women, why should his own daughter be any different? And now she was looking for what she needed from the most dangerous person she could— her grandfather.

His failure as a father was too much for him to face. He turned from Gypsy and his wife and left the room with an emotional knife twisting in his belly. The last thing he heard before going outside for a smoke was Harlan telling Gypsy to stay away from Titan at all costs. He wondered if Gypsy would listen.

Chapter 25

Master Sergeant Rakon was more intimidating up close than Gypsy thought he'd be. He always held a distant presence in her life and served under her father for a long time, but she doubted she had spoken more than three words to him in all of her nineteen years. He was a Razorback, but not like any she ever met. He was what many considered a throwback to a more primitive time in ÆEssyrian evolution. Although not as tall as most males, he nevertheless was unmistakably powerful, with a thick beefy chest and hard knotted arms. His face was weathered and attractive, but held the hardness of battle and the secrets of a man used to brutality. When Gypsy found him, he was straddling a wooden bench in an outdoor shed sharpening his saber. His uniform was unbuttoned revealing a hard muscular chest with scarring to rival her father's. He didn't look up as she approached, his attention riveted to his weapon.

"Master Sergeant?" she said, approaching him warily.

He squinted up at her. "What?" he replied as his eyes brazenly swept over her breasts.

Gypsy felt her cheeks grow warm. "I was wondering if I could talk to you in private for a moment."

He rose from his seat and gestured to a small dark storage room. They came in and he closed the door behind them. This was a little more private than she was comfortable with, but she concealed her apprehension and turned to face him. Tiny slivers of sunlight shone through the aged boards and fell across Rakon's eyes, making him look more sinister. "What?" he said again.

"I'm trying to qualify in the arena," she began, not sure what to say now that she had his full attention. She was beginning to feel foolish for even coming here. "And I need your help."

"What exactly do you want from me?" He stood in front of her with his arms folded across his chest.

"I want you to teach me how to become a better fighter and how to win despite my obvious disadvantages," she said.

He exhaled heavily through his nose and walked around her. He grabbed her shoulders and pushed his thumbs into her muscles. Then he lifted up her shirt and ran one hand down her spine. After several minutes, he grunted and came around to face her again. "You could never afford the training."

Gypsy swallowed. "Try me. Name your price."

Rakon's eyes bore into her. "There's only one thing I want from you."

"Name it."

"Sex. Whenever I want, however I want."

Gypsy swallowed hard, but didn't betray any misgivings. "All right, that's fine with me."

"I don't guarantee you'll qualify. Nobody can promise you that. But understand this, I am going to work your ass off and I expect complete obedience from you. You do what I say when I say it. If you piss me off and you give me any whiney crap we're done, and you can find someone else to baby-sit you. That goes for the sex too."

"I understand. When do we start?"

"I'm sure I don't have to tell you not to breathe a word of this to your father," he said. "He finds out, he'll shut us both down real fast."

"Tell me when and where and I'll be there. No one will know I'm gone."

Rakon smiled and it seemed an uncomfortable act for him. "Everyone thinks you're crazy, you know."

"I know they do."

He was quiet for a moment, and then he said, "Fucking me will get out sooner or later. No man will want anything to do with you after they know you've been with me."

Gypsy took a deep breath. "Don't worry about my virtue, it's already gone. And as far as no man wanting me, that's already happened. All I care about is getting the training I need to qualify."

He held his meaty hand out and Gypsy took it. "I give you my word. I'll train the fuck out of you. Whether or not you qualify, that part is up to you."

Chapter 26

It was late and the sky threatened rain. Gypsy stood in the shadows outside the arena waiting for Caraculla to emerge. Everything inside her wanted to walk away but she forced herself to stay. *He is my only chance, I have to stay and talk to him.*

Rakon agreed to train her, but he'd told her she must get some decent armor. Without it, she'd never be able to build the strength she needed. Learning to fight without armor was one thing, but she'd never achieve the proper balance required until she fought with it on. Of course, Rakon might as well have asked her to steal the emperor's scepter, so impossible was her task. She knew if she went to Gavin or her mother, they'd certainly say no. It wasn't that they didn't have the money, but they were still holding out hope that if they didn't support her, she'd eventually give up.

The only person who might consider loaning her the money was Caraculla. After all, he'd helped her in the past. A door opened to her left, and he came up talking to another warrior Gypsy didn't recognize. She cursed under her breath, desperately hoping the other man would leave, since she needed to approach Caraculla alone. They spoke for a few more minutes and Caraculla finally broke off, cutting through the back trail leading to his villa. Gypsy followed for a few yards, taking care to keep her distance. Sensing something was wrong, he turned around and pulled his saber.

"If you intend to rob me, don't waste your time. I've got nothing on me worth your life."

Gypsy came out of the woods and walked under the silver moonlight. His expression softened. "It's only me," she said. "I just wanted to talk to you alone."

He sheathed his weapon and held his arm out to her in welcome. "Come. Let's go back to my villa. We can talk there."

* * * *

They entered through the rear entrance of his villa and Gypsy took a seat in the courtyard. The clouds that gathered earlier had blown away, and the sky was as fresh and clear as she'd ever seen. Caraculla went inside, got himself a cigar and brought out two drinks. He took a seat next to her and lit his cigar after handing her one of the drinks. The scent of tobacco reminded her of her father.

Caraculla examined the end of his cigar. "What did you want to talk to me about?"

Gypsy's palms were damp and her belly twisted in knots. She didn't know if it was because she was embarrassed to ask him for money or nervous about being alone with him. "I need to borrow some money," she blurted out, regretting the delivery.

She felt him study her, but she kept her eyes down. "For what?"

She took a deep breath. "Armor."

He considered this for a moment. "Have you found someone to train you?"

"Yes." She downed the drink in one gulp.

"Who?"

"I'd rather not say," she said.

"If you want me to support you, you're going to have to trust me. I don't want to give you that kind of money unless you have some chance of being successful and the right trainer is important."

"Rakon agreed to train me."

"I'll bet he did." His tone took on a nasty edge. "What are you giving him in return? Don't tell me—let me guess—sex."

Gypsy turned the empty glass around and around in her hand nervously.

"If I didn't know better, I'd think you were jealous. But you wouldn't dare train me because if Gavin found out, you can kiss your promotion goodbye."

"If he finds out I funded you, the outcome will be the same," he said.

Gypsy, starting to lose patience, put the glass down on a nearby table and leaned forward with her arms resting on her knees. "Are you going to loan me the money or not?"

"I have a better idea," he said. "Why don't you give all this up and find yourself a good man and raise a family?"

She scoffed and stood up. "I'm not going to sit here and waste my time having this idiotic conversation with you. I thought it was obvious to everyone that I am not giving up anything to settle down and raise a family, and the next person who suggests it is going to get decked. I'm sorry I bothered you." She got up and started to walk away.

"Don't go," he said softly.

Gypsy stopped, but didn't turn around. "Do I have to sleep with you for it?" she asked sarcastically. She did not intend to do so, but she wanted to know what he would say.

He let out a low, deadly laugh. "I would say yes, but I don't like what that says about you."

"Or you," she said, turning to face him.

"Come here."

Gypsy walked over. "The money's in my front pocket. Get it out yourself."

Without hesitation, she knelt before him and dug into the front of his pants. She noticed the cigar in his fingers tremble. Her hand wrapped around a wad of bills and she pulled them out. She counted them and was delighted to find it would buy her a few decent pieces. She met his gaze and froze. His eyes were as savage as a hungry lion and for just a moment, she was afraid of him. "Can I have all of it?" she asked.

"That's why I brought it out here," he said. Then he took a deep drag on the cigar and blew out a thin steam of smoke.

She stood up and took a step back from him, feeling charged. "Thanks." She was about to leave when she hesitated. "Can I ask you a question?"

He grinned as if he'd seen her naked and loved it. "Sure."

"You're successful. Why haven't you found a decent woman and settled down to raise a family?"

"There's only one woman for me," he replied. "And right now, she's not available." A few tense seconds ticked by. "Will you kiss me before you go?"

A sexual thrill jolted her. Moving forward, she straddled his hips and wrapped her arms around his neck. Her senses filled with the rich scent of his skin and hair. Her lips touched his in the same soft, gentle way as the first time they'd kissed, but this time he wanted much more. Pushing his fingers into her hair, he returned her chaste kiss with one infused with white heat. The kiss was like nothing she'd ever experienced and sent lust blazing all through her body. In that moment, she wanted him like she'd never thought possible, but before she could seduce him, he took her arms from around his neck and peeled her off him. He looked confused and his chest rose and fell with the intensity of his passion. *What the hell is wrong with him? Why is he pushing me away?*

"What is it?" she said, her body trembling like famine victim. "What's wrong with you?"

He picked up his cigar and puffed hard on it. "I don't want to wear you out for Rakon," he said with a nasty wink. "After all, you two do have a bargain."

"You know what, Caraculla? You're a bigger fucking asshole than my father is. You'll make a great replacement for him when he retires."

Caraculla smiled. "Why, thank you, Gypsy. And here I thought you'd never notice."

For a moment, she thought about throwing his money back in his face, but then she thought better of it. That kind of money would be hard to come by. *Who cares about him anyway?* Her dream was the only thing that mattered to her right now, and she was going to do whatever it took. "Thanks again for the money. I'll pay you back when I can." She headed for the courtyard gates.

"Don't bother, I'll just take it out in trade like the others do."

Gypsy smirked and looked back at him. "Fat chance of that, you son of a bitch. Besides, you wouldn't want to suffer by comparison. I might call out the wrong name in bed."

Caraculla stared at her darkly. "You know, Gypsy," he said, crushing out his cigar. "I hope you are successful because you'd make a much better replacement for your father than I would."

Chapter 27

Gypsy met Rakon at a practice arena near the military complex early the next evening. He was dressed in a dark gray shirt, black army pants, and short black boots. She'd worn a pair of lose-fitting pants and a dark gray tank top, per his instructions. His eyes roamed down her body as if looking for something.

"Are you going to be able to buy the armor?"

"Yes," she said.

He nodded. "I got a guy who'll open up his shop for us after we're done here so we can get you suited up."

"Is he going to have something that fits me?"

"He's the best. If he doesn't have it, he'll make it and it'll fit you like a second skin."

"Why don't we just go now so I can start training with it?"

Rakon chuckled. "You're not going to need it for the first part of your training."

"Why? What are we going to do first?"

"We're gonna run." He slapped her roughly on the shoulder.

"Run?" she said, confused.

"That's right," he said, heading for the start of a dirt trail. "And you'd better be right behind me or I'll double back and kick your ass. Got me?"

Before Gypsy could say a word, Rakon took off at a fast pace. Not wanting to get too far behind, she broke into a run and fell in behind him. The pace was grueling and it didn't take long for her to lose ground. He was surprisingly fast for someone with so much bulk, but she stayed with him for the time being, at least until her lungs began to burn and the sweat from her forehead poured into her eyes, partially blinding her. She let out a groan and stopped for a moment, leaning over to catch her breath. Rakon, noticing she wasn't behind him, turned around and came back.

"What the *fuck* do you think you're doing?"

Gypsy tried to catch her breath. "I had to stop to catch my—"

"I don't give a shit!" he roared. "Pick it up and get behind me or I'll go the fuck home and you can train by yourself. This isn't charm school." With both hands, he shoved her forward, causing her to stumble and fall. For a moment, she sat on the ground staring up at him in disbelief.

"Are you gonna cry?" he said, staring down at her.

Gypsy shook her head.

"Good. Then get up and follow me before I really do kick your ass and make you cry."

Holding her tongue and nursing a newfound hate for him, she got to her feet and fell in behind him again. But if she thought he'd slow the pace out of mercy, she was sadly mistaken, if anything, he was running faster. After an hour, Gypsy was irate and nauseated.

"I thought we were going to train," she complained behind him. "All we've done is run so far. I don't exactly need you to teach me how to do that."

Rakon glanced at her, annoyed. "This *is* training, dumb ass. You run to build up your endurance. I watched you in the arena—you suck. You're slow, weak and you tire easily. You're never going to match those boys in size and strength so you've got to be at the top of your game in everything else. Getting too tired in a match is going make you dead real fast. Now shut up, we've got a long way to go."

* * * *

91

After an arduous evening run and some blade work, they finally went to the armor shop. The smith met them there as promised, and they all went inside. He was a large man who seemed to Gypsy to be pretty old. His long white hair was tied back and he wore small spectacles. While Rakon discussed her needs with him, Gypsy wandered the store, examining all of the different pieces. Some were elaborate to an extreme and didn't appear to have much function, while other pieces were bare bones metal with nothing but seams. All of the armor was huge and nothing even came close to her size, but being around all of this stuff ignited her soul, and made her stomach flutter with excitement.

Rakon snapped his fingers at her.

"Get over here and strip." He gestured to the spot between him and the smith.

Gypsy folded her arms and stayed put. "You're kidding, right? I'm supposed to get undressed in front of you two?"

"Do you want armor that fits or armor that sort of fits? He needs your exact measurements. So get on with it."

Gypsy shuffled over and slowly began removing her clothes. *This is a bunch of shit.* That guy could get her measurements without her being naked. Rakon probably promised him a peep show for his trouble. She shifted uncomfortably as the smith tightly wrapped the tape around practically every inch of her body and wrote the numbers on a little pad of paper. He didn't appear overly interested in her nakedness, unlike Rakon who leered at her the whole time, occasionally rubbing her butt.

"Are you done yet? Can I get dressed?"

The smith nodded quickly and continued scribbling on his pad. She glared at Rakon and began putting her clothes back on.

"That was a bunch of shit," she whispered to him.

He laughed at her and said, "By the time I'm through with you, all of your modesty and inhibitions will be a distant memory."

Gypsy felt herself flush from the neck up and was about to say something nasty to him when the smith spoke up.

"Five days and your armor will be ready. Here is the price." He handed her a piece of paper.

She looked down at the price and scowled. "This is more than I have. Can't you give me a better deal?"

The smith shook his head. "That is a good deal. Because of your small size, every piece you need has to be custom made from scratch. It's very time consuming."

Rakon intervened. "We'll take it. Give him what you have and I'll cover the rest when I pick it up."

Gypsy handed him the wad of bills she had taken from Caraculla. The smith took it. After counting it, he scribbled something on a piece of paper and handed it to Rakon. They walked outside as the smith began to close up his shop again.

"Thanks for loaning me the extra money," she said.

"It wasn't a loan. You're going to earn every bit of it. See you tonight." He walked down the street.

Gypsy started toward home to shower and wait for later that night, when her payment was due. She was grumpy, sore and exhausted, and she was certainly not looking forward to being sweated on by that big ape.

As Gypsy walked down the stone path, she spotted her friend, Angel riding toward her. *Oh great. Just what I need right now, an inquisition.* Because Angel was a noblewoman, she was of course, chaperoned by some large, bored-looking goon. She trotted up alongside Gypsy on her cream-colored hyperia and looked down at her thoughtfully. The goon obediently lagged behind, probably out of a disinterest in anything two young women had to talk about.

"You're looking rather dirty and smelly," she said with a slight smile.

"Really, I hadn't noticed." Gypsy continued down the path. Her muscles were aching and she knew if she stopped, she would have to sit down.

"You've obviously found someone to train with. Who is it?"

"I'd rather not say." She looked down the path away from her friend.

"Come on. You know I wouldn't tell anyone."

"It's not that I think you would tell anyone. It's that I know you won't approve of who's training me and what I'm paying him."

"Tell me. I promise I won't say anything negative."

"Rakon." Gypsy kept walking, waiting for the barrage of disapproval.

Angel stopped her hyperia and although Gypsy couldn't see her, she was sure her friend's mouth was hanging open.

"Rakon? That's gross." Angel gave an exaggerated shiver. "So what's he like in bed?"

"I'll let you know next time I see you."

"You haven't slept with him yet? Then it's not too late. You can call this off. He can't do anything to you." She looked down at her hopefully.

"Nope. I need his help. I have to pay for it and I'm okay with that." Gypsy stopped to make eye contact.

Angel leaned down and squeezed Gypsy's arm. "If you're okay with it, then so am I. I promise not to tell anyone if you promise me one thing."

"What?"

"That when you tell me all about it you don't spare any details." She giggled.

"You know, Angel, I think there's something really wrong with you." Gypsy laughed as she walked down the road.

Chapter 28

Standing by his home in the woods, she tried to convince herself it wouldn't be that bad. *Just like Gregor. A few uncomfortable moments and it will be all over.* She knocked on the heavy wooden door. Rakon opened it and let her in. His house was small, but surprisingly clean. Inside was a large wooden bed with several thick blankets, a round breakfast table and several stands with armor. The walls adorned with an array of swords, knives and a few battered shields.

The master sergeant wasted no time. Turning Gypsy around to face him, he pulled her into his arms and kissed her. Closing her eyes, Gypsy forced herself to relax. The kiss was surprisingly sensual and soon Gypsy found herself surrendering to him.

Rakon broke the kiss and picked her up, carrying her to his bed. He laid her down and moved up over her. His hands roamed under her shirt, caressing the tender flesh of her breasts and belly. He peeled her clothes off until she lay next to him, naked. Not many things made Gypsy nervous, but this certainly did. After all, Rakon was only the second man she'd ever been with and there was a substantial difference in their age.

Pulling her into his arms, he whispered beautiful erotic words into her ear. He told her she was bewitching and how much her naked body reminded him of his youth. He told her he'd never seen such a stunning, sexy woman and he couldn't wait to be inside her. It was all so strange, but he was gentle and took his time, which helped her relax.

Rakon dragged kisses down her body, stopping to worship her neck and breasts with tender kisses. The more he stroked and kissed her, the more the tight muscles in her neck eased. Then he guided her hands down his hard, chiseled body. He took his uniform off as he went, stopping every time she grew anxious. "Relax, Gypsy," he said in a voice thick with passion. "By the time I get done with you, you'll be begging me to take you."

Rakon grabbed three plump pillows and placed them under her naked hips, propping them up. Nestling between her thighs, he kissed her sex, running his tongue deep inside her. At first, she was tense, waiting for him to climb up and finish the deed, but when he lingered, she held out hope this might end up as good as he promised. It took a long time for her to enjoy his soft licking and nibbling, but when the hunger came on her, it was fierce. She whimpered as pleasure licked at her mind, and she suddenly became aware of her hips moving in rhythm to his tongue. He moved up over her and nestled his hips between her thighs.

Lifting her legs onto the back of his, he reached down and guided his thick cock to her lusty, wet channel. With agonizing slowness, he pushed himself inside her, claiming more ground every time her muscles slacked. Soon he'd filled her and Gypsy was frantic for more. He kissed her neck and groaned as he pushed the last few inches home.

"More?" he grunted.

Language escaped her as she searched for something to say. She was all instinct and hunger. "Yes," she whispered, gasping.

Rakon squeezed her buttocks and began a hard steady thrust. The sex was worlds away from what she'd experienced with Gregor. Rakon seemed to know every erogenous zone both on and in her body. She gripped onto him and snarled, wanting him more than she thought she ever would. He was a fierce lover, taking her like an animal in the woods, and making her love him for it. Her orgasm exploded, causing her to cry out and dig her nails into him.

Two more orgasms came before he grunted out his passion into her.

He rolled over, exhausted.

She laid in bed next to him for a long time, thinking about what she just experienced and listening to his heavy breathing. Without a word, he had fallen asleep a few minutes after he finished. Eventually she sat up and stretched, feeling infused with his life force. She was actually giddy and slightly disappointed he couldn't do her again. She climbed out of bed and gathered up her clothes.

Rakon rolled over and pointed toward the back of the house. "Shower," he mumbled groggily.

"What?"

"You need to take a shower. If you run into Gavin and he picks up my scent on you, he will definitely kill me and maybe you too," he said, rolling back over.

"Right. Good idea." She headed toward the bathroom.

The hot water electrified her senses even more as she stood under the steaming waterfall. She massaged soap through her hair and throughout her body until all physical traces of Rakon had slipped down the drain. When she came out, he was asleep again. She surveyed him as she dressed, and felt a hungry ache in her groin. Maybe this wouldn't be such a hard debt to pay after all.

Chapter 29

There was a unique grace to the way an ÆEssyrian man moved in battle. Stretching their long powerful arms out, they smashed their weapons into each other with bone-shattering force. A full adult male typically weighed in at three hundred pounds of pure muscle, with some larger males, like her father, weighing in well over that. But even with all that bulk, they could attack with striking speed and agility. Razorback males like Caraculla were even more fearsome, because in addition to size and strength, they could also spit lethal venom. Luckily, most Razorbacks rejected the warrior's life, but there were always those who fell outside the mold and left the queendom in search of honors and war.

Even though Caraculla was an accomplished soldier, he still needed practice to hone his skills. Once the path was chosen, being a warrior was a lifelong vocation that could end abruptly with maiming or death. It wasn't uncommon for young men trying to qualify, just as Gypsy was, to lose a limb or endure a fatal injury during practice matches. Given those risks, she didn't blame her parents for doing all they could to stop her. Most warriors didn't live longer than five or six hundred years, which was young considering their lifespan stretched to an average of one thousand five hundred.

* * * *

Gypsy had finished training with Rakon for the evening and he had duty, so she wouldn't be meeting him tonight. She stole her way into the arena and sat high in the bleachers where the practice lights couldn't reach, watching Caraculla and Gavin practice. It was hard to see them together enjoying each other's company, because it reminded her of how strained her relationship was with Gavin. It should be her down there being trained by her father, not Caraculla. But it never would be, because she was *a woman*. Some nights she'd come here just to watch them until the pain in her heart made tears fall silently from her eyes. She'd often compared her feelings to that of a wife who'd lost her husband to a mistress.

She didn't blame Caraculla for what hadn't happened with her father. After all, he'd been training under Gavin long before she was born. In some ways, she should be grateful for the friendship between the two men. According to her mother, Caraculla brought out some of the best in Gavin. She'd heard the Razorback officer had been the first one to encourage her father to be more patient with his men, and not always act on his red-hot rages. But whatever good Gavin picked up from Caraculla was offset by the general's corruption of his protégé. Gavin, although happily married to her mother, never felt as comfortable as when he was in the brothels of his youth. He introduced Caraculla to all the finest vices—drinking, whoring and gambling, and soon the young officer picked up a vice all his own—drug addiction. Although now drug free, Gypsy had seen him battle that horrible demon for years.

As she watched them packing up to leave, she remembered the kindness Caraculla had shown in giving her money for armor and loaning her his sword before the last match. She knew if Gavin found out about the armor, it would be very bad for Caraculla. He'd been the only one to openly defy her father, and she found that incredibly sexy.

Gavin slipped off to clean up and dress, leaving Caraculla alone on the arena floor moping sweat from his neck and chest. Gypsy descended the steps. The closer she got, the more her blood rushed with excitement. He turned around and stared at her with those metallic green eyes and her breath caught in her chest. She smiled at him. "Hi." She felt self-conscious and weirdly shy.

His forked tongue darted out and licked his split bottom lip. "Hello." He glanced in the direction Gavin had gone. There was no sign of him. "You get what you needed?"

Gypsy moved closer. "Yes, thank you."

"You end up getting killed, I'll never forgive myself."

She shrugged. "If you didn't help me I'd probably be dead a lot sooner."

Something smoky drifted through his eyes. "How's your training coming?"

"Good," she said softly, moving within inches of him. "I wanted to thank you in a more personal way." Wrapping her arms around his neck, she placed her lips on his. He dropped the towel he was holding and pulled her into his arms. He kissed her back with stunning passion. Gypsy drank the kiss in, savoring the heat. Her body ached for him and a lusty heat began to grow in her groin. Ever since her erotic cultivation had begun with Rakon, her sexual fantasies with Caraculla had become much more explicit. There were so many things she wanted to do to him. Sometimes she pretended it was Caraculla ravishing her instead, and her orgasms were mind-numbing. This hot, sweet kiss was not helping her situation.

In those brief few moments, her heart took flight and she couldn't remember ever being happier. If only they could be like this forever. He broke the contact with her lips to maul kisses down her throat.

"I wish you would train me," she whispered breathlessly, running her fingers into his hair.

"I can't."

"Why not? You're not afraid of Gavin. He'd be mad, but he'd get over it."

Caraculla smiled bitterly. He pulled her off him and she suddenly realized she'd made a terrible blunder. *He thinks I'm trying to seduce him into helping me, damn it.* Gypsy shook her head but it was too late. He was already suspicious.

"I've got to go." He turned his back on her and headed for the locker rooms.

She tried to think of anything that would keep him, but came up empty. She wanted him so bad it hurt and now she'd probably lost him. *What else could go wrong today?*

Gypsy made her way to the arena entrance feeling like the world was coming to an end, when who should be coming toward her, but Drake.

"Working on your combat, little girl?" he sneered.

"Fuck you, asshole," she said, surprised at the venom in her tone.

Drake reached out and grabbed her arm. Normally she would have been ready for such a move, but she'd been so distracted by her spat with Caraculla she didn't react in time. Drake pulled her up to him and seized her jaw in a painful grip. "I want you to know I lay awake at night praying for the day when you come up against me. I want the whole arena to see your battered body fall under my blade, and when I'm done smashing you, I'll use you like the whore you are!"

Gypsy broke free and stumbled back. She rubbed her jaw. "You'd have to win that match first."

He gave her a chilling smile. "There is no doubt of that, little girl. There is certainly no doubt of that."

Chapter 30

Harlan sat in the officers' lounge waiting for Gavin to arrive. While she waited she rehearsed what she was going to say, but no matter how she phrased it he was going to be pissed. *Gypsy is training with someone; she's going out running every morning.* As much as she didn't want it to be true, she suspected it was Caraculla.

Gavin came across the room as everyone scurried out of his way. She had to admit he was an imposing sight in full battle armor, with an even worse reputation. She took a deep breath as he sat down and held it.

Gavin took a seat across from her. He reached out and took her hand, kissing the back of it. "What did you want to see me about, my love?" he asked.

"First," she said, "I want you to promise you won't jump up and storm out of here after I tell you."

He let go of her hand and leaned back in his chair. "As you wish."

She looked down at the table and traced a design with her index finger. "I think someone is training Gypsy. I've been watching her and things are different."

"What do you mean—different?"

"She's up before dawn every morning running, and her body's changed. In the past weeks, she's become more muscular, harder. She tries to wear loose clothes to hide it, but I can tell. Her eating habits have also changed. She consumes a lot more meat." That caught Gavin's attention. His eye narrowed. "And the other night I

102

accidentally walked in on her and she had bruises all over. She tried to tell me she got them while hunting, but they were the big, black, nasty ones that looked a lot to me like combat injuries. She didn't get those by herself."

Gavin folded his arms across his chest. A minute passed, then two.

"Aren't you going to say anything?" she asked.

"Do I need to? I think we both know who's probably training her. It has to be Caraculla. Has enough time passed for me to jump up and go talk to him, my dear?"

Harlan sighed. "Yes, but just take it easy. We're not sure it's him and if it is, he's just trying to help her."

Gavin's face was expressionless. "May I go now?"

Harlan nodded, defeated. She sure hoped it wasn't Caraculla, for his sake.

* * * *

Gavin found Caraculla at the military complex looking over the evening's watch bill. "Colonel?" Gavin said. "May I have a word with you in my office?"

Caraculla frowned, but followed his general. Once inside the office, Caraculla closed the door, but remained standing. Gavin didn't offer him a seat.

"Excellency?" Caraculla said, referring to Gavin's official title.

Gavin sat behind his desk and clipped the end of a cigar. He offered one to Caraculla who shook his head. He lit it and squinted at his colonel through the smoke. "I just had a most interesting meeting with my wife," Gavin began. "She's under the impression someone has been training our daughter to compete in tomorrow's final match. Now, you and I both know there are not many men who are foolish enough to do such a thing. So I'm asking you as a friend, do you know who is training my daughter?"

Caraculla lowered his head and sighed. Then he looked up and met Gavin's gaze. "Yes, Excellency."

"Is it you?"

"No, Excellency."

"Who then?"

"She convinced Rakon to train her."

Gavin laughed and shook his head. The girl was sharp—he had to give her that. The master sergeant was the last person he would suspect. The man was a virtual ape. Gavin never would have thought Gypsy brave enough to ask him for anything. But he would be an excellent trainer for a beginner. Gavin looked up at Caraculla. "Go fetch the master sergeant, Colonel. He and I are going to have a little chat and put an end to this nonsense."

Caraculla dropped his head in obedience. "Yes, Excellency."

Chapter 31

Caraculla sat in his villa nursing a drink in the dark. He felt horrible about Gypsy's discovery, but Gavin was bound to find out eventually. He just wished the general hadn't found out until after the match. Was he being foolishly optimistic about Gypsy's chances? He sure hoped not, because if she died in the arena to-morrow, he would go home and end his own life. It would be the only honorable thing to do and he simply wouldn't want to live without her.

A frantic knock sounded on the door and he went to answer it. Gypsy stood there, face wet and eyes red from crying. "I hope you're happy with yourself!" she roared.

Caraculla walked away from the door with Gypsy in furious pursuit. "He sent his monkeys to Rakon's and took everything! What the hell am I supposed to do now, fight with my fists? Why couldn't you keep your big mouth shut until tomorrow?"

Without looking back at her, he switched on the living room light. He returned to his seat and sipped his drink as Gypsy continued to rage at him. Then, mid-sentence, she stopped.

All her armor and weapons were there in a corner, polished and ready for tomorrow. She placed her hand over her mouth and stared. Slowly, she sank into a nearby chair. "You did this for *me*? Are you crazy?"

He tossed back the rest of his drink and poured himself an-other. "Yes, I did and apparently yes, I am crazy. And when Gavin finds out, I'll be pursuing a new career as a blacksmith. But I've watched you practice, Gypsy, and I think you can do this."

"Do you mean that or are you just trying to make me feel better?"

"Well," he said darkly. "Let's just put it this way. If you fall tomorrow, you won't be the only casualty of the day."

Her eyes welled up with tears and she got up and went to him. She crawled into his lap and took his drink, draining it in one gulp. Hugging him around the neck, she said, "You've been so good to me. I should leave before someone sees me here. Gavin and I had a huge fight and he'll be looking for me everywhere."

"He won't look for you here. He thinks I'm on his side. Besides, he thinks he has all your equipment. He'll probably just wait for you to turn up pissed off at home tomorrow."

Gypsy nuzzled his neck. "What makes you think I have a chance?"

"I know Rakon. I've fought with him and the men he trained for as long as I've had a career. I can't think of a man better qualified to start your training. You'll be more than a match for those clumsy junior warriors. It's when you move up next year that you'll need more specialized training." He got up, picking her up as he went. "Now you need to get some sleep. You have a long, hard day tomorrow and you'll need all the rest you can get. I'll wake you when its time to go." He lowered her to the floor and gestured to a room off to the right. "The guest bedroom is in there."

Gypsy smiled at him for the first time in a long time and the room seemed a little brighter. "I don't know why you put up with me. I'm such an ass to you most of the time."

Caraculla sat down and poured himself another drink. "Yes you are, but I wouldn't want you any other way. Good night, Gypsy."

"Good night."

Chapter 32

The final fall tournament in the main arena was packed to the walls. Gypsy was sure she'd never seen so many people in one place. When Caraculla woke her this morning she'd been excited and eager, but standing in the dressing area watching all these young warriors, she was starting to have second thoughts. Caraculla pushed through the crowd with the match list in his hand. Gypsy's mouth went bone dry. "Well?" She shifted in her heavy armor. "Who am I matched with?"

"Some guy named Haydin. Never heard of him." He looked up and met her eyes. She could taste the fear on him and wished his feelings didn't matter to her. For a fleeting moment, she thought about calling all this off and leaving, but she knew she couldn't, she was in too deep.

The crowd suddenly parted and Gypsy saw Gavin approaching. His heavy boots thumped on the floor as his stride echoed off the stone walls. He shot a dirty look at Caraculla as he passed. "I'd like a word with you," he said to her.

Gypsy shook her head. "If this is about ditching the fight—"

"It's a private matter. I know nothing can stop you from this folly now."

Gavin went into a dressing room and closed the door behind them. "I've seen the man you're about to fight training with his handler and he's slow on his feet. You can use speed to defeat him." He reached into the breast pocket of his tunic and pulled out a small strip of cloth bound with silk thread. He handed it to her.

"This is a good luck charm. It's a piece of the uniform from the first man I ever defeated. I want you to have it." Before she could say a word, Gavin stuffed it into a small gap in her armor. He grabbed her face and kissed her quickly, leaving her dazed. Then he opened the door and disappeared into the crowd.

Gypsy sat there stunned. Gavin hadn't shown her that much affection in years. But his visit had a profound effect on her. A quiet serenity came over her, a sense of peace. *I can do this. I know I can.*

The referee called her name and she stepped out. She moved across the packed black sand feeling very small in such a vast place. Crowded bleachers circled all around, booming with shouts and cheers. A huge roar erupted from the crowd when they saw her, and she wasn't sure if it was for her, or her opponent. Haydin entered from his side, clad in thick gray armor that had obviously seen some battle before. She suddenly felt self-conscious that her armor looked so pristine.

They approached each other until they were a few yards away, then stopped. The announcer introduced them and the battle began.

* * * *

Gavin took his seat next to Harlan, his eyes riveted to the arena below. Harlan's mouth was in a permanent frown. "I take it you weren't able to talk her out of this," she said grimly.

"No, so I did the only thing I could. I gave her hope."

Harlan glanced down at his tunic and noticed a large chunk missing at the bottom. She put her fingers through the hole. "What happened to your uniform?"

He didn't look down at the damage. "I made a charm for Gypsy. I told her it came off the uniform of my opponent after my first victory."

"She's not an idiot, Gavin. I'm sure she would know the difference between a piece of cloth from hundreds of years ago and one off a fairly new uniform," Harlan said.

Gavin smiled and kissed her. "It wasn't the history that was so important to her, my love. It was the message. Anyway I stuffed it into her armor before she had a chance to examine it."

* * * *

Gavin was right. Haydin was slow, plodding around the arena swinging his weapon before he was even sure it would connect. A lot of what he did was designed to intimidate her. Just as Rakon taught her, she took her time studying her opponent, waiting for just the right moment to strike. After a few long minutes, her moment came.

Haydin was growing tired, not keeping his guard up as he should. Gypsy decided to wake him up a little. Taking advantage of his clumsiness, she lured him into striking at her and when he missed, she plunged her sword into his side. Haydin roared in pain and Gypsy jumped back.

Blood spilled onto the arena floor. The crowd erupted into a wall of noise so loud she could barely hear herself think. Momentarily distracted by the din, she took her attention off Haydin for a second, and that was all he needed. Lunging forward, he drove his blade between her armor and into the soft flesh of her belly. Gypsy jumped back, feeling what she thought was a cramp in her abdomen, then she saw the blood.

Summoning all her rage, she twisted, trapping his blade between her armor and struck back at the warrior, swinging her sword in a wide arc and connecting with his neck. His head came half off, lulling forward in a sickening spray of gore. Haydin's knees buckled and he collapsed to the ground.

Gypsy noticed the noise of the crowd growing softer and a sudden rush of weakness came over her. She too fell onto the ground and was surprised to find there was so much blood beneath her.

Then she realized some of that blood was her own.

Chapter 33

Harlan sat outside the treatment room with Gavin, grateful her daughter's injury hadn't been much worse. She reflected on the few times she'd had to put Gavin back together after some critical wounding. The fear and devastation she felt at those times was back, only now it focused on her child. Harlan's distress was somewhat exaggerated since Gypsy's stab wound wasn't deep, just gory. *Thank God, Gypsy would be fine, but what about tomorrow and the next day?* Her daughter was never going to stop competing, there was too much of Gavin in her. She glanced over at her husband and he looked miserable. He was at just as much a loss over what to do as she was. Perhaps Caraculla was right.

There was only one way to protect Gypsy.

She got up and patted Gavin's hand affectionately. "I'll be right back," she said. "Will you go in and sit with her while she sleeps off the sedative?"

Gavin nodded and disappeared into the room. Harlan folded her arms and went outside the clinic to where Caraculla was waiting for word on Gypsy's condition. His normally handsome face was carved with worry. "I'm so sorry Harlan——" he began.

She placed her hand on his chest to stop him from talking. He appeared puzzled, but fell silent. "I want to be mad at you for helping her, but I can't. I know you did what you did out of love and respect for her. I wish there was some way to end all this, but I know she'll never stop. She'll happily die before she gives this up.

The only thing I can think of is to train her well, so the next time she'll be better equipped to defend herself."

Harlan paused for a moment and glanced toward the glass double doors to make sure Gavin hadn't come out. She didn't want him to overhear what she had to say. "I want you to train her, Caraculla. I've seen you fight and you're one of the best—easily as good as Gavin. She needs you."

Caraculla stared down at his boots and rubbed the back of his neck. "If Gavin finds out, he'll kill me, not to mention end my career. And what about my feelings? I'd never forgive myself if anything ever happened to Gypsy. Training someone is a huge responsibility. I can't, Harlan. I just can't. Why can't you talk Gavin into doing it?"

Harlan sighed. "First of all, she is not emotionally mature enough to be trained by Gavin. It would be a disaster. Second, he won't do it because he thinks it will encourage her to continue. But that's just what he says on the outside. I know his feelings run deeper than that. I think he's terrified that it will destroy what tattered relationship they have left. God knows you grew to hate him in your first few years."

"Hate doesn't even touch what I felt toward him. His training was grueling, but it saved my life many times."

"Well now I'm asking you to do the same for my daughter. Give her the training she needs to survive. Save her life just as Gavin saved yours. If you don't, she will find someone who will, and that terrifies me." A tense few moments passed between them. Harlan pushed some dirt around with her foot. "I understand I'm asking a lot of you. But my child's life is more important than your career."

Caraculla met her gaze and Harlan saw the hunger in his soul. *My God. He doesn't want to do it because he's in love with her.* Harlan felt her stomach drop. He wasn't going to agree. He was too afraid of facing the power of his emotions. She turned around and headed back toward the clinic, wondering what she was going to do.

"I'll do it," he said behind her.

Harlan turned around and watched him. A wave of relief washed over her. "Are you sure?" she asked, to give him another chance to decline.

Caraculla frowned and lit a cigar. He took a few hardy puffs on it then squinted into the hot afternoon suns. "I said I'll do it," he repeated.

* * * *

Gypsy squirmed in bed trying to sit up. Why the hell was she hooked up to all this monitoring equipment? Her stab was not much more than a flesh wound, only a few inches deep and she didn't feel any pain. She noticed her father sitting in the visitor's chair and she froze. He was no doubt going to yell at her for disobeying him. He got up and came over. She withered under his commanding golden eye. "That injury," he began, "could have been your last. You're out of trainers and out of money. Your benefactor Caraculla has been placed on military suspension—"

"No!" Gypsy shouted, interrupting him.

"So he can't help you anymore," he continued. "I'm also putting a ban on your future competitions. I'm ending your fighting career today, Gypsy."

She glared at him. "You are not ending anything," she snarled. "The only thing ending is your interference in my life." With that, Gypsy pulled the monitoring tape from her neck and yanked out her IV. Blood flowed from the puncture site as she jumped out of bed and frantically searched for the rest of her clothes. Gavin grabbed her upper arm and she swung at him with her bloody free hand. He easily caught it and twisted both behind her back in an attempt to restrain her. Gypsy screamed in a frustrated rage that reverberated through the room and half way down the hall.

Gavin's grip was unyielding. "Stop it before you injure yourself further!"

"Let me go!" she yelled and brought both feet off the ground kicking over a supply tray in her attempt to break free. All she succeeded in doing was popping several of her stitches and making her belly wound bleed.

* * * *

Harlan and Caraculla heard the crash as they were walking back into the clinic after their conversation. Immediately, Harlan realized the mistake of sending Gavin in to Gypsy without her to act as a buffer. Simultaneously, she and Caraculla broke into a run toward Gypsy's room. Like Gypsy's initial injury, the sight that awaited them looked much worse than it was. Gavin had her partially restrained as blood dripped from her arm and seeped from her belly. Gavin's own arms were covered with her blood, and she was still fighting.

"Gavin, let go of her!" Harlan screamed at him.

As soon as he did, Gypsy launched herself back at him, her rampage not yet quelled. But Caraculla anticipated her attack and grabbed her around the waist firmly before she could get back to her target.

Harlan pulled on Gavin's arm. "Please go out so we can get her calmed down and resutured." She could tell he was barely containing his own rage. He started toward the door and then turned back toward his daughter. His eye blazed at her.

"You had better remember that until you have a husband, you are my property and I will do with you and your life as I please."

"God damn it, Gavin, get the hell out of here and stop making things worse!" Harlan yelled at him.

He turned his back on all of them and threw open the door to Gypsy's room with such force that it smashed into the back wall and cracked down the middle. He paid no attention and stormed out.

* * * *

Gypsy wiped away a few angry tears and allowed Caraculla to help her back into bed. Harlan replaced the sutures Gypsy had torn and put a fresh dressing on the wound. She then walked out without a word, leaving her alone with Caraculla.

"Are you all right?"

"I'd be much better if Gavin would stop talking to me."

He leaned against the wall and grinned. "I know how you feel. Your mother and I had a talk about you. She's worried you're going to die."

Gypsy glared at the broken door. "She doesn't have to worry. Gavin put a ban on my fighting, but I'll find a way around it."

"You mean *we'll* find a way around it."

Gypsy stared at him. "What are you saying? You're willing to train me?"

He threw his hands in the air as if to surrender. "I will if you'll let me."

"Won't Gavin demote you if you do?"

"He'll try, but I don't think your mother will let him. Right now keeping you alive is our main priority. Luckily, it's year-end and we have a few weeks before the tournaments start up again. Your arena kill gave you exactly the points you needed to move up to the next level. But I'm warning you, things get a lot harder from here on out."

"I'm ready."

Caraculla stared at her for a long time, and then said, "I know you are."

SIREN WARRIOR SERIES BOOK 2: HARLOT'S LIFE

by

Michelle Marquis & Lindsey Bayer

Chapter 1

Drake Trolis moved through the smoky whorehouse looking for the madam. He'd been told this was one of the few places in the city where he could get a human whore for the night, and his fever was riding high. The seedy weekend crowd filled every cramped gaming room and parlor. In their haste to rid themselves of money, they pushed and jostled each person who went past. Annoyed, Drake was beginning to think he'd just go home and jerk off. He stopped by one of the game tables and touched the dealer's arm. She was a tall, thin Æssyrian woman with catlike greenish-blue eyes. Her ample breasts bulged out of a tiny sequined bikini top. She gave him a jaded smile. "I'm not for sale tonight, honey," she said with a lewd wink.

"I'm looking for the madam," he replied.

She turned her attention back to the players. "She's probably in the back room with the big rollers. Why? What do you want?"

"A human."

The woman turned her attention back to him and looked him up and down. "Upstairs," she said. "First door to your left. Make sure to knock."

Drake nodded and muscled through the crowd. He ascended the stairs, feeling the hunger quicken his blood. His cock was so hard it was almost numb. Reaching the door, he knocked loudly and waited.

"Come in," a woman's voice called.

He entered and took in the stuffy smell of old sex. His passion cooled a little as he looked at the woman. She didn't look anything like Gypsy. She was short and much older, with a faded red tint to her hair. But she'd feel the same on the inside. The woman smiled at him, showing a broken front tooth. "What can I do for you, lord?"

Drake pushed the door closed behind him. He reached into his pocket and tossed the woman a tiny bottle of shampoo. "I want straight sex from behind, but I want you to wash your hair first with that."

The woman didn't look surprised by his request. She slipped into the bathroom and he heard the water turn on. He walked around the room and let his desire burn hotter. His balls were heavy and ached with need. He pulled some bills out of his pocket and tossed them on the dresser. Before turning away, he examined his reflection and admired the extra twenty pounds of muscle he recently put on. But he also caught sight of something dark and menacing in his eyes, and knew he was losing the battle to control it. It was all that damned Gypsy's fault. She was making him feel a lust that bordered on madness. What the hell was he doing *here* anyway?

The woman came out, her hair toweled dry. But the scent was there. Not exactly Gypsy's shampoo—but close, very close. He gestured to the bed. The woman went over and placed her knee on the mattress, but he grunted, "No." She gave him a questioning look. He grabbed her and bent her over at the waist so her torso was resting on the bed. He reached under her cheap orange dress and was pleased she wasn't wearing underwear. Holding her in place with one hand on her back, he unbuttoned his pants and lowered them to the floor.

Drake's erection was painfully hard. A pearl drop of seed formed at the tip. He placed his thumb on it and rubbed it around the swollen head. The sensation was pure bliss. He stroked the thick veins of the shaft, and let his mind imagine it was Gypsy licking his cock and staring up at him with those smoldering yellow eyes. Pure desire filled him and he couldn't wait any longer. Stuffing his cock into the woman, he drove himself all the way into her, and heard her groan. Squeezing her hips, he let his lust take over and pumped into her with unbridled savagery. The bed under her squeaked and thumped against the wall until he eased back on the pace. To his surprise, the woman moaned louder, becoming slicker with every punishing stroke of his cock.

In his mind, it was Gypsy moaning under his grueling lust. He focused enough to smell the fragrance of her hair and the velvet texture of her skin. His cock drove harder and faster until he thought his heart would burst from his chest. The woman beneath him was insatiable, pushing her slick pussy back onto him, crying out her pleasure. The muscles deep within her seized his cock and rippled along his shaft. His own climax was one of the most powerful he'd ever had and it took him several hard thrusts to empty his balls completely.

He backed away from the woman and let his erection soften a little before putting his cock back in his pants. The woman lowered her dress and went over to the dresser. She tossed him the money he'd left for her.

Drake stared down at the money. "What's wrong?"

She laughed and shook her head. "That was the best lay I've had in years. You can come back anytime. No charge."

He nodded and stuffed the money back into his pocket. *This was no good.* He needed a lot more, but didn't want to stay here any longer. He had to get himself a steady girlfriend and fuck the life out of her every night. Then maybe he could get that shameless whore, Gypsy, out of his head.

Chapter 2

Gypsy couldn't believe she'd made it to the second year of qualifying. She sat on her bed, fastening the buckles on her boots, marveling at what everyone said she could never achieve. Not, of course, that she wasn't infested with her own doubts. But now it was a whole new season, and year two was going to be a hell of a lot harder than the past year. Expectations for success were much higher. Combatants were judged on technique and victories equally, which meant tons more practice for her.

Gypsy got up and moved in front of the mirror in her bedroom. Her tall, feminine frame had developed a tight covering of lean muscle she worked on daily to maintain. She meticulously combed her dark brown hair back with a leather tie and began to braid it, taking care not to leave a single hair out of place. While sparring for the first time with her previous trainer Rakon, she had made the mistake of leaving her long hair loose during the fight. The mistake had cost her. During one of his attacks, she had been too slow to dodge his strike. He grabbed a huge chunk of her hair in his big, beefy hand and flung her halfway across the arena. She thought he'd ripped her scalp off. For several minutes, she'd lain on the black sand in a fetal position, holding her head and trembling from the pain as he stood over her. All he said was, "You might want to tie your hair back during your bouts. Now get up."

Every session she had with him was forever burned into her memory because of the horrific pain he inflicted upon her. Rakon never told her her mistakes, he showed her, and that was usually enough to prevent them from being made again. Although there were a lot of things she didn't miss about his training, she found herself longing for their sexual encounters. They were not exactly emotionally fulfilling, but they were physically gratifying and she had gotten used to the regular sex. When her father pulled the plug on her training, he had also inadvertently ended her sex life. But now things were looking up.

Today was the first day with her new trainer, Caraculla, and a deluge of different emotions tormented her. Her desire for him stretched back a long time and now she was going to be in close contact with him on a daily basis. Creeping down the stairs that evening, she was delighted to see Gavin was not home yet. He was aware of her new training direction, but that didn't mean he wouldn't start a fight about it. A fight with Gavin often lasted much too long and she had to meet Caraculla in half an hour.

* * * *

For the third time in as many minutes, Gypsy was on the ground, separated from her sword. Caraculla walked over, extended his black-gloved hand down to her, and grinned.

"You know, Caraculla, you're not doing anything for my self-esteem," she said, allowing him to pull her up.

"Don't be so hard on yourself. I have a few hundred years of experience on you."

She nodded and readied herself for another attack. Caraculla was turning out to be a fantastic teacher. In the few hours they'd practiced, she'd learned details of technique and attack that improved her skills tenfold.

Watching him mop the sweat off his neck and chest made her whole body hum with desire. She put her saber down, pausing to calm her thoughts. He was one of the sexiest men she'd ever met. His long, auburn hair was thick and usually loose, with two bright red braids at each temple. The crimson locks were a warning from nature telling anyone who messed with a Razorback that the species was dangerously venomous. Most people heeded the warning and avoided fights with them at all costs. Naturally, Razorbacks were forbidden to use their venom in the arena. It would be an unfair advantage and they'd surely win every time. They didn't often use their venom in close combat, because the chance of peripheral spray hitting one of their own men was too great.

Caraculla also had a beautiful body, with a thick powerful chest and a magnificent broad back. Every twisting muscle was perfectly sculptured and bulged with energy. His face was a pleasing mix of confidence and male aggression, but held a slight hint of softness she found irresistible. His full, sensuous lips seemed to beg for her kisses. As she studied him, she didn't think it was possible to want a man this much. He tossed her a towel, sheathed his saber and sat down on a stone bench to rest. "I want you to consider something," he said.

She wiped some sweat off her face. "What's that?"

"I think you should move in with me. It would make training you a lot easier. We'd be able to practice more hours each day."

Gypsy rolled the idea around in her head for a moment. There was no way she was going to say no, but she had to look like she was thinking about it. "Well," she said, casually strolling closer to him. "If I agree, there's going to be a few rules."

He squinted at her, annoyed. "What kind of rules?"

"First of all, I'm not swapping one big asshole jailer for another. You are not my boss, so you don't tell me what to do."

He remained silent.

"Second, I expect sex, lots of it. I'm not going to live here looking at you everyday and not get something out of it."

Caraculla stood up and she caught a whiff of him. His masculine scent drove her nuts, twisting her womb with a heady lust. Gypsy moved closer, daring to place one hand on his warm chest.

"Don't you think if we start having sex it might be too much of a distraction?" he said in a breathy whisper.

Gypsy, lost in his scent, moved her hands up behind his neck and pulled him down to kiss her. "Did you say something?" she said, lazily pressing her lips to his.

The kiss was like climbing into a warm bed at night—soft and comforting. Then it changed. Caraculla wrapped his arms around her and crushed her body against him. His gentle kiss turned into a hot savage claiming that Gypsy loved. She opened up her heart and devoured him right back, finding a bliss she'd never known. Every place he touched her turned to longing and desire. Moaning her name, he picked her up and carried her toward the villa, but they never made it to his bed.

Just past the courtyard threshold, she struggled with him to put her down. She couldn't wait for them to get to bed—her need was too strong. He put her down and she grabbed him, pulling him to the floor with her and kissing him wildly. His hands were all over her, undressing her as he went. When he encountered something too difficult to remove, he simply tore it off. Gypsy busied herself clawing the buttons off his uniform pants. Grabbing his pants, she yanked them off his hips, her greedy hands reaching for his enormous cock. She squeezed the base and he moaned.

They grappled like wrestlers, fighting with each other to consummate their union as quickly as possible, each one getting into the other's way.

He found her wet center with his cock, and penetrated her.

Gypsy gasped and dug her nails into his back. His lust was the most natural thing in the world and made her feel like a queen. Plunging into her again and again, Gypsy rode a sea of pleasure she never wanted to end. Deep within her body, the ridges on his cock found the tender erogenous zones near her cervix, and sent her into several frenzied orgasms. But there was more than sex in this union, there was something stronger, richer, but she couldn't place it. In the haze of her hunger, she tried to understand what it was that made this encounter so special.

Caraculla slowed his pace, rotating his cock to massage her slick, hot channel, and it suddenly dawned on her. He wasn't just fucking her, he was making love to her and she felt loved. Her heart swelled with the many delights he teased from her flesh. When he finally climaxed and exhausted himself, she felt a deep sense of satisfaction she had never known before.

He collapsed next to her, panting, sweat trickling off his chest and belly. Weakly, he fumbled for her hand, brought it to his lips and kissed it. "Before you go running off to tell Gavin you're moving out and to go fuck himself, let me talk to him first, okay?"

Gypsy smiled, a soft flutter tickling her womb. He should be good for another round in a few minutes. "Sure, whatever you say, Caraculla." She climbed up on top of him and teased him mercilessly until he was revved up and hard again.

Chapter 3

Hunting with Gavin had always been one of Caraculla's favorite activities, but not today. They'd gotten a late start after work and, truth be told, he was anxious to get back home to Gypsy. What an incredible morning they'd had, making love for over two hours. He would have loved to stay in bed with her all day, but he was already late for work and she had to practice.

Although he was officially on suspension, he wouldn't know it from the work Gavin threw on his desk. The general didn't mention the suspension, so Caraculla kept showing up for work. Every day he wondered if Gavin was going to burst in and send him home for good.

Caraculla spurred his hyperia forward and jumped a broken fence. The animal hissed and fought its bridle as he reined it around to wait for Gavin to rejoin him. Gavin took the jump with ease and rode up alongside him. The general paused to drink from his flask. "You're surprisingly quiet today," Gavin said. He replaced the metal container in its holder on his hip and squinted at the road ahead.

"There's something I've been meaning to tell you," Caraculla replied.

Gavin fixed his one good eye on him. "I suspected there was something on your mind. If it's about the suspension—"

"No," Caraculla interrupted him. "It's not that. It's about Gypsy…she's moving in with me."

"I take it this isn't entirely about her training," Gavin said suspiciously.

"I won't insult your intelligence by saying there's nothing more between us than training. But I will say this about her fighting—I think you're selling her short. She's a determined and ferocious fighter, Gavin. She has a lot of natural ability. I think she can do this."

Gavin laughed wickedly. "Let's say for the sake of argument, she does have talent and ability, and wins her two bouts this year. What is her future going to be? She'll be battered and beaten again next year in the final tournament before the academy picks in winter. And if she succeeds and wins her one big match, then what? Then she'll go into the academy and have to learn how to be a soldier among men who will do everything in their power to discredit and destroy her. And what kind of horrible injuries will she endure along the way from all that fighting? Surely, it hasn't been so long that you've forgotten how grueling military training is.

"And finally, when she gets her commission, she'll be gone for months and years at a time, fighting in some hellhole, only to be assassinated by her own men or slaughtered by the enemy...that is if she's lucky and they don't take her prisoner and torture her. By the time she's done with this crazy dream, you will have moved on with your life, and she'll be too old to have children. Do you really want that life for her?"

Caraculla felt as if he'd been punched in the gut. Gavin's brutal honesty was cruel, but truthful. He was so confused. "It's not my decision to make. Gypsy picked her own future. I don't understand what you want me to do."

Gavin pulled out a cigar, clipped the end and lit it. "You are in a unique position to help her, she trusts you. You should give careful consideration to getting her pregnant."

He was stunned. *Is Gavin so emotionally bankrupt that he would want me to do such a thing? What about Gypsy? Are her feelings and desires to be pushed aside like so much scattered trash?* "I don't think I could deceive her like that."

Gavin blew out a thin stream of smoke. "Let me ask you something. What have you gotten out of this relationship so far? Aside from the sex I'm assuming she's giving you, has she said anything about a future with you? She's just a young girl, Caraculla, what does she know about the life she's choosing for herself? You're older, wiser. You know what she's up against and what it will cost her. Shouldn't you be looking out for her well-being?"

Was Gavin right? Was he being too optimistic about her chances? The thought that she might get seriously injured in the arena weighed heavily on his soul. He loved her, shouldn't he do all he could to keep her safe, even if that meant protecting her from herself? "Even if I decided to do it, I doubt it would work. She's half-human. I don't think I can get her pregnant."

Gavin blew a few smoke rings. "I've seen her body. She's putting on muscle more like an Æssyrian than a human woman. Harlan told me after Gypsy's encounter with Gregor she gave Gypsy something to prevent an unwanted pregnancy. I could get you the antidote and we'll see what happens. I've seen this drug work before. If she's mostly Æssyrian, she'll immediately cycle once the drug wears off. Being around you in your house with your scent everywhere, I'm sure she'll ovulate. That will be your chance."

"I can't. She'd never forgive me if I did something like that to her."

Gavin chewed the cigar to the other side of his mouth. "She need never know. It could be a fluke accident." He shrugged. "It's up to you of course, but I thought you loved her."

"Damn you, Gavin!" Caraculla snarled.

"It all comes down to how important she is to you. You can do nothing, keep training her and wait for her to dump you for her career, or you can have her forever as your wife and mother of your child. But there is something else you should know before you decide."

Caraculla shifted in his saddle. He was so torn, he needed time to think. "What's that?"

"If you succeed, I'll award you the rank you've wanted for so long. How does that sound, Lieutenant General Caraculla?"

Chapter 4

Harlan entered exam room one expecting to see Gavin for his scheduled appointment and found the room empty. She tossed his chart down on the table and sighed. How is it that a man, who spent the majority of his eight-hundred-year life following orders, couldn't follow her simple instructions? It had to be because she's a woman, and worse yet, his wife. Poking her head out of the exam room, she spotted Krull, one of the visiting Kirillian doctors reviewing a patient file. Of course, Carla, her receptionist, was nowhere to be found. *She's probably on one of her eleven breaks.*

The Kirillians were human, but just barely. They looked to Harlan more like Conan rejects than any humans she was accustomed to. She stared at his large, clumsy hands as he flipped through the lab reports.

"Have you seen the general?" she asked him.

He shrugged, grunted and walked off into his patient's room. Harlan came down the corridor, scowling. She opened the door to her office and looked inside, nothing. She came back out to the waiting room to see if he'd gone back there, nothing again. *Where the hell could he have gone?* Krull came back out to the reception desk, writing in his file. "Your husband is in the medication supply room," he said, without looking up.

What? Harlan went to the medication room. The door was partially open. She pushed it hard enough to let it hit the opposite wall. Gavin looked up from a medical textbook, fixing her with his one good eye. He looked devious and she was immediately suspicious.

"What are you doing in here?" she said. *This ought to be good.*

He slammed the book shut, making her blink.

"I've been waiting for you," he said with a devilish grin.

Harlan glanced down at the book. "Did you have a question about something?"

"No, no," he said. "I was looking up things at random. Are you ready for my appointment?"

Looking up things at random? Is he kidding me?

"Yes," she said, annoyed. "I've been looking everywhere for you, and you still haven't told me what you're really doing in here."

He ignored her and went back into exam room one. Harlan came in after him and closed the door. She reviewed his chart, trying not to obsess over what he was doing in the medication room. She'd ask him about it later, when he'd be less defensive. "How is your back doing? Is the medication I gave you helping with the pain?"

"Not much," he confessed.

She leaned against the exam table. "You're going to need to have surgery, Gavin."

"Fuck that. I'm not going off-world for something like that. Why can't you do it?"

"We've already had this discussion. You need a specialist for something like this."

Gavin folded his arms and looked out the window. "Just increase my pain medication then."

"With the amount of alcohol you drink? I don't think so. Your back is only going to get worse the longer you wait. Why don't you go for a consult? At least then we'll be able to get a better idea about what needs to be done."

"No," Gavin said in his most commanding tone. "Up the dosage or I'll switch my care to the Kirillian. At least he'll give me what I want, no questions asked."

Harlan frowned. That was true. She had to handle Gavin carefully. He was very proud and it had taken her forever to get him in here in the first place. The last thing she needed was him going to someone who wouldn't say no. She folded her arms, suppressing her anger. "All right, I'll up your meds a little. But if that doesn't work, we're going to seriously talk about surgery."

Gavin brooded for a moment, and Harlan leaned forward and kissed him. It was very hard for him to face growing older. She guessed all ÆEssyrian men went through the same thing—hell, most men in general went through it.

She felt him soften as he pulled her into his arms. God, how she loved him. She wrapped her arms around his neck, inhaling his rugged scent. A stirring began within her and she gently pulled away. Although he had no qualms about it, she didn't like having sex in the clinic.

"I thought you were taking me to dinner tonight," she said.

He gently kissed her neck, awakening a bonfire of want within her. "Why don't we have dinner at home and fuck 'til dawn?"

Harlan tried to suppress her smile, but failed. "Sounds like a good plan to me. Are you going back to your office?"

"Yes, and believe it or not, I'm having lunch there with our rogue daughter." He continued to nuzzle her neck.

Harlan stepped back from him. "You're kidding? I can't imagine why she wants to have lunch with you. She's barely speaking to you."

"I have an idea of what she wants to tell me, and it has to do with her training arrangements. Don't worry, my love, this conversation won't end in bloodshed." He laughed.

* * * *

Gypsy sat in the comfy black office chair behind Gavin's desk with her feet resting on the scarred wood edge. With a small dagger, she carefully dug at a rusty u-shaped nail that had become lodged in her boot tread. She glanced at the ebony wall clock next to the bookcase and frowned. Gavin was late and she was annoyed. This was not a convenient place for her to have lunch, but she figured if their discussion got ugly, at least there wouldn't be a public scene.

She was really hoping he'd hurry up, so she could get this over with and start moving her stuff to Caraculla's. Their food had been delivered to his office almost fifteen minutes ago and it was getting cold. Gypsy sighed and continued the obsessive task of getting the nail out of her boot. She heard familiar heavy footsteps advancing from the hall. Gavin's spurs clinked lightly with each step. *Finally.* He threw open the large wooden doors and stopped just inside the doorway. His yellow eye locked on her.

"Daughter," he said, coming inside. He dropped a file on a nearby stack of others.

"Gavin," she replied, returning her attention to her boot.

"Get your ass out of my chair."

Gypsy smirked at him, resheathed her dagger and pushed herself out of the chair, slinking around to lean against the front of his desk.

"How's your back?" she said, deliberately prodding at his weakness.

"How's the fact that you're short, weak and don't have a penis?" he snapped back at her.

She plopped into one of the chairs in front of his desk. "Touché." Leaning forward, she picked up one of the two lunch containers from a side table and pulled off the top. Gavin had already made his way to the bar cart near the window to pick up a crystal whiskey decanter and a tumbler. After placing both on his desk, he slowly lowered himself into his chair, grimacing the whole way down, and poured himself a drink. Reaching into his breast pocket, he retrieved a silver oblong container and snapped back the top. He shook out three, square pills into his hand and placed them under his tongue. Then he downed the contents of the tumbler in one gulp and leaned back, closing his eyes.

"I don't think your doctor would want you mixing your pain meds with your booze," Gypsy pointed out.

"Well, she's not here, and therefore, has no need to know," he said, picking up the other lunch container and opening it.

She shrugged. "All right then, on to other matters. I assume you already know of my plans to move out."

"Caraculla and I discussed it. I think it's a brilliant idea."

Gypsy, who had been attempting to spear a piece of meat with a two-pronged fork, stopped in mid-stab and looked at him. "You do?"

"Of course. You can pursue this short-lived dream of yours, and I don't have to watch and get irritated. If Caraculla wants to waste his time training you, that's his prerogative. As long as it doesn't interfere with his military obligations, it's of no concern to me."

Gypsy watched her father with a well-deserved eye of suspicion. Something wasn't right. He was taking this too well. There was no way he would ever relinquish so much control without a fight.

"So you don't care that I'm going to move in with him. Even though you know we're having sex?"

"Gypsy, you having sex with Caraculla is the least of the things you do that pisses me off. At any rate, I think being with Caraculla is good for you. I wish you the best of luck."

Now she was really on edge. He was definitely up to something—she just wasn't sure what. The sooner she got moved out and away from him, the better off she'd be. They finished the rest of their meal in relative silence. Gypsy got up to leave.

"Well, thanks for not being an ass about this. I appreciate it."

Gavin gave her a benevolent smile. "I believe in the end, this new living arrangement will work out for the best. Goodbye, dear."

Chapter 5

Gypsy padded into the kitchen, catching up with her mother just before she'd finished breakfast and headed off to the clinic. Gypsy hadn't had time to dress, and was still clad in her loose, black, pajama bottoms and a snug, gray, tank top. She was aware that her hair was tangled and sticking up wildly, but Gypsy needed to see Harlan before she left for the day. Thankfully, Gavin was already gone, so it would just be the two of them and they could talk. Gypsy headed straight for the refrigerator and began to rummage, ignoring the earthy scent of the coffee her mother always drank. She didn't know how Harlan could stomach that vile stuff. "Mom, could I talk to you for a minute?" Gypsy asked, pulling out a small tray of freshly sliced raw meat.

Harlan smiled and wrapped her slender fingers around her coffee mug. "Sure," she said. "What's on your mind?"

There was only one way to break the news, straight up. "Caraculla has invited me to move in with him and I've said yes."

Harlan's smile faded. "Have you told your father about this?"

"Yes, and he thinks it's great. He can't wait to get rid of me and I can't wait to leave, so everybody's happy. Well, except for maybe you," she said, frowning.

Gypsy didn't have to look at Harlan to know she was upset. Living with a man without being married was almost unheard of here. Women who did so were considered little more than whores. They faced a lifetime stigma as a loose woman, and if their lives were particularly unfortunate, they could end up in a whorehouse, as her grandmother did. Harlan had been lucky. Prior to her marriage to Gavin, she was not considered a citizen, but a guest of the emperor. Therefore, she was not subject to the same societal rules of conduct. She had lived with Gavin for quite awhile before agreeing to marry him. But Gypsy was considered a deviant anyway. It was unlikely anyone would pay much attention to her and Caraculla's arrangement.

"I assume you and Caraculla are sleeping together," Harlan said, looking worried.

Gypsy shrugged and chewed some meat. She really didn't see what the big deal was. It wasn't as though she was a virgin. "Yeah, we are," she replied.

"Is it just sex or do you have feelings for him?"

"I don't know," Gypsy said truthfully. "I mean, I like him a lot and he's been really good to me. He's a great trainer, but as far as spending the rest of my life with him...well, I'm not ready to think about things like that."

"Aren't you concerned this might get complicated?"

"Like how?"

"What if he has long-term plans for the two of you?"

Gypsy sat and picked up another fresh morsel of meat with her fingernails. She wolfed it down and looked her mother in the eye. "I think I'm just a good time for him."

Harlan shook her head. "I've known Caraculla a long time, Gypsy. He wouldn't ask you to move in with him if he didn't have strong feelings for you. I think you could be getting into much more than you realize."

"I'm not worried," Gypsy said, finishing off the last of her snack. "I can handle Caraculla." Before Harlan could voice any more objections, Gypsy got up and put the tray in the sink. "I'm moving my stuff over to Caraculla's today so I won't be here when you get home."

Harlan was pale. Her green eyes were moist and clouded with sorrow. "Please be careful, Gypsy," she asked.

"Of what?"

"Everything and everyone. You are so focused on this dream of yours, I'm afraid you're not paying attention to what's going on around you. That can have severe consequences."

"Stop worrying. I'll be fine. I've come this far, haven't I? Besides, Caraculla is teaching me so much that I actually feel a lot better about my skills and my potential." Gypsy smiled, trying to reassure her mother, but she knew it was a waste. Harlan would never stop fretting, but she guessed that's what mothers did.

"Do you need any help with your stuff?" Harlan said, looking down into her cup.

Gypsy felt bad, but was sure this was the way to go. If she continued to stay here, eventually Gavin would interfere again. "Angel is coming over to help. But thanks anyway." She leaned down and kissed her mother on the cheek. Harlan hugged her, dumped the rest of her coffee down the sink, and then left quietly for work.

* * * *

Caraculla sat on the tavern patio sipping a whiskey and watching the street merchants pack their carts up for the day. A few of them cast curious glances at him, probably wondering why an Imperial officer was drinking before the workday was done. Caraculla didn't care. He was suffering and needed the time to think. Gavin's words had become a black spell in his heart. No matter what he did, he couldn't forget them. *I thought you loved her,* he'd said. *If I love her, I would impregnate her and make her dream of becoming a warrior impossible. I have the ability to protect her from herself.*

During his long career, he'd done a lot of things he wasn't proud of. He'd led women on, kept them around for sex, and used some mercilessly. The gods knew he deserved this misery, but if he did this…compared to the other things he'd done, this act seemed particularly unsavory.

Did he want Gypsy as his wife and mother of his child? Of course he did, she was everything he'd ever wanted in a woman, but never could identify. When they made love, it was like nothing he'd ever experienced before, it was fulfilling in ways he couldn't describe. She was deep in his soul and he wanted her with every fiber of his being. If he did as Gavin suggested and impregnated her, she would indeed be his alone. *It's so simple. What's the debate?*

The only problem was, if he destroyed that uniqueness, he'd take away the very thing he loved most about her. He hated to admit it, but he knew it would destroy her. Gavin was right, a warrior's life was a lonely one filled with injury and hardship. It was a long, demanding apprenticeship that took everything from a person and had few perks. Men did it because it guaranteed access to legions of women, riches, and status. Two of which women could acquire through a good marriage, not battle. Gypsy was different. She was one of the crazy few, like Gavin and himself, who did it out of love.

He sipped his drink and imagined the heady scent of her sex as he licked and kissed her luscious young body. A river of fire filled his veins. His cock felt heavy and his balls were full. He couldn't wait to get home and be with her again. Once Gavin got the antidote, impregnating her would be so easy and so very sweet.

"Will there be anything else, lord?" the waitress said, snapping him back to reality. "You look like you could use someone to talk to." Before Gypsy, he would have bedded this woman tonight. Now, he couldn't care less about her. All he wanted to do was get home.

He pulled a few bills out of his pocket and tossed them on the table. "No," he said. "I think I've worked everything out on my own."

Chapter 6

"That's the last of it," Angel said, directing her bodyguard to put a box of clothes by Caraculla's bedroom door. She turned to the burly guard. "Vitor, you may leave me for a while. Gypsy and I would like to be alone." He bowed his head and stepped outside the villa.

Gypsy went to the bar and grabbed an expensive bottle of scotch. She held it up to Angel triumphantly. "Let's have a drink to celebrate."

Angel glanced around guiltily. "Won't Caraculla be mad about you getting into his liquor?"

Gypsy grinned and shook her head. Angel was so naive. "Oh, come on. He's not Gavin. He told me this was my home now and I could have anything in it."

They sat on the plush brown couch and Gypsy poured them each a stiff drink. She held her glass up. "To a new life!" She tossed the drink back and slammed the glass on the table. Angel took a tentative sip and grimaced. Gypsy gestured for her to hand the glass over. Angel did and Gypsy downed that one, too.

Angel laughed and nestled deeper into the seat. "So what kind of lover is he?"

Gypsy smiled and remembered the fabulous coupling they'd had that morning. "He's very passionate." A sensual heat filled her sex and the thought of him naked made her groin ache with need. She glanced at the clock wondering when he'd be back from work.

"You're very lucky," Angel said, frowning as Gypsy poured herself another drink. "I know a lot of women who've been trying to bag him for years. He's a great catch."

Gypsy laughed. *Is Angel serious?* She wasn't making any marriage plans. They just started this relationship. Right now, she was just training and sleeping with him. "They still have a chance. I have no plans to marry him."

Angel sat up, startled. She looked around the room as though she'd been trapped in a whorehouse. "You're living here and he hasn't asked you to marry him?"

"No, of course not. We don't have any long-term plans. We're living together to make my training more convenient. The sex is an added bonus for both of us," Gypsy said, feeling the liquor caress the edges of her mind. *This is great.*

"By the gods, Gypsy! I'm surprised the general let you do something like this. Do you know what everyone will be saying about you when word of this spreads?"

Gypsy was getting bored with the conversation. "No," she said. "What are they going to say?" She downed another drink and made a mental note to slow down.

"They'll say you're living a harlot's life! Surely, you must give some thought to your family name. Why don't we move you back into your parents' house? You can still train with Caraculla without carrying on like a shameless whore."

Gypsy glared at Angel and replaced the cap on the scotch. She was a little buzzed and for the first time in her life, her friend was really pissing her off. "First off, my father—who mind you, grew up in a whorehouse—was more than happy to let me move in with Caraculla. Second, the reputation of my stellar lineage doesn't exactly warrant protection. And third, I don't give a rat's ass what anyone thinks of me. I'm staying. Now can we drop this?"

Angel shrugged and pulled her shawl tighter around her shoulders. Gypsy could tell she'd offended her friend. She decided to try and change the subject. "What about you? Are you seeing anyone?"

Her friend's face lightened. "Yes, I am," she chirped. "He's a young warrior from a good family and I think he's serious. You might have met him around the arena, his name is Drake Trolis."

Gypsy's buzz evaporated as if she'd been splashed with a bucket of cold water. Leave it to Angel to find the biggest asshole in the empire to get involved with. She gave her friend an anemic smile. "We've met."

"Do you think he's handsome?"

She opened the scotch again and poured a double shot. "Sure," Gypsy said, downing the drink in one gulp. "He's okay, I guess."

Angel stared at her. "You don't like him."

"What does it matter, as long as you like him?" Gypsy said, impressed by her restraint. What she really wanted to tell Angel was the man was as big a jerk as Gavin was. But Angel was looking for good bloodlines to breed with and marry. Gypsy was sure Drake had that in spades. All the big bastards did.

A knock sounded on the door and Angel's bodyguard came in. "Your curfew, Miss," he said. "It's time for us to go."

Angel hugged her tight. "Are you sure you want to do this?" Angel asked before letting go.

Gypsy pulled her friend's arms from around her neck. "This is what I want. Don't worry about me. Now get out of here before you ruin your reputation by being seen with me."

Angel got up and walked toward the door slowly. She stopped and turned around. "I won't be able to come here again."

Gypsy nodded grimly. She was turning into a dangerous liability for her friend, especially now that Angel had found a good marriage prospect. "I know. Good luck with Drake. I hope he turns out to be everything you wanted."

"Great success in the arena, Gypsy. I'll be in the stands rooting for you," Angel said. She blew Gypsy a farewell kiss and disappeared out the door.

Chapter 7

Harlan came home later than she'd hoped and found Gypsy already gone. Her bedroom stripped bare except for the bed, dresser and wing chair. The beige walls had a scattering of tape and nails where pictures had been hastily removed. The emptiness was a stark reminder that her little girl had grown up. She leaned in the doorway feeling her eyes burn and her mouth pull into a frown.

She sure hoped Gypsy wasn't making a mistake choosing to live with Caraculla. Although he was a Razorback, and quite liberal in his views toward women, his many years as Gavin's officer had molded him into a ruthless soldier. Like all ÆEssyrian men, Harlan had no doubt he'd do whatever he needed to keep a woman he felt was his. To make matters worse, Harlan was afraid Gypsy might have advanced their sexual relationship too fast and confused him. If Caraculla began to blur the lines between trainer and lover, things could get tense very fast.

She heard the front door slam and Gavin's heavy footfalls come into the house. Pulling Gypsy's door closed, she came out to greet him. He was in his black double-breasted uniform with gold piping, black uniform pants and tall boots. His spurs jingled menacingly as he walked, like a gunfighter from an old western movie. His long black hair was pulled back into a loose ponytail, except for the four long braids by his temples. The black eye patch covering his right eye made him look even more sinister. Gavin looked every inch the commanding ÆEssyrian general he was—dangerous, mysterious and deadly. Gazing at him never failed to arouse a little fear and a flood of desire in her.

He unbuttoned his uniform and collapsed on the couch, rubbing his chest. "Gypsy gone yet?"

"Yes she is. Why didn't you tell me she was planning to move in with Caraculla?"

Gavin shrugged. "It was her news to tell."

"Are you not the least bit concerned that she's making a mistake?"

"Despite your refusal to accept it, my love, she is a grown woman. It's time she began her own life. I couldn't be more delighted she chose Caraculla to shack up with."

Harlan frowned. He was hiding something from her. This was all too easy. "Don't you think Caraculla might get the wrong idea about all this? What if he's planning to marry her?"

Gavin smiled wickedly. "I'm sure he is."

Harlan threw her arms in the air. "Gavin! Gypsy's not going to marry him. She's planning to make it to the military academy. She can't be married in there. What's going to happen when she refuses him?"

"What makes you so certain she will refuse him? Anything could happen between now and the academy picks next year."

Now Harlan was really suspicious. "He's not planning to marry her by an ÆEssyrian wedding, is he?" Those weddings were a curse to every woman on the planet. When she and Gavin had first started seeing each other, he'd broken off their relationship to pursue someone else. Depressed, Harlan had decided to leave the planet and return home to Earth. To stop her, he'd almost succeeded in marrying her by force. Thank God, Emperor Megolyth had rescued her from that marital form of enslavement, or things between her and Gavin would have been unbearable. She would have never forgiven him if he had managed to go through with it. She almost didn't, for the mere fact he had tried.

Gavin chuckled and it chilled her blood. He still didn't see anything wrong with what he'd done. "You know Caraculla doesn't believe in forced marriages."

"I don't know that. I don't know him as well as you do." She watched Gavin and a creeping unease filled her. Her husband was much too relaxed. He was up to some kind of treachery. "What's going on, Gavin?"

He patted the seat next to him. "Nothing, darling. Come and sit with me."

"I should go and see how Gypsy is settling in."

"Leave her be, woman!" he roared. "I would remind you that it was you who pleaded with Caraculla to take over her training, and now you're worried about their relationship. What did you expect was going to happen?"

"I don't know. I didn't expect she would pack up and move in with him!" she yelled back at him.

"If you're done screeching at me, I would also remind you, it was I who was going to pull the plug on this ridiculous pursuit. If you hadn't interfered, she would not be training for her next fight and she would not be living with Caraculla."

Harlan advanced on Gavin, but stayed just out of grabbing distance. She glared at him. "Don't you encourage Caraculla to do anything to Gypsy against her will. I mean it, Gavin. I know you're up to something, I don't know what yet, but I'll find out."

Gavin stood up and stalked up to her until they were only inches apart. An evil cunning swirled in his golden eye. "I'd never do anything to our daughter that wasn't in her best interest. Being with the colonel is good for her. Give her a chance to grow up a little, Harlan. She has good instincts, let her use them." He reached out and pulled Harlan to him, touching his lips to hers in a smoldering, hungry kiss. Then Gavin picked her up and carried her off to the bedroom to ravage her with hot, angry sex.

* * * *

Loving Gavin was one of the hardest things Harlan had ever experienced. Not only was he a mean drunk and a dedicated soldier, but he was driven to succeed in everything he did. It never mattered who he hurt, as long as he won. Gypsy was becoming a battle she knew Gavin wanted to win.

Harlan straddled his hips, savoring his feral kisses, she couldn't shake the nagging sorrow deep inside her. How many times had she been warned about him and his horrible relationship with his children? She didn't think she could bear it if he broke Gypsy's spirit with his bullshit.

She stopped kissing him and placed her hand on his chest to get his attention. "What happens if she qualifies and makes it to the final match next year?"

He stroked her breast affectionately. "She'll be eligible for the academy picks."

"How do they make those picks?"

Gavin sighed. He clearly didn't want to be having this conversation now. "The elders usually make the picks based on talent, training and some political influence." He reached down and lifted Harlan's hips, positioning his cock to enter her. He pushed deep inside her with a satisfied grunt.

A flood of pleasure filled her and she closed her eyes. She leaned down and kissed him. "Promise me one thing," she whispered against his lips.

Gavin ran his calloused hands up her back. "What is that, my love?"

She braced her hands on his massive chest and moved her pussy up and down on his rock-hard cock. Waves of ecstasy rolled up her back and filled her brain. Her climax was close, very close. "Swear to me if she makes it through this year, you'll pick up her training for the final one."

"Yes, my darling," he said, his voice deep with animal lust.

"Swear it," she said, as her breathing sped up.

Gavin ran his fingers into her thick black hair, pulling her head back to maul kisses along her neck. "I swear it," he said, pumping into her. Then the delight overtook her. She had what she wanted—and for whatever it was worth, she had his word. She pounded her hips down until her body shuddered and they released together.

Chapter 8

The clang of steel was music to her ears. They'd been sparring behind the villa for almost two hours and she could tell Caraculla was completely distracted. Gypsy parried a horizontal chop from his saber with ease and playfully stabbed at his belly. "You're getting old and slow," she said, slicing the air.

"I have a lot of things on my mind," he said, grabbing his canteen and gulping down some water. Some of it ran down the sides of his mouth, trickling down his throat and making damp ribbons over his thick chest. He was a bewitching sight in his sexual frustration. He tossed the canteen down and his nostrils flared as he approached her for another attack. Gypsy took advantage of his poor guard and kicked him in the chest, knocking him back about three feet.

Now he was pissed.

Leaning his head back, he sent a chilling reptilian screech into the early morning air. If she'd been his real enemy, she probably would have gotten a face full of venom. As it was, she just grinned. He was so damned sexy. With startling speed, he charged her. She sidestepped him and attacked him from the side as he passed close. Despite being so close, she never made contact. He blocked her with a side slice and launched a few angry chops designed to drive her back. She tripped over a root and fell on her butt, wincing as he came down over her. He stared into her eyes, panting. Some sweat from his face dripped onto her cheek. Gypsy's cheeks flushed with heat. "That," he said, placing his saber to her neck, "is a kill."

Laying her saber down, she leaned into him and touched her lips to his. The kiss was hot and short, but potent. She scooted back to get up, but he wasn't going to accept a brief kiss from her. Caraculla put down his weapon and pulled her against him, claiming her mouth with his own. Suddenly, Gypsy was engulfed in a heated passion she never knew was in him. He pushed her down on the ground, his mouth spreading fire everywhere it went. A moment later, all thoughts of practice evaporated from her mind.

Where Rakon had been slow and steady, letting the passion build with heavy petting, Caraculla was all fervor, setting her passion on fire like gas to a flame. She inhaled the scent of him, amazed at how he could go from a spark to bonfire in seconds.

His kisses scorched a river of molten lava down her throat. He tore her armor off, pulling her tunic up and devouring her breasts, until she thought she would orgasm from that simple pleasure alone. Gypsy had to touch him. Grappling with him, she found the fastenings to his armor and peeled a few pieces off until, with a masculine snarl, he picked her up off the ground and carried her inside over his shoulder.

She laughed. He was absolutely nuts. Throwing her down on the bed, he slid her leather pants and panties off with one swift motion. He moved up over her, his pale green eyes blazing. "Tell me you love me, even if it's a lie," he said.

Gypsy stroked his cheek, her heart pounding. "I love you," she whispered.

He pulled off his few remaining clothes and began to devour her. She closed her eyes and her soul took flight. He was the most amazing lover, licking, stroking, and carefully searching every part of her that made her scream. Surrendering to him became a feverish necessity; she simply had to have him inside her like a nasty drug.

Grabbing her, he positioned her on all fours and moved up behind her. He interlaced his fingers with hers, holding her hands down on the mattress as his cock found the hungry yearning in her pussy. His chest pressed into her back as his weight overpowered her. He filled her up, stroking his long, thick cock into her until she was shaking and gulping air like a drowning victim. Her orgasm was a noisy explosive thing that sent her mind reeling. Excited by her arousal, he pumped harder and faster until, with a mighty roar, he too climaxed deep inside her.

Time melted into a steamy orgy of sex and heat until, finally spent, they lay satisfied in each other's arms.

"We need to practice more and fuck less," he said, in a voice thick with fatigue.

"If we practice more we'll be too tired to fuck," she teased, laying her head on his belly and tracing the outline of his abdominal muscles with her fingertip.

Caraculla laughed. "You are something else."

Gypsy rolled over and looked up at him with a lazy smile. "So how come you've never let any other women move in before me?"

"I didn't want to be smothered, and I like my privacy."

"So why me? It can't just be the training," she said, as she softly kissed his nipple.

"I'm not worried about being smothered by you, and there's nothing that I want to hide from you."

Gypsy took his hand and slowly ran kisses along his fingertips and down the back of his hand. "I really appreciate you letting me live here. I feel so happy and relaxed when I'm with you. I still can't believe Gavin allowed me to do this."

"I meant to ask you, how did your lunch date with him go?"

"Good. Too good. I think that treacherous old bastard is up to something, but no matter how much I rack my brain, I can't figure out what. At least I feel safe here and somewhat out of his reach."

Caraculla remained silent and ran his large hand up her back, caressing every bump in her spine. Gypsy grinned and peeled his arms from around her. She sat up, loving that she smelled like him.

She was sorry she needed to shower. "I'm going to the arena to practice. You'd better get to work or Gavin will give you some shit job for being late."

He groaned and sat up. "All the jobs he gives me are shit."

Chapter 9

Before going to the arena that afternoon, Gypsy stopped by the weapon master's shop to pick up her custom-made shin guards. Because of Caraculla, she'd gotten there later than she expected and the place was packed with warriors. Gypsy squeezed through the crowd and made her way to the merchant's wife near the back.

The woman was short and stout with dark green skin. Against tradition, she'd cut her hair to the shoulders to make it easier to manage. Gypsy opened her mouth to speak but the woman held up her hand. "I'm only fetching custom orders, dearie," she said.

A warrior with bad breath and battered armor accidentally jostled Gypsy as he lumbered past her for the front door. She shot him a nasty look. "Mine is custom," Gypsy replied.

The woman eyed her up and down. "What is it?"

"Shin guards."

"Wait here," the woman said, disappearing behind a tan curtain.

Another warrior moved up behind her, bumping his chest armor into her back. Gypsy turned around to tell him to back off, and was face to face with Drake. He glared down at her. "What could a little girl like you need in a shop for men?" he asked.

"I was about to ask you the same thing," she said. A hearty laugh rose from the men around them.

"I think your shopping trip is just for show," he said. There was a thin layer of rage under his words. "I think you're really hoping to find a husband. That is if your father isn't going to gift you out to someone else who comes into his favor. Eventually, Cara-culla will tire of being your pimp and then maybe a good man will take pity on you and keep you as his concubine."

Gypsy lunged forward, but the weapon master came between them. "Not in here, Theron," he chided. "Kindly take this argument outside."

* * * *

They moved outside and stood in the street. Gypsy rested her hand on the handle of her saber. "You leave Caraculla out of this, you filthy bastard. He's a better man than you'll ever be."

Drake laughed. "You tell him there are lots of men waiting to take you to bed when he's done with you."

"You'll never be one of them."

He leaned in close and leered at her. "I'll be the first one to bring you to heel, little girl."

A tense silence fell between them. Gypsy turned to leave. Drake said, "Gypsy, it's not too late for you. Your friend, Angel, is a good woman, obedient and chaste, and since she actually likes you, she can help. There are still men who would take you as their bride. Stop shaming yourself and your family."

"You don't know a damn thing about me or my family, so shut your mouth. Mark my words—one day I am going to meet you in the arena and force you to live with the fact that you were beaten by a woman," she snarled.

He held his hands out in welcome. "Why wait for the arena? Take me now. I'll even let you have the first blow."

"As much as I'd love to, I have other things to do right now."

"I never understood your hostility. All I want to do is help you. Why stay with Caraculla? Can't you see he's only using you and your ridiculous dream to gratify his lust? If he were an honorable man, he would have saved you from your whoredom and claimed you by Æssyrian Marriage."

"Caraculla has no interest in that primitive ritual and he has more honor than anyone else in this whole empire! He believes in me and he's going to help me go as far as I can! And if I only advance as far as being able to kick your ass, then it all would have been worth it."

Drake shook his head like she was a condemned prisoner. "And how will he do that, little girl? By bedding you more than training you? He's done nothing to ready you for the senior levels. Trust me; there is more of debauchery than duty in his service to you."

"You're talking out of your ass, Drake. You're jealous because the only sex you get you have to pay for," she said. But something in his words found the garden and planted a seed.

Caraculla had been distracted during their past few sessions, which always ended in rambunctious lovemaking. The truth was, he wasn't really pushing her. She was getting more out of practicing alone.

Drake rolled his thick shoulders in his armor, making him look even larger. "You're wrong about me, Gypsy. I'm the only one who has the guts to tell you the truth you refuse to see." He held his hand out to her. "Come with me; let me become your protector and guardian. I'll take you from this harlot's life and rent you the villa of your choice. With your beauty, I know I can find you a good match."

Gypsy laughed bitterly. "Have you lost all touch with reality? I would sooner live in a whorehouse than be your mistress while you *pretend* to try and find me a husband."

"Surely a mistress is worlds better than a common whore."

"Not if it's with you."

She shook her head and turned her back on him. His words about Caraculla sat in her mind like ghosts in a vacant house. *What if he's right and Caraculla is just humoring me until...* She shook the thought off. She couldn't believe that, because if she did, she could never trust Caraculla again.

Chapter 10

The day had been long, hard and lonely. Gavin had been locked away in meetings all day and Caraculla, as Officer of the Day, was overwhelmed with a million problems and stupid questions. Normally he loved busy days like this, but today he'd been annoyed and distracted. All he could think about was that fantastic morning with Gypsy, and how he wanted to be with her.

Coming into his villa, he felt a strange cocktail of sexual frustration and fatigue. His emotions were surprising since he didn't consider himself a romantic, but compared to the other women he'd known, Gypsy was an opiate. Even as he moved through his house smelling her, but knowing she wasn't there, he was tense. His body wanted her like a man in the desert wants water. All day long, he fought to forget her and all day long, he'd failed. She had become everything to him and, the truth was, he was little more than a pawn to her. He was kidding himself if he thought she wanted him as much as he did her. Gavin was right—there was no other way to keep her than to make her pregnant.

Tomorrow would be the first of only two matches Gypsy would be eligible for this year. She had to win both bouts to earn enough points to move on to the one big match next year and the military academy picks. Winning tomorrow would mean *more* training, *more* time in the arena, and *more* time away from him. The way he saw it, if she won tomorrow, their future together would be doomed. He *had* to do this. He *had to* for so many very good reasons.

But even as he rationalized it, he felt dirty. He moved to the bar and poured himself a drink, downing it in one swallow. Glancing out the living room window he watched as Gavin rode up. Caraculla went to the door and let him in. *Here we go, he'll have the antidote and my fate will be sealed. Let the games begin.*

Gavin came in with a wicked smile. Caraculla tried to look pleased and forced a grin. "Did you get it?"

Gavin slapped him on the back. "Of course I did, dear boy. Get me a drink, will you?"

Caraculla went to the bar and poured Gavin a double shot of Sawjack Whiskey. Gavin took the glass gratefully and sipped at it. He handed Caraculla a small, pre-loaded syringe with light blue fluid inside. Caraculla held it to the light and marveled at the color. *How innocent it looks, just like candy.* Who would guess it held the future of his lover within? He slipped it into his pants pocket and frowned into his glass. This was so wrong. "You don't feel guilty about any of this, do you?" he asked Gavin.

"No, why should I? I'm trying to save her life. I'll make no apologies for that."

"Come on, Gavin. Even I've admitted there is more to this than just the noble deed of saving her life. I'm worried about what she'll do if I'm successful. What if she rejects both the child and me? What if she never recovers from the devastation of losing her dream?"

Gavin shook his head. "She's a good woman. She'll accept both of you and move on with her life. You're forever suffering from your useless conscience. It's those scruples of yours that have cost you promotions in the past. Don't let them get in the way of having the woman you were meant to be with."

Caraculla stared out at the darkening night. By the gods, he wished Gypsy would get home. "How did you know she wouldn't be here?"

Gavin stalked over to the couch and collapsed into it. "I spotted her at the weapon master's shop being fitted for her shin armor. Apparently, she was supposed to pick it up earlier, but got into an argument with someone and they threw her out. Anyway, all those adjustments will take at least an hour." The general raised his glass. "To the miracle of life," he said with a devilish wink. Caraculla forced himself to smile and finished off his drink

Gavin got to his feet. "I'd better go before she comes home. I don't want her to get suspicious."

All Caraculla could do was nod. He felt like the lowest form of life on the planet. He escorted the general outside and watched as he retrieved his hyperia. "Good night, Gavin," he said, but the general didn't hear him. He was already on his mount and riding off.

Caraculla turned to go back inside, when he heard her riding up the road. *Gavin and his weird sixth sense.* He waited on the steps in the dark. The only light came from the open front door behind him.

She put her hyperia away and came up to join him. She was glowing with energy and excitement. "What a day," she said. "I'll be happy when tomorrow's over with and I can take a short break before the next match."

Caraculla kissed her, his guts twisting in knots. "You'd better get inside and get some sleep. Tomorrow is a busy day."

Chapter 11

"There are more people here than last year," Gypsy said, coming into the arena ready room with Caraculla. She was fighting off a serious case of nerves.

"You're at a higher level now. These competitions are more brutal and sometimes fatal. Aside from family showing their support, a lot of people come to watch the warriors die," he said, muscling through the crowd.

"Nice," she said flatly. Finally, they reached a side room with a torn brown curtain. He held it open for her and they went in.

Because of his status as a flag officer, Caraculla had managed to reserve them a small dressing room. Otherwise, they would have been like the dozens of others, struggling for a place to dress and arm up on the concourse.

Caraculla pulled the curtain closed and Gypsy stripped off her street clothes. He stayed in the dressing room with her, helping put on the bulky armor and making all the necessary adjustments. When they were done, Caraculla stepped back and looked her up and down. "How does everything feel?"

Gypsy moved her arms and legs, checking for chaffing or restricted movement. She marveled at how comfortable she was. *What a difference good armor makes.* How did she ever fight in that junk from the poor chest? "I'm fine. Everything feels good."

Caraculla checked the schedule and frowned. "I was afraid of that."

"What?"

He sighed and squinted off at the empty arena floor. "Because of your weight, you're first."

"It's okay," she said, trying to reassure herself more than him. "I'd rather be first."

They came out to the sidelines and waited on the battle line. Gypsy was painfully aware of all the strange looks she was getting from the other fighters. High up in the stands the crowd was excited and restless for the fights to begin. She scanned her father's reserved seating and spotted Gavin with her mother, looking worried next to him. Harlan met her gaze and gave Gypsy her bravest smile. *Don't worry, Mom. I'm going to wipe the floor with these monkeys.*

"That's interesting," Caraculla said.

Gypsy glanced at the arena floor and listened to the chief messenger delivering the latest news. Everyone looked bored and the messenger could barely be heard over the din. "What's interesting?" she asked.

Caraculla pointed to the noble seating area. There were very few people there. The nobles usually only showed up for the big, final matches. Then Gypsy spotted what he was pointing at. Grand Duke Molitov Von Goth's wife, Tannyth, was taking her seat, accompanied by her entourage. She was a stunning woman, with long, wavy, auburn hair carefully styled to give her a regal look. At middle age, Gypsy had been told she was more beautiful now than in her youth. And she was one of the wealthiest women in the empire, with bloodlines so pure she could have been a match for the emperor himself. For a fleeting moment, Gypsy wondered what it would be like to be such a powerful woman. She wondered if Tannyth was happy.

"I wonder why she's here," Gypsy said.

The referee, overhearing them, moved closer and said, "She's here to see you, Theron. A lot of these people have heard you're quite good and they want to watch you fight. You'd better give them a good show or they'll heckle you off the floor."

Gypsy couldn't believe it. She stared at Caraculla, looking for reassurance. He smiled at her and squeezed her arm. He was always so good at making her feel better. "Don't worry about whose watching," he said. "Your only concern is the outcome of this fight. Besides, you have natural talent. You'll do well."

* * * *

The referee went out onto the floor and the crowd roared with excitement. He announced Gypsy's opponent, a huge male called Anthos. He was startlingly ugly and he'd shaved his hair into a Mohawk, which didn't add to his looks. A nasty scar ran down the side of his jaw and through his bottom lip. The scar looked recent and Gypsy felt a sudden rush of fear. *What if I get cut up like that?* Before her fear could take hold, she angrily pushed it down. This was no place to second-guess her ambition in the name of vanity.

Gypsy heard her name and came out onto the arena floor. As before, the roar of the crowd filled her head and deafened her, but this time, she made sure to stay focused on Anthos. They circled each other and Gypsy immediately knew his weakness would be his face. He winced when she cut through the air, indicating he was still blade shy from his injury. This weakness was good luck for her, because he'd probably overreact to defend it.

For his part, Anthos growled and snorted, swinging his blade wildly through the air to try and intimidate her. He roared and Gypsy caught the unpleasant smell of rotting teeth. Puffing out his chest, he lunged forward with his blade high. Gypsy waited for him to get close, then ducked under his attack and brought her blade across the side of his face. A vicious cut opened up and blood poured from the wound.

An electric current moved through the air and she watched her opponent's eyes flash white. He was starting to panic. Anthos snarled, bringing his right hand up to cover the wound. Gypsy seized her chance. Moving in to his body, she placed one foot behind his and slammed her body into his. He lost his footing and fell backward onto the arena floor with a loud thump. Gypsy immedi-

159

ately brought her saber down over his throat, so if he moved, she'd be able to deliver a fatal cut.

The audience went wild. A wall of sound came down from the bleachers and filled the arena. Everyone was on their feet, screaming. Then another sound rose from the crowd. It began quietly at first, but rose with urgency. A sudden rush filled her heart and adrenaline spiked her blood. She listened carefully, and the chant became clearer.

"Theron!"

"Theron!"

A wave of pure joy filled her. *What life could be better than this?* The referee came out and called the fight in her favor. Anthos was removed from the floor and her second opponent came out. This man was much tougher and better trained, but after almost twenty minutes, she was able to bring him down as well. She was ready for more, but the referee told her there was no one left to fight in her class. She was done for now.

She met Caraculla at the battle line. He escorted her off the floor and took her back to the ready room. She was exhausted and her hands were shaking, but she'd never known such complete happiness. The first fight seemed to end so fast, the second felt as if it went on forever. "How many points did I get?"

Caraculla was grim, but she chalked it up to him being worried about her. "Enough to qualify you for the finals next year. You don't even need to fight in this year's final match. If you do, it'll just be for practice." He leaned against the wall and folded his arms. "They haven't announced it yet, but I know you've been reclassified to senior level."

All Gypsy could do was smile. "I'd better get busy training, so I'll be ready. But first we need to go out and celebrate!"

He helped her into her street clothes and kissed her. "I know just the place."

* * * *

Drake watched Gypsy come off the arena floor, escorted by Colonel Caraculla. She was good, no denying that. But luckily, her inexperience had left her with many weaknesses. It was fortunate Caraculla had been her trainer this year, because if her father had trained her, there was no doubt she would have been a force to be reckoned with. As it stood though, one glaring shortfall in her training was she was too slow, and left herself open far too many times. Her sloppiness took some of the edge off his worry. The first senior fighter she was matched with would bring her down instantly.

Sweating in his armor, Drake watched the referee standing on the sidelines as staff prepared for the senior matches. Medics laid out bandages and tourniquets, and the doctors took up their positions by the entrance. Both Doctor Ambrose and the Kirillian, Doctor Krull had tense looks on their faces. Injuries here could be severe and everyone knew it.

As he waited, Drake thought back to his generous offer to Gypsy. Her rejection wasn't surprising, and only led him to one conclusion—she was more corrupt than he had imagined. It must be her poor bloodline. Her father was a notorious whore's son, after all. But he had shown integrity by not supporting her in this blasphemous pursuit, and she defied even him. He guessed he'd have to be the one to teach her a lesson she wouldn't soon forget. He'd have to physically show her the error of her ways. Who knows, she was such an open harlot she might even enjoy it.

"Drake Trolis!" the referee announced. Drake pulled himself from his thoughts and smiled. He placed his hand on the handle of his saber and headed out to meet his opponent. Thoughts of Gypsy danced in his head. In his fantasy, he saw her face down on the arena floor, forced to endure the violence of his will. It fired his blood with a scalding lust. *What an excellent day for a kill.*

Chapter 12

Gypsy was ecstatic. She'd dreamt of this moment, trained for it, wished for it, and now it was finally here. Word came down the rumor mill long before it was official—she'd made it into the senior warrior class. The military academy was finally within reach. All she had to do now was win against another senior next year and she was as good as in. She beamed at Caraculla who was toying with his food. He gave up trying to eat and pushed the plate away. He was probably still fretting about her getting hurt. What an old woman he was sometimes.

She downed another shot of whiskey and picked a piece of meat off his rejected plate. "What the hell is wrong with you?" she said. She laughed at how she'd slurred her words. "I thought you'd be excited with me." The bar was quickly filling up with people and Gypsy had to talk louder in order to be heard.

He put his hand over hers and leaned in close. "I am, Gypsy, really. It's just been a long day and I'd really like to go home."

Gypsy shook her head. She was having a blast. "We can't go home *yet*. Just a few more drinks and we'll go, I promise. Surely your libido can wait that long." She broke into wild laughter. She honestly couldn't remember ever being so happy. Then she spotted Gavin stalking across the room. *Here comes the angel of death to suck the life out of my good time.*

Gavin placed his hand on her back and smiled. He rubbed it in a circle. "Congratulations on your win, Gypsy," he said. "You fought very well."

She downed another drink and smirked at him. "*You* thought I couldn't do it," she said, rising to her feet. "*You* said I should give up and get married." Gypsy laughed, vaguely aware that some people in the restaurant were turning to look at her. She lowered her voice. "I'm sure glad I didn't listen to *you*."

"How much has she been drinking?" Gavin asked Caraculla. The colonel held up an empty bottle of Sawjack Whiskey and gestured to another one, half gone.

Gypsy suddenly felt an urgent need to pee. She got up and glared at Gavin. "Excuse me," she said, deliberately getting into his space. She would have liked nothing better than to kick his ass right here and now. He grinned at her, amused, and stepped back. "And stop telling him things about me," she shot back at Caraculla as she made her way to the bathroom. All along the way, people stopped to talk to her. Peasants said how she'd won them a ton of money in the betting room, warriors patted her on the back, nobles tried to buy her drinks. It was like being a celebrity. At first, all the attention made her intensely uncomfortable, but as the alcohol soaked confidence into her cells, she began to love it.

When she got back, Gavin was gone. "Where did tall, dark and evil go?" she said, scanning the table for what was left of the whiskey. She couldn't seem to find the bottle. She knew there was still some left. "Did that son of a bitch take my drink?"

Caraculla stood up and tossed some money on the table. "There's plenty to drink at home. Come on, you'll be hung over enough in the morning."

She got up and hugged him. "You just want to get me home so you can take advantage of me," she whispered in his ear.

Caraculla pulled her arms from around his neck. He stroked her cheek with the back of his hand. "Yes, I can hardly wait."

As Gypsy rode back to the villa, she was having difficulty sitting up straight. Afraid she would pass out and take a header into the road, Caraculla slid his arm around her waist and pulled her onto the front of his mount. She nestled against his chest and fell asleep minutes from the villa. When they arrived, Caraculla put both hyperias away and carried her into the house. He took her into the bedroom and laid her down, pausing to stare at her startling beauty. Her dark brown hair was messily tousled across the sheets, and her full lips were slightly parted as if expecting a kiss. As he stared down at her, the doubts began. *Is this really the right thing to do?* It must be—there was simply no other way to stop her. He lay down next to her and pulled her into his arms. Burying his face in her neck, he knew. He knew he loved her more than any woman he'd ever met, and if he didn't do this, her career would tear her away from him forever.

Death was an ever increasing possibility too. The odds were terrible. Someday, she would meet up with someone who was better, and would kill her for the mere fact that she was a woman and that would be it. He'd be forced to watch her die. The thought made his heart ache and his eyes water. He couldn't take that chance.

Taking a deep breath, he pulled the loaded syringe from his pocket and prayed Gavin had obtained the correct medication. For all he knew, he could be injecting her with poison. But Gavin wanted this almost as bad as he did, so he was fairly confident he'd done his research. Caraculla unbuttoned her pants and yanked them and her panties off. If she had woken up, he might have lost his nerve and stopped, but she didn't. The whiskey was keeping her in peaceful oblivion. He disinfected a small area of her buttocks and positioned the needle over the site. "I love you," he whispered, then hesitated only a moment before sticking her with the needle and pushing down the plunger. Gypsy never stirred. Afterward, he disposed of everything and changed her into loose-fitting sleep clothes. He covered her up and sat in a chair by the window staring out at the night.

The deed was done. All that was left was the sex. It was almost too easy.

A knot sat in his belly and mingled with his grief. *I've done the right thing. Everything will be better now. You'll see. She'll be safe at last.* But no matter how many times he repeated it, he couldn't bring himself to believe it.

Chapter 13

She was twisted in the sheets and sweating like a fever victim. Gypsy opened her eyes, feeling sick and desperately thirsty. Rolling off the bed, she unsteadily made her way to the kitchen and poured herself a huge glass of water. She drank it down and poured herself another. Leaning against the sink, she suddenly realized her pussy was very wet. A deep hungry ache twisted inside her groin and she frowned. Something wasn't right, everything felt so weird. *I've never been hung over like this before. What am I, sick?*

Taking her glass with her, she returned to the bedroom. Caraculla lay on top of the sheets completely naked. His body was power itself, a masterpiece of sculptured muscle. He was also partially erect. The sight of him froze her in her tracks. From some dark place within her, a savage lust was born, and set fire to her whole body in seconds. Never in her life had she felt anything like it. Its power over her was so complete she dropped the glass and didn't flinch as it shattered on the floor.

Caraculla startled awake. Those stunning pale green eyes drew her in and all she could think of was having him inside her. *Now.* She crawled up over him on all fours, her mouth finding his and kissing him with demonic passion. Grabbing his hands, she guided them up under her shirt to her breasts, gasping in delight at his touch.

"Gypsy," he murmured, as he dragged hot kisses along her throat. His hands moved quickly, peeling off her clothes and tossing them to the floor. His fingers found the tortured wet center of her pussy. Gypsy arched her back and gasped.

Reaching down, she grabbed his erect cock and pushed it deep inside her. Pleasure exploded inside her, increasing in intensity with every stroke. He felt so good she knew she had to have him all day long. Forget practice for now. This moment was all that mattered to her.

Rolling over on top of her, he rode her passion until she was right at the edge of climax. "*Don't stop,*" she gasped grappling with him like a wild animal. "*Harder...harder...please don't stop.*"

Then he pulled out.

His cock looked painfully hard and Gypsy watched as he stroked it to climax, spilling his seed on the bed between her legs. It took Gypsy a moment to realize what had happened. Pain gripped her pussy as her passion went berserk. Gritting her teeth, she pushed him back onto the bed and straddled him. His cock was still rock-hard. She grabbed the pulsing shaft and pushed it back inside her. The ecstasy was a narcotic rush, sending her into a delirium of hunger. Slamming down on top of him over and over, she sweated and groaned in her desperation, trying to reach another climax like the one just robbed from her.

The passion built again, punishing her by making her clit tender and a little numb. She tossed her head back and let the orgasm seize her. A bottomless rush hit her like a tidal wave and the climax lasted much longer than any she'd ever had before. Her pussy throbbed with the last spasms of lust when suddenly Caraculla tossed her off. She watched in disbelief as he rolled away from her and stroked his cock to climax, once again spilling his seed on the sheets.

"What the fuck are you *doing?*" she said, unable to contain her fury. He'd never done this before when they made love. *What the hell is this all about?*

He set his mouth in a grim line and shook his head, climbing off the bed. She could tell he was in a lot of pain. "Why are you doing this? You've never been afraid to come inside me before. What's the matter with you?"

Caraculla collapsed into a wing chair by the window. For the first time ever, she was worried about him. He looked haunted. "I don't want to make you pregnant."

Gypsy sat there for a moment rolling those words around in her head. "I've taken the shot. It's good for five years. I can't get pregnant."

He took a deep tortured breath. "Yes, you can. Last night while you were passed out, I gave you the antidote."

The room fell into a suffocating silence. "What are you talking about? Where the hell did you get…" She let the sentence die on her lips. *Gavin, of course. Who else?* Tears of rage filled her eyes, blinding her for a moment. Then her mind exploded. She lunged at him. He was up and out of the chair in a split second, grabbing her wrists before she could slam them into him. "I can't believe you did this! Why would you do something like that to me?"

"I wanted to end your career. That's why," he said, letting her go.

She rubbed her wrists and stared at him. He was suddenly a stranger to her. She watched him pace the room like a caged lion. "I don't understand," she said.

"Yes, you do. I wanted a life with you, Gypsy. Getting you pregnant was the only way that was ever going to happen."

She shook her head, desperate for none of this to be true. "You wanted to *trap* me by getting me pregnant—you of all people? I *trusted* you. I thought you believed in me and what I was doing. But you wanted to stop me all along, and that's why you agreed to train me?" Gypsy stepped backwards and fell against the wall. Sinking to the ground slowly, she wrapped her arms around her knees and pulled them to her chest, feeling like she had been punched in the stomach.

"It wasn't like that, Gypsy," he said, as he crouched near her. "The more time I spent with you the more I wanted to be with you. The thought of losing you to someone's blade or a military career was killing me."

Harlan had been right about him. He is Gavin's man. "I was an idiot to think that I could ever escape Gavin's reach! You're his boy and always will be, won't you?"

"Obviously, I changed my mind."

"You didn't change your mind fast enough not to fuck me. You probably didn't even pull out in time."

"I did. I know I did."

She sat there feeling like her entire world had caved in. How stupid she'd been. Why had she thought Caraculla was so different from any of the other treacherous men in her life? Drake had been right about her training, and that hurt most of all. There really was no one she could trust. She had to get to her mother and make sure she wasn't pregnant. She pushed herself to her feet and walked around the room in a daze, gathering her clothes. Caraculla moved toward her and she shot him her most venomous look.

"Stay the hell away from me. Don't you ever touch me again," she said through clenched teeth.

He pulled back, stricken. "I'm sorry, Gypsy. I made a mistake. Please don't let this come between us."

"You should have thought of that before you joined forces with that colossal asshole, Gavin!"

"All right! Okay! So I fucked up! I'm not perfect. I make mistakes like everybody else. Don't you see *why* I did it? Don't you realize all I wanted was you?"

Gypsy stopped buttoning her pants and looked at him, amazed at his ignorance. "But you don't want me the way I am. You're just like the rest of them. You only want me the way I'm *supposed* to be.

Now, get the hell out of my way. I need to get to the clinic and find out if you've actually succeeded with your shitty little plan. I'll be back later to get my stuff."

"What are you going to do, move back in with Gavin?"

"At least I expect this kind of shit from him," she said, her voice shaking with a combination of pain and rage.

Caraculla held up his hands. "Please don't leave. I want to try and work this out."

"Work what out? Another plan to confine me and trash my career? Go fuck yourself, Caraculla!" She angrily threw the shirt she was holding at him. He caught it and held it out to her. Gypsy snatched it back and pulled it on. Caraculla sat on the bed with his elbows on his knees. He hung his head in defeat.

"Don't move out. Moving back home will be a mistake. You don't have to stay in here. I'll move your stuff into one of the spare rooms."

Gypsy hopped a few steps, pulling her last boot on and stormed out of the room. Caraculla stood up and took a step forward. "Gypsy...please."

She stopped just outside the threshold, with her back to him.

"How can you expect me to live here? You hurt me like I didn't know I was capable of being hurt. How can I ever trust you again?"

"All I can do is offer my word that I won't ever do it again. I wasn't able to go through with it. That should count for something. Give me a chance to make this right."

"I don't know what to do right now. My decisions are going to depend on whether or not you and Gavin have succeeded in killing my dream."

Chapter 14

Harlan was about to go into her next patient's exam room when Gypsy stormed into the clinic. Her cheeks were flushed and she looked like she'd ridden hard all the way here. A few waiting patients glanced at her with mild curiosity then returned to their reading. "I need to speak to you," Gypsy said, breathless. "It's an emergency."

Harlan turned to the Kirillian doctor, Krull. He was taking his lab coat off to go to lunch. He was a tall, strikingly handsome man with long, dirty-blonde hair pulled back into a loose ponytail. Unfortunately, he was the kind of man who had little patience with the unexpected. He enjoyed his life boring and predictable. Their eyes met and he frowned. His gaze shot to Gypsy, then back to Harlan. Harlan gave him her warmest smile. "Could you please do a routine check-up on the patient in room one?" For several seconds, he didn't move and she was certain he was going to refuse. Then he held his hand out for the file and Harlan handed it to him. "Thanks," she said, but he ignored her, burying his nose in the file and disappearing into room one.

Harlan gestured to her office. "We can talk in here."

Gypsy came in but didn't sit down. She was stiff and gave off the smoldering anger her father perfected so well. How alike they were at times. Harlan wondered what could have upset her so. Usually her daughter was very relaxed in here, taking a seat and putting her dirty boots on the desk. But there was none of her usual bravado this morning. Gypsy waited until Harlan had closed the door. "I need another shot," she blurted out.

"Another shot of what?" Harlan said, confused.

"Whatever that stuff was you gave me to stop my ovulation."

"Why? What's happened?"

Gypsy paced, running her fingers through her hair, hung in wild strands partially covering her face. She clenched her jaw, obviously trying to fight back any tears that dared venture out. Her lip trembled and she bit it hard, making Harlan wince. "Gavin gave Caraculla the antidote and he used it on me while I was passed out last night. I might be pregnant with his child."

Harlan lowered herself in her chair, unable to believe what she was hearing. The more she thought about it, the more it made sense. Everything suddenly fell into place. *That's why he was in my medication room. That's also why he was so supportive of Gypsy moving in with Caraculla—he thought he had her.* A rush of fury filled her. She took a deep breath and remained calm. She'd deal with Gavin later. "It's too early to check for pregnancy, but I can give you another shot, for all the good it'll do. Just make sure you don't have sex for forty-eight hours. That's how long it takes for the hormones to build back up in your system."

"What if I'm pregnant? Will the shot hurt the baby?" Gypsy asked, looking miserable.

"No, the fetus will be fine, but hopefully there is no child," she said. She got up and headed for the door. "I need to prepare another injection, wait here." Harlan went into the medication storage room and prepared the syringe. She was so angry her hands were shaking. Sitting on a rolling stool, Harlan took a moment to calm down. The thought that Gavin had done something so despicable to stop Gypsy was mind-boggling. *Is there no end to that man's deceit?*

Harlan came back in and Gypsy wiped a few stray tears away.

"I'm going to take some blood from you and then I'll give you the new injection." Gypsy nodded and Harlan swabbed her daughter's arm, pulled a small syringe full of blood from her and placed it on the counter. She then swabbed her other arm and gave her the injection. "I'm so sorry, Gypsy. I should have known Gavin was up to something."

Gypsy shook her head and stared at her fingers, unraveling threads from the bottom of her shirt. She pulled a loose thread away from the others and twisted it around her finger. Harlan couldn't remember ever seeing her daughter so sad. Gypsy looked into her eyes and Harlan's heart melted. "He said he pulled out before...you know. Maybe I'm not."

Harlan felt a tiny glimmer of hope. "ÆEssyrian men have excellent control. If he says he pulled out before ejaculation, I'm sure he did. Also, keep in mind, you have a lot of human blood in you, which may hinder your ability to conceive. That might be a good thing at this juncture in your life."

"This whole thing is so fucked up. Why did he have to do this to me? I thought he was my friend. I thought I could trust him."

"Well, for what it's worth, at least he told you the truth," Harlan said. "He could have easily said nothing and waited to see what happened, and you'd be none the wiser."

"That's basically what he told me. But I can't believe anything he says anymore."

"Are you going to move back in with us?"

Gypsy laughed. "Oh, hell no. I couldn't stomach living with that bastard for one second, especially if I'm pregnant. Caraculla said I could live in one of the spare bedrooms, so that's what I'm going to do for now." She got up and hugged Harlan. "Thanks for everything, Mom, but I've got to go. If I sit around here I'll drive myself crazy obsessing over this test. When will you have the results?"

"About two days to be sure," Harlan said, squeezing Gypsy into a tight embrace.

Harlan tried to ignore the block of ice in her gut. *God, I want to kill Gavin.* "Gypsy," Harlan said as her daughter opened the office door. Gypsy looked back at her. "*Please* be careful and remember, forty-eight hours."

Gypsy shook her head. "Don't worry about me. I don't want to have sex ever again."

Chapter 15

Harlan went straight home right after closing the clinic that evening, and slammed the front door. Gavin was exactly where she expected him to be, sitting on the leather couch drinking a glass of whiskey. The living room smelled like fresh cooked meat and cigar smoke. There was a small covered plate on the dining room table for her. His thoughtfulness took a tiny grain of anger off her fury. She marched up and glared down at him. "Guess who came by the clinic this morning?"

He gestured to the plate. "I made you dinner."

"I don't care about that right now. Take a wild guess."

Gavin gave her a belligerent look. She itched to slap it off his face. He slowly pulled out a cigar from inside his tunic and clipped the end. Taking his time, he lit it and blew a few smoke rings toward her. They drifted past her cheek like tiny clouds, filling the room with the rich scent of his tobacco. She remained stoic. "I have no idea," he said. "Surprise me."

"Gypsy," she said. "Gypsy came by my office and she was upset. You'll never guess why."

Gavin put the cigar in his teeth. "Female troubles?"

"More like father and boyfriend troubles."

Gavin grunted. He downed the liquor in his glass and poured himself another. "My dear Harlan," he said, raising an eyebrow. "What the devil do you mean?"

Harlan sat down in the matching leather chair next to the couch. Her fists were clenched and her palms sweaty. She hadn't been this mad at him in years. "I'm not even going to get into what a stupid and dangerous thing you did *stealing* the antidote from my clinic. You could have killed her if you'd taken the wrong bottle or overdosed her. But then *convincing* Caraculla to get Gypsy pregnant because you want to *win* is an all-time low, even for you."

He gave her an icy look. "I'm sorry, my darling," he said, his voice dripping with sarcasm. "I thought we were both on the same page about this. I thought you *wanted* to save her from certain death or maiming in the arena, I apologize that I misread you."

Harlan stood up enraged, and pointed at him. "Don't you try to put this back on me! I hate the fact she has chosen this life, but I have accepted that she won't stop. That's why I asked Caraculla to train her and you know it!"

He waved his hand dismissively. "Well, I refuse to concede defeat in all of this. And anything I do—no matter how much it upsets her—is better than standing by watching her get slaughtered. What else would you have me do? As I recall, the last time she got her ass beaten in the arena, you turned to me and said, 'Gavin, do something.' Well, I have done something, my darling. I've probably saved her life."

"You haven't done a damn thing, Gavin. Caraculla put a stop to the plan and told her. All you've accomplished is to drive them apart and probably make your relationship with her irreparable. She'll never trust him again after this, and it's all your fault," Harlan said, feeling her heart racing in her chest.

Gavin downed another drink and got up. He put his hands behind his back and paced. "Do you truly believe I did what I did out of selfishness alone?"

Harlan sat there for a moment, unsure of what to say. She knew how deeply he loved Gypsy. However corrupt he was, she did know that about him. "No, I don't believe that. But some of this is a contest to you. When it comes to her, it always has been. Even in her defiance as a child, you always had to win. But it's different now. You must see that you can't keep forcing your will on her like this. She's an adult woman. She has a right to make her own decisions about her life and her future, no matter what the ultimate cost is. Don't you understand that?"

"I want you to say those words to me when a warrior has lopped off her right arm," he said grimly. "I'm getting the fuck out of here."

"Where are you going?"

"To the bar, where else? And don't wait up."

"Oh, you can be sure I won't. You need to apologize to her," Harlan said, following him to the door.

He opened the front door and glared back at her. "You're my fucking wife, albeit sometimes in name only. You make my damned apologies for me," he said, slamming the door behind him.

Chapter 16

It was late and Gypsy wanted to be anywhere but Caraculla's house. She'd come to the arena to practice, but spent most of the day doing more thinking than anything else. A few warriors were standing by the exit, talking and ignoring her. "Anybody want to spar?" she called to them, slicing the air with her saber. They glanced over at her, a few of them chuckling.

"We've got families to get home to, Theron," one of them said, and they all laughed. It was an insult, implying no one wanted her. She was used to it. She was going to insult them back, but decided against it. There were more of them than there was of her. They disappeared out into the night and a sudden quiet filled the arena. Some of the overhead lights shut off, leaving just a few to cast ominous round circles on the black sand floor. *Might as well go home.*

"I'll spar with you," a deep, familiar voice said.

Gypsy looked up and watched Drake coming onto the arena floor. He was dressed in gray practice armor, not nearly as elaborate as what he wore to regular matches. His expression was grim, highlighting the dangerous scowl of a seasoned fighter. He carried his thick saber over his left shoulder as if it were a terrible burden to carry. She hesitated, they weren't exactly friends—in fact, she was pretty sure he hated her guts. He probably wanted to spar with her so he could rub her face in his superior skill. Unfortunately, if she left now, she had no place to go but home, and she wasn't ready to face Caraculla yet. He would want to talk and right now, there was nothing she wanted to do less. Besides, it was just a spar and she could use the practice.

"Okay," she said. But even as the words left her lips, something was telling her to leave and go home. Ignoring her apprehension, she came out into the partially lit arena, and held her saber out in the ready position.

Drake moved up to her, lifting his saber off his shoulder and slicing the air playfully. "I didn't congratulate you on making it into the senior class," he said.

"Uh...thanks," she replied, feeling the muscles tense in the back of her neck.

She kept her eye on him, circling around, trying to stay out of striking distance. She'd had a lot of luck with this defense so far, and was getting good at it. In a blinding flash of speed, Drake moved in and slammed his weapon into hers. He hit her with several devastating blows, sending her on an immediate and unbalanced defensive.

Gypsy struck back and realized a second too late that she'd fallen into his trap. Her counterattack left her chest unguarded, and Drake took advantage of the opening to hit her with his fist. The impact was like being hit by a charging bull. She flew four feet through the air and hit the ground hard on her back. The landing knocked the wind out of her, and for a few precious moments all she could do was fight to pull in air.

Drake strode over and slammed his boot into her ribs twice. Gypsy grunted in pain and rolled away from him. Her lungs finally remembered their function and she gasped in several raspy breaths.

Her mind reeled and suddenly snapped in a panic.

This was a *real* fight and she was hopelessly outmatched in size and skill. How could she be so naïve? Scrambling, she jumped to her feet, but was a second too slow. Her opponent tackled her, grabbing her saber and tossing it to the other end of the arena floor. It hissed like a serpent as it slid along the sand. Gypsy slammed her fist into his throat, and Drake's iron grip slacked just long enough for her to break loose.

Jumping to her feet, she raced for her saber. Sand and debris flew off the arena floor as she struggled to keep her footing. She could hear Drake's thick boots scraping the sand behind her, closing the distance, and only an inch from her weapon, he slammed into her back and drove her to the ground. He came down over her, turned her over and slapped her so hard, she thought he'd knocked out all her teeth. The pain aroused something primal inside her. Gypsy exploded in violence, punching him with every ounce of strength she could summon. Every punch she landed was met by two bone-jarring backhands, until she was so dazed she could barely think. The distinct taste of blood filled her mouth.

Drake leaned down and leered at her. "I told you this day would come," he said, flipping her onto her stomach. She hated that tossing her around was so easy for him. A million thoughts came flooding into her mind as his knee pushed hard into the small of her back. She tried to push herself up, but was completely immobilized. *He's going to break my fucking back.* Black pain filled her body and she marveled that her death was going to be such a horrible experience. She'd always thought it would be quick, but this was going to be slow and filled with agony. Her left eye was swelling shut and a doomed calm came over her. *This is it—the end of my life. He's going to kill me and there's nothing I can do about it.* Breathing hard in her ear, Drake slid the blade of his saber under her chin and rested it against the tender flesh of her throat.

Then he unfastened her pants and pulled them down to her ankles. The sudden realization of what was happening filled her with a dark sense of irony. *Of course, he has to rape me first. It's not good enough to kill me—he has to beat me down and humiliate me. What a fucking piece of shit he is.*

The rape was violent and painful, but mercifully quick. The blade of his saber made several long, thin cuts against her throat as he sweated over her, until he grunted his release and finally moved off. Her heart burned with a hatred she'd never felt for anyone. She vomited the limited contents of her stomach as he pushed his knee into her back getting up. He weighed a ton. Crouching next to her, he reached down, grabbed her by the neck, and pulled her face close to his. He squeezed her throat, digging his fingers into the bloody cuts. "Next time, little girl, I'll make sure there's an audience." He dropped her, stood up and walked off toward the exit, whistling.

Gypsy rolled onto her back, coughing and gasping for air as she choked on the blood that had filled her mouth. She had to get out of here before he decided to come back and finish her off. Every muscle in her body screamed as she got to her feet. Her head swirled and her back hurt so bad she was starting to think he'd ruptured some of her disks. She pulled her pants up, staggered over to her saber, and sheathed it. She wiped her nose and mouth on her sleeve and was surprised at how much blood covered it when she pulled it away. *I need to get cleaned up and get this fucker's scent off me, but where can I go?* There was only one place she could go—her parents' house. She only hoped Gavin was out drinking, or she'd have to wait until morning to come in and shower. Thankfully, her injuries were superficial and could wait for treatment.

It was torture mounting up on her hyperia, and every step he took sent a current of pain through her. Every part of her was in torment. Her whole body ached, her heart suffered in agony, and her mind was beating itself up over her stupidity. What she believed to be her world had come crashing down around her today. The realization that she was such an easy casualty shook her to her core, and the pain of that truth pulled her spirit into a black, bottomless pit.

Chapter 17

Gypsy rode to her parents' house as fast as she could. Stopping at the stable, she leaned into the archway and saw with relief that Gavin's hyperia was gone. *He's probably at the bar, but who knows when he'll be back?* After putting her mount in an empty pen, she limped up to the front door and banged hard. The lights inside came on and Gypsy heard Harlan trotting down the hall to the door. "Who is it?" Harlan said through the thick wood.

"It's me, Mom," Gypsy said.

Harlan pulled the bolt back and opened the door. Without a word and keeping her head down, Gypsy rushed past her and ran up the stairs. Her mother was right behind her, trying desperately to catch up. She went into her old bedroom and hastily stripped off her armor and clothing. If Gavin came home and smelled Drake on her, he'd surely grill her, and she was too fragile right now to keep what happened from him. The last thing she needed was his involvement. He'd kill Drake and all her credibility as a warrior would be pissed away.

Harlan came in with panic etched on her face, and froze in the doorway. There were dark circles under her eyes and she looked like she'd been crying before Gypsy got there. "My God, Gypsy, what happened?" she asked, staring at the dark purple and red bruises covering most of Gypsy's back and left side. Before she could answer, Harlan rushed over to her, gently pushed her hair back from her face and gasped. In a voice close to tears, her mother asked, "Who did this to you?"

"Mom, I need to take a shower. I'll answer all of your questions when I'm done." Gypsy picked up her clothes and held them out to Harlan, who took them. "I need you to wash these for me."

"Gypsy, please—"

Gypsy couldn't answer any questions yet. Holding her hand up to ward off any further inquiries, she rushed into the bathroom and locked the door behind her. She turned on the water and stepped inside, resting her back against the cool stones.

Then the agony came.

Putting her hands over her face, she let her battered body slide to the floor. Waves of pain and rage seized her and the tears, denied the whole way here, burst from her eyes. Gypsy placed her hand over her mouth, so her sobs wouldn't be heard. How could she have been so stupid? Why had she accepted Drake's offer to spar? She knew he hated her. Gypsy realized then that she had been blundering along for a while now, oblivious to the dangers around her. She'd taken Drake's offer to spar because she'd really believed he wouldn't hurt her. She'd had success so quickly, she'd taken the arena for granted. Never realizing what everyone was saying was true. She wasn't ready for the senior classes.

Gavin's fateful words echoed in her head, *All they have to do is get their hands on you.* Even Drake in his clumsy, half-wit way had warned her she wasn't ready. Now every scrap of confidence she had was stripped away. Perhaps everyone was right. Maybe her dream was a horrible mistake and she should stop before she was killed. A shudder moved over her flesh when she thought how close she'd come to being butchered by Drake. As sick as it sounded, thank the gods all he'd done was rape her. That she could at least avenge someday. Dead was dead.

Grabbing the soap, she stood up and forced her sorrow inside. She lathered herself carefully, taking great pains to scrub every inch of skin that might have touched Drake's. When she was done, she sat cross-legged on the stone floor and let the hot water pour down her neck and back. She fumed, letting her rage fill and comfort her. What the hell was she going to do now? Her future looked as black as night. She needed to make decisions, and she needed to make them now. Perhaps she should go to Caraculla, marry him and forget all this, if he even still wanted her. The thought of giving up on her dream hurt more than the beating she'd taken. *No, this is who I am. It's in my blood and I can't give up, even if it kills me.*

After almost an hour, she finally came out. She wrapped a towel around herself and went into the bedroom, taking a seat on the bed. Her wet hair dripped onto her skin, causing goose bumps. Harlan was sitting in the large wing chair Gavin usually sat in when he was going to lecture her. Gypsy almost grinned, but her lips seemed stuck in a permanent frown. For some strange reason, she no longer felt the same anger toward that evil old man. What he and Caraculla had done seemed to lessen in the face of what she was now feeling. It was more than the trauma of the rape, she was losing her dream, and the desperation she felt was devouring her. Without the right training, she'd never be ready and she'd probably be killed or maimed next year in the senior matches.

Harlan's legs were pulled up to her chest with her arms wrapped around them. She looked miserable. "Are you all right? Those cuts on your throat—"

Gypsy touched her finger to the wounds and frowned. "They're not deep. It's okay."

"I brought you an ice pack," Harlan said, gesturing to the bedside table. "And a drink. You looked like you could use one." Gypsy picked up the ice pack and held it over her swollen eye. She wished she had one big enough for her whole body. With her other hand, she grabbed the tumbler and downed its contents. The whiskey bit into her throat, but did nothing to warm the chill in her core.

"Now please tell me what happened."

Gypsy stared down at her discarded armor. "If I tell you," she said, "you have to promise me you won't tell anyone, especially Gavin."

Harlan nodded quickly.

"Or Caraculla."

Harlan frowned but nodded.

"Drake tricked me into sparring with him at the arena, and he ended up raping me." Harlan gasped, putting her hand over her mouth. Gypsy scowled, she shouldn't have told her mother. "It's all right, Mom. I've come to terms with it and I'm okay. It could have been much worse."

"Gypsy, you have to report this! What he did was a crime!"

"I know. I know. But this wouldn't have happened if I wasn't being an idiot."

Harlan was out of her chair in an instant. "Don't say that! This is not your fault and I'm not going to allow you to share any responsibility in this. You need to tell your father so something can be done. He had no right." Tears fell from her mother's eyes and it was making Gypsy feel even worse.

Gypsy stood up and grabbed the clean clothes Harlan had folded and left on the bed. She started dressing. "No, Mom, I can't. If I do, no one will ever take me seriously as a warrior. Besides, Gavin would probably be the first to say I had this coming."

"You're wrong about that. He loves you and if you think for one minute that this wouldn't break his heart, then you truly don't know him. Please don't ask me to keep this from him," Harlan pleaded.

"Mom, you promised. I don't want Gavin's help. Drake's not going anywhere. I'll handle this myself in my own time."

"You can't seriously be thinking of fighting him again? Let your father and Caraculla deal with..." Gypsy shot her a nasty look and Harlan stopped cold before she sent her daughter into a rage.

"This is my fight, not theirs," Gypsy said.

"I think you're making a terrible mistake," Harlan said quietly.

"Well, it'll go well with the many others I've made so far."

"What are you going to do now?"

"The same thing I've always done. Find a way to prepare for my match this year," Gypsy said, collecting her armor.

"So you're going to keep going...even after this."

"Yes. I know this is the only life that will fulfill me. I have a better understanding of my weaknesses and I know what I have to do. This year is going to be different." She leaned forward and kissed her mother on the forehead. "I'm going home. Thanks for letting me use the shower."

Harlan stood up and followed her to the door. "You need to come by the clinic in the morning and let me take a better look at your injuries. I also need to take some more blood and submit another pregnancy test."

Gypsy coughed out a bitter laugh. "With the way my luck is running, if I am pregnant, he's probably the father. Wouldn't that be an ironic ending to all this?"

Chapter 18

Caraculla awoke when he heard the villa's back door close softly. It was Gypsy. It had to be. No one would dare break into a Razorback's home. There wasn't anything here anyone would want badly enough to die for. He climbed out of bed, pulled on some loose-fitting gray pants, and made his way down the hall to Gypsy's bedroom. He knocked.

"What?" she said, without opening the door.

"It's very late. I was just wondering if you were okay."

"I'm fine. I just want to go to bed."

He hesitated. What he wouldn't give for the right words to say to her. He hated this problem he'd caused between them. "Please open the door. There's something I want to say to you."

A full minute passed. He was beginning to think she was going to ignore him. The door opened. Looking down into her beautiful face, he was shocked by her appearance. One of her eyes was swollen shut and there was dark bruising on her cheek and jaw. His eyes fell on the linear wounds across her throat, obviously left by someone's blade. She'd had the shit kicked out of her by someone. He was going to find that someone and tear his head off. "What happened to you?"

"I got into a fight and I don't want to talk about it. What do you want?"

He leaned in the doorway, trying to control his anger. "I want to know who did this to you," he demanded.

Gypsy sighed. "Look, it's late and I'm very tired. This hasn't been the best day for me and I need some time by myself. Now tell me what you want to say to me."

Placing his hand on the upper part of the door, he forced it open and came inside. Gypsy stepped back stiffly and glared at him. "You're not helping things by doing this," she said. "Say what you want to say and get the hell out or I'm leaving."

She was right. This wasn't the time to talk to her about the beating, but if she thought he was going to drop it, she was wrong. No one beat up on his woman—no one. He took a deep breath and reined in his temper. "I wanted to say…"

"What?" she said, with growing impatience.

"I wanted to say I'm sorry."

She nodded. "Is that it?"

"No," he said. "I also wanted to say I love you."

Gypsy looked up into his eyes and he saw so much there, but couldn't define it. She was always carefully guarded around him, probably more so now. "You're just saying that to get laid."

"That's right," he said. "That's all I've ever wanted." He pulled her into his arms and buried his face in her neck. Gypsy hugged him back, surprising him by squeezing tight. Her body melted into his and it felt so good. Perhaps she could forgive him and they could find their way back from this. Caraculla kissed her, but she pulled out of his arms.

"I really need some time alone," she said.

He nodded and turned to leave. He stopped, blocking the doorway, and looked back at her. "I'm going to find out who put their hands on you, Gypsy," he said darkly. "And when I do, that bastard is as good as dead. There won't be any arena rules to stop me from doing what I want. You understand me?"

Her eyes watered. She kissed him once and pushed him from her doorway. "Good night, Caraculla," she whispered.

"Good night, my love."

* * * *

The suns hadn't even cracked the horizon when the demons of doubt began chattering in her mind, pulling her from restless slumber. There was no possible way she could fall back asleep, so she decided to run until she could numb the pain. At least she didn't need a trainer to do that. Caraculla was still asleep when she left. He would be hurt by her early departure, even though it had nothing to do with him. At least now, her feelings for him were clear in her mind. He was the love of her life and no one else made her feel so complete or so loved. But she was incapable of giving him what he wanted, and his frustration was both apparent and warranted. Love is about sacrifice, and she wasn't willing to sacrifice her desire, not even for him. They needed to talk about all of the things that had remained unsaid throughout their relationship. But not now. First, she needed to run, to quiet the villainous voices devouring her thoughts. Only then could she try to come up with a plan before her dreams slipped away forever.

Gypsy felt the cool morning breeze evaporating some of the sweat covering her body. She was nearing the end of her hour-long run, and the fatigue that enveloped her only bolstered the contempt she felt for herself. Less than six months ago, she could have run for three hours and barely broke a sweat. Now she wanted to pass out in less than half the time. Her training with Caraculla had wasted precious time, time that she didn't have. She didn't blame him. After all, the sexual distraction was most often initiated by her. Gypsy also recognized that he didn't have the experience necessary to train her with her unique deficiencies.

As she forced her body into the second hour, the combination of physical pain and fatigue began to dull some of the ache in her soul. How she wished she could go back to the beginning, knowing what she knew now. The attack forced new realizations on her every passing moment. She understood why her parents had fought so hard to quell this desire for combat. She also understood why Caraculla had been lured into Gavin's plan so easily. So much more could have been accomplished if only she had listened to what was being said, instead of assuming everything was a ploy to bring her down. Her oblivion to the world around her had caused her to squander time and resources. Now she was looking at a dead end. The depression sank into her bones and threatened to consume her entire being. *I've got to fight this off. I can't give up. I need to go back to the practice arena, even if he's there.*

Chapter 19

Angel came out of the dressing room clothed in a stunning white sequined ball gown. The white set off her olive green skin to perfection. She flashed Drake a dazzling smile and turned around so he could see her from all sides. He shifted in his chair as his cock stiffened in his pants. A rogue memory of Gypsy on the arena floor as he raped her flashed through his mind, and his lust melted away. Shame burned in his gut and he did all he could to hide it from his fiancée. She gave him a schoolgirl frown and stopped twirling. "You don't like it," she said, disappointed.

Drake stood up and shook his head. "No, darling," he said, kissing her on the forehead. "All the dresses you've tried on are beautiful. I just need to get some air."

Her eyes were sweet and questioning, but she didn't say anything as he walked outside. He folded his arms across his chest, wishing the horrible feelings inside him would go away. Vendors nodded to him as they set up their wares and bullied their assistants to hustle up customers.

He'd *raped* her. Even as he remembered the deed, he could hardly believe it. Of all the things he'd done in his life, last night's attack was probably one of the most puzzling. Drake didn't consider himself a villain. On the contrary, he was trying to *help* the wretched woman. But when he'd had her down and under his power, the most extraordinary desire had taken him over. Even now, the shame twisted inside him and a new thought was born.

What if he'd made her pregnant?

There was only one thing left to do, to save both of them from this terrible dishonor, he'd have to ask her father for permission to lay claim to her. As his concubine, he would be able to tutor her in the proper behavior of a young woman. It was no secret the general was beside himself with Gypsy's wild and willful ways. Perhaps this was a solution for all of them.

And what of her current lover, Caraculla? Drake had seen him with enough women to know the man wasn't interested in settling down. Besides, a man with Caraculla's position and rank had his pick of any woman in the empire, why would he settle for a wanton whore like Gypsy Theron? He'd already had her several times over, and Drake felt sure the colonel was done.

This was the perfect time to bring it up to her father, since Drake was confident Gypsy's beating in the arena was enough to make her reconsider her foolish dream to be a warrior. All Drake had to do was find a good time to talk to the general and Gypsy was as good as his.

* * * *

Gavin came home from being at the bar all night to find Harlan in the kitchen, crying. This was unusual for her, they often fought and, so far, nothing had ever been serious enough to keep her from a day of work at her beloved clinic. He came up and sat down next to her, running his fingers through her hair. Watching her weep was a torture he couldn't bare.

"Have I hurt you so much, my love?" he said.

Harlan tried to pull away when a heartbreaking sob erupted from her chest. Something was wrong and it had nothing to do with their fight earlier. Gavin pulled her to him and forced her to sit on his lap. She resisted him, trying to get up, but he held her firm until she stopped. He fixed her with his one good eye. "Now," he said firmly. "What's wrong?"

"I can't tell you," she said softly. "I swore I wouldn't."

"Has something happened to Gypsy?" he asked.

Tears streamed down Harlan's face and talons of pain tore at his heart. "Please," she said. "She made me promise. She'll never trust me with anything again."

Gavin took her face in his hands and kissed her. He kissed her with the gentle kindness that always broke her will. "Harlan, you must tell me. In many ways she is still a child and under my protection. If something has happened, then I have a right to know."

Harlan shook her head. "She doesn't want anyone to know, least of all you and Caraculla."

"You know as well as I do, secrets don't have any longevity in the empire. Caraculla and I will find out eventually, and whatever situation she's in may be much worse by then. Tell me what's happened and let me determine what must be done."

Harlan wrapped her arms around him and wept in his chest. After a few shaky breaths, she pulled back and gave him a hard stare. "You can't do anything about it or tell her you know. If you do, she'll know I told you. Promise me."

"I promise."

"Swear it."

Gavin frowned. *This must be very bad indeed.* "I so swear."

"Gypsy was in the arena alone last night and a warrior named Drake Trolis offered to be her sparring partner. She's had issues with him in the past. Somehow, during the course of that practice, he managed to get her on the ground and rape her, after beating the snot out of her." The tears rolled down her cheeks. "I don't know what to do! She refuses to report it and said she wants to deal with Drake herself. She is adamant—she doesn't want you or Caraculla interfering."

Black fury roared from the depths of his soul. Gently but firmly, he pulled Harlan off his lap and stood up. Every muscle in his body was tense and ready to fight. His rage was so consuming and deep, he had to go out into the courtyard to have a smoke and get it under control. He hadn't been this angry for a very long time.

The morning was sweet and calm. A tiny breeze caressed his skin. He lit his cigar and puffed hard on it, sending smoke billowing into the air. *So they think the girl is easy prey, do they? And so she is. She has talent and heart, but no real training. And that last shortfall is because of me.* Agony filled his heart when he realized how he was partially to blame for this disaster.

But Gypsy was right, if Gavin—or even Caraculla for that matter—went after Drake, her reputation would be salvaged, but her career would be done. No one would take her seriously as a warrior if her family fought her battles. She would have to deal with this herself. But Drake was a nobleman's son, handed a saber and trained for combat from the time he could walk, and Gypsy was a girl.

Correction—a woman. His daughter, and he'd failed her in so many ways. He'd been a horrible and negligent father, and he was deeply ashamed for taking her for granted. But there was still time to make things better between them, and now she would need him more than ever.

By the time he was done training Gypsy, all those men who'd dismissed her would be running from the very mention of her name.

Just the thought made him smile.

* * * *

Gavin's back was to her when she ventured into the court-yard, still in her sleeping clothes and bare feet. Harlan sat on the garden table where they had first consummated their relationship so long ago. She kept a reasonable distance between them as she usually did when he was pissed off. In twenty years, Gavin had never laid a hand on her in violence, but that never stopped him from launching an unprovoked verbal assault on her when he'd lost control of his temper.

She watched as he turned around and closed the distance between them. Standing before her, he brought his hands up to her face, with his thumbs pushed her tears away, and kissed her forehead softly.

"What are you going to do?" she questioned cautiously.

"What I should have done from the beginning. I'm going to assume the responsibility for her training," he said, wrapping his arms around her.

"Oh," she scowled.

"You don't want me to train her?"

"I do. I was hoping you would say you were going to find Drake and tear him to pieces. That's all."

Gavin grinned down at her. "If it wouldn't mean the end of her career, I wouldn't still be here talking to you. He'd be dead already."

Chapter 20

Gypsy practiced in a corner of the arena by herself. She had forced herself to come here today, and staying was proving to be no easy feat. Drake was always watching her. Normally outgoing, she avoided the other warriors, now painfully aware of the rumors that were circulating about her. They were cruel and mean-spirited, implying she'd somehow brought the attack upon herself. She sighed and tried to shrug it off. She shouldn't be surprised. But the fear had already taken up residence within her. What if others thought they could do the same?

She cast a wary eye on Drake, who'd been hanging around the dressing rooms all morning keeping her under his surveillance. The sight of him made her skin crawl, and the bad memories dominate her mind. There was a time before the rape when she would have ignored him and felt no fear. But that violent act had changed everything. Only a few days had passed since the assault, and she couldn't rid herself of the constant presence of her naked vulnerability. Every time Drake got anywhere near her, she felt edgy, and quickly put some distance between them.

From high in the bleachers, she saw Gavin and immediately wanted to leave. He walked with his familiar lethal grace, looking like a predatory cat waiting to pounce. He paused to talk to some soldiers, and Gypsy scanned the arena for the closest exit. She wasn't ready to face him yet. Even her practice wasn't giving her any joy.

Who was she kidding? This was never going to work. She'd never be as fast as the senior class warriors. She was giving serious thought to forfeiting her slot next year. *What was the use?* All these warriors were better than her and they all knew it.

She was about to walk off the floor when she spotted Drake heading for Gavin. He walked up to her father and started talking in earnest, occasionally gesturing to her. *What the hell is he talking to Gavin for?* Suddenly her father glanced around and pointed to a small dark alcove used to store equipment. *Oh crap, what is that moron telling him?* She thought with mounting dread.

After what seemed like an hour, Gavin emerged from the alcove looking stiff, and slammed his shoulder against Drake's as he passed. The impact was hard and it was clear to everyone watching that it was an obvious provocation. Drake didn't take the bait, however. He just stood there looking unhappy and confused.

Her father descended the stairs with all eyes riveted on him. He was pissed and no one wanted to miss what he was going to do next. Gavin came onto the arena floor and headed right for her. *Goddamn it! He knows about Drake! I should have known my mother couldn't keep quiet about this. Now he's going to make a huge scene and embarrass me.* Gypsy's belly twisted in knots as she waited for him to reach her.

Sheathing her saber, she folded her arms across her chest and prepared for the worst. He was going to put a stop to everything and she didn't know if she had the will left to challenge him.

Gavin stopped and stared down at her with that chilling golden eye. Angry black energy flowed from him like sorcery. "Do you still want to be a warrior?" he said, loud enough for everyone to hear.

Gypsy felt her stomach drop. Her palms were starting to sweat. "Yes," she replied. Looking him in the eye was extremely difficult. It was as if he could see the whole rape play out in her pupils and the shame she felt at her weakness was almost unbearable.

"If I agree to train you, will you swear complete loyalty to me?"

For a moment, she wasn't sure she'd heard him right. A flicker of hope filled her. Was he going to do this in front of everyone? She searched his face to make sure he was serious. He was. "Yes," she repeated.

"Before you agree too quickly, know what I'm asking of you will change our relationship forever. I will no longer be your father, Gypsy. I will now become your general. No disobedience will be tolerated. I will treat you as any other military academy prospect. Do you understand?"

She understood completely, she'd seen what they did to disobedient recruits often enough. Most discipline involved severe beatings and jail. "I understand."

"Get on your knees," he said.

Gypsy slowly dropped to her knees before Gavin, feeling everyone's eyes on her. Excitement began to take root in her. The prospect of returning to the matches next year with better training was igniting her soul, which minutes before had been in a death spiral. *Please let this be real.* She'd seen this done a thousand times and never dared dream it would happen to her one day. She knew what was expected of her. Her breath caught in her throat a few times, as she inhaled deeply and bowed her head.

"Swear your loyalty to me," Gavin said, in a voice as loud as thunder.

"I so swear, Excellency," she said. "I am your woman in all things from this day forward."

"Good," Gavin said. "Come to my office after you've changed and we'll discuss your schedule."

Gypsy was so confused. "Yes, Excellency," she said, wanting to smile but still unsure if this was really happening.

Chapter 21

Gypsy came into Gavin's office still dazed from what had happened in the arena. The room held the heavy, earthy scent of cigar smoke even with the window open. A lazy breeze toyed with the curtain. Gavin was sitting behind his desk puffing on a cigar with two sheets of paper in front of him. He handed them to her. She took them and was surprised that her hand was trembling.

"One of those is your new diet and the other is your training schedule. The diet is essential to build up your muscle mass. I believe you have more Æssyrian blood than human, and I think with the right diet you can become stronger. You and I will have one lesson in the morning and one in the evening. The rest of the day you will use to practice technique and sparring."

"Excuse me, Excellency," she said, feeling self-conscious. It was weird calling her father by his official title, but she was required to. *I'm like any other trainee now.* Gavin leaned back in his chair and watched her. "What is it?"

"No one will spar with me."

"All that nonsense is behind you, Gypsy. When you show up at the arena to spar, you'll have a partner. I'll be there as well to supervise the session. We don't have any time to waste." He stood up and crushed out his cigar. "I want you to follow that schedule to the letter, do you understand me?"

"Yes, Excellency."

"Now for that other matter," reaching into his desk, he took out a small, clear vial with purple liquid inside. It looked like a capsule of ink. He came around the front of his desk and leaned against it. "Has your mother gotten the results back from your pregnancy test?"

Gypsy's throat tightened. She wanted to yell at him for his part in that mess, but held her tongue. This was her last chance. If she allowed her temper to detonate, she was finished. Instead, she shook her head.

Gavin held up the vial. "This is a potent aphrodisiac. It's been long enough. It should work well. When I break it, you might feel a carnal hunger and that's what we want. If you are pregnant, you'll feel nothing. The pregnancy hormones will block any response to this pheromone. Are you ready?"

"How come Mom doesn't have this?"

Gavin laughed. "Because she thinks it's Æssyrian voodoo, not science."

"Does it really work?"

Gavin's yellow eye shined brightly. "Like a charm."

"I'm not going to want to jump you, am I?" she said, crinkling her nose.

"No. It won't give you feelings you don't have. It'll enhance the ones you do. Let's just say you'll be very forgiving toward Caraculla this evening. Are you ready?"

"Have you ever used it on Mom?" She grinned at him devilishly.

"Not that I needed to, but yes. Naturally I didn't take into consideration that she is not Æssyrian." Gavin winced as if struck by a bad memory. "She ended up in bed vomiting for two days and nursing a hellacious migraine. She was of course, upset with me for quite some time."

Gypsy bit her lower lip and shifted around in the chair. "Can that happen to me?"

"Possibly, but as I said, I believe you tend to favor your Æssyrian genetics in many subtle ways. If not, there may be a slight delay in the commencement of your training."

Gypsy tried to relax. *Great, either I'm going to be horny, sick or pregnant.* "Okay. I'm ready."

Gavin pushed his thick black thumbnail into the capsule and it snapped open. Dark purple vapors rose from the capsule and Gypsy waited nervously for something to happen. A most extraordinary scent reached her nose. It didn't smell like anything she could define, but it was wonderful, and made her body feel warm and relaxed. A gentle lust filled her belly and she closed her eyes to enjoy it. Images of Caraculla came into her head and all her anger and pain drifted away like mist. She wondered how fast she could get the hell out of here and find him. Her mind played with images of him at home, masturbating like a fiend, missing her. Her lust for him moved up a notch. Then the images melted away as Gavin invaded her space. His scent was rich and dark, reminding her of black leather. His familiar smell always managed to get her hackles up.

Gypsy frowned as the pleasant sensation drifted away. "Why do you have that?" she said, opening her eyes and blinking. She needed to get some of that stuff for later.

Gavin gestured toward the door, indicating she should leave. "Never mind. Go home and get some rest because we're going to the weapon master's first thing in the morning, and I expect that will be a long visit."

"How long will this feeling last?"

Gavin shrugged. "Probably well into this evening."

"Can I have another one of those things?" she said, pulling herself out of the chair.

"Fuck off, Gypsy. Your training starts tomorrow and you are not to be exhausted from ravishing Caraculla all night." He grinned and pointed again to the door.

"Yes, Excellency," she said, turning and heading out.

"And, Gypsy?" Gavin said. She turned around, inwardly groaning and trying to get the thoughts of Caraculla out of her head. *What the hell does he want now? I need to go look for Caraculla and he keeps talking.* That little purple thing didn't look like much, but it was strong. "I suggest you make up with Caraculla," he said. "You'll need his support during all of this. If anyone is at fault for trying to get you pregnant, it's me. Please don't blame him. I knew his weaknesses and exploited them to do what I thought was best."

She let his words linger for a moment. Her gaze wandered over the many books and papers piled on the floor. She wondered if he ever touched any of it. A nagging doubt about her ability made her heart ache. "Do you still think what you both did was the best for me?" It was a risky question but she needed to know the truth. Did he think he was wasting his time, or did he think she had a chance?

"No," he said. "What we did was a mistake. It was easier for me to deny you than accept who you really are. I've made a lot of mistakes when it comes to you, Gypsy, but I intend to make amends for them all. I've seen you fight and you do have natural ability. As Caraculla told me numerous times, you can do this. All I need you to do is trust me and do everything I say, no matter how absurd. Together we can succeed. No—not succeed—triumph. The question is, can you give yourself over to me completely?"

Chapter 22

Old man Narone was said to be one of the most knowledge-able people in the empire. If there were rumors and secrets circulating through the nobles, Narone knew all the details. As janitor of the arena, Narone heard everything the men talked about in hushed whispers as they came and went through the dressing rooms on their way to their matches. Better yet, it was common knowledge that any information anyone wanted was always for sale for the right amount of money or trade.

Caraculla waited that afternoon until most warriors were on the arena floor. Then he came into the showers where the old man was working. He glanced around to make sure they were alone. When he was sure everyone was gone, he advanced on Narone, the echo of his spurs jingled ominously off the stone walls. Narone didn't look up and continued his work, leaning over his mop and occasionally holding his back. Caraculla stalked up and stopped by the old man's bucket. He pulled a few crisp bills from his pants pocket and waited for Narone to look up from his work. The old man wrung out his mop and glanced at Caraculla. Meeting Caraculla's eyes, Narone immediately dropped his gaze to the floor. "Please excuse my insolence, lord," the old man said.

"I've heard you tell good stories," Caraculla said.

"None that I don't believe to be true, lord. I won't spread lies if you know what I mean."

Caraculla played with the bills in his hand. "Tell me a story about a female warrior getting a beating on the arena floor."

Narone looked around nervously. Confident no one was listening, he reached out and snatched the money in Caraculla's hand. He stuffed it into his pocket. "Not only a beating, lord—a most foul violation! A warrior tricked her into a spar when he was sure everyone was gone. The warrior barely let that poor girl escape with her life! Word is he has gone to the general to lay claim to her." The old man shook his head. "Shameful behavior to treat a woman that way."

A wild animal let loose inside Caraculla's soul and clawed pain into his heart. Blind fury exploded inside his head and all he could think of was revenge. Venom flooded his mouth and he spit some onto the stone wall. It sizzled and burned a hole right through to the outside. Whomever it was who'd done this would pay dearly for it. Caraculla clenched his fists. "Name?"

The old man took a cautious step back and cowered. "Please, lord...I had nothing to do with..."

"*Name!*" Caraculla snarled.

Narone dropped to his knees and bowed his head. "Drake Trolis, lord. He is on the arena floor as we speak."

Pulling his saber, Caraculla turned and stormed with steady purpose from the room.

* * * *

Gavin stood at the bar sipping his drink and talking politics with some of his officers. He was pleased with his decision to take over his daughter's training and decided a celebratory cocktail was in order. The serene quiet was smashed when three young warriors raced into the bar running so fast their boots slid on the floor. All three were pointing toward the arena.

"Excellency!" one of them said, his voiced laced with terror. "Come quick! Colonel Caraculla is going to fry a senior warrior right in the middle of the floor!"

That took less time than I expected. Gavin downed the rest of his drink. He followed the warriors back over to the arena and raced down the steps to the floor. As he descended, he slowed down and felt his blood cool in his veins. Few things were as terrifying as a Razorback in a blind fury. Except for Caraculla and Drake, the floor was completely deserted. Indeed, it felt like the entire arena was. A few jumpy guards stood by the entrance, too frightened to make a move against the Razorback.

Gavin didn't blame them.

As Gavin continued down the steps, he noticed several places where scorch marks were all that remained of a few seats and part of the stairs. Every place Caraculla had spit was still smoking from the corrosive fluid.

For his part, Drake looked like a lion had mauled him. Cut and beaten, he didn't utter a word. He lay on his belly, his arms outstretched with Caraculla over him. The Razorback's blade was pointed directly at his victim's skull. But Gavin knew Caraculla didn't plan a quick death for Drake. He was sure his colonel had something much worse planned. Something that had to do with that horrible venom of his.

Gavin stalked onto the arena floor and stopped a few feet from them. "Colonel Caraculla!" he said in his most commanding voice. "Stand down!"

Caraculla turned and looked at Gavin with death in his eyes. He barely seemed to know where he was. Leaning his head back, he let out an ear-splitting screech. It was usually the last thing any- one heard before being spit on.

The guards that had been peeking in through the door broke and ran.

Gavin took a few more steps forward. "I am commanding you to stand down *now*!"

Caraculla spit venom to Gavin's right. It hissed and smoked like molten lava, but Gavin didn't move. Caraculla's eyes burned into him as a glossy string of venom dripped down and sizzled on the ground next to Drake's chin. The warrior's eyes ignited with blind panic. Gavin stayed completely still, willing himself not to show the fear bubbling inside him.

"You filthy *bastard*," the colonel snarled at him. "You knew this happened and you did *nothing*. What's worse than that is you couldn't even be *bothered* to tell me what he did to her. Does she mean so little to you?"

"I understand your rage," Gavin said, keeping his tone neutral. "But he is not yours or mine to correct. His discipline belongs to someone else."

The colonel shook his head. "No. He's mine."

"You *must* let him go."

"*No!*"

"She doesn't want this, Caraculla. You, of all people, have respected her wishes more than anyone else. Don't take this away from her. There are so many other ways you can help her, my friend."

Caraculla glared down at Drake, and for a few tense moments, Gavin was sure he'd lost. The warrior was shaking so hard, Caraculla's blade kept nicking the back of his head. Then the colonel took his boot off the warrior's back and kicked Drake in the head. The impact was so hard Gavin thought he'd fractured the warrior's skull. Caraculla took a few stiff steps back and let Drake get to his feet.

Gavin stalked forward and picked up Drake's saber. Handle first, he held it out to him and said, "I would suggest you not be a common fixture here for awhile. Also, if you need to go to the medical clinic, I would suggest you see the Kirillian." Drake glanced at Caraculla and stumbled off the floor as fast as his legs could carry him.

Gavin turned to Caraculla. The colonel slid his saber back into its sheath, still swearing under his breath. *What a day.* He wondered if Drake truly appreciated how lucky he was. Being forced to watch your own arms and legs melt off would definitely ruin a young noble's career.

Caraculla came over, still fuming, and Gavin slapped him good-naturedly on the back. "What say we go and get a drink?" Gavin offered. "I'll buy."

Chapter 23

Gypsy walked down the white hallway, enjoying the sound of her boots clicking on the gray tile. The sterile smell of medicine seemed to decrease her arousal with each passing breath. She'd received a message to come to the clinic when she was done with Gavin, but apparently, the aphrodisiac made a person ravenous for food as well as sex. So Gypsy had first stopped in one of the local cafés and gorged herself on a huge plate of sliced meat. The food had satisfied some of her lust, so she hadn't felt the need to rush to the clinic. Instead, she chose to meander around in some of the shops for a bit.

At first, she was confident at Gavin's pregnancy prediction, but as she advanced down the hallway, a nervous tingle began to swirl in her belly. *What if he was wrong?* She felt herself resisting the urge to run like a maniac to her mother's office at the end of the corridor. Not rushing ended up being a wise decision because halfway to the office, Krull came out of an exam room and walked toward her, scribbling notes in a chart. She was sure he had no intention of acknowledging her, or even making eye contact, so Gypsy intercepted him, deliberately standing in his way. "Hey, Dr. Krull, have you seen my mom?"

Krull stopped short of smacking into her, and kept writing in the chart he was holding. He stopped writing long enough to regard her with an icy stare and instantly returned to his task. Gypsy held her ground, wondering if he was going to answer her question. After an entire minute went by, she finally stepped aside. He continued walking down the hall without so much as a grunt.

"Thanks, Doc, you've been a big help," she called after him. *What a complete prick that guy is.*

When she reached the end of the hall, she barged into the familiar dark wood door with the polished brass sign that read, *Dr. Harlan Theron-Chief of Staff.* Her mother looked up from behind her desk and smiled warmly. "I wish you would learn how to knock. I could have been in a meeting."

Gypsy smirked and dropped into one of the two chairs in front of Harlan's desk. With her foot, she turned the other chair to face her and propped her boots up on the seat. "I know all about your *meetings.* And as far as I know, Gavin's still at his office, so I knew I wouldn't be interrupting any *meetings.*" She sat back satisfied as her mother flushed.

"My *meetings* are none of your business. So if we can move on, I have your test results back. You'll be pleased to know they're negative."

"I know," she said, nodding.

"How do you know?"

"Gavin broke a vial of purple crap under my nose and now I am desperate to find Caraculla and do bad things to him."

Harlan rolled her eyes. "That purple crap is nonsense. It's an aphrodisiac, not a pregnancy test. You're part human, it could have made you very sick."

Gypsy shrugged. "So what's with that Kirillian doctor? Why's he such an asshole?"

Harlan sighed. "He's not bad. He just isn't very personable. But he is a very good doctor and that's what matters to me."

"Do you think he ever has sex? I mean, unless he pays for it, he would have to actually talk to a girl. I don't see him doing that. Maybe he prefers other men?" Gypsy said, looking at Harlan and tapping the side of her nose with her index finger.

"All right, this portion of our conversation is over. I'm not going to discuss his sex life or lack thereof. I don't care and I am certainly not interested in you putting creepy images in my head." Harlan pointed at her as a warning and Gypsy burst into peals of happy laughter. It felt good to laugh.

Harlan got up and walked around to the front of her desk. She leaned down and wrapped her arms around Gypsy, kissing her on the cheek. "I'm so happy things are finally working out for you. You deserve it. Now go make up with Caraculla. He loves you so much and I just heard that he has had a very bad day today."

"What happened?"

Harlan stepped back and leaned against the front of her desk. "He found out about the rape, probably from that nosy janitor, and almost melted Drake into the arena floor. Somehow, your father managed to talk him out of killing that piece of shit. I know you want to take care of Drake yourself. But I'm not ashamed to admit I'm on Caraculla's side for this one."

Gypsy frowned, feeling needles of anguish pierce her heart. She sat forward, pulling her boots off the chair. Running her fingers through her hair she said, "I was really hoping he wouldn't find out about that. *Damn it!*" She suddenly stood up and began to pace.

"He didn't kill Drake though. You'll still have a chance at your revenge," Harlan said, obviously unhappy with the idea. Gypsy stopped pacing and dropped back into her chair. Resting her elbows on her knees, she hung her head. The long wild locks of her hair partially obscured her face.

"It's not that. I don't care about that."

Harlan reached out and stroked some of the hair away from her daughter's face.

"What is it, Gypsy?"

"It's just that I feel really dirty from it, and even though I know it's crazy, I'm afraid Caraculla won't want me anymore."

"Oh, Gypsy, you have so much to learn about love and men. Caraculla is devastated that this happened to you, and he blames himself. I know him and mark my words, he's going to carry this with him for years. You don't need to feel dirty and unwanted. You need to go and share your strength with him. He needs to know you're okay and that you still want *him* even after, in his mind, he's failed you."

Gypsy felt the muscles in her jaw tighten, and her eyes start to water. She got up and gave Harlan a bear hug. "Thanks, Mom. I know this has been tough on you too, and I really am okay."

"I know you are. Now go help Caraculla be okay."

Chapter 24

Harlan had climbed into bed and nestled down for the evening when she heard Gavin come home. It had been a long day and although it was still early, she was emotionally exhausted. Now that Gavin was stepping in and her daughter would finally get the training she desperately needed, Harlan was feeling much better. Even though she still wasn't happy about Gypsy's career choice, at least her chances of survival just increased substantially. Gavin's heavy footsteps thumped along the floor as he made his way to their bedroom.

She sat up in bed and turned the light on.

He came in dressed in full battle armor and her breath caught in her throat, as her eyes feasted on him. Even after all these years, he could still do it for her. Standing at a towering six foot seven and close to three hundred and twenty pounds, General Gavin Theron was a commanding figure. He was also the best-looking ÆEssyrian man she'd ever seen, even if it was a more rugged handsomeness than most. His face was hard and masculine, with a muscled jaw and a piercing yellow eye. The other eye was covered with a black patch, having been destroyed on campaign many years ago. Like all ÆEssyrians, he had a mouthful of sharp predatory teeth and Harlan wondered why her daughter hadn't inherited that trait. Gypsy had sharp canine teeth, but that was about all. Except for her eyes and lean muscles, Gypsy could have passed for any athletic woman back on Earth.

Unfastening his armor, he pulled it off his generously muscled chest, and hung it on the stand. His skin was a rich olive green, except in the places where his many scars marred his flesh. In those places, his skin was lighter. Down the center of his back was a thick raised spine with tiny glands on either side of the lumbar that, once caressed, would make an Æssyrian man insane with desire. Heavy knotted muscles covered his chest, back and arms, and at a respectable eight-hundred-and-twenty years old, he was a very healthy middle age.

Luckily, for her, the planet's atmosphere had slowed down her human aging process. On Earth, she would have been a woman of fifty-five but here she still looked a youthful thirty-five.

Coughing a few times, he stripped naked and climbed into bed with her. His thick twelve-inch cock was already erect and ready for her. She loved how he filled her up to the point of almost hurting her. It made her feel deliciously used and conquered. He pulled Harlan into his arms and hugged her tight. "I've done it, my love. She's my trainee now. She swore loyalty to me this morning."

Harlan ran her fingers through his hair. Her pussy was already throbbing with sexual hunger. "I know, I heard. So what actually happened at the arena? I've only heard bits and pieces. I don't suppose you killed Drake, after all."

Gavin laughed. "No, but he almost was done in by Caraculla. Seems as though the colonel found out about the assault and he was quite upset. I thought I was never going to calm him down." He kissed her deeply and she pushed her breasts into his chest. He massaged them and groaned her name.

"Why is Drake still alive?" she asked, not hiding her disappointment. Not many people escaped the wrath of a rampaging Razorback.

"I stopped Caraculla with my superior negotiating skills," Gavin said, licking down her throat. Harlan paused to enjoy the rush of lust filling her belly. He was such a great lover. Always very attentive.

"Why did you stop him?" she whispered, losing herself by the second.

"Because Drake is Gypsy's. She deserves to have her revenge, and I'm going to see that she gets it." His voice had taken on that deep, sexual sound she adored.

"Do you think Caraculla would have gone through with it?" she said, as her breath came in quick pants.

"There is no doubt in my mind, and it would have been a slow agonizing death."

Harlan gently bit his lower lip and pulled. "Maybe I should use my own superior negotiating skills and convince Caraculla to go ahead and kill him," she said, stroking the thick shaft of his cock. He growled in her ear and dragged kisses down her body, pulling down her pajamas and panties.

"Only if I can watch the negotiations." His forked tongue caressed the swollen bud of her clit and Harlan moaned, rolling her hips up to give him better access. She smiled and leaned her head back. He liked to talk a lot of shit, but she knew he'd never share her with anyone. Not even his beloved Caraculla.

When they'd first been married, she'd almost been overwhelmed by his voracious sexual appetite. But as time went on, she got addicted to how beautiful he made her feel. He never just had sex with her; he worshiped her with his hands, mouth and tongue. A rush of happiness burst through her senses and she smiled. The orgasm was coming and it was going to be a long one.

Digging her nails into the bed, she arched her hips up to his mouth, but he was already gone. She groaned in protest as he moved up over her. Opening her legs wide, he braced them back with his forearms and eased his enormous cock deep inside her.

Harlan gasped and cried out his name as he rocked back and forth until her climax exploded with the frenzy of a wild animal.

He released her legs and Harlan wrapped them around him. "Do it," he said. Harlan shook her head and laughed. He was so kinky sometimes and really loved to hear her get loud when they made love. Harlan cried out his name as loud as she could and bucked her hips up into him. Snarling like a fearsome beast, he exploded inside her, murmuring benign threats into her ear.

Gavin was still very erect and stayed inside her until she signaled him that she was ready to go again. *This was going to be one hell of a long night.*

Chapter 25

Drake sat in the temple with his head bowed thanking the gods he was still alive. His early afternoon encounter with Colonel Caraculla had been one of the most jarring experiences of his life and he wouldn't soon forget it. How could he have been so wrong about the colonel's feelings for Gypsy? *What could a man like that see in her? He must not be finished with her yet. Men could be very proprietary over what they think is theirs.* His attempt to lay claim to her was a miscalculation that almost cost him his life.

But now a new horror dawned on him.

This misunderstanding with Gypsy would cost him his slot at the academy and subsequently any hope of a military career. Everything he'd worked for all his life was lost. He would end up being a mercenary or degenerate bounty hunter or something equally distasteful. That was not the life for a nobleman's son.

There was only one answer to this nightmare. He'd have to kill Gypsy Theron and dispose of her body in a place no one would ever find it. But there was only one problem with his plan. The general was now her teacher and mentor, he'd never let anyone near her until she was ready for combat. Of course being a half-breed human woman, she'd never be ready for combat. It baffled him that a great military mind like the general would waste his time attempting to train her. Drake was eager to save him the trouble. She was weak and had no skill to speak of. It would be so easy to kill her and probably take less than a few minutes. But how was he ever going to lure her someplace alone where he could do the deed?

The answer came to him like a divine message from the gods. *Angel*. His fiancée and Gypsy had grown up together. With the right excuse, he was confident Angel could get Gypsy alone. Angel was the perfect accomplice for his plan; all he had to do was convince her that it was in her best interest to help him. But he needed time to work on her and mold her into an obedient wife. With enough physical persuasion, he was sure he could coax her into helping him with the deed. All he had to do was pressure her to marry him now, before the fallout from his disgrace became common knowledge. Once she was his, he would tell her everything, and then remind her that their fates were intertwined. If he failed to get into the academy and make rank, then she would flounder for the rest of her life in disgrace, too. She was as ambitious as he was, so he was sure he could convince her of the wisdom of this.

Gypsy's disappearance would cause quite a stir, but without knowing what had happened, what could her family do? He would join General Theron and Colonel Caraculla in their exhaustive searches and weep with them in the bars as if he'd been Gypsy's own brother. Who would suspect a man so devoted to finding her? Then, when time had passed and the pain of her loss had faded, he'd beg forgiveness from those two powerful men and work his way back into the life he'd lost. The plan was brilliant.

All he needed now was Angel.

* * * *

Angel wrung her hands and walked in tight little circles. Her delicate features tensed and relaxed as she tried to reach a decision. "I don't know," she said. "An elopement is so unexpected. My family will be very angry."

Drake leaned against a tree and folded his arms. He focused on keeping his tone neutral. "Why not?" he asked. "There is no one else, is there?"

"Well," she said nervously, "no."

He went over and pulled her into his arms, kissing her. "You want me, don't you?"

She ran her hands down his chest. "I don't understand your urgency. We can be married in a few weeks. Why elope?"

This was going to be harder than he thought. He decided to try a new angle. "Because I've been tempted by someone else."

"Who?"

"What difference does it make? It's you I want, Angel, but my flesh is weak. I need you in my bed. Let's go to the temple and be married now. We can always do the public ceremony later. I would never disgrace you, but I need to douse this lust within me."

She smiled weakly. "I could please you in other ways."

"I don't want that. I want to consummate our relationship, and the only way to do it, is to do this my way. If you will not obey me in this, I'll have no choice but to put an end to our engagement."

Tears welled up in Angel's eyes. She softly kissed him on the lips. "All right. When do we leave?"

Chapter 26

Caraculla sat in the courtyard with his boots up on the table, smoking a cigar and nursing a whiskey. He was close to drunk and was planning to get much drunker as the night wore on. Regret tore at his gut and he cursed himself for not ignoring Gavin and killing that son of a bitch Drake when he had the chance. The man would probably avoid him from now on. He had lost the element of surprise. *Damn.*

She was home. Her sweet, luscious scent filled his senses and drove his buzz to the back of his mind. His body started to heat up and it was all he could do to keep his seat and not ravage her. The vivid memory of her body under him was total bliss and his desire flamed high. Ever since their fight, he had been lost without her. She was as essential to him as the blood that flowed in his veins, and his soul was withering without her.

He heard her boots coming up behind him. They scraped along the stone pavers as she moved closer. His cock grew hard in his pants and he reached down to shift it into a more comfortable position. She came around and took the seat opposite him. Grabbing the whiskey bottle she took a sip, grimaced and put it back on the table.

"I understand you have had a very bad day," she said.

Caraculla smiled, despite his dark mood. He shook his head and rolled his drink around in the glass. "I should have killed him."

Gypsy stared at him, her eyes burning with passion. "That's very sweet of you, Caraculla, but Drake is mine."

"I wish you had told me what he did to you."

"I didn't tell you for just this reason. Look at you, you're a mess." She smiled, but it was weak and her eyes pulled away from his. They dropped down to her hands, which began to fidget with each other.

"Is that the only reason?" he said, daring to open the door for a rebuke on how he had destroyed her trust in him.

She shook her head, still not looking at him. After a few moments passed she said, "He made me feel so dirty and so used, that I was afraid. I was afraid you wouldn't want me anymore."

Caraculla couldn't believe what he was hearing. He remained still for a moment. Then he reached out, taking her chin in his hand, and pulling it up until she looked at him. A few stray tears made their way down her cheeks and the pain in her eyes tore at his very being. He gave her a hard stare.

"That will never happen, not ever. I will always want you, all the time, no matter what."

Caraculla watched the sadness fade from her face and a guarded smile return.

"Really?"

"Gypsy, I have had to train myself not to think about you, or I would be walking around with an erection all day long, every day," he said, grinning.

A soft laugh escaped from her lips and she wiped her eyes with her sleeve. Then she got up and took his cigar out of his fingers. Grabbing his glass, she tossed back what was left of his drink and set it on the table. She put the cigar in the ashtray and climbed into his lap backwards, facing him. Pulling off her shirt, she let it drop to the ground.

"Both of my parents think I should make up with you," she whispered, running her fingers through his hair. "What do you think?"

Caraculla slid his hands over her soft round breasts while gently dragging his teeth along her throat. The feel of her flesh was like being reborn, and he let the rage within him transform into something far more carnal. Lifting her up, he pulled one nipple into his mouth and mauled it. Gypsy cradled his head and gasped with delight.

"Please, Gypsy," he said into her skin as his hunger blazed high, "please let me kill him. I'd love for you to be there and watch. I can make it horribly slow and painful."

She tossed her head back and gave another hearty laugh. Her mouth came down over his. She softly sucked on the corner of his mouth. "Right now I can think of better things you can do with your mouth than talk."

Caraculla rose, picking her up as he went. Gypsy pushed her tongue into his mouth and consumed him with wild frantic kisses. He pushed her against the courtyard wall and stripped off her pants and boots. They struggled with each other, each one trying to undress the other faster. Gypsy was so frantic, she tore his shirt, lifting it off his chest. Her hands stroked his back, boldly running down the tender glands of his spine and awakening him in an entirely new way.

He braced her against the wall and squeezed her long thighs as they wrapped around him like a viper. With a deep primal growl, he pushed his thick cock into her, encasing himself in her soft, wet heat.

"*Caraculla*," she groaned, in a voice that almost made him orgasm. "*More*," she whined. He drove his hips into her, moving them in a slow circular motion to maximize her pleasure. Gypsy's nails dug deep into his back, and her breath came in desperate pants as she worked her pussy over his throbbing rod. Her body stiffened and he felt the gratifying ripple of her orgasm around him. A moment later, he too, climaxed and filled her with his seed.

Lowering her legs to the floor, he interlaced his fingers with hers, keeping her hands pinned to the wall. They kissed like they'd never see each other again. Then he said, "I heard Gavin took over your training."

"Yeah, I swore loyalty to him this morning."

"So I guess you're not pregnant."

"No," she said. "The test came back negative."

"That's good. I'm glad." He was surprised that he meant it.

She nodded. "I start with Gavin tomorrow."

His heart sank. Although he was sure she was willing to fuck him all night, he knew she needed her sleep. "Go to sleep then," he said, nuzzling her neck. He let her hands go.

Her eyes grew soft and she stroked his face. "Did you mean what you said to me the other day?"

Caraculla walked back to the table and picked up his cigar. "About loving you?"

"Yes," she said.

"I've always loved you, Gypsy. I thought you knew that."

Gypsy reached out and grabbed his forearm. "Come to bed with me. I want to lie naked with you." There was a childlike joy to her voice.

"No, you need your rest. Gavin will not be kind to you if you show up on your first day exhausted." He took her hand from his arm and held it. She gave him a mischievous grin and gently pulled him forward.

"Come on," she said warmly. "I'll be all right. I promise I'll behave."

"I never could say no to you and mean it," he said, following her off to bed.

SIREN WARRIOR BOOK 3: OUTLAW BRIDE

by

Michelle Marquis & Lindsay Bayer

Chapter 1

For the first time in her life Gypsy Theron was up at dawn, dressed and ready to accompany her father to the weapon master's shop to purchase a weapon for *her* to use. As a child she'd often gone there with him to pick up a custom sword he had ordered or just to see what was new on display. Sometimes they'd spend hours there as Gavin fussed at the weapon master over this detail or that and she'd wander the aisles imagining what it would be like if one of those magnificent weapons was actually hers.

After her father was done shopping, he'd drag her off to the bar where he'd have his soldiers watch her while he busied himself drinking and gossiping with the other officers. It was at that seedy old bar that Gypsy learned to play cards, dice and drink. Her mother would have been horrified if she knew. The memories of those times seemed ancient now but made her smile anyway.

She waited outside the villa she shared with her lover Caraculla. She sat on top of her hyperia as it shifted restlessly. The creature wanted to be on his way but his predatory instincts made it impossible for him to stand still. Instead of waiting calmly, he busied himself snatching small lizards off the ground and eating them. For her part, Gypsy just thought about the road ahead and picked at a broken nail.

Her relationship with Gavin was like a dark cave with twists, turns and dead ends and she was worried about him training her. She had misgivings about so many things. For one thing, she was afraid he was going to spend more time abusing her, than actually teaching her. It would be so like him to do something like that to make her quit. Well—she'd had enough of his treachery and was not going to stand for anymore of it. She'd give Gavin a chance to make good on his word but this alliance would be short-lived if he thought she was just going to stand there and be his punching bag until she gave up. The sound of another hyperia coming toward her pulled her from her thoughts and she looked to see him approaching.

General Gavin Theron was dressed in his trademark black battle armor and looked every inch the famous warlord he was. A lot of what he wore was for just for show, like his ornate black and gold muscle cuirass, thick leather gloves, and cloak. His mount was dressed up too in hand-painted body armor and a spiked faceplate, but everything added to the feeling of power that rose off her father like smoke. The man knew how to make an entrance. She had to give him that.

Spurring her animal, she cantered up alongside him and they rode in silence for a while. Then, just a few yards from the weapon master's shop, he said, "I've been hearing some snide remarks directed toward you, Gypsy and I'm telling you, you are not to stand for it. From now on, I need you to think like their commander because one day you will be. You must not allow any comment to go unchallenged. Do you understand me?"

Gypsy understood him. She just didn't much like what he was saying. Most of her life had been spent ignoring those snide comments. "Yes, Excellency," she replied.

The moment Gavin walked through the door, the weapon master was at his side, showing him the latest weapon designs and armor. But soon he realized Gavin wasn't shopping for himself, but for Gypsy. The old man stepped back to let her father browse and watched them puzzled.

Gavin stalked up to a weapon on the new designs display and pulled a long, thick saber off the wall. He handed it to Gypsy who frowned at how heavy and awkward it was. The damn thing must have weighed six pounds.

"This will be your new weapon," Gavin said. "You will fight with it, eat with it, and sleep with it. If I catch you without it, I'll have Master Sergeant Rakon give you the thrashing of your life. Do you understand those instructions?"

Gypsy so wanted to complain that no one could fight with this damn big thing. So she settled for, "It's kind of long and heavy."

Gavin turned on her in a flash and leaned in close. His one good eye seized hers and he said through gritted teeth, "Are you questioning me?"

She felt the hairs on her neck and arms prickle and she forced herself to look at the shop floor. "No, Excellency. It wasn't a question. It was just a statement."

Gavin seemed to relax. "The reason for the heavy blade is to build up your strength and increase your stamina. Once you become proficient with a bulky, graceless weapon such as this, every other sword will seem easy. Do you have any other statements to make?"

"No, Excellency," she said, attaching the scabbard to her belt.

"Good. Now hand over your other saber."

Gypsy scowled and hesitated for a moment. This was Caraculla's sword he'd given to her when she'd needed it most. It was so comfortable to fight with that it felt like an extension of her arm. It was tough parting with it. But before her father lost patience, she pulled it from the sheath and held it out to him. He took it and attached it to his belt opposite his sword. She examined her new saber and instantly decided she hated it.

"Shouldn't you be using an adolescent blade, Lady Theron?" a young warrior said from a few rows away. He was standing with two of his buddies and they chuckled at the comment. Gypsy could tell he was eager to impress his friends.

She could feel Gavin's eye boring into her with savage intensity. *This is it. I have to call this guy out.* Gypsy sheathed her new saber and walked up to the warrior. "Did you have something to say to me?" she said, fighting to keep her tone cool. "I couldn't hear you clearly while you were hiding behind your buddies."

The warrior stared at her shocked. He obviously hadn't expected her to call him out on an innocent comment like that. "What? You want to go outside and fight me?"

"Come on, little boy," she taunted over her shoulder while heading out into the street. "Let's see how impressed your friends will be when a girl kicks your ass."

The warrior came out after her looking even younger under the harsh Æssyrian suns. He emerged from the shop slowly, keeping his hand on the hilt of his saber but never actually drawing it. Gypsy pulled her weapon from its sheath with a long fluid motion. The saber was so heavy it felt like a battle axe in her grip. She wished Gavin hadn't ordered her to use it. Her usual weapon was much lighter and easier to use.

Confronted by the very real possibility of being killed, the youth took his hand away from his weapon. He bowed his head in respect. "I'm sorry if I offended you, lady," he said.

Gavin came out into the street his spurs jingling ominously. Gypsy moved to put up her weapon and Gavin held his hand out to stop her. "No," he said in a heavy growl. "Don't you accept this pathetic apology from him. If he won't kneel and apologize, then you mark him."

Gypsy glared at the warrior. "On your knees," she ordered.

The humiliation was too much for the youth. Pulling his own weapon, he lunged at her awkwardly and Gypsy easily sidestepped him. She toyed with him for a moment enjoying the feeling of being the one in control. "This is your last chance," she said when she'd grown tired of the game. "On your knees and apologize."

The warrior snarled and swung his saber, striking blow after blow against her blade with no real planning behind it. He got within inches of cutting her arm and Gypsy danced back delivering a deep cut to his forehead. Her opponent stumbled back falling on the ground. He ran his hand over the fresh wound. It came away soaked in blood and he got to his feet.

"Next time you won't be getting up," Gypsy said.

The warrior was about to make another foolhardy attack but one of his friends grabbed his arm and shook his head. After a brief pause, the youth went down on his knees and repeated his apology.

Gavin gave the young men a wicked smile as Gypsy replaced her weapon. "There, you see, gentlemen? Was that so hard?" he said in a mocking tone. "Now if you'll excuse us, we have a tournament to prepare for. Why don't you boys run along and play soldier?"

Gavin stalked toward his hyperia whistling a happy tune. Gypsy glanced at the warriors expecting them to glare at her with unbridled hatred. That was what she was used to. But they didn't. Instead they bowed their heads in respect as she mounted up. *Who would have thought a little ass kicking would finally get me some respect?*

It was one of the best feelings she'd ever had. As she climbed on her own mount she decided to enjoy her recent confidence boost before Gavin found some way to ruin it for her.

Chapter 2

Angel stormed into their bedroom and pulled the drapes back flooding the room with brilliant sunlight. It was late morning and her new husband Drake Trolis was still sleeping soundly as if he didn't have a care in the world. He groaned and rolled away from the light. She marched up and stood over him trying and failing to control her temper.

"My sister just told me you *raped* my best friend Gypsy Theron. Please tell me that's not true," she said through her teeth.

Drake glared at her as he sat up. He ran his fingers though his hair pulling it back from his face. "Does every bit of news in this Empire travel by gossip?" he grumbled.

"You're not telling me what I want to hear."

He sighed and frowned. "It's true, but it was a mistake and I'm deeply sorry for it."

Angel couldn't absorb the words that had just come out of his mouth. By the Gods, she hoped he was joking. She felt as if she'd become the butt of a terrible joke. "How did this *happen*?"

Drake shook his head looking miserable. "I honestly don't know. We were sparring in the arena and, of course, I won." He stared at the opposite wall and seemed very far away. "The sight of her beneath me...I don't know what came over me." He waved his hands as if to ward off a terrible dream, then he got up from the bed and went into the bathroom.

Angel sank down on the mattress. Now suddenly this rushed marriage made sense. He wanted to trap her before she found out and dumped him. The thought made her stomach turn. "What have you done to apologize to her?" she said not recognizing the sound of her own voice.

Drake came out of the bathroom wiping his face with a towel. It was amazing how quickly he'd become an ugly brute in her eyes. He snorted. "I'm not going to do *anything* to apologize to her. She's the one carrying on like a cathouse harlot, or have you forgotten that?"

Angel barely registered a word his said. *My family is going to disown me for running off with this disgraced son of a bitch. Why didn't I wait! No decent man will want me now. What the hell am I going to do?*

"There's only one thing I can do to restore my name," Drake continued as he lumbered around the room getting dressed. "And I'll need your help to do it."

It felt like she had woken up in a terrible dream. She rubbed her face and leaned down over her knees wanting to throw up and wondering how she was ever going to make this up to her family. She felt like such a fool. "What's that?" she said, distracted.

"You have to help me kill her."

Angel looked up at him confused. "*What* did you say?"

Drake walked over and stood in front of her. She thought about the night they'd had together and felt even more nauseous. He was never touching her again. Gods, she hoped she wasn't pregnant.

"I need you to help me kill Gypsy."

"Have you completely lost your *senses?* Your big plan is to *kill* my best friend to save you from your shame?" Her life was slipping down into a waking nightmare. *He is completely insane. I'm trapped in marriage to a lunatic.*

"Don't you see, Angel? Killing her is the only way. I just need you to—"

Angel held up her hand. "Just stop right there. I don't know how you came up with this sick little plan but there is *no way* in a million years I would help you kill Gypsy. So you can just keep the sordid details of that to yourself. Second, I am going to fight like hell to get out of this farce of a marriage. Perhaps my family won't believe I didn't know about you but someone out there is *bound* to take pity on me and help me get rid of you. I can't believe you committed this dishonor and tricked me into marriage."

She launched from the bed and grabbed her bags. Opening drawers and racing around the room, she threw everything of hers she could find inside. Drake stood there watching her with smoldering rage in his eyes. Stepping in front of her, he tried to grab a handful of clothes from her but she easily sidestepped him.

Then something within him snapped.

"No!" he roared, hurtling her bags into a corner of the room. "You're not going anywhere! You are my wife and you *will* obey me!"

"Like *hell* I will!" she barked back.

Drake lunged for her and Angel knew it was time to run. Nothing in those bags was so important it was worth losing her life over. In a flash of speed, she darted out of the bedroom and took off at a full run for the front door. Drake was right behind her closing the distance so fast, she screamed and ducked even before he'd touched her. His beefy hand grabbed a handful of her hair and pulled her up to him. "You will *not* leave me!" he screamed into her face. "I will not *allow* you to!"

With every ounce of energy she had, Angel attacked him, biting and clawing like a wildcat. She tasted blood in her mouth and heard him cry out in surprise. His grip on her hair loosened, and for just a fleeting moment, she thought she might have fought herself free.

But unfortunately Angel was wrong.

Chapter 3

Doctor Harlan Theron went back to the medical clinic after a light lunch and checked the appointment schedule. Her first check-up was Banta, one of Doctor Krull's patients. The doctor had taken a rare day off to go hunting and Harlan had been happy to take his patients. It was the least she could do for all the times Krull had covered for her last year. He might have been a man of few words but he'd never refused to help her out when she needed it. The quiet Kirillian doctor also intrigued her. Like her, he was a transplant from another planet with no family to speak of. His entire life was work and she sometimes wondered if he was lonely here.

His patient was a warrior who'd had an arm severed in the arena a few months back. She remembered that fight as being a particularly violent one and it still sent chills down her back. Krull had spent six hours reattaching the arm taking great pains to do the best job he could. It was impressive since not only didn't he know the man, but she'd heard Krull had had an altercation with the family just minutes before he'd gone in for surgery. Apparently they didn't like the idea that Banta would never be able to fight in the arena again. A lesser doctor would have done the bare minimum. But that was never Krull's way. He always strived for perfection and Harlan felt his dedication made her a better doctor too.

She grabbed the file and went into room two. Banta was a shorter male with a thick mane of dark-brown hair. His eyes were a captivating bright silver and looked even more striking peering out from his forest-green skin. He only had one scar on his chin and thus still retained a youthful look to his face. She guessed his age at just barely one hundred. He had already taken off his shirt and sat on the exam table watching her curiously. "Where's Doctor Krull?" he asked.

Harlan smiled. "He took the day off to go hunting. Would you rather reschedule and see him?"

"No," Banta said. "I'd rather see you."

For a moment, Harlan felt uncomfortable and considered asking the security guard to come in. She looked into his eyes and didn't sense any aggression in him so she dismissed it as just harmless flirting. "I'm just going to take a quick look at your arm."

Banta lifted the arm up and turned his wrist. He flexed and unflexed his fingers which moved a little stiffly. A deep, nasty scar marred him just above the elbow but other than that she couldn't tell anything had ever happened to him. *Amazing. I have to assist the next time Krull does one of these reattachments.*

"Do you have any pain?"

Banta shrugged. "Sometimes, but nothing I can't handle."

"Good. Are you still going to therapy?" she asked.

"Every week," he said with a smile. "I'm very grateful to Doctor Krull."

Harlan made some notes in his chart. "You can put your shirt back on," she said.

She heard him getting dressed. "I've seen your daughter in the arena," he said. "She's good. You must be very proud of her."

Harlan glanced up to see if he was mocking her but he seemed sincere. God how she wished pride was what she felt but all she could feel was dread. She worried every waking moment that Gypsy would be her next patient. "She's definitely dedicated to it," she said, escorting him out.

"My uncle thinks she'll be one of the great ones," Banta continued. "Wouldn't that be something? A woman winning a tournament and a senior match at that!"

Harlan nodded impatiently. "You don't need any more fol-
low-up appointments for the arm unless you start having problems.
Just be mindful if you have any severe pain, swelling, tingling or a
loss of sensation. If any of those things occur, get in here immediately. Okay?"

"Sure, Doctor Theron. Thanks."

Harlan leaned in the doorway and watched him leave. She
thought about Gypsy in the arena and felt a deep sense of sorrow.
The only thing that made her feel any better was that at least Gypsy
was in Gavin's hands now. If anyone could prepare her for combat
it was him. But training under her father was no charm school and
Gypsy had never been very good at controlling her temper. She
only hoped her daughter was wise enough to listen to everything
Gavin taught her no matter how much she hated it. Harlan didn't
know much about war, but she did know one thing, Gavin was the
only chance Gypsy had of surviving in this violent and deadly world
of men. All her daughter had to do was listen to her father but
Harlan knew that would be the hardest part of all.

Chapter 4

It was early and Harlan had already gone to bed. Gavin entered the house as quietly as he could and closed the door behind him. Her scent was everywhere and his nostrils flared to take it all in; he caught the scent of her skin, her hair, and the intoxicating elixir of her tender sex. He paused in the living room and pulled a deep breath in letting the magic of her perfume excite and arouse him. The infernal beast in his soul awoke in a firestorm of lust. The primal excitement quickened his blood, pushing his desire to a fever pitch. His heart sped up, pounding in his chest like he'd been running for miles.

Normally his hunger was a caged thing, like an animal in captivity but with all the fighting he'd been around today, he was more sexually aggressive than normal. He ached to go into the bedroom and ravage his wife, to let the beast loose to do as it willed but he could never allow that. Harlan knew how to please him. He would get what he needed. All he had to do was keep his passion under control.

Gavin moved into the room and undressed watching her sleep. Once naked, he opened the hamper and found her underwear, placing the cotton panel up to his nose. He took in her perfume reveling in the private scent of her body. His cock, already painfully hard, grew harder until he had to put the garment back and squeeze the shaft of his cock to ease some of the pressure.

He climbed up onto the bed and it squeaked under his weight. Harlan stirred and turned to look at him stretching. He kissed her with a smoldering, carnal heat and a nervous fear came into her eyes. "I need you to do exactly as I say," he said as calmly as he could. Her caution was an aphrodisiac to him, baiting the animal within, tempting it to savage her. It took everything he had to keep himself under control.

"Anything you want?" she whispered with a soft smile. Her apprehension was melting away. *Good.*

Wordlessly, he reached up and tore her underwear off flinging it carelessly to the floor. She shifted onto her back and looked annoyed but said nothing. Harlan had seen him like this before and knew exactly what to do.

"Open your legs," he growled.

Harlan opened her legs and let him move up over her. She turned her head away and avoided looking him in the eye and the tension in him eased for a moment. Grabbing his throbbing cock, he placed the glistening, swollen tip against her pussy and stroked the shaft. He didn't enter her, he didn't dare. He needed more control than he had right now or he'd surely hurt her. With a few forceful strokes, he brought himself to orgasm while running the tip of his dick through her drenched curls.

Harlan licked her lips and he could smell the excitement in her. "*Do you want me to fuck you?*" he said in Æssyrian.

A tiny grin played on Harlan's lips. "*Please, lord,*" she replied in his native tongue. "*I love how you feel inside me.*" The sweet sound and imperfection of her Æssyrian made him crazy. Grabbing her, he turned her over and pulled her up on all fours easing her back against his hips. She was soft and compliant as he positioned her and he almost orgasmed at the sight of her beautiful pussy laid bare before him. Pushing his face into her sex, he tickled her clit with his long forked tongue. He teased and tortured her, watching with private joy as she wriggled her hips to enjoy him more. Then he tasted the slight shift in her body chemistry and knew she was ready.

Mounting her from behind, he stuffed his cock deep inside her taking care not to put all his weight on her back. Harlan cried out as loud as she could and the sound was the sweetest music he'd ever heard. She reached up and braced herself on the headboard as he drove his dick deep inside her. The heavy wood slammed into the wall over and over again adding to the many scars he'd already made on so many other nights. Deeper and deeper he went, working himself into a punishing rhythm. She was growing very wet which made his claiming much easier. While he labored, he moved his mouth over to her ear and spoke to her in ÆEssyrian.

"Look at what you've done to me, my love," he growled. *"You are in my blood like no other woman I've ever known. There is witchcraft in your kisses, one kiss from you and I am undone like a bridegroom on his first night."*

Suddenly Harlan gasped and cried out, pumping her hips against him and screaming out his name. The muscles within her contracted around his cock, milking the seed from him as his balls spasmed in release. She collapsed onto the bed panting and their physical connection was lost. He, however, was far from done. Tenderly he kissed her back, dragging his tongue between her shoulder blades to catch a trickle of sweat.

I'll give her a few minutes to rest. As soon as she was ready, he'd be on her again and again and again...

Chapter 5

Harlan stepped out of the shower feeling sore and deliciously used. Standing in front of the mirror she could see the pink, raw flush on her neck and light bruising on her breasts from Gavin's marathon lovemaking. She loved it when he got like that. Running her fingers through her hair she marveled that there was still no sign of gray. Although she was just past fifty in Earth years, she could easily pass for a woman in her early thirties. In fact, she looked younger than when she'd arrived on Æssyria over twenty years ago. She couldn't be happier with this planet for slowing down her normal aging process. It wasn't just vanity. What really mattered to her was being able to spend a long life with Gavin without becoming old and frail while he lingered at middle age. The thought brought a smile to her face. It still amazed her that she had stayed here this long. Of course, there had been times when she had seriously considered leaving but her love for Gavin always won out.

Gavin. She dressed in the bedroom. She could hear him making her something to eat in the kitchen before they both had to run out to work. The hardy smell of cooking meat filled the house and coaxed a rumble from her belly. He always made such a colossal noise banging and clanging around.

Brushing her hair, she thought about how much she loved him. He was so much more to her than her husband and lover, he was her soul mate. She grinned at how corny that sounded but it was true. Who would have thought they'd end up together? Certainly not her. He was everything she hated in a man: boisterous; rude, and a natural bully. But there was another side to him too that was brave, passionate, and surprisingly tender. Much to her surprise, she loved all his conflicting elements.

She went into the kitchen and made herself a cup of coffee. Over the years he'd tried to master the art but always managed to make her tar in a cup. After his last attempt made her sick for two days, she told him never to touch her coffee stuff again and he was happy to comply. He was sitting at the kitchen table wolfing down an enormous plate of raw meat. She walked over to sit down with him and he pushed a chair out for her with his boot. That was his idea of chivalry.

"What time are you meeting with Gypsy?" she asked.

He grabbed a cloth napkin and hastily wiped his mouth. The napkin came away smeared with blood. "Seven."

Harlan smiled and sipped her coffee. It tasted like heaven in a cup. "That's pretty early for her."

He grunted and stuffed more food in his mouth. After washing it down with some water, he said, "Anything bothering you other than your daughter's career choice?"

Harlan blinked. He knew her so well sometimes it was scary. "No. Why?"

Gavin shrugged. "You seem…preoccupied."

She traced a design on the side of her cup. "A patient of Krull's came in yesterday. You might remember him. He was the warrior who got his arm cut off in the arena a few months ago."

"Yes, I remember," Gavin said, nodding. He'd finished off his food, pushed the plate back and belched.

"Krull reattached that severed arm and it looks as good as new," she continued, ignoring his table manners. "It made me feel…well, kind of inadequate. I'm not sure I could have done as good a job as he did."

Gavin leaned forward and draped a lock of her black hair behind her ear. "You are a brilliant doctor, Harlan," he said. "But I think the burden of being the Chief of Staff has made you somewhat aloof. Perhaps if you assisted Krull the next time something like that comes up, you'd feel more prepared to do it yourself."

He was right. Afraid to appear weak, she'd avoided getting too involved in Krull's cases. Now she realized she could learn a lot from the surly Kirillian doctor. She resolved to try harder to get to know him.

"How is Gypsy doing?" she asked as Gavin got up and fastened the buckles on his boot.

"Fine for now, but we're still on our honeymoon. Real school starts today. I'm going to bust her ass."

Harlan smiled despite her worry. She got up and dumped the rest of her coffee in the sink. Gavin grabbed her and gave her a lusty kiss. She kissed him back then giggled. "Have a nice day, Gavin," she said as he let her go.

He grunted then paused before leaving. "Harlan," he said. "Have you considered what will happen to our marriage if Gypsy's killed in training, or even in the arena for that matter?" He took a deep breath as if a great weight had been placed on his shoulders. "I've trained a lot of sons and I can tell you, anything can and does happen. I've never had a marriage survive the strain of training a wife's child. The process is so brutal and punishing and…"

Harlan placed her fingers against his lips. "Don't," she said softly. "This was her choice. You didn't push her into it and if you hadn't stepped in when she needed you, I have no doubt she'd probably be dead already. Besides I trust you. I know you didn't want this, but I also know you'll train her to the best of your ability."

"I love you, Harlan," he said. "No matter what happens, I always will."

She kissed him feeling like her heart was about to break. "I love you too, Gavin. If anything does happen I'll need you more than ever."

Chapter 6

The afternoon heat baked into Gypsy's skin causing her to sweat. Not the light uncomfortable glow she got while riding under the harsh Æssyrian suns, this was a fearful sweat, the kind that ran down her face in rivulets and burned her eyes. This was the sweat born of pure adrenaline and terror but she stood there holding that heavy, awkward saber her father had given her and watched.

There were two of them; great hulking warriors in full battle gear charging up the path at her roaring like a pair of hungry cannibals.

She lifted her saber and waited, not daring to waste an ounce of precious energy advancing on them. Her arm muscles trembled under the weight of the horrible weapon. Close behind them mounted on his hyperia was her father riding at a full gallop as he chased after them bellowing orders, commanding them to kill her if they could. Gypsy backed into a tree blocking access to her from behind. The first one, Makkai skidded to a stop in front of her and launched a barrage of blows designed to carve her body in two. Gypsy fought back with every ounce of strength she had left, blocking every strike he tried to land. The other warrior Falken, then attacked her on her right and in the blur of flashing blades, Gypsy was cut on the right shoulder.

"Stop!" Gavin roared.

Everyone lowered their weapons and the two warriors moved back giving Gypsy some room. Gavin rode up to her and leaned down. He wiggled a finger for her to come over to him. Her wounded shoulder burned like it had caught on fire. She came over and kept her eyes down.

"Look at me!" he commanded.

Gypsy lifted her gaze to look him in the eye. Removing his glove, he struck her with such force she fell to the ground. A cauldron of white-hot rage howled to life in her gut and in that moment, she hated him even more than her sworn enemy Drake. She pulled herself to her feet and stood there staring straight ahead. Gavin grabbed her under the chin and forced her to look at him again.

"You feel that?" he said through clenched teeth.

"Yes," she said, not bothering to hide her hatred for him.

"Not the slap, girl. The fury."

"*Yes.*"

"I want you to bring that every time we train," he said his golden eye blazing at her. "Understand?"

Gypsy glared at him. "Yes, Excellency."

Gavin let her go and nodded to the two warriors to continue. They rushed her but this time she was ready for them. Harnessing her anger, she let it grow and consume her. The violence that erupted from her shocked and frightened her. In that brief pause she had become faster, stronger and more focused. She drove both warriors back, slamming her blade into them with devastating force, the tip of it cut Falken in the jaw. He snarled at her and broke off his attack for a moment.

Seizing her advantage, she turned on Makkai, striking blow after punishing blow at him until he lost his footing on a tree root and went down. Gypsy leapt on top of him and placed her blade against his throat. "This is a kill," she said to the warrior.

Something stabbed her between the shoulder blades. It wasn't a deep cut, but it hurt enough to get her attention. "And so is this," she heard Falken say.

"Good," Gavin said, dismounting and coming over to crouch by Gypsy. "Do you understand what you did wrong?"

Gypsy sighed and got up off Makkai. He rolled away from her and used a low-hanging tree branch to pull himself to his feet. He had an obvious and impressive erection straining in his pants.

"Not really," Gypsy confessed, feeling her anger at Gavin fade as fatigue took over.

"You were so intent on a kill that you forgot your other enemy. When Makkai went down, you should have dispatched Falken right away. Then you could have focused on killing Makkai," Gavin said. "Now let's keep going."

Gypsy barely had time to get to her feet before the warriors were on her again. She deflected them as best she could but knew she was making mistakes. Everyone was exhausted and as a result the warriors were softening and not taking advantage of her errors. Of course Gavin saw it.

"Stop!" he snarled again. He came over to Gypsy.

She sighed. Her hatred for him arose anew. *If he hits me again I'm going to lose my fucking mind.*

"Do you see what is happening here?" he asked.

Gypsy stared at him blankly. Gavin pointed his saber in the direction of Makkai's erection. The warrior glared at him and backed up several feet. "You're fighting so pathetically, he thinks this is foreplay."

Falken and Makkai laughed and Gypsy shot them both a nasty look.

"Are we here to fight or fuck?" Gavin asked her.

"We're here to fight, Excellency," she said.

"Then you'd better butch up and get these two fuckers." Then Gavin turned on the warriors. "You're both supposed to be senior-class warriors. You mean to tell me you can't bring down a little girl like this? So far, I'm not impressed. Now get her and put her on the ground!"

Gypsy lifted her saber and reignited her rage. Even through leather gloves her hands were raw and blistered from wielding this piece of shit saber all day. Her shirt was drenched with sweat and stuck to her body in every uncomfortable way she could imagine. Her mouth was desert dry and her arms felt like they'd been twisted on a rack for hours. But there was no time to dwell on her many miseries, because a second later the two warriors were on her again. And this time they were determined to win.

But Gypsy was pissed and Mr. Erection was going down and staying down. The thought Makkai was so unafraid of her that he became aroused sent a frenzied anger through her. Her anger was not only directed at him but also at herself for fighting so lamely. Quickly she drove off Falken knowing she only had a few moments before he returned. Turning to Makkai she came at him with a savage ferocity striking his blade high and kicking him in the hip between his armor plates. It was enough for him to lose his balance and go down again. Not willing to make the same mistake twice she kicked him as hard as she could in the side. Immediately she turned to face Falken who was almost on her. They erupted in a burst of violence, each intent upon bringing the other down.

"Stop," Gavin said, holding up his hand. "That's all for today. You two boys can go."

Gypsy smirked as Makkai groaned getting to his feet. She was glad she'd hurt him. "You still think I'm sexy, asshole?"

Makkai glared at her and without a word walked off down the road toward his mount with Falken in tow.

After they were out of earshot Gavin mounted his hyperia and rode over to her. She resisted the urge to fold her arms and just stood there.

"Here is what I want you to do," Gavin said.

Gypsy prickled. *Oh great. I have no strength left. What could he possibly want from me now?* •

"I know you're bone-weary and the desire for sleep is all-consuming but you need to go home eat, drink—not alcohol—and fuck Caraculla. Then you can sleep. Understand?"

"Yes, Excellency."

Without another glance, Gavin rode off leaving her to walk back to the military compound. Gypsy had been required to leave her hyperia stabled there at the start of today's torment. Learning to fight mounted up was apparently much further down the road which left her walking to all of the training sites. She wouldn't have minded the walk had she not been so tired. But at least she had some time alone to think.

Think about how much she hated this fucking saber.

It was ridiculous to make her fight with this thing. Her arms were barely long enough to pull it from the scabbard. As a result, she had needed to saw several inches from the top and reconnected the hardware. It wasn't perfect but it seemed to be holding together. Her father never missed a thing but for whatever reason he hadn't seen fit to comment on it. *I'm going to get butchered in the arena with this stupid weapon that I can barely control.* She continued to sulk as she walked. *What the hell did he mean by go home and fuck Caraculla? The last thing I feel like doing right now is having sex. I'm going to bed and that's it.*

Chapter 7

It was late by the time Gypsy rode home to Caraculla. She entered the villa pulling her armor off as she went and leaving a trail of it scattered down the hall. Reaching the couch she collapsed onto her belly wishing the pain in her body would subside. Caraculla came out of the bedroom in just some loose-fitting black pants and his bare feet; his scent was intoxicating. She heard him laugh wickedly. Picking her up off the couch, he carried her to the bathroom and stripped the last few pieces of clothing off. The thoughts of sex that had been so far from her mind a few minutes ago were now crowding her senses. He filled the tub with steaming water and lowered her aching body into it. The liquid heat soothed some of the aches and made her think she'd found eternal bliss.

"Why don't you come in here with me?" she said as she swiped at his arm but missed.

"I think you need to relax for a little while," he said, turning off the water.

Gypsy sank down into the tub with just her forearms and head sticking out. The water had taken on a reddish brown tinge as it cleansed the dried blood from her wounds. "I love you," she said as he picked up her clothes and carried them out. He came back in a moment later with two thick fluffy towels. He placed them on the sink.

"I really mean that you know," she said.

He smiled at her. "I love you too." Then he disappeared returning a few moments later with a bowl of meat. He fed her as she soaked, then lifted her out of the tub and carried her into their bedroom. She loved how safe and special he always made her feel. Sometimes she was afraid she wasn't grateful enough for what they had. But the truth was that she was thankful for Caraculla's quiet support every day. He was the one man she would love until the day she died even if they never did make it to a high priest.

He got into bed with her and she curled up pressing her body against him. "How did the training go?" he asked.

"It was a nightmare. I don't know which I hate more—that mean old bastard or the crummy saber he's forcing me to use," she said, feeling relaxed.

"I probably shouldn't ask about the bruise on your cheek."

Gypsy rubbed the spot self-consciously. "Probably not. The last time my face was bruised, you almost melted someone into the arena floor. Man, I wish I'd seen that."

"There's a big difference between one bruise, albeit a large one, and half of your face black and blue with an eye swollen shut." The statement alone seemed to agitate him.

"I guess that's true enough," she said, stroking his chest.

"Seriously, how'd you get the bruise?"

Now it was her turn to get agitated. "That filthy bastard slapped me so hard that the ground came up and hit me before I even realized what he'd done." She could see Caraculla suppressing the urge to laugh.

"Do you think that's funny?" she said, twisting his nipple.

"No. No. I don't. I promise. Just tell me what happened."

"I was so enraged that I wanted to do major violence to him. But you would have been very proud of me because I did nothing." She smiled triumphantly.

"Nothing?"

"Well I glared at him a little but I kept my mouth shut and just stood there."

"That *is* amazing," he said, stroking her back. "It's all part of his training method. He spends most of his time finding your rage and then channeling it. That's how he knows if you've got *it*."

"I'll bet he never slapped you."

"No he never slapped me. He punched me so hard once that he knocked out one of my back teeth." He said as he ran his tongue to the back of his mouth.

"What did you do?"

"Same as you. Nothing. I just stood there hating him."

Gypsy laughed. "You're a better man than me."

"Why is that?"

"Because if it were me I would've spit venom on him," she said, then laughed.

"Yes I'm sure you would have. I believe it is by divine intervention that none of the Therons are Razorbacks."

She nodded. "You're probably right about that. Still you have to admit the son of a bitch has some pretty big balls to drive a Razorback into a fury in the name of training."

Caraculla squeezed her tightly and buried his face in her neck. She played with one of the blood-red braids at his temple.

"Well, I may as well tell you now that you won't be the only one training your ass off," he said. "I have to go back into the arena too. The council has decided that in order for Gavin to award me the rank of lieutenant general, I can't just be a master. They are requiring me to attain the level of grandmaster."

"Aren't you skipping a few military ranks going from a colonel to a lieutenant general?" she said, tracing the knotted muscles along his ribs.

"All the more reason why I have to reach the level of grandmaster before they'll promote me," he said. He toyed with a lock of her hair. A grandmaster was the most skilled and violent of all the levels in the arena. Her father was one of only five on the whole planet. Men fought on with horrific injuries and didn't leave until their opponents were dead. If Caraculla had to fight a warrior at that level, he might not come out alive. Everything in her wanted to tell him not to do it but she felt she didn't have the right.

"I guess for once it's my turn to be worried about you," she said as she laid back and stared up at the ceiling.

"Don't be," he said, climbing up over her. "I've had to train for difficult fights before. Everything will be fine. You just focus on getting through your own training."

In that quiet moment, her exhaustion melted away and all that remained was her overwhelming love and desire for him. Running her hands down his back, she pulled him into a carnal kiss. He returned her passion, allowing her to push him onto his back so she could straddle his hips. Gypsy climbed up over him surprised at how wet she was. Reaching down she touched the tortured center of her swollen throbbing nub. Her clit was shockingly tender making her gasp every time she touched it. Hungry to taste her arousal, Caraculla pushed her fingers aside and ran his own through her. Gypsy jumped. He dipped his fingers into her moist channel and placed her essence on his tongue, licking her off him with perverse delight.

Gypsy smiled and kissed him, stroking her tongue along his in a frenzy of primal need. Driven by hunger, she moved her hips up over his mouth and groaned as he buried his forked tongue deep inside her. He wiggled it within her until her feral orgasm drove her to the edge of sanity. As the last spasms rocked her body, he pulled his tongue out to caress and tease her aching button.

A desperate flutter shook her womb and all she could think of was getting him inside her. Lowering herself down to his hips, she stripped off his pants, seized his cock and pushed it deep inside her. Blinding pleasure erupted from her pussy and before she was aware of what she was doing, she was pounding down onto his shaft like she hadn't had sex in months.

He moaned her name with such genuine emotion that the tiny hairs stood up on the back of her neck. Every time he touched her she fell more and more in love with him. Caraculla devoured her with kisses as his hands massaged her breasts. Her whole body became a symphony of love and lust as she grappled with him to roll on top of her. The weight of his body and the pounding between her legs made her wild with excitement.

But as her fourth climax seized her she couldn't help feeling a tiny bit lost and afraid that the only man she'd ever loved would be facing the biggest danger of his professional life.

What the hell was she going to do if she lost him? *That's impossible. There isn't a warrior alive except for Gavin who can beat him in the arena. Stop your worrying.*

And so she did.

Chapter 8

Loss was one of three moons circling the great, green planet of ÆEssyria. As the largest of the three, *Loss* had one purpose— monitor space in all directions in the unlikely event ÆEssyria was attacked by a fleet of alien starships. Of course it was possible that such a thing could happen but highly unlikely. Most of the other alien races were busy dealing with their own problems, let alone trying to conquer a planet as inhospitable as this one. So the truth of *Loss* was that it was really a duty station of exile, a punishment for disobedience or insubordination.

The control room was a small stuffy space filled with clutter. Complex computer systems blinked impressive lights and uttered the occasional beep, but for the most part nothing in this room really needed watching. Still the Imperial Council insisted someone had to stand watch here twenty-four hours a day *just in case*. Attached to a far wall were a collage of naked women: most Kirillian; some ÆEssyrian and a couple Asgardian.

Desmond Theron slumped in his chair flipping through the empty computer screens hoping to catch a meteor shower or comet. He was the only man on duty in the control room today monitoring fleet traffic as it passed by the ÆEssyrian moon. He hoped someone would stop by for a chat or this was going to be a long watch. It was only an hour in and already he was fighting off mind-numbing boredom. Propping his boots up, he stretched and tried to take a nap. He pulled a flask from his jacket for a nightcap and shook it. It was empty. *This is definitely going to be a long watch.*

For the thousandth time since he'd arrived here, his mind brought him back to the fight with Gavin that landed him on this forsaken duty station. Not that this was the first isolated duty locale Gavin had given him. Since his father had slaughtered his half-brother Northe over forty years ago for treason, their fights had steadily escalated to the point where they could barely talk to each other anymore. Their fights always ended the same, with Desmond getting orders to ship out to some shithole. He wanted to feel bad that he and Gavin didn't get along but all he could ever manage was indifference. They'd never been close. His father had tried to dig his hooks into him when he was a child just like he had all his other children.

Countless times Gavin had tried and failed to make Desmond the great warrior he was forever trying to forge in his sons. But Desmond wasn't as ambitious as Northe. He thwarted every effort Gavin made to mold and drive him. After a few years, Gavin walked away and left a gaping wound in Desmond's soul. Desmond became an ordinary soldier just like he'd always wanted to be.

There was never any desire in him to command legions. A platoon or a company was about all the men he wanted to deal with. He'd made the rank of sergeant and master sergeant more times than anyone else in the empire. Unfortunately, with each fight and each isolated duty assignment, there usually came a demotion. Desmond always struggled to regain the ranks he'd been stripped of. Not out of any ambitious desires but just to piss Gavin off.

There was so much emotional distance between them now that Desmond hoped he never saw the bastard again. Sooner or later Gavin would tire of this little game of 'punish Desmond for being ordinary' and let him transfer to someplace else. He hated not having a war to fight in. At least then Gavin could care less about oppressing him. In fact he usually sent Desmond to the front lines, which is exactly where Desmond wanted to be. But for now all he could do was wait the old man out. Who knows, maybe someone would actually succeed in killing the son of a bitch.

The thoughts of Northe tore the scab off of an old emotional wound and Desmond cursed under his breath that it still caused him so much suffering. Northe had been the best of the best, a skilled warrior and the most likely heir to Gavin's impressive military career. He had also been Desmond's big brother and best friend. But Northe and Gavin were too much alike to ever get along. It wasn't long after Northe's training was complete that he escaped his father's influence and went to serve another monarch's general.

Northe had begged Desmond to come with him.

Regret filled him daily for not having the guts to follow his brother. When Northe had approached him, Desmond was still so young and afraid of what Gavin would do to him or his mother. Gavin could be a spiteful fucker, there was no denying that.

In his new kingdom, Northe rose quickly through the ranks and soon used any excuse to bring his troops against his father in battle. The two devastating wars between father and son were legendary.

Then one fateful day, Northe's luck ran out. Separated from his men after a nasty skirmish, Gavin cornered his rebellious son. A heated battle ensued and Gavin, knowing Northe would never stop trying to destroy him, cut Northe down in a monstrous rage. Desmond had been unfortunate enough to have been there when it happened. The bloody scene haunted his dreams to this day.

The pressure doors slid open startling him from his thoughts. Corporal Tolbert came in with an odd look on his bland, fleshy face. *What now?*

"You have new orders," the corporal said. He looked down at the transmission transcript as if it had appeared out of thin air.

Desmond blinked trying not to get his hopes up. *Could Gavin have possibly found some place worse than this?* "Where's that bastard sending me this time?"

"Your new assignment is Military Central Command on ÆEssyria. You report directly to the general. I'm supposed to relieve you and you're to leave for the planet right away."

A black rock formed in Desmond's gut. Gavin must be bored. It must be time for yet another evil game of cat and mouse. Desmond got up and arched his back. "Anything on there say what my assignment will be?"

The corporal just shrugged and took Desmond's seat. He tossed the paperwork on the control panel. "The only other thing it says is you're to assist with some kind of special training. Good luck."

"The ÆEssyrian Central Command, huh? This won't last long."

Chapter 9

Gypsy raced up the narrow mountain trail trying to keep some distance between her and her pursuers. Sweat poured down her face and throat drenching the skin beneath her battle armor. She stumbled several times, fighting off the desperation slowly taking hold of her emotions. Her legs were cramping and screaming in pain so she stopped for a moment to catch her breath.

Her pursuers were almost on her and she was forced to pull her saber and ready herself to fight. The first one to round the corner was Makkai. He was a large and muscular warrior with polar-blue eyes, dark-brown hair and forest-green skin. Like her, he was decked out in full battle armor—something Gavin insisted they all wear every time they trained. Close behind him was her old mentor, Master Sergeant Rakon looking as fresh as if he'd just woken up from an afternoon nap. She marveled at how fit he was then she remembered he'd been with her father on military campaigns hundreds of times. He was probably used to this kind of crap.

As usual, Gavin brought up the rear mounted on his hyperia. He yelled at the men to keep the pressure on and not give Gypsy an inch. Makkai was the first to attack her. He lifted his saber and charged, roaring so loud he startled a flock of birds from the trees making them take flight. He crashed through the brush and reached her with his saber flying. Gypsy kept her cool, deflecting his blows as best she could while trying to keep her footing. She needed to keep tabs on Rakon because he had a lot more experience and wouldn't hesitate to hurt her. Out of the corner of her eye, she spotted him trying to circle around behind her.

Sprinting around Makkai, she engaged Rakon long enough to put some distance between her and the two men. To her right, she spotted the only escape route she had. Bolting down a hill, she ended up losing her footing and rolling a few feet into a shallow river with a splash. The water refreshed and revived her but she didn't have much time to enjoy it. The warriors were on her in minutes slicing at her and driving her into a deeper part of the river.

Gypsy slipped on some rocks and fell under the surface. The world melted away and all she could hear was the soothing rush of the water. Then she felt hands grab her. One around the neck, the other grasping her arm and they weren't pulling her to the surface. Her mind reacted to the confinement with a crazed panic as flashes of her ordeal with Drake played through her mind. Dropping her saber she tore at the hands and arms trying to free herself but they remained frozen in place holding her underwater. Gypsy continued to fight until she inhaled her first liquid breath and a new terror set in. Before it completely registered to her that she was drowning, she was lifted out of the water and hurled onto the riverbank landing flat on her back with a hard thud. Rolling over she coughed and wretched violently as her lungs fought to expel the water from them.

"That's a kill," Rakon said, still standing in the water absently looking around by his feet.

"Indeed it is," Gavin confirmed in disgust as he rode over to Gypsy who was spitting out the last of the water she'd breathed in. His hyperia blocked the sun as he looked down at her curiously. "You panicked when he put his hands on you and lost all focus. We'll have to fix that." It was more a statement of interest than a reprimand. Her father looked in thought as though trying to figure a way to address this new problem.

Rakon emerged from the river with her saber in his hand and threw it at her like a dagger so it stuck in the ground next to her. "Here. You dropped this."

Gypsy frowned and got up. "Thanks for finding it," she said flatly. *Yeah thanks a lot, Rakon.* Pulling it from the ground she looked up at Gavin waiting for him to sic his dogs on her again. Reaching behind him, he pulled two shorter sabers from his saddle and tossed them on the riverbank by her feet. "Put up your weapon, Gypsy, and continue with those."

Makkai slogged out of the river muttering and shaking off as much water as he could. Gypsy sheathed her own heavy, mammoth saber Rakon was kind enough to locate for her. She picked up the two small sabers and felt her stomach drop. *This is going to suck.*

Rakon crashed from the water like a charging animal. Jumping on the bank, he snarled and tried to cut her in the face but she managed to deflect him with her right saber.

"Use *both* of your fucking weapons!" Gavin roared.

Makkai came at her from the left, slicing near her face and neck making her flinch. It took every ounce of concentration for her to fight with both sabers at the same time but she forced herself to do it. And in one frozen moment in time, she suddenly forgot what she was doing and just let the movements flow out of her like music. It was pure sorcery and *somehow* she was holding both Rakon and Makkai back without really thinking about *how* she was doing it.

"That's *it*, that's *it*, Gypsy," Gavin said in a voice laced with real admiration. "Stay with it."

She struck flesh and heard Makkai hiss in pain. Suddenly he broke off. The distraction broke the spell and Rakon managed to strike her right saber out of her hand. When she looked down, he had the tip of his weapon pointed near her heart at a gap between her armor pieces. It definitely would have been a kill. Gypsy felt exhausted and defeated. "I'm sorry, Excellency," she said, picking up the dropped saber and carrying it back to Gavin.

Then she realized how badly injured Makkai was. Gavin had dismounted and stripped off his tunic to hold it over the bleeding wound in the warrior's neck. Gypsy stood there shocked.

Rakon grabbed her arm and pushed her toward Gavin's mount. "Get the kit," he said calmly.

Gypsy grabbed the first aid kit from Gavin's saddlebag and brought it over. Gavin took it from her, his hands covered in Makkai's blood. Rakon seized Gypsy's trembling hands and placed them over the soaked tunic. "Apply pressure," he said.

Gypsy did as the master sergeant told her. Makkai was in obvious distress, bleeding and fighting to get up as Rakon held him down. Keeping pressure on the wound, Gypsy watched as Gavin loaded surgical staples into a plastic, disposable gun. Then her father settled back on his haunches and knelt in close to the wound. Gavin glanced at her and she looked for any sign of anger in him. There was none—just a sober sense of purpose. "Take the tunic off when I tell you," he said.

All she could do was nod. She'd never felt so guilty in her life.

"Take it off now," Gavin said. Gypsy took the tunic away and the wound bled but not nearly as much as it had before. Rakon's arms bulged with the strain of holding the struggling warrior. Three loud snaps made Makkai's body jolt violently. Glaring at her and Rakon, he snarled for a moment then just lay there moaning. Gavin tore bandages open with his teeth and covered the wound.

When he'd secured the bandage in place, he stood up and wiped some blood off his cheek with his sleeve. He glanced at Rakon who was already picking up the warrior and putting him on the back of Gavin's mount. Without a word to her, Gavin mounted up and rode off at a full gallop.

Gypsy felt horrible and lost. She looked at Rakon who busied himself picking up anything of value to take back with them.

"I'm so sorry," she said.

Rakon stopped what he was doing and stared at her. "What for?" he replied. "You did what you were trained to do. In the field, that would have been a kill. Now let's get back before we miss lunch."

Chapter 10

Harlan was just about to retreat to her office and update her reports when Gavin burst through the double glass doors into the clinic carrying a wounded warrior over his shoulder. Gavin's chest was bare and the young warrior's blood was smeared all over him. Harlan raced up and did a quick check of the wounded man's neck. It was hard to tell how serious it was. She needed to get those staples out and have a better look.

"Take him to exam room three. How much blood has he lost?" she said, falling into step behind her husband.

"A lot I imagine."

Gavin kicked the door open to the exam room making Harlan flinch from the noise. He laid the warrior on the table and held him down. Harlan pulled on some gloves and moved in to get a closer look at the wound. The field staples had done their job in closing the wound and slowing the bleeding. She prepared a sedative and injected the warrior. While she waited for it to take effect, she dug out some skin staple removers and placed them on a tray with some other things she would need.

"Who put the staples in?" she asked as she loaded fresh staples into her own gun.

Gavin eased his grip on the warrior to see if the drug was working. When Makkai didn't struggle, Gavin stepped back and leaned against the wall. "I did," he replied.

Harlan pulled the tray of instruments closer. "You did a good job," she said, smiling at him. Gavin grunted. She knew how he hated playing nurse to his men. It wasn't that he didn't care about them. He was just oddly squeamish about anything medical.

Harlan looked down at Makkai. "How are you feeling?"

The warrior nodded drowsily. "Better."

"I'm going to take those staples out of your neck now. You shouldn't feel anything but if you do, just hold your hand up and I'll stop. All right?"

Makkai nodded and relaxed.

Harlan took the staple removers and gently pulled the staples from his neck, taking care to watch Makkai for any sign of pain or discomfort. She didn't need him becoming violent while she was this close. He laid there with his eyes closed and she thought he may have even drifted off to sleep.

"What happened?" she asked Gavin as she carefully pulled each staple out and dropped it on the tray.

"He was sparring with Gypsy and she stung him," Gavin said, sounding bored.

Harlan glanced back at her husband. "Is she alright?" She knew it was a stupid question but she had to have some reassurance.

"Yes, of course. Although I think she may be plagued by some guilt over this. Injuries come with training."

"How is her training coming along?" She normally wouldn't have asked but she was curious. A part of her hoped he'd say Gypsy was useless and he was going to stop her from competing but she knew that wouldn't happen.

Gavin went to the sink and washed the blood off his hands and chest. "Her training is going well. Caraculla was right about her. She is a very gifted fighter."

Great. Harlan tried to focus on her work and not be disappointed. "Good," she said without meaning it.

"In fact," Gavin continued. "She's so good I've had to recall my son Desmond from *Loss* to help me train her. I can't use Makkai anymore, next time she's bound to kill him."

"I don't remember you mentioning Desmond before," Harlan said, stepping back to admire her handiwork. Makkai's eyes were not only still, but now he had begun to snore. *So much for being traumatized.*

"I don't mention Desmond," Gavin said bitterly, "because he's too much of a disappointment."

Harlan was about to ask him more but Gavin had *that* look on his face. It was a look full of old pain and she knew if she pushed him, he'd say something nasty that would piss her off. She decided to drop it. Gesturing to Makkai, she said, "He'll be fine. I'll keep him here for a few hours until the sedative wears off and he builds his blood supply back up. If he feels okay after that, I'll let him go home."

Gavin pulled her into his arms and kissed her. Burying his face in her neck, he held her close and she was surprised the mention of Desmond had bothered him so much more than she realized. She wrapped her arms around him and squeezed pressing her cheek against his warm chest. He felt large and powerful. Taking her hand, he put it over the outside of his pants so she could feel the urgency of his erection. All of Gavin's emotional pain was dealt with through sex.

Touching his lips to her ear, he said, "Meet me at Lady Neice's Brothel when you break for lunch."

"I hate going there," she said. "I know they let people watch us."

"So what?" Gavin growled against her cheek. "Let them watch. You're a married woman. What do you care?"

"It just creeps me out," Harlan groaned in protest.

"Very well let's just go to your office," he said, crowding her toward the door.

"No! You are way too noisy."

"I don't think it's me who makes *all* the noise." He grinned still pushing her toward the door.

"All right, you win," Harlan said. "I'll meet you at the brothel, just give me an hour."

* * * *

Gypsy went by the clinic to see Makkai fully expecting him to throw her out of his room. Instead he greeted her like they'd been best friends since childhood. She gave him a sheepish smile. "I'm really sorry," she said, moving up to his bedside. "I feel just awful."

Makkai sat up in bed with a medium-sized bandage covering the left side of his neck. His arctic eyes sparkled with admiration. "What for? You were fantastic. I've never seen someone wield two sabers like that. It was incredible."

She shifted feeling embarrassed. "Really?"

"Even Gavin was impressed, and I'm sure I don't have to tell you how hard it is to impress that man."

"But…" Gypsy said, unsure how to continue. "I could have killed you. Aren't you mad about that?"

Makkai shrugged looking unfazed. "That's the way for all warriors, isn't it? Both Falken and I were trying to kill you, so I guess we're even. Besides, I could get taken out at the Academy anytime. It's all about survival there. By the time graduation comes, less than fifty percent make it out."

"You mean over fifty percent are killed during their three years?" Gypsy asked amazed.

"Not exactly. There's a high dropout rate for those who just can't cut it. But a lot die in military exercises too." He squinted at her as if trying to read her thoughts. "You must have known all this with your father being a general and all."

Gypsy folded her arms. "Sure I did." A moment of silence filled the room, and then she asked, "What's Gavin going to do with you now?"

Makkai rolled his eyes. "Remedial training with Rakon. I can't wait."

Gypsy laughed and unfolded her arms. She was feeling less defensive than she had earlier. "Wow that sucks for you," she said. "Speaking of Rakon, he's waiting for me in the mess hall. I'll probably see you later."

"Sure. See ya, Gypsy. And good luck with your upcoming bout. I've got money riding on you," he said with a wink.

Chapter 11

Harlan arrived at the brothel just after lunchtime and followed the madam up the stairs cursing to herself for letting Gavin talk her into this little afternoon tryst. Although she didn't share her husband's kinky taste in rendezvous locations, she never denied him anything he asked for. Over the twenty plus years she'd been married to him, she had come to learn many of Gavin's deep, dark secrets.

One of his best hidden was that, although he almost never showed sorrow or pain, he suffered deep emotional scars from his past mistakes. That was never as true as when his sordid history came back to haunt him, as it occasionally did. Recalling his son Desmond from a remote duty station was obviously reigniting one of those painful memories. Even though she wasn't familiar with this part of his past she knew there must be years of tragic history between them.

So, during difficult times like this, Gavin would seek her out more often for sex. For him it was a way of letting his defenses down and seeking her love and approval when his emotions ran high. Sex was also a ritual, a way of purging the weakness within his tortured soul.

For Harlan, sex with Gavin was a treat as well, for it was one of the rare moments she got to see her husband for the man he really was. Not the great general always on display for everyone else or the brooding drunk everyone believed him to be, but the flesh-and-blood man he was underneath all that. The man who loved his wife and daughter with a ferocious passion she'd never seen in anyone. And in those moments when she found the real him again, she was reminded of how desperately she loved him.

The madam stopped at the last room on the left and winked at Harlan. "He's been waiting for you for almost an hour. Let me know if you need anything."

Harlan nodded and opened the door. The room was small with barely enough room for the large bed and a nightstand. It was decorated in a sickly faded pink: torn pink bedspread; sheer pink drapes; a worn dark-pink carpet. Gavin sat in a white chair positioned by the window with his boots on the sill. He smoked a cigar and stared out at the city as the street vendors aggressively hustled the pedestrian lunch crowd. Dressed in black from head to toe, he was a stark contrast to the soft pastels that adorned the room.

Harlan closed the door behind her but stayed by it trying to read his mood. "I thought you'd be naked in bed by now," she joked.

Gavin didn't look at her and didn't smile. *This must be bad.* Harlan glanced around for an empty bottle but saw nothing. She relaxed a little.

"Desmond was one of my greatest blunders," he said quietly. "Such a grand talent wasted."

"What happened with him?" Harlan asked, venturing into the room and sitting on the bed. She casually looked for obvious stains on the linens and crinkled her nose.

Gavin crushed out his cigar on the sill and glanced at her. "Nothing happened with him. That's what the waste was. He is a gifted swordsman, the only man to remain undefeated in the arena to this day. Unfortunately he never had the ambition to be anything more than a common soldier."

"Not everyone is cut out to be a general," Harlan said.

Gavin got up and joined her on the bed. Taking her face into his hands, he tenderly kissed her and she closed her eyes to enjoy it.

He broke the kiss and nuzzled her cheek. "I'm afraid for Gypsy, my love," he said. "I think she's gifted but I fear her ambition will tear both her and us apart."

Harlan looked into his golden eye. "Hopefully that won't happen. I know you didn't want to train her but I appreciate that you did. I can promise you that I will never hold you responsible for her decisions. She's an adult and has fought for this choice of hers." She leaned forward and wrapped her arms around him, burying her face in his neck. His scent was rich and masculine. What good did it do to worry about what *might* happen?

Pushing him back down on the bed, Harlan climbed up over him and straddled his hips. She lifted her shirt off and unhooked her bra, smiling as he massaged and cupped her breasts. With great flair, Harlan tossed the discarded clothing to the floor. Gavin grinned. He took each taut nipple in turn pinching and rolling it in between his thumb and forefinger.

Then he surprised her by letting her be the aggressor. Relaxing beneath her, he passively helped her as she stripped him making two piles of 'his and hers' clothing next to the bed. When they were both completely naked, she hugged him and cradled his head to her breasts. The feel of his hot mouth was ecstasy on her flesh and she reveled in the carnal bliss of his hungry kisses. Deep within her, her lust quickened making her womb flutter with pure excitement. Her flesh danced to life, wanting and *needing* him in such a desperate way she couldn't even put it into words. Gavin moaned her name, squeezing her tight as he continued to kiss and maul her breasts and belly. Sucking in a deep breath, she could feel the feral need burning within her. She needed him like she needed air to breathe.

Peeling one of his hands off her waist, she guided it down into aching center of her pussy. He dipped his fingers into her *very* wet heat and froze. She knew that would do it. He couldn't resist her when she was *this* hot for him. Snarling something unintelligible in

Æssyrian, he rolled over on top of her and lifted her legs around his hips.

Harlan ran her fingers down his raised spine over the gland that drove him wild then lifted her hands to brace herself against the headboard. Throwing her head back, she whispered in rough Æssyrian, "*Yes, my love. Come into me. I love the way you feel deep inside. Fuck me, Gavin. Please.*"

Gavin bared his teeth, letting out a low, dangerous roar and arched his broad back. The swollen tip of his cock teased her labia, parting it and probing through the slick walls of her contracting pussy. He filled her, devoured her, and took her with the savage passion of a man who hadn't been with a woman in years. Her pussy clamped down on his pounding cock and the orgasm came over her in a rushing tide of complete pleasure. His body shuddered as he ejaculated inside her, but he continued his conquest unfazed until he'd coaxed two more mind-blowing orgasms from her.

Afterward they lay on the soiled pink bedspread letting the rickety ceiling fan cool the sweat on their naked bodies. Gavin moved closer and kissed her on the ear. "I love you Harlan," he said so softly she almost didn't hear him.

Harlan smiled feeling like all the tension had been fucked out of her. "I love you too, Gavin."

Chapter 12

Gypsy had improved greatly in the past few weeks and Gavin attributed much of it to her natural talent and willingness to practice. When it came to keeping her practice schedule she was always there and he'd come to use her as an example to all his other students. He watched her in the private arena he'd reserved for her as she fearlessly battled three men at once. Despite being cut many times, she never stopped or asked to take a break and his heart swelled with pride for her bravery. She definitely had a warrior's soul. And to think he'd almost overlooked her.

A heavy metal door banged shut off to his right and he glanced over. Caraculla came in dirty and sweaty from his own training. He wore light gray armor accented in bronze. The colors were a good choice; they suited him. The colonel joined Gavin at the railing and they both watched Gypsy in silence for a moment.

"You've done wonders with her," Caraculla said.

Gavin grinned slightly. "She has a lot of heart. I couldn't have done anything without all her effort. You were right about her. I'm sorry I didn't listen to you."

Caraculla glanced at him as if he couldn't believe what Gavin had said. Gavin didn't apologize very often. "Do we know who she's fighting?" Caraculla asked.

"I bribed the game marshal to match her with Drake Trolis," Gavin said. He heard Caraculla's teeth clench and waited for his colonel's fury.

Caraculla shook his head slowly and watched Gypsy on the arena floor. "Why would you do something like that?"

"Because it was necessary. If she is ever to have a successful military career, she *must* put this rape issue to bed. She *must* defeat Drake in the arena—not just for herself—but also to prove that Drake is not the better warrior."

Caraculla was quiet for a long time. Then he said, "Does she know yet?"

"No. I'll tell her today, when she's done here."

"I've never questioned you before but I think that—"

"Then don't question me now."

Caraculla turned on him, his green eyes blazing. "You can't do this to her! What if he gets her down and rapes her again?" His voice was so loud it caused the training to stop dead. Everyone looked over at them.

Gavin shot Caraculla an angry look. "Take a break for a few moments," he called to Gypsy and the three warriors. Gypsy responded by falling to the ground on her back in exhaustion. Her three combatants laughed and tossed her a canteen of water, which she took and poured over her face.

"You," Gavin said, pointing to Caraculla. "Outside."

They walked outside and Gavin moved into Caraculla's space glaring at him. "I understand that you love her and want to protect her but you must trust my judgment on this. Gypsy has asked me not only to make her an arena champion, but to get her into the Military Academy. She could fight the best man in the Empire, win and still not be chosen by the council to attend. Why? Because as things stand now, rumor has it Drake is the better fighter and that won't change until she *proves* he's not. And as far as that warrior ever getting her down again, it will never happen. Gypsy would fight to the death before she lets him get his hands on her."

Caraculla hung his head. "I just hate the thought of her getting pounded by that brute again."

"That's not likely to happen because this time she'll be more than ready. Drake won't stand a chance against her by the time she steps into that arena. I suggest you focus the majority of your energy on your own match. Who are you fighting?"

"General Kharon," Caraculla said.

Gavin rubbed the back of his neck. General Kharon was head of the military in an allied kingdom and a peerless combatant. Like most grandmasters, he had a specialty weapon. His choice was called a *meteor hammer*. The weapon consisted of a large spiked ball at the end of a six-foot chain. The wielder swung the chain continually, striking devastating blows with the ball until either a head was smashed or a limb was torn off. Caraculla didn't have a lot of experience battling a warrior with mastery in that kind of weapon and Gavin was worried.

"I hope you've been practicing," Gavin said grimly.

Caraculla shrugged. "No one here has mastery in using a meteor hammer. I'm doing the best I can with what I have to work with. All I can do is train and keep from getting distracted by the ball."

Gavin grunted. "When is your match?"

"Tomorrow night," Caraculla said.

Gavin slapped him on the back affectionately. "We'll all be there to cheer you on. Just don't get killed."

Caraculla laughed. "Well that's the point, isn't it?"

Chapter 13

Angel had never been beaten in her life and she was going to make damn sure it never happened again. For the past week and a half her new husband Drake had done everything he could think of to make her submit to his will. He deprived her of sleep, waking her in the middle of the night to rape her, he'd threatened to kill her family, and when she persisted in resisting him, he'd threatened to kill the first child out of her womb.

That was the last straw for her.

She didn't care who the next man she laid eyes on was—if he looked like he could beat Drake in a fight, she would throw herself on his mercy and take her chances.

Unfortunately it was late and there weren't many travelers on the road. Mounted on the back of Drake's hyperia, they headed for Caraculla's villa for one main reason; Drake knew Caraculla would be at the arena late tonight preparing for his fight tomorrow and Gypsy would be alone. Drake's feeble-minded plan was to have Angel lure Gypsy out on the pretext that Angel had run away from Drake. Angel was to ask Gypsy to escort her to seek Gavin's protection. When they were on the road away from the villa, Drake was to jump Gypsy, kill her, and hide the body.

The only part of the plan Drake wasn't counting on was where Angel begged a stranger to help her. That would be a big surprise. She was also taking a terrible risk. If she came across someone unsympathetic or if the person she beseeched lost to Drake, she knew he would be hiding two bodies tonight, Gypsy's and hers.

As much as Angel wanted to ask her friend for help, she knew she couldn't let Drake make it to Caraculla's villa. Gypsy would feel compelled to defend Angel and would certainly fall victim to Drake a second time. No, this was Angel's problem and she was going to find a way to solve it.

Then a miracle happened, a rider came up the road toward them. At first, Angel couldn't make out much, but soon she saw it was a Kirillian warrior with an Imperial uniform on. The humanoid Kirillians were rare in the Æssyrian Empire, usually choosing to serve in their home kingdoms on Kirillia. The man had the hardened look of a seasoned soldier with a wide jaw and piercing hazel eyes with a starburst of gold around the pupil. There was also something reminiscent of an Æssyiran warrior in his bone structure, something in the way he carried himself. *Probably a half-breed. By the Gods, I hope he wants me.*

As they rode up to pass the Kirillian, Angel took a chance. She jumped off Drake's hyperia and fell to the ground in front of the Kirillian. His animal hissed and snapped at her in surprise and it was all the Kirillian could do to keep it from biting her with its razor-sharp teeth. Angel scrambled away from it and went down on one knee. "Great lord, I realize you do not know me," she said breathlessly, "but I am begging you for your pro—"

"Bitch!" Drake roared, jumping off his mount and grabbing her by the hair. Angel screamed and fought him but he was much too strong. Just as Drake was about to mount up and drag her with him, he suddenly let her go.

Angel lowered her hands from over her head where she'd been trying to prevent Drake from tearing her hair out at the roots. She blinked and looked over to see the Kirillian off his mount with his blade at Drake's throat. The move had been so quiet and fast, Drake hadn't even had time to touch his hilt.

"I don't think the lady had a chance to finish her conversation with me," the Kirillian said coolly. Angel raced over and threw herself at the soldier's feet. "I beg you for protection, lord. I'll do anything you ask. I am yours if you'll have me." Tears erupted from her eyes but she forced herself not to sob. *Please don't refuse me; please don't refuse me…*

Drake shifted uncomfortably as the blade scraped his throat. "Who is this man to you?" the Kirillian asked.

Oh no, here we go. She wanted to lie but the truth would come out eventually. Taking a deep breath, she said, "He's my husband."

"He must be a pretty bad husband if you'd throw yourself at the first man you see," the soldier said.

Angel nodded. "Indeed he is a horrible man, lord. He's been beating me for days and he wants me to help him commit a murder."

"Shut up, you filthy whore!" Drake bellowed.

The Kirillian glared at Drake and cut him under the chin. The wound wasn't life threatening but it bled a lot. "If you open your mouth again, I'll cut out your tongue before the next word leaves it. Is that clear?"

The Kirillian looked down at her. "First you need to realize I am the bastard son of a bastard. You're obviously nobility, so becoming my concubine will ruin you."

Angel silently thanked the Gods for their kindness to her today. "I don't care. I would be honored to be your woman, lord. And as far as my reputation goes," she said, glaring at Drake, "I am already ruined."

"You're setting her aside as your wife," the Kirillian said to Drake. Angel couldn't really tell if it was phrased as a question or a statement of fact.

Drake glared at Angel. "She is the queen of lies and she's lying now so you'll rescue her from her new home in the whorehouse. A fitting place for a vicious bitch like that. She's yours if you want a scheming, lying harlot for a consort."

"Good," the Kirillian said, sheathing his saber. He watched with amusement as Drake rode off at a full gallop.

"What's your name?" Angel said as the Kirillian mounted up. He held a hand down and pulled her up behind him.

"Desmond. Desmond Theron," he said.

"Funny," Angel said, hoping he didn't take offense. "I've never heard of you."

Desmond laughed. "And that's just the way I like it. So who did he want you to help him murder?"

Angel wiped her tears away with her sleeve. "Your half-sister and my best friend, Gypsy Theron."

"Why?"

"It's a very long story," Angel said as relief flooded over her. She squeezed her arms around him hoping he found her attractive. She hadn't felt this safe in weeks.

"You'll have to tell it to me sometime," Desmond said. "But really, you're under no obligation to come with me. I can witness he put you aside. Is there some place I can take you, maybe back to your parents?"

"No they have probably disowned me by now. There's no place for me to go. Please I would like to be with you if you'll take me," she said with tears welling in her eyes again.

Desmond frowned. "I just got back to this planet and was going to bed down in an empty barracks. That's not exactly an ideal place for a woman. I guess we should head into the city and find something more suitable." With that, he turned his hyperia around and headed back the way he'd come.

Angel watched him with burning curiosity. "I thought all of the general's sons were dead and—" Angel felt his muscles stiffen and stopped talking. She was ashamed at how rude her statement was. "Oh, I am so sorry. That was an awful thing for me to say. I can't believe I just blurted that out. I'm not usually that insensitive, it's just that I've had a really bad week and—" *You're babbling. You need to shut up before he thinks you're crazy and drops you off at the next stop.*

"It's alright." His voice was rich and calm. He didn't sound angry or offended. "All of Gavin's sons *are* dead except for me. I'm the unlucky one."

* * * *

It had been a long time since Desmond felt the soft lips of a woman—much too long. He had to hand it to that bastard Gavin though for exiling him to places not even prostitutes would go. With the stroke of a pen, his father not only sent him to the ends of the known Empire, but he'd also essentially doomed Desmond to long empty sexless nights. The only reprieve being an occasional cargo freighter passing through their restricted space. Most of the large ones had resident prostitutes that could be bought for a few hours. Of course, they knew they had a desperate man and would charge him a whole paycheck. Desmond hated that he was so glad to be back in civilization. It hurt to know Gavin's treachery had such a powerful effect on him.

Desmond brought Angel into a modest room above Tiller's Tavern suddenly feeling as awkward as a youth on his first date. It was the nicest place he could find on such short notice. She entered the room frightened, and he knew immediately she hadn't been bedded by anyone but her husband. The extent of her sexual experience being but two weeks. She was a beauty though—with dark-brown hair, olive-green skin and a long, shapely body. She was also very young. *I need to take my time or this is going to suck for both of us.*

Angel entered the room and stood before the bed expectantly. She knew what Desmond needed and she was willing to pay the price. Perhaps if it hadn't been so long for him he might have given her longer to adjust, but as it was, he was so hungry for her he just couldn't think straight. Unbuttoning his tunic, he took a seat in a corner chair and flung one leg over the armrest.

Angel folded her arms. "What would you like me to do?"

He ran his index finger over his bottom lip thoughtfully. The urgency of his erection was torture. "Undress," he said.

Lowering her arms, she looked past him at a spot on the wall and unbuttoned her blouse. With long elegant fingers, she peeled it away from her generous bosom and let it fall to the ground. Desmond's eyes roamed over her torso and he could see many dark bruises just starting to fade. A sudden anger rose in him and he wondered what kind of lowlife asshole would beat a woman like that.

As he watched her, she continued to strip until she stood before him completely naked. He thought her the most beautiful woman he'd ever seen and he knew he had to touch her. Climbing up out of the chair like a jungle cat stalking his prey, he moved toward her amused she couldn't look him in the eye.

"Did you ever enjoy it when he touched you?" he asked before softly kissing the side of her mouth. He took both of her hands in his and softly caressed them while continuing to kiss her jawline.

Angel closed her eyes for a moment to savor his gentle kiss. "No," she said. Her voice was light and delicate like an early morning fog.

Desmond slid his hands up her arms to the sides of her face and pulled her into a smoky, carnal kiss. His tongue moved past her lips and rubbed against hers in a tender claiming that made her swoon against him. He caught her just as her knees buckled and laid her on the bed.

"I'm sorry," she said. "It's just the stress of everything."

Desmond's excitement rose to a fever pitch. The animal within him was driving him, forcing him to pursue his need. Moving his mouth over her right then her left breast, he mauled the velvet flesh, sucking and licking the nipples until she gasped and ran her fingers though his hair. Her scent was changing, going from terror to something far more pleasing. All he had to do was hold off a little longer and the sex would be much better. Dragging his mouth down her lush young body, he nestled between her legs and pushed them apart. He knew she wanted to resist him but he watched with satisfaction as she grabbed great handfuls of the blanket instead.

With the greed of a starving man at a banquet, he buried his tongue into her tender folds and devoured her. Her scent was bliss itself, awakening and arousing him in ways he'd missed for so long. He slowed his pace painstakingly searching out every tender spot that made her jump. She was close now, so close to climax and he wanted to be within her when she achieved it.

Hastily stripping off the rest of his clothing, he moved on top of her and nestled his hips between her legs. The tip of his swollen cock found the moist passion of her pussy and he eased his way home. Like a hot bath after a long day, he was engulfed in delicious heat. She was tight and decadently wet. Within her was an intoxicating cocktail of pleasures he'd been too long without. Forcing himself into a steady rhythm, he buried his face in her neck and listened to the magical sound of her quickening breath. Her hands ran down his back, stroking, caressing, as her beautiful mouth whispered his name over and over again like a prayer.

Her noisy orgasm was the purest flattery he'd ever known and enhanced his own climax making it last longer than usual. He took her two more times, delighted in how easy it was to please her. She fell into a quiet sleep beside him and after he too took a quick nap, he found he couldn't sleep any more. He attributed it to his temporary time confusion. Living in space for long periods of time did that to people.

Leaving her sleeping, he decided to go downstairs and have a drink. He took care to leave his gear where she could see it if she woke up. Otherwise her first thought at noticing his absence would be that he had fucked her and ditched her. Besides he would be an idiot not to hold on to this deal for as long as he could. Desmond grinned to himself. Less than an hour back on the planet and already he had a girlfriend. Maybe this visit home wouldn't be so bad after all.

All he had to do now was get along with Gavin.

Chapter 14

Desmond went down to the bar surprised by how crowded it was. Muscling through the cliques, he found a spot at the end of the bar and ordered a whiskey. As he waited for his drink, he glanced around at the soldiers and townsmen to see if he recognized anyone. Many of the patrons were young warriors who were probably born during his last few exiles. Then, to his relief, he recognized his old mentor, Master Sergeant Rakon. *Now maybe I can find out what the hell I'm doing here.* The old warrior was arguing some point with three other hard-looking soldiers. Desmond walked past him and deliberately rammed his shoulder into the master sergeant.

Rakon turned toward him glaring and was just about to insult him when he saw who it was. Snarling in mock aggression, he grabbed Desmond's hand and pumped it hard. "Desmond, by the Gods! When did you get back, you old bastard!"

Desmond smiled. It felt so good to be home. "Just a few hours ago. I was barely off the shuttle and I managed to snag a girlfriend."

Rakon slapped him on the back. "Now we've talked about this before. A prostitute is *not* a girlfriend," he said, slowly enunciating.

"It's good to know age and senility haven't doused your sense of humor," Desmond said flatly. "Seriously, Rakon, a girl just fell into my lap."

"What girl?"

Desmond sipped his drink trying to avoid being jostled by the crowd. "Some woman named Angel Trolis threw herself at my feet begging for protection from her husband. That guy was a piece of work."

Rakon nodded grimly. He grabbed Desmond's elbow and dragged him out back where they could talk without shouting over the noise of the crowd. "That poor girl married badly indeed," he said. Then he grinned and gave Desmond a brief bear hug. "It's damn good to see you, boy!"

"So what's going on?" Desmond asked. "Gavin didn't bring me back for a family reunion. He didn't find a worse place to send me, did he?"

Some soldiers at a nearby table left and Desmond and Rakon sat down. "No, nothing like that. Gavin's got a new prospect, your half-sister Gypsy."

Desmond shook his head. *What an asshole my father is.* That man never gave up in finding a worthy successor for his military legacy. Out of sons to bully, now he was picking on his daughters. "I'm surprised he'd lower himself to train a woman considering he's a bigger misogynist than anyone in the Empire."

Rakon downed his drink and signaled the barmaid for another. "She's not just any woman," Rakon said. "She's got the goods. This'll be hard for you to hear, but there's a lot of Northe to her moves."

The mention of his half brother's name brought an unexpected agony and Desmond fought hard to push it down. When he could speak again, he said, "So if he's found *the one*, what the fuck does he need me for?"

"You're still one of the best swordsmen in the Empire. I expect he wants you to help him train her. She's already tagged one of her sparring partners out of commission."

Desmond studied Rakon for a moment. He saw in his old mentor something he'd not seen in a long time. Admiration. Rakon really thought highly of this girl. *Interesting.*

"How do the two of them get along?"

"Gavin and Gypsy? Like fire and water, but she's sworn loyalty to him and she's obedient." Rakon lit a cigar and offered Desmond one. Desmond took it and they both sat for a moment smoking. "I think she'll be the first woman to make it," Rakon said thoughtfully.

Desmond frowned. "Are you telling me she chose this herself? No interference from Gavin?"

"You nailed him with the misogynist part. He did everything short of throwing her ass in jail to keep her out of the arena. She defied him every step of the way even using armor and weaponry from the pauper's chest. Gavin refused to train her and she refused to give up."

"That's pretty determined. That pauper's chest is pretty much scrap metal with straps." Desmond laughed while shaking his head.

"That's nothing. She came to me out of the blue one day and asked me to train her in exchange for sex." Rakon sighed. "Now that was a nice arrangement while it lasted."

"So what happened?"

"Gavin found out. He was so fucking pissed he threatened me with all kinds of torturous punishments if I continued," Rakon said then sipped his drink.

"I'm surprised he didn't bust you down a rank 'cause he sure loves to hit his military personnel with that demotion stick."

"Don't think he didn't threaten me with it. But as it turns out he only suspended me a few days without pay. Funny thing is, that just made Gypsy more tenacious and she showed up in the arena anyway. She won her match," he said, glowing with pride. "Unfortunately she took a stab to the belly bad enough for her to end up in the clinic."

"So then Gavin finally relented?" Desmond asked.

"Are you kidding me? He dug his boots in and wouldn't budge, told her she was finished."

"That sounds just like him." Desmond nodded.

"Next thing you know she's moving out and in with Caraculla—her new trainer."

Desmond broke out a hearty laugh. "I think I like this girl already."

"Well they have a lot of chemistry and pretty soon there was more fucking than fighting."

"She doesn't want a husband and family?" Desmond asked, unable to picture a woman who didn't want those things.

Rakon shrugged. "I'm sure she does but she's willing to wait and risk it all. As far as a husband goes, I know Caraculla, he's crazy for her and he'll hold out. I think she loves him too but like all of the Therons, her career is her first priority."

Desmond smiled and shook his head. Caraculla *loved* tough women. "What's he going to do if she goes into the Academy?"

"Not my problem," Rakon said.

Desmond figured he was right. It wasn't Desmond's problem either. "So when did that asshole finally grace her with his training?"

"One night she got tricked into sparring with a senior warrior who beat the shit out of her and raped her," Rakon said, grimly crushing out his cigar.

Desmond couldn't believe what he was hearing. "Who would be stupid enough to rape the daughter of the man who runs the military?" Even if Gavin didn't give a shit about his kids, he was very proprietary.

"You know, your girlfriend's husband—ex-husband—or whatever he is."

"That little piece of excrement, Drake?" Desmond said, almost shouting.

"The same."

"Now I wish I'd killed him back on the road."

"Don't bother. I'm pretty sure Gavin has plans for him." Rakon downed his drink and slammed his glass on the table.

"What time does Gavin get into the office?" Desmond asked.

"Why? Are you that eager to see him?"

"No, but if I get in there before him, I can dip into a few cups of his whiskey. I can be halfway drunk before he gets there and I have to talk to him. That way I'll be better prepared to deal with his shit. The bastard thrives on conflict in the morning," Desmond said, feeling that old unease building in his gut.

"He'll probably be in at seven. He gets in earlier now that he's training Gypsy," Rakon said. His new drink arrived and he over-tipped the barmaid.

Desmond ordered another drink. Seven in the morning was only about three hours off so he might as well start his buzz before the fireworks began.

Chapter 15

Desmond stood at attention in front of Gavin's desk waiting for his father to tire of ignoring him. Finally Gavin pushed aside his paperwork and looked up. "Have a seat," Gavin said.

Desmond sat down with a million feelings bubbling in his gut. He tried to think of what to say to his father but finally decided to stay silent. *If I keep my mouth shut I can get out of this meeting sooner.*

Gavin leaned back in his chair. "You must be wondering why I sent for you."

"I assumed you'd get around to it eventually," Desmond said.

"I need your help in training your sister, Gypsy," Gavin said simply.

"There are plenty of people in the Empire who can help you train her."

"I didn't want just anyone," Gavin said. "I wanted the best."

Desmond shrugged. "You're my general. I'll do as you command," he said, willing to say anything to get out of this room.

Gavin watched him like a predator ready to pounce. "I also asked you here for another reason."

Desmond sighed. *No use hoping for a quick exit. It was time to fuck with Desmond.* "The suspense is killing me."

Gavin paused for a moment. Then he said, "I think we have some things to talk about."

"What could *you and I* possibly have to talk about?" Desmond said, glaring at him. "If you're going to start in on how much of a disappointment I am, you can save it. I'm not listening to your crap anymore."

Gavin watched him for a moment and Desmond couldn't even begin to guess at what his father was thinking. Usually his father showed visible signs of getting pissed off by now. But he just sat there looking thoughtful.

Finally he said, "The issue of my disappointment in you is my problem, not yours. I want to talk about Northe."

A boiling fury twisted in his heart. Desmond shifted in his chair. Suddenly the room felt much too small. "I don't. You want me to help train my sister—fine. You want me to play the good soldier and do as you say—fine. But I have nothing to say to you on the subject of Northe."

To Desmond's surprise and disappointment, Gavin didn't fly into a rage and throw him out. "I'm not asking you to forgive me for Northe. But there are things I need to say to you that should have been said a long time ago. Then I need to move forward because your help is necessary in getting Gypsy the right skills to win her upcoming arena match."

Desmond shook his head bitterly. "That poor girl doesn't know anything about you."

"What exactly does that mean?"

"Forget it. I told you I'd do it," Desmond said. "What more do you want?"

"I loved Northe as much as you, Desmond," Gavin said, leaning forward for emphasis. "I mourned his death just as you did."

"I doubt that, Gavin," Desmond said, fighting with every ounce of restraint he had not to explode into a barrage of angry accusations. "You're not capable of loving anything."

"I loved him and I love you."

Desmond had had enough. He got up out of his chair. "That's enough of this. Is there anything else you wanted, General?"

Gavin got up and pursued Desmond to the door coming to stand in front of it. "I killed Northe because he left me no choice and you well know it!"

"All I know is you *butchered* him on the field like an animal," Desmond said through his teeth. The pain within him was sucking the life out of his soul. He had to get out of here and away from Gavin. "Get the *fuck* out of my way!"

Gavin stood his ground blocking the exit and Desmond clenched his fists to keep from drawing his saber. As much as he hated Gavin at that moment he was still a soldier and Gavin was his superior. Besides he really didn't want to be exiled again so soon.

"How could I let Northe go after he'd led *two enemy* armies against me? You know how driven he was. He wasn't going to fail a third time. When he challenged me on the battlefield there were no other options left. Should I have stood there and let him cut me down?"

"You could have imprisoned him! You seemed to have liked that option for everyone else at the time!" Desmond roared, trying to get around Gavin. When he couldn't get Gavin to move, he paced like an agitated panther in a cage and slammed his fist into the wall. "I don't want to have this discussion now *get out of my way!*" Desmond snarled, feeling his grasp of his emotions quickly slipping.

Gavin held up a hand as if to ward off Desmond's anger. "Alright, alright. Calm down. I'll tell you what. If you want out so badly I'll give you your choice of duty stations and you're out. All I ask is that you listen to what I have to say and you're done."

"I'm not in the mood for another one of your tricks," Desmond said guarded.

"It's not a trick. I'll write the order now, as you're standing here and hand it to you. You can be gone in an hour." Gavin returned to his desk and pulled out an order form. "Anywhere," Gavin said. "Name it."

Desmond leaned against the wall folding his arms. "Say what you want to say while I stand here and think about where I want to go."

"Out of all my children I have treated you the worst and you have deserved it the least. I am through trying to make you suffer for not living up to my expectations," Gavin said, still holding the pen.

Desmond stared at the floor for a moment trying to digest the words his father had just said to him. "Are you...apologizing to me?"

Now it was Gavin's turn to pause. He put the pen down and took a deep breath as he pondered Desmond's question. "Yes. Yes I am. I realized how I have failed you, and Northe, and so many of the others. I don't want to fail Gypsy the same way. I need your help. She has wanted this more than all of my other children combined. I almost dismissed her and drove her off because she didn't come in the right packaging."

Desmond's emotional turmoil was momentarily numbed. *Could Gavin really believe this girl Gypsy is that good?* The thought seemed close to impossible. "Is she as good as everyone says she is?"

Gavin locked his yellow eye on Desmond. "She is."

That was a sobering admission from a man who believed women were only good for sex, birthing babies and making men miserable. Desmond's anger began to fade. "Then you probably need to know that Drake Trolis was planning to assassinate her. I have custody of Drake's wife who threw herself on my mercy just as her husband was taking her to lure Gypsy out for the kill."

His father's dark fury showed in his face and Gavin was silent for a long time. "Do you understand now why I need you?" he said finally.

The words were the closest thing to paternal love he'd ever felt from Gavin and it wore him down. Was there still some affection in him for this black-hearted bastard? Maybe there was. "How long do I have to stay?" he said, walking back over to the door.

"However long you want," Gavin said.

"Then I get to choose my next duty station?"

"I swear it."

"What if I choose to stay here?"

"That's fine. You can select who you want to report to. I'll stay out of it."

Desmond pointed at Gavin and placed his hand on the doorknob. "Don't fuck me, Gavin," he said. "I know I'll regret it, but I'm trusting you on this."

Chapter 16

The night was pleasant and cool and the arena was packed. People sat shoulder to shoulder in the stands, with some latecomers forced to sit on the stairs. Gypsy had never seen it so crowded and it did nothing to calm her nerves. From where they were in the ready pit, people rushed across the metal grating above shouting at each other excitedly. The ready pit smelled like stale sweat and old blood. Gypsy couldn't help but wonder how many warriors had stood here for the last time. She swallowed and glanced over at Gavin. His face was an expressionless mask of concentration as he told Caraculla what to watch for. It was her father's best poker face and she knew it hid his worry.

Caraculla was nervous too, getting aggressive over minor things, fidgeting as Gavin checked his armor to make sure nothing was restricting his movement. Finally, after another tense argument between the two men, Gypsy came over and grabbed Caraculla's hand. He looked at her and his features softened. He pulled her into his arms and she inhaled his rich masculine scent. Nuzzling his ear, she said, "I know you'll do fine but please be careful."

He kissed her and she thought her heart was going to break. "I'll be alright. Don't worry about me."

The referee came over and signaled them it was time for Caraculla to enter the arena. He released Gypsy and walked out to the ear-splitting roar of the crowd. High in the bleachers, soldiers chanted his name and stomped their feet with each syllable. Gavin grabbed her arm and led her over to the sidelines where they'd be able to watch the battle. The noise was a great fortress of sound cutting her off from talking to her father. He wouldn't have heard a word she said and that made her feel even more isolated. The very real possibility that Caraculla could die in this fight was making her heart palpitate in anxious frustration. She chewed the inside of her lip and shifted her weight back and forth on each leg.

From her right Caraculla's opponent General Kharon came out. Like her father, he was a colossal ÆEssyrian standing well over six foot five and weighting at least three hundred pounds. He wore light gray armor and carried his meteor hammer coiled on his hip. He paused for a moment to unbuckle his scabbard and hand it to the referee. In that brief moment in time, she noticed that his eyes were two different colors. One was a chilling artic-blue and the other a more normal brownish-green. Her eyes fixed on the small chain tattoo near the blue eye that defined his humble beginnings as a slave.

He fixed his gaze on her for a second and she felt a nervous chill. She caught the current of sexual hunger in him and it didn't repulse her as much as she expected it would. Something about him was vaguely familiar. Then she realized that the artic-blue eye was the exact color as Makkai's. But before she could dwell on the significance of that, Kharon was walking into the arena.

From the left side of the arena, his supporters roared, calling out encouragement to him. She spotted Kharon's three wives, all beautiful and well dressed sitting next to each other giving off the explosive tension of three wildcats in a small box.

The referee was talking to the noisy crowd, giving background on the fighters but no one could hear a thing. It didn't matter anyway, all the crowd came to see was blood and death. Gypsy looked over to the side benches at her mother and Krull waiting in the emergency medical area. Her mother had to lean in close to Krull as she talked in his ear. She gestured to the arena floor and he nodded in agreement. Then the noise rose from the audience in a great tidal wave of jeers and cheers.

The fight had begun.

Kharon had the meteor hammer in full motion over his head and around his body. It moved around and around in lazy circles looking more like a child's toy than a weapon. The weapon was a six-foot chain with a spiked metal ball on the end. In the right hands, it was almost unbeatable and terribly lethal.

Kharon sped the looping up until it blurred like a propeller. It was almost impossible to see where the ball was at any given time in its rotation around its master. The ball encircled him completely, never leaving the general's body unprotected for more than a second. Kharon launched the ball at Caraculla several times, connecting with his sword as the colonel used his blade to deflect it. The motion of the meteor hammer was hypnotic as it flew around its fighter seemingly with a mind of its own. At the most unexpected times, it would launch at Caraculla, and it was all Caraculla could do to not be hit by the speeding weapon.

For endless minutes the fight continued, each man trying to outthink and outmaneuver the other. Caraculla finally took a big risk to win. Waiting for the ball to return to Kharon from a launched attack, the colonel threw his saber at a gap in his opponent's armor. The blade traveled through the air in a wide arch and found its mark, sliding past Kharon's protective armor and into the soft flesh of his belly. The powerful force of the throw knocked Kharon backwards as the blade embedded into the arena floor pinning him there. The general's body convulsed in pain and blood began to leak from his mouth.

But the battle wasn't quite done, because the meteor hammer had enough momentum to find its own mark at last and slammed into Caraculla's temple with a sickening thud a split second before he could dodge out of the way. Gypsy could swear she heard a crack when it made contact. Then the ball fell to the ground with a metallic clank.

For an eternity it looked as though the colonel was alright despite the blow. But then his right eye clouded crimson and he collapsed face first on the ground.

Gypsy threw herself toward the guardrail to get to him but Gavin brought her down with a hard tackle. "You can't go out there! You'll disqualify him," Gavin said, holding her arms to her sides.

"I don't give a fuck if I disqualify him! You let me go!"

Gypsy fought and screamed but no one could hear her and as always, she wasn't strong enough to break her father's grip. She thought she was in hell. Her mother rushed to Kharon with her medics and Gypsy couldn't believe what she was seeing. *Don't bother with him, go to Caraculla, damn it!* Krull and the others had already reached Caraculla and were carrying him out on a stretcher with a spit guard secured to his mouth. Gypsy fought her father to go after them but he dragged her outside instead.

The outside air made her breathe a little easier. She was having a hard time absorbing what had just happened. "What the hell is wrong with you!" she screamed. "Get the fuck off me and let me get to the clinic!"

Gavin pointed at her still holding her by one of her upper arms. His grip was like a tight manacle. "First I need you to get a hold of yourself. I don't need any wild hysterics while your mother and Krull are trying to save these two men's lives."

"Why didn't she go to Caraculla *first*? Who gives a shit what happens to Kharon?" she said, feeling tears stinging her eyes.

"Because she's too close to Caraculla, my dear," he said calmly. "You need to trust her judgment."

"I hate that guy Krull and I don't want him taking care of Caraculla!" she yelled still unable to keep the hysteria from her voice.

Gavin gripped her arm tighter and shook her slightly. "Now you listen to me. Your mother thinks very highly of that Kirillian to the point where she has insecurities about him being a better doctor. She is also very fond of Caraculla and knows what he means to both of us. You know she wouldn't do anything to jeopardize his life. Now you need to pull yourself together or we're not going anywhere. Do you understand me?"

Gypsy's guts twisted in knots and she angrily swiped at the uncontrollable tears pouring down her face. "Okay," she said. "I understand. Can we please go to the clinic now?"

He frowned at her not quite convinced but he released her arm. "If you cause any problems or interfere in any way, I'll have you removed and placed under guard. Do I make myself clear?"

Gypsy nodded quickly and looked at Gavin with defeated sorrow. "I promise. I'll behave."

Gavin placed his arm around her waist and led her over to their hyperias. She pushed down a sob that was threatening to choke her when she saw Caraculla's mount. "What about—" she said, pointing at the colonel's hyperia. It was becoming increasingly difficult to form coherent thoughts. The stupidity of her question dangled in the back of her mind. But Gavin seemed to know what she needed.

"I'll send Makkai to get him and take him home. Are you alright to ride?"

Gypsy gave a faint nod and climbed on to her own hyperia. She never thought anything would feel worse than the rape. But it was barely a blip to her senses compared to this. The frailty that invaded her body and thoughts made her feel like a newborn lost in the woods. *What if he dies? What am I going to do without him?*

Chapter 17

After almost two hours in surgery, Harlan got Kharon stabilized. Lucky for him nothing vital was severed when the saber entered his gut, but he'd be on a liquid diet for a few weeks. She came out of surgery like a sleepwalker, feeling as though all her energy had been drained out through her feet. She didn't need to be Caraculla's treating physician to know he was in bad shape. Everyone close to the arena floor had heard the crack when that awful weapon struck him. Both she and Krull had shared a look immediately after, knowing the crack was his skull. God, how she hated the violence of life on this planet.

She went into the break room and stripped her soiled scrubs off. Then she stepped into the shower and cleaned the rest of the blood and gore off her. As she stood there under the steaming water, she realized she was terrified. Terrified for her daughter—terrified for Caraculla—and even terrified for Gavin. Caraculla was such an integral part of their lives, nothing would ever be the same without him. *I'm sure I made the right decision by turning his care over to Krull.*

She dressed carefully, giving herself plenty of time to collect her feelings. Once she was ready, she came out to talk to Kharon's wives who were waiting in the quiet room. Before she could say a word, one of them stood and said, "Is he going to live?" The woman was tall with a contrasting petite bone structure. Her completely straight hair was dark with white tips and like his other wives, she was strikingly beautiful.

"Yes he's going to be fine. He'll need to stay out the week here so we can watch for infection and make sure he's tolerating his temporary diet. With any luck he should be back to normal in a few months." Harlan addressed the one who stood but made eye contact with all of them.

"When can we see him?" one of the two still sitting asked. Harlan had been looking at the one standing so she wasn't sure which one had asked the question.

"He is still under sedation from the surgery but he should be well enough for a visitor in a few hours. I am going to have to ask that you take your visits one at a time to avoid any unnecessary stress."

The women exchanged irritated glances but agreed. Harlan was sure none of them wanted any of the others to have too much alone time with him. *Multiple wives indeed.* That is one situation Harlan would have no tolerance for. Now it was time to talk to her own family before she went to check on Caraculla.

Gypsy jumped out of her chair the second she entered the waiting room and rushed over to her. "Have you had a chance to see Caraculla yet?" she said desperately. Harlan glanced around for Gavin. He was probably outside smoking and waiting for word. That was what he usually did. He was an old pro at waiting for injured men.

"Not yet," Harlan said. "I'm going to check on him now."

"Can I come with you?"

Harlan held up her hands. "No, Gypsy. I need you to wait here until I know he's out of surgery and stabilized. Let me see what's going on and I'll come out and talk to you and Gavin. Then I'll have a better idea of when you might be able to see him."

Harlan waited for Gypsy to fly into a rage but she sat down instead hanging her head and clasping her fingers behind her neck. Harlan breathed a quiet sigh of relief that Gavin had been teaching their daughter some self-restraint. She made her way down the hall remembering all of the horrible injuries Gavin had sustained she'd had to fix. Back then, she didn't have a doctor on staff of Krull's caliber and right now she was unbelievably grateful for him. She scrubbed up at the dressing station, donned a mask and gloves and went in to help Krull.

The room was surprisingly quiet and Harlan could see that Caraculla was already in deep hibernation. He lay on the bed with the side of his head shaved and black stitches showing over the nasty slice in his temple. He was hooked up to several monitoring devices that hummed much too quietly for her taste. Krull came over and pulled Harlan aside. His blue eyes searched her face. "He's not responding," he said. "His brain is continuing to swell and I've already drained fluid from it three times. I want to put him in a medically induced coma and shut down his immune system. Then maybe we can get his swelling to abate."

Harlan was stunned at his suggestion and began to wonder if she'd made a mistake entrusting Caraculla's care to him. She'd never heard of an ÆEssyiran coming out of a coma. According to the literature, if they went into a coma they died. "Do you realize what you're saying? He'll die. He's ÆEssyrian," she said, not recognizing the sound of her own voice.

"No," Krull corrected. "He's a Razorback."

"There must be alternatives."

Krull shrugged. "We don't have time for alternatives. Repressing the swelling must be our first priority before he incurs any brain damage. If we wait, he'll be a vegetable. If we wait longer, he'll be dead. I believe this is his best chance for survival. This *can* work."

Harlan looked at Krull for any signs of wavering doubt. She saw none. She then looked at the color monitor on the wall that showed a continuous 3-D image of Caraculla's brain. It was swelling fast. She needed to decide right now. *What am I going to tell Gypsy?* "Okay," she said. "We'll do this your way."

Krull nodded to the two medics helping him and they used the life support system to lower Caraculla's blood pressure and heart rate until he went into a coma. Krull prepared an immunosuppressant and injected it into Caraculla's central line. Harlan thought she was going to be ill. "How are we going to bring him back out of this if your treatment is successful?"

Krull folded his thick arms and stared down at his patient. "Let's let the swelling go down and see how much he can heal on his own. Then we'll play it by ear."

"I don't know what I'm going to tell Gavin and Gypsy," Harlan said more to herself than Krull. She'd never felt so lost in her life.

"You're going to tell them the truth," Krull said. "You're going to tell them he's alive and that's all."

Harlan nodded and walked out. She stripped off her gloves and mask and went out to Gypsy. She forced herself not to look too worried. "Come on," she said. "Let's go outside and talk to your father at the same time. I don't think I have the energy to repeat myself."

As Harlan expected, Gavin was leaning against the building smoking a cigar. He watched them guardedly as they came over to him. "What news?" Gavin asked.

"He's alive," Harlan said. "But he's still very critical. I can't give you a prognosis yet."

"Can I see him?" Gypsy asked.

"Yes, but only for a few moments." Harlan glanced at Gavin. "Are you coming?"

Gavin didn't look at Harlan and she knew he was hurting. "No," he said, watching a few coaches pass by. "I'll wait here for Gypsy. How is the general?"

"He'll be alright. Despite the dramatic flare of being pinned to the arena floor his wounds were not life-threatening."

Gavin nodded. "Good."

* * * *

Gypsy entered the room and moved over to Caraculla's beside. She wanted to take his hand but there were just too many devices hooked up to it. She didn't know anything about medicine but he looked pretty bad to her. She finally found an uncluttered spot on his left forearm and placed her hand on it gently squeezing. She looked at the flexible glass tubes that traveled up under his spit guard. The other ends were attached to opaque containers secured to the floor.

"What are those things going in on each side of his mouth?" Gypsy said without looking up. She sounded so sad that Harlan could barely stand it.

"They drain any excess venom he's producing so the sacs don't overflow and leak out under the guard and onto the bed. Which, as you know, will melt."

Gypsy looked up into Harlan's eyes and Harlan felt her own start to tear up. "Please don't let him die," her daughter whispered in a voice so soft and fragile that Harlan barely understood what she said.

Harlan came over and stroked her hair. "You know we will do everything possible to save him, Gypsy."

"I know *you* will. I guess I just don't know the Kirillian very well."

"It's because of Krull that he's still alive. I understand you're upset that I'm not his primary doctor. But you need to understand that I'm heartbroken over this too and I'm afraid it will impair my judgment."

Gypsy nodded. "Gavin told me all of that. I do understand even if I don't like it. Can I please stay here with him for a little while? I promise I won't interfere with anything. I'll leave if you or Krull tell me to. I just really want to be here with him."

Harlan hated seeing Gypsy in so much pain. There was a frailty to her that Harlan had never seen before. "Yes. You can stay with him for a bit. I'll let your father know and he'll come and get you when he's ready." Harlan brought a chair over to Gypsy and set it down. "Here. Sit before you pass out." Gypsy sat and Harlan watched for a moment as Gypsy pressed her face into the bed next to Caraculla's arm and sobbed quietly.

Chapter 18

Angel woke Desmond at the crack of dawn and said, "I need to buy some things. I have nothing here."

He blinked trying to focus and she thought if he'd just drink a little less, it might be easier to wake up in the morning. He was such a typical soldier.

He tried to go back to sleep and she shook him again. "Did you hear what I said?"

"What kind of things?" he growled, shielding his eyes from the rising suns.

"For one thing I need clothes. Like I said, I have nothing here. Everything I have is at Drake's villa," she said, growing impatient with him. "Just tell me your account number and I'll go out shopping for what I need."

"Why don't we just go to Drake's house and get your stuff?" he said, sitting up.

"I really don't want a confrontation."

"Well," Desmond said, climbing out of bed. "I do. Let's go."

Angel frowned. He obviously didn't understand how much stuff a noblewoman had. "It's not quite that easy. I'll need a coach and a few men to help me."

Desmond scratched his head looking confused. "I thought all you had to get was some dresses?"

"I also have furniture, a trunk and jewels. You and I can't do it alone. We'll need help."

"What the hell do you need furniture for? We have furniture."

"That is my furniture and some of those pieces are family heirlooms," she said, folding her arms.

"Family heirlooms? You didn't care about the family heirlooms when you were offering to empty my credit account to go on a shopping trip for new things."

"Desmond, if I am going through the trauma of setting foot back in that villa, I want *all* of my things."

* * * *

An hour later they had rented a very expensive coach, and enlisted the help of two of Gavin's trainees, Falken and Makkai. The young noblemen were nice enough but it annoyed Desmond to no end that they were always defending Angel and jumping at her every whim. It didn't take Desmond long to realize he and the nobles were worlds apart.

Walking up to Drake's door, Desmond dispensed with the usual pleasantries and kicked it open. Drake came down the hallway seconds later with his saber in hand dressed just in his pants and boots.

"What the hell do you think you're doing?" he shouted at Desmond.

Desmond ignored him and walked into the villa followed by Falken and Makkai. "I'm here to get your wife's things. Any questions?" He could see Drake toying with challenging him to a fight, then thought the better of it and sheathed his saber.

"Go ahead, just make sure you get all of the stupid whore's stuff," Drake taunted.

Desmond was on Drake in less than a second and had pinned him against the wall with one hand gripped tightly around his throat. "I am not in a good mood. So to keep me from taking my bad mood out on you, I would strongly suggest that you not talk the rest of the time we're here." He let Drake go and walked back outside muttering.

Then the heavy lifting began.

Desmond had never seen a woman with so much stuff. Angel must have owned half the furniture at the villa and three trunks of clothes. As it was, Desmond was forced to rent her an apartment to put everything in and that's when he knew he had to get rid of her. She was an expensive woman with expensive tastes. She was way too high maintenance for a simple soldier like him. He would rather go back to his *other girlfriends*. In the long run, they would be much cheaper.

As he brooded in the coach on the way to the apartment, he finally spotted his way out. Makkai was stealing looks at Angel and she seemed to be encouraging him. *Thank the Gods.*

"You know," Desmond said, pretending he hadn't seen them flirting. "I won't be able to see you as much as I'd like while I'm helping my father train Gypsy," he said to Angel. "Maybe Makkai would be nice enough to take you out in the evenings so you don't get bored." *He's a nobleman's son. He can surely afford your ridiculously expensive tastes.* "Would you be willing to do that for me, Makkai?"

Makkai stared at him with those chilling artic-blue eyes. "I'd be happy to, sir."

"What about you, Angel?" Desmond asked. "Would that be alright with you?"

She feigned disinterest and stared out the window. "I suppose," she said.

"Good," Desmond said, breathing a secret sigh of relief. He knew it wouldn't be long before the two were sleeping together. He expected Makkai would come to him in the near future and offer to take Angel off his hands and the sooner the better. Desmond would play the wounded boyfriend then he'd say all he wanted was what was good for Angel. He'd be the hero again and she would be out of his life. "I'm glad that's settled."

Chapter 19

Gypsy went to the arena that morning feeling her anguish drag her down into a cavern of despair. The truth was if it hadn't been for her father, she didn't know how she would have coped thus far. He'd stayed with her all night and took her to the clinic first thing in the morning. Of course Caraculla was no better, but Gavin didn't let her dwell too long on her lover's condition. It felt strange to rely on her father's strength. Usually she was at such odds with him. She had gone through the motions of her morning practice session and went to eat lunch alone. Now she was back for her second lesson of the day and Gavin was there waiting outside.

"I have something for you," he said, taking a saber off his mount.

Gypsy stood there unable to respond one way or the other. She had been numb since last night and wasn't reacting right to anything around her. Gavin took her old bulky saber from her and replaced it with the one Caraculla had given her so long ago. She wrapped her hand around the handle and a rush of mind-wasting sorrow filled her. Before she could say anything, Gavin pulled her into his arms and held her tight.

"I don't know if I can do this anymore," she said, her words muffled in his chest. Without warning a sob escaped from her and before she could clamp down on her emotions, a few others joined it.

"That's just the pain speaking, my dear. Take Caraculla's saber—use it. He was the first to support you. He wouldn't want you to give up now."

The dark void in her soul opened up and her father's warmth filled it. How long had it been since he'd shown her this much affection? She couldn't even remember. She wrapped her arms around him for the first time since she was a small child and squeezed. A kindling of joy soothed her and she felt like she'd come home after a very long journey. She sniffled a few times and pulled back. "I'm not sure if this is what I want anymore."

Gavin placed his hand under her chin and lifted her face to look at him. "Don't worry about any of that, just trust me. Do as I tell you. If the time comes for your match and you don't want to go through with it, I'll scratch you. But remember this, no matter what you decide, nothing will change Caraculla's fate. You can't bring him back by quitting. Trust your mother. She has saved his life before and I believe she can do it again. But we must give her and Krull room to work—to take chances. Brooding around the clinic helps no one. You are a soldier. Caraculla isn't the first or the last person you'll love to fall by a weapon. Embrace your loss and move forward."

Gypsy took Caraculla's saber and stared at it. It was the most beautiful piece of steel she'd ever seen. She managed a nod.

Gavin lit a cigar and moved with her to the center of the arena. As was common the day after a big match, the place was empty. Only a few custodians moved through the bleachers like ghosts cleaning up. "We'll start with First Position, Practice Four," Gavin said.

Gypsy took a deep breath and lifted Caraculla's weapon. She let her memory take over, gliding the weapon through the air in the memorized movements of Practice Four. The blade was so light, she found herself picking up speed and settling into her practice. Over and over again she cut through the air, cutting, parrying, slicing, deflecting—each move as clean and precise as she could get it. Everything melted away but her, the blade, and Gavin's commanding voice. She lost herself in the practice, surrendering to a more primitive state where nothing existed but the thrill of battle. Gavin circled around her, encouraging her, directing her, suggesting she try new things.

Then Gavin stepped away and she stopped to see what had distracted him. She was surprised to notice she was sweating and wondered how long she'd been doing the same moves over and over again. It must have been a long time because the muscles in her arms were trembling from fatigue.

"Nice of you to join us," Gavin said to a large Kirillian soldier who'd just come in.

The Kirillian came down the steps stripping his uniform tunic off and pulling out his blade. He was an older man, probably a little younger than middle age for a Kirillian and ruggedly handsome. Then Gypsy caught sight of his eyes. They were hazel with a starburst of yellow around the pupil. They were very familiar to her. She glanced at her father in confusion. *That's got to be one of his sons, but I thought they were all dead.*

"Gypsy," Gavin said as the Kirillian came down onto the arena floor. "This is your half-brother Desmond. He's going to help me train you."

Gypsy nodded to him. Desmond grinned and looked back at Gavin. "You do produce good-looking kids, I'll give you that."

Gavin paused while passing Desmond and said, "I hope you brought your best game today because she's going to eat you alive."

Desmond laughed. "We'll just see about that, old man."

Gypsy reached deep inside and found the horrible pain plaguing her soul. With an angry snarl, she launched at Desmond forcing him on the defensive. He growled and slammed his saber into hers to send her back. He rolled his arms and got into a ready position. She attacked again taking care not to leave any openings for him. Desmond deflected each of her blows with such speed and ease she found herself trying to think of new ways to strike.

"Stop!" Gavin bellowed across the arena. He strode out from the side and wiggled his index finger at them. Desmond looked away, obviously irritated.

"Me?" Gypsy gestured toward herself.

"No. Him," he said, pointing at Desmond, who slowly moseyed over toward his father with a definite attitude.

"What the fuck are you doing?" Gavin said, moving into his personal space.

"I'm sparring with her. Isn't that why you brought me here?" Desmond replied.

"You're sparring with her like an old noblewoman."

"I don't want to hurt her," Desmond said, absently scratching his muscular chest.

"Either train her to kill or tell me where you want me to send you and I'll draw up your orders. But don't waste my fucking time," Gavin snarled.

Desmond broke off from Gavin angrily and walked back over to Gypsy. She could tell he was pissed and now she was probably going to suffer for it. He launched a vicious attack on her and it was all she could do to keep her footing. For the next five minutes, he wailed on her and all she could do was defend herself.

Then he started talking.

"So what does your mother look like?" he said, smiling wickedly. "Is she good looking too?" He swung his blade wide and purposely missed taking her head off. She ignored the question and tried to keep her focus.

"You realize your future is severely limited by your sex. Your lack of size and strength will eventually be your undoing," he said, circling around her.

"I'm prepared to do whatever it takes," she said, letting her fury fuel her.

"I suppose you do have other attributes. Maybe you can use those to get ahead," he said, grinning evilly and striking her blade over and over to drive her back again. No matter how hard Gypsy looked, she still saw no opportunity to get on the attack.

Gypsy glared at him. "That's not what I meant, you bastard."

"Stop!" Gavin yelled again.

Now what?

He walked right up to Gypsy and got into *her* personal space. He leaned down and his golden eye squinted at her. "Why are you talking to him?"

"Because he won't shut up! He just keeps going on and on."

"That is his strategy, dear, and it's working. He could have easily killed you at least three times in that last minute. You do not yet have the skill to carry on a conversation with your opponent. Too many things can go wrong with even the smallest distraction. Don't let his words wield your emotions. Learn to ignore his comments and focus only on the fight."

Gypsy nodded and returned to her position. They engaged again and she resisted the urge to respond to his shitty comments. She was, however, in awe of his skill. She had never seen anyone with so much grace and precision. He commanded every molecule of that sword and it yielded to his will like a smitten lover. Desmond stopped his attack and backed up a few steps giving her the opportunity she was waiting for.

Gypsy flew at him determined not to be put on the defensive again. As her saber crashed against his, she barely noticed a movement out of the corner of her eye. In a blur Desmond brought his other hand up and smashed his palm into the flat side of her saber as it was locked with his. The force of the blow sent her saber flying out of her hand and onto the arena floor.

She bolted for it and Desmond threw himself forward tackling her to the ground. As the panic exploded in her mind, she lost her focus and blindly struggled. Desmond immediately let go of her and got up. He took a few steps back and looked back at Gavin. He pointed at Gypsy with the tip of his blade and said, "What are you going to do about that little problem?"

Gavin sighed and folded his arms. "I'm not quite sure yet. This is not the first time it's cropped up." Gypsy got to her feet and retrieved her saber. She felt like an ass for freaking out like that, but she couldn't help it. Every time she was grabbed and restrained, her mind just went crazy. It was the rape all over again.

Desmond got into a ready position and motioned for her to attack. She tried another attack strategy but he deflected it easily and put her back on the defensive. His fighting style was definitely a hybrid of many styles. There were both Æssyrian and Kirillian qualities and who knew what else. It was very difficult to predict his moves and this was becoming as much a mental challenge as a physical one. But what annoyed her most was that he continued his conversation with Gavin while they fought, as though she were a minor distraction. *I wonder what it would be like to be that good.*

As she stole a few glances at her father she saw him watch Desmond with a strange mixture of admiration and disappointment. She knew both of those looks well but had never seen them together before. With another bizarre move Desmond hooked the top of his blade under the hilt of her saber and sent it tumbling to the ground again. Gypsy darted for it but this time Desmond did not pursue her. Instead he addressed Gavin.

"You need to desensitize her. You're focusing too much on her not getting caught and not enough on what she's going to do if someone does get a hold of her."

"The problem with that is she cannot match the strength of her male counterparts," Gavin said thoughtfully.

"She doesn't need to match their strength. We just need to teach her a few dirty tricks to buy her a chance to get loose. That's all," Desmond said, driving her backward again.

"Is that all?" Gavin said with bitter sarcasm. "Then I will put that part of her training in your hands. Maybe you can think of something too. Now it can be *our* little problem."

Despite being engaged in conversation, Gypsy noticed that Desmond watched her intently the whole time. He seemed to know every move she was going to make. Before she realized it, her strategy had shifted from a sparring mentality to a fighting one. Now she understood why Gavin had recalled him. She could fight with him without holding back from the kill because he was that good. So she spent the rest of the afternoon purging her pain the way her father taught her—by trying to inflict it.

Chapter 20

Harlan leaned into General Kharon's room and was happy to see him awake and sitting up. "May I come in and check your bandage?" she asked.

"Of course. I was hoping for an opportunity to thank you for your good work on my injury. Sometimes medical care for foreign combatants can be, shall we say, substandard and here I am graced with the emperor's personal physician."

Harlan walked over to the bed grinning and shaking her head. "I may be his personal physician but not his exclusive one, much to his annoyance. Although I'm sure the emperor would prefer I sit around all day waiting for him to stub his toe." She pulled the sheet down to the upper portion of his hips and began to peel off the bandage covering his abdomen.

"You are as charming as you are alluring. The rumors of your beauty do not do you justice," Kharon said with a smoky seductive edge to his voice.

Harlan softly giggled at his flirtatious attempt to flatter her. "Gavin warned me about you."

"Oh? What did he tell you about me?"

"He said to keep my ears covered from your serpent tongue because you usually catch whatever you pursue," she said as she cleaned the incision and checked his staples.

Now it was Kharon's turn to laugh, grimacing with each chuckle. "May I ask you for a favor?"

"Sure. What is it?" Harlan said, placing a fresh bandage over his wound.

"Would you ask your daughter to come see me before she leaves today?"

"I'll ask her, but I can't promise that she'll come. Her emotions are still very raw," Harlan said, frowning.

* * * *

Gypsy sat in the chair by Caraculla's bed looking for any sign of life. Her lover lay there barely alive and cold to the touch. Every time she thought about his injury in the arena she wanted to break down and sob. She didn't though. She was forcing herself to be brave. Gypsy got up and was about to leave when her mother came in. Harlan looked exhausted. Her black hair was pulled back into a tight ponytail with a few rebel locks hanging free and her eyes had that warm sorrow that always made Gypsy want to cry. She felt bad for her mother because Gypsy knew she was doing everything she could think of to save Caraculla. Gypsy focused on what her father had said—that if anyone could save him it was her mother. That had to be enough for now.

Harlan sighed, folded her arms and leaned against the wall. "General Kharon wants to see you."

"What for?"

"I don't know, Gypsy. He's probably just curious about you. You're quite famous in gossip circles."

Gypsy grimaced. "I don't want to talk to *him*."

Harlan nodded as if she'd anticipated that. "Just stop in for a moment. He's very nice and I think it would be good for you. You don't have to stay long."

"Fine," Gypsy said, fully expecting to hate the guy. She walked the few doors down and knocked on Kharon's open door. The general was propped up in bed with a white sheet covering his hips. Gypsy felt her cheeks warm as she realized he was naked under that sheet and the bulge of his cock was very visible. He was a huge, powerful man with a massive chest and thick arms. His attractiveness was all raw animal power and she found herself responding to his authority, taking care not to stare him in the eyes. His face was harsh and brutal, a strong-willed man accustomed to being obeyed and she found herself very curious about the slave tattoo by his right eye. She'd never heard of anyone becoming a freeman from a slave and she was sure that must be one hell of a great story.

"How is Colonel Caraculla?" Kharon asked.

Gypsy came in noticing the half-empty bottle of pureed meat on the table next to him. *Yuck.* She sat down next to his bed. Thick bandages were wrapped around his stomach. "He's not doing very well."

"I'm sorry to hear that," he said with such sincerity, her animosity toward him melted. "He's an excellent soldier and a brave warrior. I hope he recovers." She wanted to hate him but she just couldn't. What happened between Kharon and Caraculla wasn't personal—it was how soldiers made rank. It was as simple as that. "I hear you are also quite the warrior," he said.

Her face grew warm again and she suddenly didn't know what to do with her hands. "I'm still learning. A lot depends on my big match coming up soon."

"I know." Kharon studied her so closely she could almost feel his gaze moving across her skin.

A sudden primal hunger awoke in her and she pushed it down annoyed. *This is not the time or the place to get turned on.*

"I've seen you spar," he said in a thick whisper. He sounded like he'd seen her having sex and wanted so much more. "You're very talented."

Gypsy looked up and met his gaze. In that split second she felt naked and unprotected. She was ashamed to admit she liked how feminine he made her feel. His piercing mismatched eyes sliced into her and recognized her hidden desire for him. "I intend to watch your senior match if I'm able," he said.

"I understand you and Caraculla were on campaign together a few years ago," she said.

He grunted and nodded. "The Battle of Amarick. That was the first rebellion Emperor Megolyth had to deal with after he won the throne. I've been on campaign with your father too."

"He speaks very highly of you."

"Your father is a shameless flatterer."

Gypsy let the conversation drop for a moment. Then she said, "May I ask you a personal question?"

Kharon shifted to get comfortable and gestured to the water bottle on the side table. She handed it to him. "Ask me anything." He took a long drink and handed it back to her.

"How did you get that chain tattoo? Were you really a slave once?"

Kharon grinned but there was no humor behind it. "I was, but I bought my freedom at a young age. Now it's my turn to ask you a personal question."

"Okay."

"Is it true you were raped while sparring with another warrior?"

Gypsy sat very still unable to believe he would ask her such a thing and horribly embarrassed he even knew about it. But she guessed it was only fair since she'd asked him about his slavery. She knew some slaves suffered terrible cruelties. Thankfully it was not a common practice in the empire.

"Yes, it's true," she said, looking him hard in the eyes, her fingers nervously fidgeting.

"Why would you continue to pursue this life, knowing full well it could happen again? Why not give all this up and marry Caraculla? You claim to love him."

The question had bite and Kharon knew it. He was testing her, wondering how strong her commitment was to being a soldier.

"I know I could get raped again but crummy things happen sometimes, don't they? I'm sure lots of shitty things happened to you as a slave but you didn't quit. As for Caraculla, I do love him but this is who I am and he understands that, which is why I love him. Does that make sense?"

"Yes," he said. "But now I wonder what kind of a career Gavin will allow his little girl. I think he'll let you reach the top only to hold you back in the end."

Gypsy shook her head not wanting to listen to this. "He wouldn't do that."

"Yes he would, Gypsy," Kharon said. "He did it to your brother Northe. Northe had to leave the Empire to find a position worthy of his training and skills. You will too."

Gypsy got up to leave. This was too much for her right now. "It was nice meeting you, Kharon."

"Maybe you'll stop by again before I get discharged."

Gypsy took a deep breath and let it out slowly. Fatigue made her eyes burn. "Maybe," she said.

Chapter 21

Gypsy hadn't expected to like her brother Desmond, especially after their spar, but as they sat together over drinks at the local tavern, he kind of grew on her. He told her about his problems with Gavin, how they'd never really gotten along and how—maybe, just maybe—things were starting to change. After a few more drinks, the crushing pain of Caraculla withdrew to a dull ache in her heart. The buzz helped a lot too. "So," she said. "Tell me about Northe."

Desmond looked as though she'd thrown a drink in his face. Then, after a long pause, he said, "He was the best. Gavin's crowning jewel and his most likely successor." Desmond twisted his drink on the table making a wet pattern in the condensation. "It was hard for me when I came here. You see Kirillians all over the place now, but back then, there weren't any. I'm sure I don't have to tell you how hard it is to be different.

"Northe wasn't just my brother, he became my best friend. He was the best swordsman I'd ever seen and he taught me a lot, but his fights with Gavin were terrible things to watch. They were two colossal egos battling for the top spot. I want to believe Gavin did everything he could to reach out to my brother, but the truth was they were rivals in every sense of the word. There were rumors Gavin had even bedded Northe's girlfriend, Bethany.

"Northe was always talking about going to a rival kingdom and one day destroying Gavin. After Northe got wind of the rumors about Bethany, that was it. He became convinced they were true and left to serve another king. I like to say I regret not going with him, but even then I knew where his fate lay." Desmond shrugged and downed the rest of his drink. "The rest I'm sure you know."

Gypsy nodded. "Northe led an army against Gavin, lost and was killed."

"Actually, he led *two* armies against Gavin. The first time, Gavin let him go. It was during the second attack that Gavin killed him. Northe's biggest problem was his arrogance. He was convinced he could best Gavin. Don't get me wrong, Northe was really good, just not as good as he perceived himself to be. That was why he let himself get killed."

Gypsy considered this for a moment. "Did Gavin sleep with Bethany?"

Desmond signaled the barmaid for the tab. Then he gave her a sober look. "He says no, but no one knows the truth. I'm sure he did but I doubt Gavin would ever admit it. He has a hard time owning up to his mistakes."

"So what about you? How come out of all of Gavin's sons you managed to survive?"

Desmond shrugged. "I lack ambition to put it in his words. I like being a soldier. I like fighting and I like not having a big office filled up with paperwork and a shitload of responsibility. As for my survival, I owe a lot of that to Northe. You see Gavin was so focused on making Northe in his image that he didn't waste a lot of time trying to crush my personal rebellion against him. By the time Northe was dead, I was already a seasoned soldier and too old to bully. So he punished me in other ways."

"Why?" Gypsy said, pouring herself another drink. She was riveted by his story and feeling kind of good.

"Why do you think? All of his most promising progeny are dead and the one who lives is his biggest disappointment. I may as well have been a daughter," he said and burst out laughing. "So we would fight and he would get pissed, bust me down and find crappy remote duty stations to send me to. Then he'd bring me back for a campaign or a police action and after it was over, we'd fight again and off I went." Some old soldiers started singing an ancient battle song at the bar slurring each word. Desmond glanced at them and shook his head.

"That's awful," Gypsy said.

"I got used to it. But *Loss* was the worst and he knew it. When he brought me back, I would have done almost anything not to go back there. I think prison would have been preferable. You want to hear something amusing?"

"What?" Gypsy leaned forward eagerly.

"I have made master sergeant so many times and subsequently been busted down again, that I've memorized all of their tests. Now, every time I go up for another promotion, they have to write a new test just for me."

Gypsy leaned back and broke into peals of happy laughter. "It must irritate Gavin to no end every time you make rank again."

Desmond got up and grinned at her. "You'd better believe it. Ready to go? Gavin will kill me if I keep you out too late."

"One more question?" she said hopefully.

"Alright, go."

"Is it true that you could have been one of the arena grandmasters?"

Desmond ran his hand up the side of his face to the back of his neck and rubbed. He looked at her and let out a heavy sigh. "I don't know, maybe."

"I can't imagine why you wouldn't want to hold such an honor," she said.

Desmond smirked in disgust. "With that *honor* comes a lot of responsibility. You have to defend that title every time your name comes up on the rotation when someone new is trying to make rank. It doesn't happen that often since not many people climb to that high of a rank but still. Besides there are few things I find less appealing than trying to kill someone you've served in combat with. To me it's just twisted and I don't understand what it proves to kill an ally. I mean what if Caraculla had succeeded in killing Kharon? Would either military be better off?"

Gypsy nodded. "I never thought of it that way. It kind of makes sense. Anyway maybe things will change some day."

"That is going to be up to you."

"Me? I doubt I'm going to be able to change anything," she said, shaking her head.

"Baby, you already started changing things the minute you stepped into the arena for your first fight. I think you're going to turn most of these stuffy traditions upside down and I for one am looking forward to watching it. Now let's get out of here."

Gypsy smiled and tossed back her drink. "Okay I'm ready," she said.

* * * *

"Who the hell is that?" Gypsy said to Desmond as they rode up to Caraculla's villa. There were three Razorbacks there, two women both with cheap-looking armor and one with a long braid down her back, and one man who looked rather tall and skinny. Gypsy disliked them immediately.

The trio were wandering around the villa looking like they were trying to find a way in. Although the doors were usually unlocked, Gavin had made Gypsy promise she'd lock them until Caraculla got out of the hospital. Now she was glad she'd listened to him.

Gypsy rode up to the three with Desmond close behind. They both drew their sabers. "Who are you and what the hell do you want?" she said.

The Razorback woman with the long braid came forward. "My name is Cassy and I'm Colonel Caraculla's cousin." She gestured to the skinny man. "This is Reese, my husband."

"And I'm Celina," the other woman said, stepping forward. Gypsy could see now that she was older with a square muscular body. "I'm Cassy's mother. We've come to collect the colonel's things."

Gypsy glared at them and sheathed her weapon. It probably wasn't a good idea to get into a fight with a venom-spitting Razorback. "What are you talking about? He's not dead."

Celina gave Gypsy a patronizing smile. "He's dead. We've already petitioned the emperor to remove him from life support."

"The fuck you *will* remove him from life support!" Gypsy snarled.

Desmond came forward and touched her arm to calm her. He studied the three. "Listen, it's late and obviously the petition hasn't been granted yet or we would have heard about it. So why don't you people go back to wherever it is you're staying and we can settle this in the morning?"

Celina mounted her hyperia. "That's fine with me," she said. She arched her back and gave Gypsy a nasty, condescending look. "But I want to warn you, young lady, don't try to take anything out of here without our permission because we will charge you with theft."

Before Gypsy could react, Desmond grabbed her arm and gave her a strong look shaking his head. She hated that he was right. She had no right to even be here. Caraculla was not her husband.

"We'll see you in the morning," Celina said. She rode off with Cassy and Reese in tow.

Gypsy ran her fingers through her hair and felt her tears fighting for release. *Great, Caraculla isn't even dead and already the vultures are trying to pick away at his stuff. What the hell am I going to do now?*

Chapter 22

Harlan wanted to be grateful but she wasn't. Although Caraculla was stable, he hadn't improved since his admission and she was losing hope he'd ever be able to come out of this. To make matters worse, as she'd told Krull before, there was no case study for an injury like this. Usually the victim died within days. It was a miracle Caraculla lasted this long. She was worried they were causing him undue suffering with no hope of recovery. She checked his vital signs and frowned. Krull came in, leaned against the wall and folded his arms.

"I've just been notified that the colonel's relatives have arrived from the Razorback Queendom. They've petitioned the emperor to take him off what they're calling life support. They want to sell his villa and take his belongings back with them."

Harlan glanced down at Caraculla. To tell the truth, he looked worse than dead. "What do we do now? We can't keep him like this forever, it's inhumane."

"Before we get an order to cut him off, there's one more thing I'd like to try," Krull said.

She sat down in the chair next to Caraculla's bed. "What?"

"I want to put him deeper."

Harlan rubbed her face. She was so confused. Sending him into a deeper coma just seemed to prolong the inevitable. "I don't know. How much deeper can he go?"

Krull unfolded his arms and went to the monitors. He draped his dark blond hair behind his ears. His handsome face was grim and filled with dark purpose. "I can take him down a little more."

"What good will that do?"

"It may restart his internal healing process. As you said, he's practically dead already. We should risk everything since there's nothing left to lose."

She stared out the window. "We don't have a lot of time. The emperor is going to call me in there and ask me what he should do. What am I supposed to tell him?"

"Tell him that we still have some hope and we haven't exhausted all of our options."

"How much longer do you need?" she asked, hoping Emperor Megolyth would side with them.

Krull nodded as if he knew she'd come around. "At least one more day. I'll order the revival machine for the morning. He'll either wake up tomorrow or he won't. Either way, we'll know and it will be over."

"I'll try and get you until tomorrow afternoon. But after that, I'm afraid we'll be out of options."

* * * *

Emperor Megolyth was the kind of ÆEssyrian man who got better looking the older he became. His towering six-foot-six frame was a fortress of large, thick muscles and his long black hair showed no sign of gray. Today he wore it in an elaborate braid that ran down his back. His skin was a pleasing forest-green and his face, with its powerful jaw and high cheekbones was heartbreakingly handsome. He sat in his favorite place, the palace balcony watching the groundskeepers tending to the spring flowers. He wore a long red and gold robe with nothing underneath. It was just barely covering his nakedness.

Harlan walked out and he got up to kiss her. A tiny flutter of excitement tickled her belly but she pushed it down. She took a seat next to him.

"You haven't come to see me in a long time," he said after a long pause.

"You are a very busy man and you know it. Besides, the clinic and Gavin keep me pretty busy myself," she replied.

"You must be here about Colonel Caraculla."

"Yes, Highness."

Megolyth fixed her with a sober stare. He ran his index finger over his lips. "Is he going to live or not?"

Harlan took a deep breath. *Here it goes.* "I don't know but we'd like until tomorrow afternoon to try one more thing. If he doesn't respond, we won't contest the family."

Megolyth stared out at the gardens. He reached out, took her hand and squeezed it.

"Beautiful out here, isn't it?"

"Yes, Highness."

Megolyth fixed his gaze on her again. "I'm sorry about what happened to him," he said. "I know how close you all are." He paused, and then said, "You have until tomorrow at noon." He tugged her hand and she got up and went over to him. "Kiss me," he said in a whisper she barely heard.

Harlan leaned down and kissed him. It was a tender, sensuous kiss from a time long ago when they'd briefly been lovers. "Thank you," she said against his lips.

Then he let her hand slide out of his and she quietly walked out the door.

Chapter 23

At the crack of dawn Gypsy rushed to Gavin's office to tell him what had happened with Caraculla's relatives. Her father sat behind his desk listening quietly. When she had finished, she threw her hands up in the air and said, "I don't see how they can do this. He's not even dead yet!"

Gavin rocked back in his chair thinking. He interlaced his fingers over his belly. "I don't know how we can stop them. Unfortunately, my dear, because you're not married and there's no will, you have no right to his home or property."

"I don't give a shit about his home or property. They can have it for all I care. Please. You can't let them just turn him off!"

A knock sounded on the door and Harlan came in. There were dark circles under her eyes and tiny frown lines around her mouth. She wore her white lab coat and looked like she'd been up all night. "I take it you both know about Caraculla's relatives."

Gavin nodded grimly and Gypsy threw herself into the chair opposite his desk. "What are those snakes trying to do now?" she asked her mother in a biting tone.

Harlan leaned against the wall by the door. "They wanted to turn him off yesterday but I managed to convince the emperor to give us until noon today. Krull wants to try one more thing. If it doesn't work…"

A desperate silence filled the room. Gypsy pulled herself out of the chair and began to pace. "That's it? Today at noon? That's bullshit!" She looked back at her father with a volatile mixture of fury and anguish. "I will stop anyone who tries to turn him off and then you can bury us together. Because no one is fucking touching him!"

Another knock sounded. "Come in," Gavin said. "Join the fucking party."

Desmond and Rakon came in looking guilty. They took two seats by the far wall. Finally Desmond cleared his throat and said, "Rakon has an idea."

Everyone looked over at the master sergeant surprised. Rakon wasn't known for his brilliant ideas.

"Well," Gavin said, obviously not holding out much hope. "What is it?"

Rakon glanced around the room nervously. "If they can kill him and get his stuff because he's not married, then let's get him married."

Gavin sat up a little and squinted at Rakon. "I don't follow you."

Rakon shrugged as if it were obvious. "Why not have Gypsy marry him by Æssyrian Marriage?"

Everyone sat in stunned silence as they rolled this possibility around in their heads. Gavin looked at Desmond. "Have you ever heard of a woman calling an Æssyrian Marriage before?"

"No, but I don't know why it *couldn't* be done. I don't believe there's a law against it," the Kirillian said.

Gypsy felt all her fear and pain ease. She sat up in her chair. "Would the High Priest do it?"

Harlan made a face and paced the room. "Wait a minute here. Gypsy, you need to think about this. You could be a bride and a widow in the course of a few hours. Are you sure you want that?"

Gavin was lost in thought. His eyes seemed to gleam with pure evil. "Of course," he murmured. "How brilliant. Those corrupt priests will do almost anything for money. The real question is whether the emperor allow it."

"I know what could happen, Mom," Gypsy said. "I love him and I want to do this. Besides, if I'm his wife, I say when he comes off life support, right?"

Harlan looked at Gavin. He nodded and she said, "I suppose you're right."

Gypsy grinned. "Then it's all worth it."

* * * *

Gypsy had seen Megolyth lots of times riding through the city but never this close before. He exuded a cool sexuality that was very erotic. The emperor's long black hair had a silky sheen and hung loose around his shoulders. Brilliant yellow eyes calmly took in everyone and everything around him. She had to try hard not to stare at him as he sat on his throne thinking about their proposal.

Off to his right, Caraculla's relatives were fuming. "Your Highness," Celina said. "May I say something now?"

Megolyth glanced at her. "No." He looked over at his adviser and the resident High Priest. "Well?" he asked. "Is there any law against a woman calling an Æssyrian Marriage?"

The two men glanced at each other. The advisor, a short, thin man who reminded Gypsy of a rat spoke first. "There is no Æssyrian law on the books, Highness, that forbids it," he said in a voice full of intelligence and authority. Gypsy was prepared to hate him but decided she liked him after all.

The High Priest fidgeted and spoke next. "Highness," he began, "although there is no *law* against it, it is a forbidden practice. If the lady should do such a thing, she would be considered an outlaw bride to the temple."

Megolyth stared at the High Priest not hiding his contempt. "Why is it forbidden? Men do it all the time."

"Because women are considered…" He paused, looking embarrassed. "I mean, in the scriptures, they are considered property."

Gypsy rolled her eyes and blew out a disgusted gust of air. Harlan frowned at her and shook her head ever so slightly.

The emperor ignored Gypsy's outburst. "But they are not slaves," Megolyth countered. "They own property, conduct business on behalf of their husbands, and can inherit everything their husband owns."

The High Priest nodded. "That is correct, Highness."

"So basically, what Gypsy is asking for is to become Caraculla's property in the eyes of the temple. She would become another piece of his property, just like his equipment and his villa. They already have a well-known, long-established relationship. I don't see how that would make her any kind of outlaw."

Everyone looked at each other. "But, Highness, he's a dead man!" Celina wailed.

"Unconscious is not dead, you asshole," Gypsy snapped at her.

Megolyth glared at both of them. "Be silent."

The High Priest was clearly flustered. Finally he shrugged in surrender and said, "As always, you are correct, Highness. But may I point out that he is not Æssyrian."

"He is a member of our military," Megolyth said. "He has taken an oath to fight, and if necessary, die for this Empire. Are you telling me that he is not subject to Æssyrian law? That is the weakest argument you've given me so far. Besides she is Æssyrian and as I believe, only one party need be. Am I correct in that assumption?"

"Of course, Highness." The priest held up his hands in surrender.

Megolyth looked back at Gypsy. "Are you sure this is what you want?"

"Yes, Highness," Gypsy said, trying to hide her excitement. *I'm going to win, I'm going to win!*

The emperor gestured from the priest to her and said, "Then do the ceremony now."

The High Priest knitted his brow. "But, Highness, I need to…"

"I said do it *now!*" the emperor roared. The High Priest rushed over and recited the oath to Gypsy. She repeated everything he told her to and that was it. Not exactly how she'd envisioned her wedding day but she had what she wanted—more time for Caraculla.

"What are your plans now?" Megolyth said, staring at Caraculla's relatives.

Celina bowed to him. "We'll be returning to the Queendom, Highness."

Megolyth got up. "Good," he said, barely hiding his anger. "An excellent idea. The sooner the better."

Chapter 24

Harlan entered Caraculla's room feeling like the bottom of her stomach had dropped out. Krull had brought the colonel's body temperature up to normal but there was still no significant brain activity showing on the monitor. Large electrodes were attached to Caraculla's head and thick leather straps held his arms, wrists and legs firmly to the hospital bed. It looked disturbingly like he was about to be tortured.

The room was empty except for Krull making last-minute adjustments, his two assistants and Harlan. He turned and fixed her with his piercing blue eyes. "Can you lock the door please, Doctor?"

Harlan went to the door and realized her palms were sweating. She glanced at the clock. It was just past noon. If Gypsy hadn't married Caraculla, they'd be taking him off the machines right now. She sighed, turned the lock and wiped her damp palms on her pant legs. She walked back over and watched Krull making the final power check. She'd never seen this done before, but knew from reading up on it that shocking the brain was a brutal process. She wondered for the tenth time today if she shouldn't just call this off. But something inside her hung on to that little bit of hope. Krull was right; they owed it to Caraculla to *try* everything.

Krull moved up alongside Caraculla and nodded for his assistants to take their places. He looked at Harlan. "Once we begin this, we cannot stop until we're sure he's dead. Do you understand?"

Harlan swallowed. "Yes," she replied, moving up on the other side of the bed.

Krull signaled the assistant by the revival machine to begin.

Caraculla's body jolted as if a bolt of lightning had hit it. Every muscle stiffened and went rigid as his teeth drove deep into the rubber bit in his mouth. A high-pitched screech filled the silence sending violent shivers down Harlan's spine. A rush of pity and fear filled Harlan and she fought hard not to call the exercise off. The machine hissed like a serpent as it was put on idle. The colonel relaxed and all eyes looked to the brain wave monitor.

Nothing.

Krull glanced at Harlan, his face a determined mask. "We go again," he said.

Harlan opened her mouth to protest but forced herself to close it. She had to trust his judgment. She was much too close to the situation. *He told you this would be rough.*

The machine powered up again and Caraculla convulsed, his back bowing off the bed. Muffled screeches filled the room forcing tears from Harlan's eyes. Under her breath she prayed for it to stop. Perhaps death was better than this horrible torture. Impatient with her emotions, she dried her tears with her sleeve and was relieved to see Caraculla relax again. She looked over at the monitor.

Something was happening.

Like fireworks back on Earth, the neurons in the Razorback's brain began lighting up, moving faster and faster until it resembled normal activity. Harlan couldn't believe what she was seeing.

"What do we do now?" she asked in awe.

Krull removed the electrodes from Caraculla and applied some salve to the burn marks. "Now," he said, exuding the same determined confidence as before. "We wait and hope he wakes up on his own."

Chapter 25

It was early afternoon when Gavin stopped practice and called Gypsy aside. Desmond came over with her. "Since the match is tomorrow," Gavin said to Gypsy, "I'm going to show you one last thing then let you off for the day."

He turned to Desmond. "You've done an excellent job. Take the afternoon off and report back to me after the match."

Desmond stared at his father in disbelief, then shrugged and left whistling a happy tune. Gavin turned his attention back to Gypsy. "Come with me," he said, stalking out to the middle of the arena. Gypsy followed him nervously, wondering what new form of torture this might be.

From a sheath behind his back, Gavin pulled out a small, thick, double-bladed knife with finger holes where the handle should be. "See this?" he asked, holding it up for her inspection. Gypsy nodded. "When I was a boy at the whorehouse, many of the women had these and learned how to use them with deadly precision." He paused, looking uncomfortable. "My mother taught me how to use the small blade and it often came in handy in the rough neighborhood where I grew up.

"The first time I saw her use it was when I was just coming into adolescence. She had a john in the room we shared who liked beating his women while he fucked them. Finally, after an hour of this, she'd had enough. Pulling the weapon from under the mattress, she cut his throat from ear to ear. We spent the rest of the night riding to the outskirts of the kingdom and disposing of the body. I used this small blade to cut up an adult Æssyrian male and it took me less than an hour.

"After that night, I never lost a fight because I always had this as a back-up weapon. I think in your case, you should wear yours on your hip, that way if someone gets you on the ground, you can pull the blade quickly even if you're pinned." He gestured to the arena floor. "We'll practice a few scenarios. Get down on your belly," he said.

Gypsy felt a tense nausea twist her gut. As slowly as she could, she went down on the ground. Gavin knelt down over her and she felt panic filling her head. "I hate this," she complained.

He ignored her and put the blade in her hand. With his hand over hers, he mimicked her pulling it from her side so she could feel the movement of the strike. He did the same thing from several angles, showing her how easy it was to strike at her attacker even with someone pinning her to the ground. Suddenly, the intense revulsion of being on the ground lifted leaving only a dull unease.

Gavin made her practice over and over again as he loosely held her in various positions to the arena floor. Because he didn't use much force, the feeling of being trapped didn't overtake her and she could concentrate on getting the blade out of the sheath and attacking. When they were done, he held his hand out to her and helped her up.

She secured the sheath to her hip concealing it under her armor. "Won't I be disqualified for using this?"

"No," Gavin said. "Anything is fair as long as we declare you have it on you."

Gypsy sensed vulnerability in her father. He was showing her something she'd never seen before. He'd told her about a part of his past she was sure he'd never told anyone. "I'm the only one you've ever told that story to, aren't I?"

Gavin met her gaze and she saw the walls go back up. "Go home and get some rest. Tomorrow is going to be a demanding day."

"I was going to stop and see Caraculla."

"No," Gavin said. "Your mother said they're running tests and she'll let you know when they're done."

Footfalls echoed through the arena and they both looked up to see Grand Duchess Tannyth Von Goth approaching. Assuming she wanted to talk to him, Gavin went over to her. "How can I serve, lady?"

Her gaze never wavered from Gypsy. "I'd like to speak to your daughter in private, if I may," she said.

Gavin gestured for Gypsy to come over and left the arena.

Gypsy approached the grand duchess wiping the nervous sweat from her palms. "What can I do for you, lady?" Gypsy asked.

Tannyth smiled at her. "I want you to know I think you are a tremendous talent and if you win tomorrow, I would be honored if you would allow me to be your sponsor."

Gypsy didn't know what to say. A sponsor was a huge coup. They paid for training, arena time, equipment, you name it, and they always had deep pockets. "I think the honor would be mine."

"I also wanted to tell you it's no secret how much I *hate* your father. He's rude, impulsive and much too aggressive, but that being said, he's also the most gifted general in our history. If anyone can help you win tomorrow, it's him. So," she said, holding her hand out to shake Gypsy's, "good luck and beat that bastard Drake to a pulp."

Gypsy laughed despite her nervousness. She shook Tannyth's hand. "Thank you."

The grand duchess held Gypsy's hand for a moment longer than was comfortable, then she let go and quietly walked out of the arena leaving a confused but elated Gypsy in her wake.

Chapter 26

Gypsy waited on the sidelines with Gavin listening to the roar of the crowd inside the arena. One would think after all this time, she'd be used to it but she wasn't. The pounding and shouting never failed to fuel a nervous adrenaline that coursed through her every time she waited for her turn. As much as she hated to admit it, it was comforting to have her father nearby chewing and puffing on his cigar. He was so calm and confident it made her feel as though everything was under control like this was just another training exercise.

From the other side of the arena, she could see Drake. He looked confident too, impatiently gesturing for his assistant to adjust this piece of armor or that one. She could see him stealing an occasional glance her way and it made her slightly ill. Gavin placed his arm around her and squeezed her shoulder once. She looked over at him and he grinned. "Don't worry, dear," he said. "He'll never know what hit him."

Gypsy sure hoped he was right. Running her hand down to her hip, she felt the reassuring sheath of the small blade Gavin had given her. It filled her with the confidence of knowing she wouldn't be completely unarmed if she should lose her saber.

The announcer, who'd been droning on about the prior combatants finally stopped. The noise of the crowd died down, leaving only the dull buzz of a thousand hushed conversations.

Conversations about her.

Drake, being the more senior fighter, was announced first. He came onto the field waving and holding his saber up high. He obviously had quite a following. Many of the military men stomped their feet chanting his name. Gypsy wondered about the loyalty of his fans. She had the distinct feeling he could have been anyone, as long as he wasn't *the girl*.

Gypsy came out next. As Gavin had taught her, she held her saber up saluting the crowd and they responded with whistling and a wave of cheering noise. She turned to face Drake who looked as though he was enjoying a private joke. He pointed to the arena floor and she understood his meaning. *No rapes for you today, you big piece of shit.*

Silence fell over the arena and they began to circle each other.

"Decided you needed another good fuck, little girl?" he said.

Gypsy was surprised the taunt didn't bother her. In response, she launched a punishing attack, slamming her weapon into his with a speed that shocked even her. Drake stumbled back and glared at her. He was obviously not expecting her to take the offensive. With an ear-splitting roar, he charged her and she easily danced aside.

As the battle between them raged on, Gypsy began to realize Gavin was right. Drake—who'd seemed so invincible before—was slower and clumsier than she remembered. When he couldn't strike a blow, which was every time he swung at her, he would get more and more frustrated, taking wild chances.

So Gypsy decided to punish him for being sloppy.

He came in close trying to deliver a cut to her leg and Gypsy easily hopped away, tagging him with a nasty slice to the cheek. Blood poured from the wound and he snarled in pain and rage. Time and time again he lunged at her, leaving himself open in tiny ways she would never have noticed before. She took advantage of each one, slicing her blade across his flesh over and over again.

Then, in a careless frustration born of wrath, he leaped on her like a predatory cat. The move caught her off-guard and brought her to the ground on her belly pinned under him. Panic exploded inside her but she forced herself to focus.

As they grappled together on the ground, Gypsy resisted the urge to punch him and grabbed the small knife instead. The metal rings fit over her fingers like an old friend and relief flooded over her. In that tiny moment, she loved her father more than words could express. He'd given her an escape hatch from a horrible and humiliating prison. No one would ever be able to rape her again.

Drake was fumbling with her armor, trying to remove some part of it that would allow him to violate her and complete his threat. But Gypsy was ready. Twisting back, she gripped the knife tightly and drove the blade deep under his chin right into his soft palate. Blood sprayed down on her and he scrambled off her in seconds. Thanks to the finger holds, the knife stayed firmly in her hand despite the slick blood.

Gypsy rolled away from him, sheathing the knife and grabbed her saber. As she jumped to her feet, she saw Drake was obviously hurt, shaking his big head and spraying blood everywhere. The referee came over to see if Drake wanted to concede but before he could reach the wounded warrior, Drake lifted his saber and charged her again. The crowd, who up to this point had been cheering them both on, suddenly fell into a tense silence as everyone realized this had turned into a fight to the death.

Gypsy had no love for Drake but she certainly didn't want to kill him. She stalled the warrior, dodging him and staying out of striking distance. Then one of his slices almost took her head off and she realized he was never going to stop. He was determined to kill her and she had to defend herself.

As the realization became clearer, a terrible sorrow filled her heart. She knew even if Drake decided to stop now and live, he was finished. Her mind touched on the story Desmond had told her about Northe and Gavin. At that moment, she fully understood *why* Gavin was forced to kill his son. Northe was so determined to kill his father, Gavin had no other choice.

Drake lumbered around the arena on the attack, his reputation and career in ruins. He could never live with her defeating him. He *wanted* her to kill him. It was suicide by opponent. Drake's exhaustion and blood loss were manifesting themselves in weak, uncoordinated attacks but he never let up. Then, when he came a little too close and the wind of the missed blow brushed her cheek, she landed the death strike. It drove deep into the belly gap of his armor. She shoved the blade from side to side, opening him up and spilling his guts all over the packed black sand. The pungent, moist smell of gore filled the air.

Drake collapsed to his knees, blood flowing from his mouth and gut. "*Finish me*," he rasped.

Gypsy raised her blade as a rush of adrenaline spiked her blood. She brought it down in a dazzling strike and took her opponent's head clean off.

The crowd went wild.

Staring down at the severed head she felt all kinds of emotions resurfacing, emotions she had locked away for too long. She wanted to cry but forced her expression to remain stoic. With little drama, she raised her blade triumphantly and walked off the field.

Chapter 27

Gypsy stood under the harsh light of the arena washroom feeling drained and a little sad. Drake might have been crazy but surely there was some future for him other than death. Unfortunately, so many Æssyrian men thought that way. For those proud stubborn men, pride was everything.

With a soiled, wet rag she washed the blood off her face and armor. A longing for Caraculla twisted her heart when suddenly the curtain pulled back. She turned to tell whoever it was to fuck off when she realized it was her mother.

Harlan came over and hugged her. That was it. Tears began running down her face and she was powerless to stop them. Like a little girl, she pushed her face into Harlan's shoulder and softly cried while her mother held her.

"I didn't want to kill him. I just wanted to win. He left me no choice," she sniffled.

"I know. You were never in charge of his fate. He made his own decisions. You fought a good and honorable fight. It was all you could do." She pulled back and stroked Gypsy's cheek. "I am so proud of you," she said softly. "When you're ready I need you to come with me. I have something to show you."

* * * *

Gypsy entered Caraculla's room terrified of what she would find. She walked in slowly, tentatively, but filled with hope. She could barely believe what she saw before her. Caraculla sat up in bed naked with just a sheet covering his waist, wolfing down a small plateful of meat. To his right seated in a large wing chair was Kharon dressed in his pants and boots. The large white bandage still circled his thick waist but otherwise he looked well. He shuffled a deck of cards glancing at Caraculla impatiently as he waited for them to start their card game.

Spotting Gypsy, Kharon got up and offered her his seat. She walked over slowly unable to take her eyes of Caraculla. *Please let this be real.*

"He's a little weak," Kharon said. "But he's surprisingly full of shit." Then he stepped out of the room and left them alone.

Caraculla put his plate aside and gestured for her to come to him. She moved closer and leaned down already feeling tears welling up in her eyes. Caraculla pulled her into his arms and there wasn't a feeling in the world better than that. He moved over and she climbed onto his bed lying her body down next to him. "I missed you so much," she whispered.

He squeezed her. "Me too. I heard you won."

She smiled wiping her tears on her sleeves. "Yes, I did."

He nuzzled her. "My beautiful warrior woman." A beat passed. "I also hear we're married."

Gypsy nodded grimly. "Your cousins showed up to finish you off and pillage your stuff."

"I have cousins?"

"*Apparently*," she said, scowling.

"Well then, I'm glad I have you to protect me."

Gypsy wrapped her arms around his large arm and pressed her face into his bicep. Her eyes were closed in blissful relaxation. "Are you really okay?"

"That's what they tell me."

Krull came into the room. He didn't seem surprised to see Gypsy in Caraculla's bed. He checked some equipment and made some notes on Caraculla's chart. He stared at Gypsy. "No sex in the clinic," he said.

She glared at him. "*Okay.* When can he go home?"

"Tomorrow. But go easy on him. He might be confused or have some memory problems for a while. Don't let him do anything too stressful," Krull said.

Krull went out and Harlan passed him coming in.

"I hate that guy," Gypsy complained after Krull had disappeared down the hall.

"Don't," Harlan said, walking over to the side of the bed. "He saved Caraculla's life and in the process taught me a lot."

Harlan pulled out some scissors and carefully snipped and removed the stitches from his head. "There," she said, taking a step back and smiling. "Good as new."

Caraculla gestured for Harlan to lean down and she did. He gave her a warm kiss on the mouth that made her mother blush. Gypsy smiled. "Better than new," Caraculla said.

Chapter 28

"Those fucking nobles are trying to screw Gypsy out of the Academy!" Desmond roared, barging into Gavin's office. He tossed a thick sheet of paper on the desk and glared at Gavin like this was all his doing. "She's not on the admission list!" he said, stabbing angrily at the center of the paper.

Gavin had expected something like this. It had been almost two weeks since Gypsy's win and if she was admitted, they'd have heard by now. The old boys' club was a hard one to get into and had never been violated by a girl. He picked up the sheet and read down the list. Desmond was right. She wasn't on it anywhere, not even under honorable mention. *What a snub.*

"What the hell are you going to do?" Desmond demanded.

"Calm down," Gavin said impatiently. "This silly little list isn't the final word." He tossed it back on his desk trying not to let Desmond's outrage infect him too. This called for a cool head. "We'll just have to go to the hearing this afternoon and appeal the decision."

"What if they still won't let her in?" Desmond asked, still fuming.

Gavin stood up and frowned. "I wish you'd been so passionate about your own career."

Desmond glared at him. "Are you seriously going there *now?*"

Gavin held up his hands in surrender. "If they still won't let her in, we'll work around it. Like you, she'll come with us on campaign but not receive a commission."

"That's bullshit, Gavin. She earned a spot on that list and you know it," Desmond said.

"I know that, Desmond. But before you start spouting off at the meeting, let's try and handle this the diplomatic way. It's obvious we're going to have to play by their rules. Go and get Gypsy from her fuckathon at Caraculla's and take her to the council meeting chamber. I'll meet you both there," Gavin said.

"Do you want me to tell her why?"

Gavin grinned. "Of course, you don't think I want to be the one to tell her, do you?"

* * * *

The council chamber was an enormous room with terrible acoustics. The half-moon-shaped hall was aligned with crescent-shaped leather and wood benches that faced the high platform table where the council members sat. The chamber was empty but for them and the council. The nobles were obviously stalling them. Gypsy sat between Gavin and Desmond straining to hear what they were mumbling about and waiting for some sign the council was going to hear their protest. Two hours and several of her father's smoke breaks later, they were still waiting. Desmond leaned over and complained to Gavin who seemed determined to wait the council out. Gypsy was miserable. All that hard work for nothing.

The double doors behind them slammed open and the council fell into a fearful silence. Tannyth Von Goth came in dressed in a stunning red and gold dress. Her dark hair was up in an attractive loose bun with wisps of wavy locks framing the sides of her face. Her eyes were blazing. She strolled up to the council bench and tossed the list at the chairman. It fluttered through the air like a bird trapped in a room full of windows.

The chairman gave her a strained look. "How can we ser—"

"Don't give me that patronizing drivel." She sneered. "How do you all justify leaving Gypsy Theron off the Military Academy list?"

Gypsy glanced at her father and saw him smiling. It was a dark, evil smile and she knew immediately he'd had a hand in Tannyth finding out.

She looked at Desmond who leaned into her ear and whispered, "He's a sneaky bastard. I should have known he was taking this too calmly."

"Baron Eldis," Tannyth called out in a voice as strong as any general's, "your son hasn't competed in the arena for months! His last match didn't even qualify him for the senior class. How is it he's managed to rank *first* on this list?" She pointed to another noble. "Duke Pollick, it's common knowledge your son Makkai isn't even your blood kin with his beautiful blue eyes. Are you so blind you didn't notice neither you nor your wife had such a rare eye color? When your son was conceived, everyone but you knew she was sneaking to the neighboring kingdom to join General Kharon in his bed. How is it Makkai's ranked so high on the list?"

Duke Pollick stood up squeezing his fists. "Now, Tannyth," he said, sounding very much like a henpecked husband. "Let's not get nasty and start hurtling accusations. Your husband isn't exactly beyond reproach."

Gypsy's mouth hung slightly open. She'd never seen anything like it. *They're terrified of her.*

Tannyth gave him a scalding look. "If you have something to say about my husband, then I suggest you say it. But before you do, I would remind you that General Theron is my husband's champion and his daughter is mine. So unless you think you can best *both* in the arena, I suggest you shut your filthy mouth."

Duke Pollick scowled but wisely retreated from the fight. "No, no, just give us a moment to review the list," he said. "I'm sure if Miss Theron was left off, it was just an oversight." After a brief pause he pretended to review the list with the other council members. There was more mumbling. He suddenly looked up and gave a forced smile. "Yes, yes. It's just an oversight." He looked at Gypsy with a mixture of disgust and revulsion. "Congratulations, young lady. You've made it to the Imperial Military Academy!"

Chapter 29

Gypsy rolled over in bed and curled up into the inviting warmth of Caraculla's arms. Burying her face in his neck, she inhaled deeply and was filled with an instant joy. His scent was rich and masculine—pheromones and body heat. She loved it. He smelled like home. Reaching up she ran her fingers over the shocking red fuzz growing back around the scar on his head. She really liked the way it felt and rubbed the area affectionately. Too bad he'd never shave his head.

Nuzzling along his cheek, she found his lips and kissed them keeping her eyes closed. *How I have longed for this moment and here he is in my arms again.* He returned her kiss with tenderness and the underlying sexual aggression he always had. She felt his erection grow quickly between them.

Reaching down she stroked the thick shaft, smiling when he gasped in pleasure. "Haven't you had enough yet?" he teased as she ran her hand down his bulging cock.

"Looks like you haven't either," she replied. She gazed up into his metallic green eyes and her heart swelled with love. "I was so afraid I'd lost you."

He squeezed her close nestling his hips between her legs. Shifting his body, he eased the length of his cock between the thickening lips of her labia. The hard feel of him was bliss and her pussy responded by lubricating to be ready for his penetration.

"We need to talk about our marriage," Caraculla said between running kisses down her neck.

"*Now?*" Gypsy groaned, wriggling to get his cock inside her.

He held her hips still. "Yes now," he said, grinning. "I think you should annul the marriage and put me aside."

Gypsy forgot about his cock for a moment. "Why?"

Caraculla played with a lock of her hair. "First of all, you can't stay in the Academy if we're married. You know that. And second, I think you're too young. I want you to be able to explore and enjoy your sexuality but you won't feel right about that if you're married to me. After you graduate, we can get married again if you want."

She wanted to argue but she knew he was right. She just didn't want to do it until the deadline for the Academy was on her and she *had* to. "Okay, but let me just enjoy being your wife for a little while."

He responded by claiming her mouth and rolling onto his back. Gypsy took his cock in her hands and ran the swollen tip through her labia. Hunger roared to life inside her but, unlike in the past, it was much more intense and demanding. Gavin had warned her about that. The more she fought, the more hormones she produced and the more sexually driven she would become. No wonder Caraculla wanted her to go out and sow her wild oats.

Her clit peeked out from her labia slick with her womanly juices. Guiding his shaft in, she eased her hips down on Caraculla and stopped to enjoy the sensation. Pleasure ravaged her as the ridges on the underside of his cock found the tender erogenous zone within her pussy. Unable to control himself, he pumped into her sending her into a delirium of pleasure.

They rolled around in a sexual haze for hours when finally Caraculla fell into a deep sleep. Normally she would have woken him up for another round but he was still a little worn out from his injury so she let him sleep. Instead, she curled up against his body heat and listened to the welcome sound of his beating heart.

* * * *

"You're up early," Gavin said, entering his office at first light. Gypsy, who'd been waiting in the hall for him to arrive, didn't say anything. She just followed close behind him and took a seat inside. He turned on the lights and took his seat behind the desk. Opening a cigar box, he took one out, clipped the end, and lit it. He offered Gypsy one but she shook her head.

"What do you want?" he asked.

Above his desk mounted on the back wall was the heavy saber she'd trained with all those months ago. It almost seemed like she'd been a different person, which she guessed she had been. There was a deep notch in the blade by the handle and a rush of heat burned her cheeks. She was embarrassed her father was proud of her killing Drake. *Men and their trophies.*

She sighed. "I came to thank you for training me."

"Nonsense. I wish I hadn't waited so long to do it. You're a magnificent fighter, Gypsy. You earned all of your success."

She nodded and got up heading for the door.

"How is Caraculla?" Gavin asked as she touched the handle.

She stopped and turned around. "He's good, better than ever. Mom said she would release him back to duty in a week."

"A week! What the hell kind of bullshit is that? You and your mother are conspiring to keep him home longer for your own self-ish needs. I have real work I need him to do. He's spending too much time being wet nursed by all the women in my life." He sneered as he stood and poured himself a drink.

Gypsy stalled for another few seconds then said, "He wants me to put him aside before I go into the Academy."

"I think that is a wise choice," Gavin said, returning to his seat. He sipped his drink.

"Interesting. I didn't think I'd ever hear you say that," she said.

"Well, my dear, you have fought me and everyone else around you for this direction in your life. Now that you are finally on your way, you'll have to continuously make difficult decisions to ensure your success. Besides you're very lucky Caraculla will always be there waiting for you."

Gypsy smiled. "I know he will."

Gavin got up and joined her by the door. He tilted her face up to him and kissed her on the forehead. "Why did you really come here?" he said.

She wrapped her arms around him and hugged quickly, then she let go. "I just wanted to say...well, um...that I love you, Dad."

Gavin stood there for a moment and squinted down at her with his one golden eye. "*Dad?* You've called me many things before but never that." A beat passed. "Interesting. I love you too, Gypsy. Good luck at the Academy."

She nodded fighting the urge to cry. She opened the door and Gavin pulled her back. Gypsy turned around and Gavin gave her a huge hug, just like the ones he used to give her when she was a child. It was too much, she started to cry.

Gavin released her and helped her wipe the tears off her cheeks. "Save that sentimental crap for your mother and your boyfriend in the future. All right?"

Gypsy smiled. "Yes, Excellency," she said. Then she slipped out of his office and went to the arena to practice.

Just because she won her match and gained entrance into the Academy didn't mean her training was over. In fact, this was just the beginning. One never knew when a girl would have to defend herself.

ABOUT THE AUTHORS

Michelle Marquis and Lindsey Bayer have written numerous erotic romance stories together. For more about them and their books, please visit their website at www.michelle-oneill.com

For your reading pleasure, we invite you to visit our web bookstore

WHISKEY CREEK PRESS TORRID

www.whiskeycreekpresstorrid.com